The Sister Returns

Joanna Rees, aka Josie Lloyd and Jo Rees, is a bestselling writer of eighteen novels, including rom-coms, blockbusters and big-hearted adventures such as *The Tides of Change* and *A Twist of Fate*. Based in Brighton, Joanna is married to the author Emlyn Rees, with whom she has three daughters. They have co-written several novels, including the *Sunday Times* number one bestseller *Come Together*, which was translated into over twenty languages and made into a film. They have written several bestselling parodies of their favourite children's books, including *We're Going on a Bar Hunt*, *The Very Hungover Caterpillar* and *The Teenager Who Came to Tea*. As Josie Lloyd, Joanna has also written *The Cancer Ladies' Running Club* and *The Salty Sea-Gals*. When she's not writing, she likes walking in the countryside with her dog, Ziggy, and swimming in the sea year-round. Joanna is always delighted to hear from readers, so please visit her website joannareesbooks.com. She's also on Twitter @joannareesbooks.

BY JOANNA REES

As Josie Lloyd

It Could Be You
The Cancer Ladies' Running Club
The Salty Sea-Gals

As Josie Lloyd, with Emlyn Rees

Come Together
Come Again
The Boy Next Door
Love Lives
We Are Family
The Three Day Rule
The Seven Year Itch
We're Going on a Bar Hunt
The Very Hungover Caterpillar
The Teenager Who Came to Tea
Switch It Off
'Twas the Flight Before Christmas
The Joy of Socks
Shabby: The Jolly Good British Guide to Stress-free Living

As Joanna Rees

A Twist of Fate
The Key to It All
The Girl from Lace Island
In the Shade of the Blossom Tree
(previously published as *Forbidden Pleasures*)
The Tides of Change (previously published as *Platinum*)
The Runaway Daughter
The Hidden Wife
The Sister Returns

Praise for Joanna Rees

'A riveting rollercoaster of a tale, full of intrigue, high-stakes drama and [illegible] will keep you hooked from beginning to end'
Hello!

'An ideal beach read'
Books Monthly

'Genuinely exciting, extremely well crafted and long enough to be perfect beach reading'
Daily Express

'If you like losing yourself in epic tales by the likes of Penny Vincenzi and Lesley Pearse, you'll love this'
Woman

'A gripping tale'
Glamour

'It's freakin' ace. Pack it in your hand luggage and expect to spend a day of your summer hols reading . . . and refusing all food, drink and conversation'
Heat

'Addictive'
Metro

The Sister Returns

Joanna Rees

PAN BOOKS

First published in paperback 2022 by Macmillan

This edition first published 2022 by Pan Books
an imprint of Pan Macmillan
The Smithson, 6 Briset Street, London EC1M 5NR
EU representative: Macmillan Publishers Ireland Ltd, 1st Floor,
The Liffey Trust Centre, 117–126 Sheriff Street Upper,
Dublin 1, D01 YC43
Associated companies throughout the world
www.panmacmillan.com

ISBN 978-1-5290-1891-2

1 3 5 7 9 8 6 4 2

A CIP catalogue record for this book is available from the British Library.

Typeset by Palimpsest Book Production Limited, Falkirk, Stirlingshire
Printed and bound by CPI Group (UK) Ltd, Croydon, CR0 4YY

FSC
www.fsc.org
MIX
Paper | Supporting
responsible forestry
FSC® C116313

For Minty, with all my love

The Sister Returns

1

An Unexpected Summons

'Where is everyone?' Vita asked, taking another bite of her bagel while bouncing Bertie on her hip. He giggled and she grinned down at him, her heart melting at his cherubic face and blond curls.

Evelyn, the Delaneys' trusted housekeeper, was over by the row of dented silver domes on the sideboard, clearing the rest of breakfast in the light-filled morning room.

'Nancy and Mrs Delaney have gone to see the venue,' Evelyn said, with a raised eyebrow that showed just how much she disapproved of Nancy's forthcoming nuptials. She glanced at the door, although there was no one to overhear her. Mr Delaney had left for his brokerage hours ago. 'All those people. You'd think Miss Nancy was marrying royalty.'

Evelyn, like Vita, secretly thought that Nancy could do much better than her father's protégé from his firm, Delaney's Brokerage. Nate Materson was a chinless man from Baltimore who reminded Vita of the snake-oil salesman Hammer in that Groucho Marx movie, *The Cocoanuts*. But Vita knew better than to try telling her best friend, who had a remarkably thick skin, the truth.

'And I don't approve of folk getting married in November,'

Evelyn added. 'Why couldn't she have a summer wedding? The garden is big enough. It ain't right.'

Vita didn't enlighten Evelyn as to the reason: that the spectacular venue for the wedding – the ballroom at the Metropolitan – was booked up so far ahead, it was either get married in November or wait for two years. But before any incriminating words of agreement were spoken, the service door moved and a small white dog nudged his way through.

'Mr Wild, that naughty dog,' Evelyn harrumphed. 'What's he doing in here? Shoo.'

Mr Wild yapped and barked, and Bertie started crying.

'He hasn't been out yet,' Evelyn said.

'Oh, poor Mr Wild,' Vita said, handing Bertie to Evelyn, who comforted him on her ample bosom.

Vita picked up the dog and he panted, trying to lick her face. 'You are such a coward. Why won't you play in the garden like a normal dog?'

When Vita had arrived in New York on Paul's illegal boat, having escaped from Paris, her vengeful brother and disastrous marriage by the skin of her teeth, Nancy had received her at home as if Vita had only come to return her beloved dog. Mr Wild had taken all the attention, with Nancy acting as if he'd been miraculously revived from the dead (which, in a manner of speaking, he had). She'd lavished the little dog with affection, even commissioning a diamond-studded collar for him. But soon Nancy was back to her old ways, and for the last few months it had been Vita who'd ensured the little dog had his daily walk.

'Why don't you take him out?' Evelyn asked.

'I can't. If I take Bertie out now, he'll nap all morning in the pram. As soon as he gets into that thing he falls fast asleep, and I'm trying so hard to get him into a routine.'

'Well then, he can stay here with me and help me in the kitchen,' Evelyn said, her eyes twinkling at Bertie as he smacked his lips. 'And you know what? I'm cooking up some sweet potato. Why don't I try him with some?'

'You think we should?' This wasn't the first time they'd had this conversation. Evelyn, who had four grown-up children of her own, was insistent that Bertie should be started on solid food.

'It's time. You leave it to me. Have some time for yourself. Go on.'

Taking the opportunity Evelyn had given her, Vita headed out with Mr Wild. She stopped for a second by the bevel-edged mirror in the hall, adjusting her dove-grey felt hat and arranging the fur stole around her neck. She inspected her face for signs of tiredness, but her blue eyes were still bright above her high cheekbones and she patted the honey-blonde curls by her ears, then smoothed the red Helena Rubinstein lipstick Nancy had given her over her full lips. Even though Nancy, with her striking looks, would always be the centre of attention, Vita wasn't so bad, she thought.

Opening the front door, she paused on the wide stoop of the Delaneys' mansion with its white Doric pillars, wrapping her wool coat around her against the chill of the morning. The sky was blue and the sun was bright above the large silver maple trees that lined the avenue.

The mailman was heading up the steps and he smiled at Vita, touching the peak of his navy-blue cap.

'Here's one for you today,' he said, handing her a pale lilac envelope with her name on the front. 'Hand delivery.' She thanked him, and he put the rest of the mail in the mailbox by the front door before petting Mr Wild.

Vita opened the envelope. The first thing she noticed was the embossed gold letterhead spelling out a name: *Renata King*.

Renata King was Irving's mother, and now Irving rose up in Vita's mind's eye. *Poor Irving*, she thought, remembering how suave and debonair the rich American had seemed when he'd been shopping for his spoilt daughter, Daphne, at Madame Sacerdote's salon in Paris. How he'd taken a shine to Vita and how he'd wooed her, wining and dining her and lavishing her with expensive gifts, until she'd given in and agreed to marry him.

She'd sincerely hoped that she would develop stronger feelings than the affectionate gratitude she initially felt towards Irving; but they had never materialized. And, although it had come as a terrible shock to learn that his quick 'Paris divorce' from his previous wife, Alicia, hadn't been legal – meaning that Vita's marriage hadn't been either – looking back, that revelation had somewhat let Vita off the hook. It was strange, though, being in this awful limbo, not married but not a divorcée either. It made things very difficult to explain – especially when it came to Bertie.

Vita had entirely forgotten that Renata King, her ex-husband's mother, lived here in New York. Irving's daughters, Daphne and Hermione, had given Vita the impression that their grandmother was very much on the side of their mother, Alicia. Daphne, in one of her more toxic moments, had claimed that her grandmamma considered Vita to be a gold-digger and would never receive her in her home; so Renata King hardly came with a favourable introduction. In fact, Irving himself had always been disparaging about his mother, saying that it was altogether for the best that they lived on separate continents.

So, given all of this, why was Renata contacting Vita now? Could it mean that Irving was here – and if so, what then? She felt a shiver of alarm at the mess she'd got herself into.

In order to make Vita's 'predicament' socially acceptable to the Delaneys, who were not only morally upstanding, but devout Christians, Vita had foolishly allowed Nancy to handle the matter. She had had several chances at the beginning to tell Nancy the truth about her night with Archie on her honeymoon, and how Irving couldn't possibly be Bertie's father; but she'd been frightened of how Nancy might react. There was no love lost between her friend and Archie Fenwick, and Nancy had made so many assumptions about the circumstances of Vita fleeing her marriage.

So she'd stayed silent while Nancy railroaded her, fabricating a story for her parents that Irving had been nothing more than a brute, claiming that Vita had been lucky to escape her terrible marriage with her life (and that of her unborn child) and that she deserved the Delaneys' charity. After all, Nancy had reasoned, her own mother couldn't very well be on the committee at the mission and then turn away a needy person from her very own door. When Vita had protested that the story went too far, and that Irving had actually been more than a gentleman – even offering a gentle reminder that he'd been the one who'd paid for Nancy to leave Paris and straighten herself out in a plush California clinic – Nancy had simply flapped her hand as if that were all ancient history. She didn't like to be reminded that she'd once been hopelessly addicted to alcohol and cocaine, not now that she was society's darling.

Vita scanned Renata's letter. *It has come to my attention that you have applied to live in an apartment in one of my buildings . . .*

One of the few things she knew for certain about Irving's mother was that she was rich as Croesus, and this casual remark about owning several apartment blocks set alarm bells ringing. Perhaps Vita shouldn't have used her married name on the application.

I shall receive you this morning. Call on me before noon.

The letter concluded with a flourish of indigo ink: *RK*. Vita turned it over. That was it. There was nothing else. No clue as to the woman's meaning.

'Damn it,' Vita cursed, realizing that the timing meant she would have to go straight there now, without stopping to sort out her appearance. Could she ignore the letter and pretend she'd never seen it? But the mailman had handed it to her personally, she remembered. Claiming it had gone astray would only get him into trouble.

Besides, Renata King was bound to move in similar circles to the Delaneys. Perhaps it wouldn't be wise to snub such a powerful woman. And, as she'd implied, she most probably decided whose applications were accepted and rejected. Might it be possible that Renata, far from being unfriendly, would actually approve Vita's application? Because, much as she'd enjoyed living on the Delaneys' charity, once Nancy and Nate had moved into their new apartment, Vita couldn't stay. It was time to start out on her own.

She checked her watch. It was already eleven fifteen. She studied the address again and, calling to Mr Wild, set off.

2

The Sky is the Limit

The Delaneys' mansion was just a stone's throw from Fifth Avenue in the most fashionable of neighbourhoods. Vita strode down the wide sidewalk, the wind whipping up piles of golden and brown leaves into mini tornadoes as she passed the tall mansion houses. Even though they were well-established homes, they had a shiny newness to them that the buildings in London and Paris didn't have. And on such a scale! Everything here in New York was bigger and more boastful.

She turned onto Fifth Avenue and, on the next corner, passed a couple of women in maroon Salvation Army uniforms who were handing out leaflets, a man behind them decrying the sin of alcohol. With Prohibition firmly in place, Vita was amazed by how pure this city seemed on the outside, when she knew full well that there was an altogether seedier side if only you knew where to look.

She thought now of her crossing from Europe on her friend Paul Kilkenny's ship. She still couldn't believe she'd been so naive as to think Paul was a struggling artist when in actual fact, all along he'd been 'Le Monsieur', the famous bootlegger and gambler. When he'd rescued Vita from Irving's house and offered her a safe passage to America on his ship, she'd been shocked to find out that it was full to bursting with illegal brandy and champagne. She remembered the crew, who'd all played poker and tried, but mostly failed, to curtail their bawdy talk and swearing in her presence.

Paul had boasted that he was friends with someone called Madden – a mobster, from what Vita could gather, who owned the Cotton Club on 142nd Street, where Duke Ellington and his band played. Paul had said that Madden had helped him find the perfect location for a speakeasy of his own. It was also in Harlem, tucked away at the back of a milk bar, in the hollowed-out building of a bakery next door. Vita had suggested he call it Le Monsieur's, after his mysterious Paris identity.

She remembered the tense atmosphere as they'd arrived in the dead of night; how the ship had chugged slowly past the Statue of Liberty, eerily lit by cloudy moonlight. Paul had been standing on the deck in the dark, his eyes trained on a signal at the end of the dock. She'd seen the red light with its pulsing code and they'd sidled up to the mooring, the thick truck tyres lashed to the wooden struts, cushioning the boat in the oily water. Nobody had spoken as Vita had stepped up onto the dock: her first footstep on a new continent.

She'd had no time to mark the moment, as Paul had ushered her straight down the gangplank to where a large truck with a canvas back was waiting. She'd climbed into the front with Mr Wild and Paul, and an Italian man had driven them silently to the city.

They'd gone to a speakeasy known only as 'the back of Ratner's' – a 'joint' run by Paul's friend Lansky, behind a kosher dairy. There they'd left the truck and walked to a garage under the Williamsburg Bridge, where Paul's fancy car had been waiting with his driver. They'd driven to the Delaneys' address and Paul had kissed Vita on the cheek, wishing her good night as casually as if they'd just been out for a quick drink rather than crossing the Atlantic together.

She wondered where Paul was now. It would be fun to visit his speakeasy, but now that Nancy was sober, she hadn't exactly had a chance. It was a shame, Vita thought. She was pleased for Nancy, of course, that she'd straightened herself out; but sometimes Vita missed the old days, when the two of them had had all sorts of adventures. These days Nancy was a changed woman – and Vita had changed too, she supposed. She was a mother now.

She stepped out into the road to cross over, not noticing the WALK sign had stopped, and a car honked at her.

'Hey, watch it, lady,' a cab driver shouted.

'Sorry,' she cried, holding onto her hat and swerving around the bonnet of the cab. When would she get used to the traffic being on the wrong side of the street?

Two Polish men were arguing loudly behind a butcher's truck, the back of which was open to reveal swaying pig carcasses. An Asian man was delivering laundry to a hotel, whistling loudly. He smiled at Vita.

Then, in just one block, the neighbourhood suddenly changed again, the shops catering for a smarter crowd. She could never get over the array of goods from around the world that were available here in New York. It was an exciting melting pot of cultures, but even so, she missed the sedate elegance of Paris. She pined for the wonderful clothes she'd left at Irving's house: the couture dresses from Maison Jenny, the Hermès scarves and Tiffany necklaces, drawers full of camiknickers and silk stockings. What had happened to all her things? Alicia, Irving's reinstated wife, had probably taken them for herself – or given them to their awful daughters.

Thinking about Paris made Vita remember what had happened with Marianne, and now she caught her breath as she thought of her former friend.

Nancy wouldn't have Marianne – or Marie, as Vita still thought of her – mentioned in the house. It was as if Vita's lapse of judgement in allowing Marie to infiltrate her life to dupe them both was a mistake that Nancy tolerantly, tactfully continued to overlook. But in cutting off all conversation about what had happened, Nancy had only magnified the distress Vita felt. She was still astonished by the massive deception Marie had perpetrated, testing the pain of those events in Paris as if testing her thumb on a blade. It was still painful, but also laced with the hard-boiled fury she reserved for her sister-in-law, Edith. *Not to mention Clement*, Vita thought bitterly, thinking of her sadistic brother.

They had caused Marie's death. They'd caused that little girl to lose her mother and Marie, who'd obviously been under terrible strain, to lose her life. Edith was just as responsible as Clement and now, as Vita pictured the two of them in Darton, manufacturing Vita's designs – the ones they'd made Marie steal from her – it made her seethe with resentment.

Well, there's only one thing for it, Vita thought. When she cashed in her stocks and shares, she'd have enough for the lingerie enterprise that filled all her thoughts. Not the little tin-pot, one-person operation she'd been striving for in

Paris. No. This time, it was going to be bigger. Better. Successful enough to blow Edith and Clement out of the water. She'd show them, if it was the last thing she did. She'd provide brassieres for every woman in America. Why not aim big? Wasn't that what New York was all about – the sky being the limit?

3

Argosy Books

Vita walked on a few more blocks with Mr Wild, who let out a little yelp as steam hissed up from a grille on the sidewalk. Then, passing a smart-looking drugstore, she thought of Evelyn with Bertie and remembered that he needed new pacifiers, so she went in to buy a few. It was always satisfying to cross a few errands off her list. Back on the street, she turned and saw that she was near Central Park, recognizing the gates of the zoo on the corner. She strained to listen out for the rare birds in the menagerie, the monkeys and bears she'd read about.

She checked her watch, wondering if she had enough time to pop into Argosy Books, which she knew was just down East 59th Street between Lexington and Park Avenue. On her various trips around New York with Bertie in the pram, Vita had made it her mission to find all the good bookstores, although nothing could really match Book Row – the seven blocks between Fourth Avenue and Astor Place, where almost every shop front was a bookstore.

But now that she was here, it would be a shame to waste the opportunity. She hurried towards the bookstore and, as she made her way through its glossy black doors, had a sudden feeling of nostalgia for the bookshops on Charing Cross Road in London and Shakespeare and Company in Paris.

The studious old man behind the counter squinted at her through his tortoiseshell glasses, taking a moment to focus. His stooped shoulders spoke of years spent hunched over manuscripts. She browsed the shelves for a while, then looked at the books piled on a small wooden table, published by Scribner's.

She picked up a copy of *The Great Gatsby* by F. Scott Fitzgerald, feeling a flash of recognition. She wished she had someone to tell about her brush with the celebrity author and how she'd met him in Zelli's in Paris when she'd been there with Irving.

Blushing slightly, she picked up the book and headed to the till, but a small publication on the corner of the table caught her eye. She picked up the white cover and ran her finger over the title – *Sylvine*, by A. S. Fenwick – and for a moment, she held her breath.

Archie's novel. The one he'd told her was inspired by her. And she remembered now the girl with the mole on her arm who had been so vividly and erotically described in the book. She held the book now, feeling as if she was holding a very real piece of Archie, the only man she'd ever truly loved. Maybe the only man she ever would truly love.

But then she pictured Irving in their bedroom in Paris – how he'd flung the then unpublished manuscript down on the bed, accusing her of infidelity. How he'd got hold of the manuscript, she'd never know, but the shame she'd felt then washed over her now.

The man behind the counter seemed to know all about *Sylvine* and how it had been published first in Paris, then picked up by a British publisher, and had now made it to the States. He hadn't read it, he said, popping it into a paper bag, but he was going to order another copy right away.

As she left the shop, burying the book deep in her bag, Vita imagined Archie with his wife Maud, chinking glasses of champagne, celebrating his success, and she shuddered. Her Pandora's box of feelings about Archie Fenwick was best buried away, under lock and key. And the book was best kept under lock and key too, so that nobody could read it and have cause to embarrass her again.

4

An Audience with the Other Mrs King

The address of Renata King's prestigious apartment building was 1001 Fifth Avenue, overlooking the Metropolitan Museum of Art. After her detour to the bookshop, it was almost noon by the time Vita arrived and she was perspiring from the fast walk. As she approached, she saw a doorman in a brown and gold uniform with epaulettes and a hat that fastened under his chin. He was standing under the canopy, guarding the red carpet that stretched across the sidewalk in front of the building to the kerb like a dragon's tongue.

She showed him her letter and his demeanour changed. He led her courteously inside and across a speckled marble floor to the gold elevator doors, gestured to them with a white-gloved hand. Mr Wild emitted a low growl as the elevator operator pressed the brass button for the penthouse.

After what seemed like an age, the doors pinged open and the operator nodded for Vita to step out. She checked her reflection in a large gilt mirror, seeing two high spots of colour on her cheeks, a flush on her neck.

She was in a lavishly marble-clad corridor leading to a room that occupied the entire top corner of the building.

Floor-to-ceiling windows revealed a panoramic view of the city; Vita stopped, awestruck.

A maid in a smart navy uniform approached her.

'Please come this way, Miss,' she said in a hushed voice before leading a path across the shiny parquet floor, her footsteps silent in the cloth slippers she wore, the only sound the rustle of the fabric stretched over her ample derrière. Vita wondered what kind of scaffolding she was wearing beneath her dress to hold those curves in place. Certainly not the kind that put anyone in a good mood.

Vita followed her past several thickly padded fourteenth-century-style sofas on silk rugs, and sideboards bedecked with china ornaments and figurines. The maid opened one of the ornate doors and Vita was shown into an even larger salon. Just on the other side of a square window she could see construction workers on the huge steel arm of a crane, hundreds of feet up in the air.

'Goodness!' she exclaimed out loud as one of them glanced into the building and winked at her, his face sooty like a miner's. The thought of the cheery worker being up so high without a harness made her stomach turn.

'Oh! Them. They're quite ruining my view,' a reedy voice said, and Vita looked across to a pale pink chair with scrolled arms. In it sat a wrinkled woman with dark curly hair poking out from underneath an old-fashioned lace cap.

Renata King had pink-powdered cheeks, which did little to detract from her heavy jowls that instantly reminded Vita of Irving. She was ancient, Vita realized – almost certainly in her late seventies.

Sixty seconds, Vita told herself, repeating a mantra of old.

She just had to get through the next sixty seconds. She would conduct herself politely and be honest. She would tell the truth about the current status of her relationship with Irving and explain why she had put her married name on the apartment application. And maybe, just maybe, the old woman might take pity on her.

'So,' Renata said in a deadpan voice, her beady eyes looking Vita up and down, 'you're the whippersnapper who married my son. He always did have an eye for the women. Although how he managed to snare anyone so pretty, with his looks, is beyond me.'

'Mrs King, I—' Vita hesitated, then began again. 'There's been a misunderstanding. You see, Irving and I aren't exactly together—'

'The business with Alicia. In Paris. Yes, I know all about that.' She held up a hand, her fingers so laden with rings that they looked like a gangster's knuckledusters. 'That phoney divorce.' She made a *pah!* sound and flapped her hand in dismissal. 'Typical of Irving to cut corners. He thought a Paris divorce would solve his problems with Alicia. How wrong could he be?'

She knew. That was a relief at least, Vita thought, still scanning Renata's face for clues.

'So you're not properly married. But that hasn't stopped you parading around town as Mrs King.' Vita hadn't expected the old woman to have a high opinion of her, but her barefaced rudeness was still a shock. 'And I hear you have a son.' Her beady eyes glinted. 'My grandson.'

Even on the way here, it hadn't once occurred to Vita that there was any connection between the old woman and

Bertie. Bertie was a baby. *Vita's* baby. She would do whatever she could to protect him from the world, and from the mistakes she'd made. But now, it seemed, this woman was asserting some sort of claim on him.

Mr Wild wriggled, but Vita clamped him in her arms. She couldn't risk putting him down.

'Well?' Renata demanded. 'What have you got to say for yourself? Where is my grandson? I was hoping you'd bring him. Not this . . . creature. I want to meet my heir.'

Had Vita heard her correctly? 'But, ma'am, surely Irving is your heir?'

'You know as well as I do that if Irving carries on the way he is, he'll die of another heart attack before long. It's a miracle he survived the last one, and I hear he refuses to change his ways. Besides, he made his feelings perfectly clear when he left me here and went to Europe. *Can't get far enough away*. Those were his exact words.'

'What about Daphne and Hermione?' Vita said.

The old woman waved her hand. 'Don't talk to me about those dreadful girls. Girls are worth nothing. Everyone knows it's the male line that counts. Do you have a problem letting me see the child?' Her black eyes were on Vita now.

'No, but . . .'

'I resent your resistance, young lady. Perhaps you don't understand that I have the power to make it either possible or *im*possible for you to get an apartment anywhere reputable in this city,' Renata said. 'And I always get what I want. You see, what I say in this town goes. You understand? Because, when I don't get my way, I have a habit of making rumours . . . well, shall we say . . . fly.'

'Rumours?'

'Oh yes, a word here or there from me can ruin reputations. And it would be so unfortunate if, say, the Delaneys were to come . . .' she paused, her beady eyes twinkling with menace, '. . . *unstuck*, just before Nancy's wedding.'

5

The Pocket Watch

At the far end of a cobbled Lancashire street, Clement Darton waited in the Mill Wheel public house, his walking stick beside him at the brass-lipped bar and his eye on the door. It had been raining incessantly, which made his crippled back and leg ache, but now a weak dribble of sunlight filtered through the etched glass of the pub doors, casting a strip of yellow across the sticky floorboards. At just gone noon on a Tuesday, there weren't any regulars in here yet; just an old woman mopping the floor, and the landlord putting glasses away from the washing-up tray. Clement had made it clear that he didn't want a conversation. The cloth on the glass seemed to squeak unusually loudly, jangling his already frazzled nerves.

He took out his father's watch from his waistcoat pocket again, casually flicking the release with his thumb and remembering how his father had looked at it in the same way. Somehow, wearing it made him feel like he had triumphed – especially as the watch had been specifically left to his sister, Anna, in their father's will. Their father had always preferred Anna. Or Vita. Wasn't that what she called herself these days?

Yes, she'd always been the favourite child – a fact that was doubly hard to swallow because of the way their father had treated Clement. And now the event that so often scorched a path through the landscape of his memories came, like a heart palpitation: his father calling Clement to his study as a boy. How he'd made him kneel down, and . . .

Clement slugged back his whisky, feeling the raw hit on his gut – a feeling that usually helped to banish the shaming memory. It wasn't so bad, he tried to tell himself. He'd heard awful stories of what had happened to blond boys like him at boarding school and at least in that regard he'd got off lightly – although there had been a few late-night fumbles with that boy in the upper year. He forced the shaming memory away, signalling to the landlord to pour another shot. The landlord didn't meet his eye as he measured the amber liquid.

Clement thought about the telegram from Mr Decker, secretary of the gentlemen's club in Manchester, requesting this meeting. Somewhere they could 'talk discreetly', he'd explained, suggesting this pub, a safe distance away from the club. Clement braced himself for the difficult conversation ahead, starting to tally up in his head just how extensive his debts were.

But Mr Decker was a reasonable man, he assured himself. He would understand Clement's predicament, as long as Clement could make clear the circumstances that had led to his current situation. Perhaps he should start at the beginning and explain how he'd won a thousand pounds on Gregalach in the Grand National in March, but then the winning streak Clement had thought was his to enjoy hadn't lasted, and his luck had disappeared like water down a plughole. He'd thought that the poker game at the club might revive his chances, but it hadn't – and he'd been too proud to stop as the stakes had become higher and higher.

He hoped his current debts were not significant enough to put his membership in jeopardy. He liked the club, where he deserved a place as one of the influential businessmen that graced its dining room and oak-clad bar. He enjoyed rubbing shoulders with other mill owners, lawyers and factory bosses, and he hoped that by eavesdropping on their conversations he would find a way to make his own business flourish.

Edith was determined that they should move their business from cotton to textile production at Darton Mill, and the investment they'd had with the sale of the shares had quickly disappeared in her modernization plans. She'd outlined a clear blueprint to make this business direction work, but Clement had insisted that they remain cautious and continue as they always had done. Before he'd died, Darius Darton had re-equipped Darton with more modern ring frames, hoping to compete with Holden Mill and Elk Mill near Stockport. He'd hoped they would keep up; but they hadn't, and Edith had no real idea of how much trouble the mill was in.

Now the pub door swung open. Clement arranged a smile on his face, ready to introduce himself to Mr Decker. But instead, two men approached – one was bulky, with a stubbly roll of a neck like a bulldog, and half his earlobe missing. The other was dapper, with swarthy skin and deep blue eyes. They were both dressed in tweed with flat caps.

'Mr Darton?' the good-looking one asked, touching his cap. He was Irish, Clement realized, a sudden shimmer of fear making him stand taller. How did this man know his name?

He cast a glance towards the landlord, who now disappeared into the other bar behind the screen of diamond-etched glass.

'I think there's been a mistake,' Clement said, his discomfort turning to alarm as the burlier man came around to his side. He smelt of woodsmoke and sweat, and Clement caught sight of the tattoos on his knuckles. 'I was waiting for Mr Decker.'

'We came on his behalf,' the thuggish man grunted. Clement felt a flash of anger, followed by a sobering dose of panic.

'Please, let's talk about this sensibly,' he said, hating the way his voice sounded. Scared. Whiny.

The good-looking man chewed a match in the corner of his mouth and rubbed his finger up and down the polished brass lip of the bar.

'Mr Decker wants you to settle your business, Mr Darton,' he said, reasonably. 'He's been very patient with you.'

'I will. I will, very soon. He knows I will. I just need a little more time.'

The fat man now twisted Clement's arm painfully and he rose up onto tiptoes, his shattered hip screaming with pain. The man casually leant forward and plucked off the gold chain from Clement's waistcoat, along with his heavy pocket watch.

'Please don't take that,' Clement said.

'You own Darton Mill. Raise the money. Pay back what you owe, and we can be reasonable, and you can get the pocket watch back.'

'But—'

'Calm yourself, Mr Darton,' the man said. 'We can be patient. Mr Decker is prepared to wait a few months. But only a few.' He swung the gold chain around and flipped the watch into his hand, then buried it deep in his trouser pocket.

'I'll get the money,' Clement said. 'Give Mr Decker my word.'

6

The Gypsy Tea Room Confession

Vita didn't tell Nancy about her meeting with Renata King. Even if she'd wanted to, she didn't have much chance; with less than two weeks to go until the wedding, Nancy was so consumed with plans that she didn't notice how preoccupied Vita was.

She went over and over Mrs King's words in her mind. If Vita would bend to her wishes, then not only would she get an apartment, there was a chance that her son would have everything in life he could possibly need. It was a carrot, Vita knew. A golden carrot.

But if she refused? Then Renata would crush her. As in, completely. That's what she'd said. And topping off all of this confusion and doubt was the most important fact of all: even if she *were* to present Bertie, Mrs King would surely see straight away that Vita's angelic blond boy bore no resemblance at all to Irving. Surely she must know that Hermione and Daphne, her granddaughters, were not Irving's natural offspring but 'procured' from a clinic because of Irving's little problem. It would only be a matter of time before Renata realized that she didn't have a genetic link to Bertie either. How would Vita – or Renata, for that matter – deal with that?

Then again, those words 'rumours' and 'unstuck' were still rattling around in Vita's head.

On Tuesday, Nancy insisted that Vita go shopping early for shoes, even though she already had a dozen pairs to choose from in her trousseau. Vita didn't mind. She was all too aware of the ticking clock, counting down to the moment that Nancy became Nate's wife. Because what would happen then? How would Vita cope when she was on her own in New York, without Nancy around for back-up? It was only now, as she was contemplating leaving the Delaneys', that she realized how blissfully protected she'd been since her arrival in New York.

Walking back from the shoe shops with Nancy, past the lake in Central Park, Vita looked at the clouds reflected in the water. Nancy strolled beside the pram, swinging her bag. If not beautiful, she was certainly striking-looking, with jet-black hair and an aquiline nose inherited from her father. Her brown eyes were heavily outlined in kohl. To Vita, though, it was Nancy's confidence that was her most attractive quality – the way her friend seemed to be lit up from within. It had been the first thing Vita noticed when Nancy whisked her off the street and took her to the Zip Club in London, where they'd had a riot as dancing girls. Oh, those days had been so much fun.

Framed as she was, with the skyscrapers and blue sky behind her, Vita couldn't help thinking that Nancy had become even more confident and attractive. In fact, even though Vita was biased because she was her friend, Nancy really did look like a movie star. For a split second, Vita longed to beg her not to marry Nate.

What would happen if she were to remind Nancy that she'd once wanted to be in the movies? That her dreams had once been limitless; certainly a damned sight bigger than getting married in order to please her parents. Because if Nancy – who was far and away the most likely of anyone Vita had ever met to succeed in life – *settled*, somehow it made Vita's own ambitions seem almost impossible to achieve.

'I wish it were November already,' Nancy said, turning around and walking backwards to face Vita. 'I just want to get the wedding done. All this waiting and worrying is no good for my complexion.' She lifted a hand to her perfectly smooth cheek.

'Sometimes I think it would be so lovely if one could arrive in the future,' Vita mused. 'Just for a moment. Just to be sure everything turns out as one wants.'

Nancy stopped suddenly, then put her hand on Vita's arm. 'That's it. Oh, you're a genius, Vita. That's exactly it. Come on.' She did a dramatic dancer's twirl, taking in the crossroads in the paths ahead, then pointed off to the right. 'Come on,' she repeated, setting off.

'Where are we going?'

'You'll see.'

Vita had never been to the Gypsy Tea Room, the famous home of Mikette Cuba, but she'd heard of its reputation. As they approached after Nancy had led her here at a brisk pace, she thought about how disapproving Mrs Delaney would be if she could see them now.

'You've been here before?' Vita asked.

'Oh, yes, a few times,' Nancy said. 'The police hate all of

this fortune-telling but I'm telling you, Vita, as mystics go, she's quite astonishing. I believe everything she says.'

Nancy had always had a penchant for what she called 'having a little peep into the future'. Her eyes danced at Vita as the elderly waitress moved another table out of the way so that Vita could bring in Bertie's pram.

They sat at a small table by the window and the waitress brought over menus.

'How much does it cost?' Vita asked, nodding to the red curtain at the back of the tea room.

'You don't have to pay as such. You just have to tip generously. Let's have a sandwich first. I think we should have the special.'

Vita ordered a tuna fish salad with mayonnaise dressing, while Nancy chose the nut bread and pimento sandwiches. 'Let's have dill pickle on the side,' Nancy said, closing the menu.

'I like the look of that angel cake,' Vita said, eyeing the cake behind the counter.

'Not for me. Not if I'm to look my best for the fitting tomorrow. I can't have you designing my dream dress and then not be able to fit into it. But you should have it. It's delicious.'

Bertie woke up now, and Vita lifted him from the pram. He snuggled into her neck.

'Don't you think it's a bind, having a baby?' Nancy asked, watching her comfort him.

'I suppose it is, but I can't change it now,' Vita said, putting Bertie over her shoulder.

'Nate wants babies.' Nancy curled her lip. 'Three of them.'

'And you don't?'

'I hate the thought of being fat and losing my waistline.' Belatedly, Nancy picked up on how insensitive she sounded. 'Oh, it doesn't matter for *you*. You're so pretty, especially with those ridiculous blue eyes of yours, you'll always have suitors falling over themselves for you.'

Vita smiled coyly at this rare compliment. 'Tell him that you don't want children, if that's really how you feel.'

'It's not so much the children, it's what you have to do to get them.' Nancy leant forward and said in a low voice, 'I don't like all that business.'

Vita blushed, astonished that her friend had confided something so personal. Why was Nancy bringing this up now, in public? While Vita was holding Bertie? But she knew better than to shut down the conversation. After all, she'd been wondering if Nancy and Nate had had sex, so it was a relief to find out that they had. Vita had married Irving without sleeping with him, and what a disaster that had been.

'Don't you?' she asked, hoisting Bertie further up on her shoulder. 'Why?'

'Because . . .'

'Because what?' Vita pressed. She ran her finger over the flower-patterned tablecloth.

'It's not Nate's fault. It's mine.'

'Why is it your fault?'

'You know why,' Nancy said. Her eyes were large and bright as she looked at Vita, who suddenly saw her meaning. Once, a lifetime ago in London when she'd got high with Nancy at a party, they'd had a bath together and had kissed.

When they'd run away from London to Paris, Nancy had confessed that she was in love with Vita.

'I thought . . . I thought that was a passing phase?' she whispered now.

'Oh, don't fuss, Vita. I've made my choice. Ignore me. It's just pre-wedding nerves. Oh, look, she's free,' she suddenly said, seeing a woman stepping through the curtain with a flushed smile on her face.

'What about lunch?' Vita asked, as Nancy got up and made her way towards the curtain.

'You eat. I'm not hungry anymore.'

7

Mrs D's Seal of Approval

Nancy didn't mention their trip to the Gypsy Tea Room when they got back to the Delaneys', but she was in a strange mood all evening and went to bed unusually early. Perhaps she was embarrassed that she'd confided in Vita, or maybe the fortune teller had told her something shocking.

She was back to her usual bossy self the following morning, though, and Vita hardly had time to finish breakfast before they were on their way across town for the final fitting of Nancy's dress.

Vita glanced at her friend across the plush buff leather seat of her father's chauffeur-driven car. Nancy was opening her compact mirror. She'd had exactly the same habit for as long as Vita could remember – as if travelling might somehow dislodge her carefully done make-up.

'What on earth shall I do with my hair? Do you remember that fabulous hairdresser we had in London? Oh, what was his name?' Nancy asked, patting her perfect bob.

'Raymond. Hanover Square.' The first time Nancy had 'taken Vita in hand', she had booked her an appointment with the famous hairdresser, who'd shingled her hair.

'That was it. Do you think it's too much to contact him?'

Vita shook her head and laughed, astonished at Nancy's ability to think that the world revolved around her.

'He'd never be able to get here in time. Unless he has a special pass with those aviation boys.' They'd been talking over dinner the previous night about investing in Boeing. Mr Delaney was convinced it wouldn't be long before affordable transatlantic passenger flights were a reality.

'You're right. I'll use Mother's. She'd be too upset if I used anyone else, in any case. Lord, you know how controlling she is.'

Vita laughed, and Nancy did too.

'Oh, Vita. Isn't this fun? You and me, getting ready for my wedding.' She turned to Vita and laid a hand on her wrist. 'I know what you're thinking. You're nervous about the dress. I can see it in your eyes. But don't be. I have absolute faith in you.'

Vita smiled weakly, vividly recalling the conversation with Camilla Delaney when Nancy had insisted that Vita should design her dress. Camilla hadn't been keen, and Vita knew what was at stake; all of the Delaneys' friends would be at the wedding and they'd be judging Nancy's dress. It had to be perfect.

But Nancy was clever. Insisting that Vita design her dress meant that Camilla had to stay out of the decision. Vita had baulked under the pressure Nancy heaped on her, but soon the skills she'd learnt at Madame Sacerdote's had come back and, after several attempts, she'd cut a pattern she was happy with. Nancy's mother had found a seamstress, Miss Tucker, and they'd already been for a fitting of the calico.

Miss Tucker was waiting for them at her small shop and,

as they entered, she turned the sign around to CLOSED. Nancy's dress was on a mannequin, the train laid out across a bench; countless tiny rhinestones glittered on the lace. Vita knew how much work it must have taken to sew them all in place. She saw that two of Miss Tucker's fingers were bandaged up, and gave her a sympathetic smile.

Nancy put a hand to her chest and, for almost the first time ever, Vita saw her eyes fill with tears.

'Oh, Vita. It's beautiful.'

Relief washed over Vita. The dress had turned out much better than she'd expected. She wished Laure from Madame Jenny's in Paris could see it.

'It's like something one of those Hollywood actresses would wear,' Miss Tucker said in an awed voice. Nancy smiled, delighted at this comparison.

'Let's see what it looks like on,' Nancy said, beckoning Vita. They went into the changing room and Miss Tucker pulled the heavy curtain across.

Vita helped her friend step into the bodice of the dress and then set about doing up the tiny buttons along the back seam. Nancy stared at herself in the mirror as if she couldn't quite believe what she was seeing.

Then the doorbell chimed again and, from the other side of the curtain, Vita heard Mrs Delaney arriving.

'Everyone has been talking about the dress,' Miss Tucker said confidentially, once she'd explained that Nancy was changing. Her voice was filled with pride. 'We haven't been able to say who it's for, of course,' she hurried on, 'but everyone has been asking.'

Nancy grinned. 'What do you think, kiddo?'

'It's a knockout,' Vita said, standing back and clasping her fingers beneath her chin. 'But don't take my word for it. Go on . . . show them.'

She drew back the curtain and stepped aside so that Nancy could present the dress to her mother. Mrs Delaney stood up, towering above Miss Tucker. No stranger to high fashion herself, she was wearing a cream coat with royal blue buttons and a royal blue and cream hat to match. There was a tense moment, and then she let out a long breath of relief.

'I take it all back, Vita,' she said, her eyes shining as she clasped her hands to her lips. 'You know I had my misgivings, but quite simply, my dear, it's astounding.'

'Thank you,' Vita said, accepting her praise and feeling suddenly ten feet taller. This was how it had been at Madame Jenny's, she remembered. This was how good it felt to do the thing she loved.

'Will you make more dresses?' Miss Tucker asked Vita. 'Only, everyone has been asking who the designer is.'

'We'll get you some business cards, Vita,' Mrs Delaney said before she could reply. 'Once my friends see this, they'll all want commissions, I'm sure of it. And to think . . . I found you first.'

8

Nancy's Secret

Vita stayed at Miss Tucker's to discuss a few details along with the incomplete bridesmaids' dresses, leaving Nancy to go home in the car with her mother. After the excitement of the morning Vita was glad of the break from wedding talk, and happy to travel back on the subway alone and wallow in her success.

She remembered feeling so modern when she'd caught the Nord–Sud line from Montmartre to Montparnasse in Paris; now, as she sat on the subway, she felt the same fascination, watching her fellow New Yorkers. Only this time, she was viewing them as potential customers.

Today's endorsement from Mrs Delaney had filled her with confidence and, as the train jolted along, she let her mind wander to a future version of herself occupying a suite of offices, just as there had been at Madame Jenny's. How thrilling it would be, to be in charge of a buzzing team!

And then, biting her lip, a smile playing on her face, she shifted her bag on her lap and let herself dream even bigger. Because what if she was wildly successful? What if she could employ enough skilled machinists to make her clothes available all across America? Surely there was no limit to what she could achieve, if she really focused?

By the time she got back, it was late. She climbed the stairs two at a time, eager to wake Bertie from his afternoon nap.

'Oh, Vita, there you are,' Nancy called from her room, and Vita went in. Mr Wild was settled in the middle of the mint-green eiderdown. 'I picked you up a dress for Friday night,' Nancy announced, holding out a striped box with a bow wrapped around it. 'It's the least I could do to say thank you.'

'Friday night?'

'How can you have forgotten?' Nancy said, as Vita unwrapped the box. 'The party.'

Of course. The pre-wedding party.

Vita pulled out a demure shot silk cocktail dress in midnight blue. 'Oh, Nancy. It's lovely,' she said. 'Thank you. But there was really no need.'

'It's a gift – and a bribe. As my chief bridesmaid, I'm expecting you to work the room. I want to make sure that everyone knows this is going to be the best wedding *ever*. Aren't you going to try it on?' Nancy asked, before Vita could respond. 'Oh, and you should wear these earrings with it.' She took some diamanté paste earrings from her jewellery box and held them up against Vita's ears. One of them slipped through her fingers and fell on the floor, disappearing under her bed.

Vita put the box down and dropped to her knees to get the earring, while Nancy picked up Mr Wild. 'You little scamp,' she said, nuzzling into his neck.

'I've got it, I think,' Vita said, stretching her arm right under the bed. Then her hand connected with something, and there was a clinking sound. Confused, she put her head down, her cheek on the rug as she looked under the bed and saw empty bottles stretching away like fallen skittles. She grabbed the nearest one and got to her feet just as Nancy turned to admire herself and Mr Wild in the long dressing mirror.

Vita unscrewed the lid and sniffed, then took a sip. Vodka. 'You're drinking again?'

Nancy glanced at her in the mirror and in that split second, the look in her eyes told Vita everything she needed to know.

'Shhh.' Nancy ran across the room and shut the door. Her cheeks were pink as she pressed herself against it. She let Mr Wild jump down from her arms.

'Don't lie to me,' Vita warned. 'Where did you even get this?'

Nancy exhaled and squeezed her eyes shut for a long moment, then opened them and looked at Vita. Her face was full of shame. 'It's just . . . it's just a tiny sip here or there,' she implored. 'Hardly anything at all.'

'But you're sober? You said you'd given up! Your parents have made such a fuss of how you've beaten it.'

'And I have. I just . . . well, oh, Vita, I can't expect you to understand, but sometimes I need something, just a little something to . . . take the edge off. And there's a caddy at the golf club who gets me—'

The edge off what? Her perfect gilded life? 'Does Nate know?'

'Nate?' Nancy looked up in alarm. 'Of course not. He'd tell Father.'

And in that moment, Vita could see what a bind Nancy was in. She was marrying Nate to vindicate herself with her parents. To be the one who'd been wild for a time, but had now come home to toe the line and take her place in the society her parents cared so much about.

'But, Nancy, don't you love him?'

'Does it really matter?' Nancy said in a conspiratorial whisper as she walked towards Vita, imploring her to understand. 'Because Father said that if I made it sober to the wedding, it'd be worth a million dollars to him.'

'So?'

'So. He means to give me a million dollars, Vita.'

'It's not all about money.'

'Of course it's all about money,' Nancy snapped, grabbing the bottle from her. 'The whole world runs on money. It's the only thing that means anything.'

Did she really think that? That her life was going to be the best it could be when she was Mrs Nate Materson? Being the wife of a city man, and spending her days judging his colleagues' wives at the golf club?

'But what about your dreams? You were going to be an actress. In the movies, remember?'

'That was in the past,' Nancy said, her face grim now. 'Don't talk about that. Not here. Not ever. And don't tell anyone about this,' she added urgently. 'Promise me. Promise me on Bertie's life.'

'I promise . . . But, Nancy, *please* don't make the same mistake I did. Don't marry for all the wrong reasons.'

'It's too late,' Nancy said. 'Nothing can stop the wedding now. Nothing.'

9
Black Thursday

Mrs Delaney, who was usually so charming, embarked on a series of heated arguments with Nancy over the seating plan for the wedding reception over the following days. Miss Kotin, the renowned society calligrapher, had delivered the hand-inked place cards and the dining room table had been commandeered for the task of negotiating positions for the guests.

With tensions running high, it didn't help that Bertie had been keeping Vita awake at night. Ever since Evelyn had given him solid food, he'd rejected Vita trying to feed him. It had made her feel emotional and bereft, not to mention sore. Evelyn had given her iced cabbage leaves to put in her bra.

Vita was folding clothes in Bertie's room on Thursday morning when she heard voices talking urgently in the hall downstairs. Stepping out of her room, she saw Evelyn.

'What's happening?' Vita asked her, but Evelyn only gave her a dark look and nodded downstairs to the hall.

Larry Goldblum, or 'Goldie', as everyone called him, was the Delaneys' family lawyer. He was a tiny man, and Camilla Delaney towered above him as they both stood by the ticker tape machine in its glass dome on the hall table.

Vita could hear Goldie saying, 'No, no, no. It can't be . . .' as she ran down the stairs to Nancy's floor.

'What's happened?' Nancy asked. She was coming out of her room, blearily tying up her silk gown. She looked hung-over and wouldn't meet Vita's eye.

'I didn't believe it when he telephoned,' Camilla said, looking up at the girls as they reached the bottom of the grand staircase.

'What is it?' Nancy asked the lawyer.

He held up the ticker tape. Vita went over to him and lifted it to see for herself. Nate had taught her how to read the tape, and the numbers she was looking at now didn't make sense. Under Nate's guidance, she'd amassed quite a portfolio and with the returns looking so healthy, Vita had borrowed ever increasing sums over the past few months to invest – in companies and consortiums, in cinemas, motorcars, oil . . . the list went on and on.

Nate had told her that in New York it was impossible *not* to make money, and he had personally helped several bellboys become fantastically rich. He always maintained that one just had to be bold and take the bounteous offers out there for investors. *It's boom, boom, boom*, he always said, his eyebrows dancing.

But what if he was wrong? What then? The motor company shares were now way below what she'd paid for them and, for the first time, Vita realized that the money Nate had promised might vanish. And if she lost all her investments, what would happen to her and Bertie? What about her plans to start her own business?

Goldie now explained in a sombre tone that the market

had opened, but the stocks had gone into free-fall. Traders were dumping stock as fast as they could. The ticker tape machines couldn't keep up.

'How bad is it?' Camilla asked.

'Bad. Very bad.'

'Oh, Goldie, don't be so dramatic,' Nancy said, jabbing him on the shoulder as if he were joking. But the lawyer didn't smile, and the dark expression on his face made Vita's stomach flip.

They listened to the radio in the drawing room all afternoon, hoping for better news. Nancy ran out into the street to get the late bulletin from the newspaper boy.

'I refuse to believe it,' she said, passing it around. Vita read the headlines about a crash and the bull market swinging like a pendulum to a new bear market, predicting overnight a new financial landscape that would affect everyone who'd invested.

'Let's wait to hear what your father has to say when he comes home,' Mrs Delaney said, placing the playing cards on the table in front of her. She liked to play solitaire. 'Please stop fretting, Nancy. You're making me anxious.'

They sat in silence until eventually Mrs Delaney said, 'Vita, I had a very interesting letter today.' She continued to concentrate on the cards in front of her.

'Oh?'

'It was from Renata King.'

'Renata King? *The* Renata King?' Nancy said. 'Isn't she richer than God?'

'I gather you went to meet her, Vita. Is her apartment

very grand?' Camilla Delaney asked. 'I heard from Lotta Tribitz that it's one of the most expensive penthouse apartments in all of Manhattan.' Mrs Delaney was clearly cross that Vita had withheld this information.

Vita described the meeting, and how Renata had offered to help.

'Well, that's wonderful. I think it's excellent news that you've found somewhere,' Mrs Delaney said. Vita caught the exchange of looks between her and Nancy and realized that she must have been the topic of several conversations. 'And of course, Mrs King must meet Bertie.'

Vita noticed a peeved sadness to the way she said it. She'd stepped into the role of a surrogate grandmother for Bertie, but now that would be taken away from her.

'I can't imagine why you haven't contacted her before,' Mrs Delaney continued. 'She has every right to see her grandchild. You were wrong to keep away. You mustn't make an enemy of a woman like that. Not in this town. I mean, the poor woman has a monster for a son, but that doesn't mean we should judge her. I always say that parents should not be held responsible for the actions of their children.'

Vita glanced guiltily at Nancy, willing her not to embellish the Irving situation any further, but just then they heard the sound of the front door. After a few moments, Mr Delaney came into the room, his face ashen.

Camilla Delaney stood and rushed to him, flinging her arms around him, but Patrick Delaney stood motionless. He was a tall man, with distinguished silver flecks in the dark hair above his ears. He was wearing a grey pinstriped suit and a pink club tie with a diamond clip at his neck, but something about his demeanour made his outwardly smart appearance seem dishevelled.

'Is it as bad as Goldie says?' Nancy asked.

'Probably worse.'

'Worse!' Nancy's face fell.

'I could never have imagined it. Not what I saw today. All our investments are wiped out. Everything. It's . . . well, unless it rallies, it's . . . it's a disaster.'

'But the market will rally?' Vita checked.

'Yes, because what about the wedding? We can't have everyone in a bad mood,' Nancy added.

'Nancy. Is that all you can think about? Yourself? At a time like this?' Mrs Delaney cried furiously.

Vita wanted the floor to swallow her. The Delaney household was usually so civilized, but this unseemly scene was altogether too raw.

'Don't you worry, my dears,' Mr Delaney said, with a sad sigh. 'Now, if you'll excuse me, I need to go to the study.' He unlocked the sideboard and swiped a decanter of brandy. Nancy watched, clearly ashamed that her father had taken it upon himself to lock up his liquor. Vita remembered how she'd also hidden the brandy from Nancy, under the sink in their apartment in Paris. Perhaps Mr Delaney was more wise to Nancy than Vita had given him credit for.

10

Holding One's Nerve

The news about the markets was shocking enough, but the conversation with Mrs Delaney had confirmed Vita's worst fears. Mrs King really did have a hold over her, and there was no way she could back out of applying for the apartment now that the Delaneys knew about it. She would have to present Bertie and deal with the consequences. But she couldn't help picturing Renata King as a black spider, spinning Vita and her baby towards her.

It was with a heavy heart that she sat down to write a grovelling letter to Mrs King, requesting a suitable time to visit, this time with Bertie.

Mr Delaney came into the breakfast room as she was finishing the letter. He looked cheerful, chucking Bertie on the chin with his knuckle. Bertie blew a raspberry of delight and Mr Delaney mimicked the sound back to him, making Vita smile that the serious banker could be so playful.

He sat down at the head of the table with his eggs and bacon, tucking a large linen napkin into his collar. 'You look very serious, Vita. Who are you writing to?'

Vita held up the envelope to show him the name.

'Ah,' he said. 'Mrs King's a formidable woman, so I hear.'

Vita tried to smile. 'She is, rather. I applied for an apartment in one of her buildings. And, well . . .' She paused, and Mr Delaney looked up at her. He had a bushy moustache and long sideburns, but his eyes were bright and young. They were the same as Nancy's. 'You see, I'll need a deposit, so I was wondering . . .'

'Yes?'

'Is it going to be possible to liquidate my assets? I tried to talk to Nate about it, but, well, I'm worried about the markets and my investments—'

Patrick Delaney shook his head. 'No, no, no, my dear. Hold your nerve,' he said. 'Look at the papers.'

He nodded to the folded-up copy of the *New York Daily Investment News* next to him, and Vita picked it up as he tucked into his breakfast. The headline read, 'Stock Market Crisis Over'. She opened the paper out and read on: 'Stock Houses Survive the Worst Day in History.' Scanning the article, she noticed that it was by Waldo Young, a reporter she recalled meeting at one of the Delaneys' dinner parties.

'Read what he says at the bottom,' Mr Delaney instructed.

'*It is over. We have seen the worst. Heaven forbid that anything worse than yesterday on the Stock Exchange should be possible*,' Vita read out.

'Trust me. The market will swing back up. Hold on until next week and you can get your money. This has just been a scare, that's all.'

Vita nodded and got up so that he could have his breakfast in peace. She headed to the door, holding Bertie, then turned back as Mr Delaney called her name.

'We'll miss you both, when you're gone. You will come

back to visit, won't you?' he said. 'Whatever happens, you'll always have a home here.' He pointed his fork at her. 'Don't you forget that. You promise me?'

Vita nodded. 'I promise,' she said, but as she left the breakfast room, she found her eyes filling with tears.

She'd wanted independence for a long time, but even so, it had been deeply reassuring to be in Nancy's family home for the first few months of Bertie's life. Very soon, she would be on her own. And what then?

11

The Lancashire Cotton Company

Clement sighed, his breath clouding against the leaded glass of the office window as he looked down at the small group of men from the LCC leaving from the mill's forecourt.

Once they were gone, he turned back towards his chrome desk and the art deco chair that hurt his back. Edith had had smart new offices fitted. On the way past the desk he crushed out a still-smouldering stub of cigar, left by one of the men in a heavy glass ashtray. He could feel the man's spittle on his fingertips.

It was frustrating that the government had foisted the problems of overproduction and dwindling markets onto the Lancashire Cotton Company, when it was the government themselves who, in Clement's opinion, were to blame. They'd taken all the technology developed over decades in places like Darton and allowed mills to be established in South-East Asia, where people would work for a fraction of what Clement paid the workers at Darton. They simply couldn't compete. He'd seen for himself how many spinning mills and weaving sheds had closed down all over the valley.

Over at the other wall, he now glanced through a porthole window that looked down over the factory floor where the machinists made the bras they were exporting. The bobbins were whirring, the steam machine hissing. He scanned the line of girls in their brown Darton smocks and hairnets, backs hunched over their machines. Instinctively, he looked for Marianne – or Marie, as she'd let him call her – remembering a second too late that he would never see her again.

Recently he'd started to dream about her as she had once been. Years ago, when they'd first started their liaisons, Clement had offered to marry her; to make an honest woman out of her. Marie, thinking he was joking, had refused. He'd been humiliated. After that, there'd been a break while he punished her with his silence. It had only been when Marianne's mother had been maimed in an accident at the mill and the girl, Susan, had come to the house, that Clement had even realized Marie had borne him a child.

He'd given Marie money after that. Not much, but more than her wages, to make up for punishing her. And she'd let him visit her cottage; and sometimes, with a little more force, visit her bed too.

When he'd found out that Edith had used Marie to get to his sister, he'd been unable to believe that she'd masterminded such an audacious plan. He'd gone straight to Paris to find them both. And, unbelievably, Marie had been there with his sister in that grand house.

He vividly recalled the scene in that top room, how torn he had felt when he'd seen Marie, with her halo of blonde hair and blue, blue eyes. He hadn't meant to hurt her, of course he hadn't – only to make her take notice, and to wipe that defiant expression off her face. But then Anna – or Vita, as she called herself – had hit him, catching him exactly on the place on his back where she knew it would cripple him with pain. And Marie, sweet Marie, had fallen to her death.

He'd been so shocked at the sight of her dead body on the railings outside. He'd wanted nothing more than to trap his sister and make her pay. But there'd been a man with a gun, and a car, and in his shock and pain, Anna had slipped through his grasp once more.

He'd thought of that moment continually ever since. It consumed him with hatred and fury that his sister was still free. Still not paying for Marie's life.

At the time, he'd been so shocked that he'd blindly followed Edith's instructions to bring Marie's – *his* – child home from Paris to Darton. The child, Susan, was strange and unlikeable, but sometimes, when he was drunk, he could see so much of Marianne's defiance in her eyes that he imagined, if he touched her, some of her goodness might pour out of her and into him.

He heard the faint sound of laughter and then saw one of the workers glance guiltily up at the porthole, her smile fading when she saw him looking down. Clement wasn't paying them to laugh and they knew it. It was that girl Clarry. If she wasn't careful, he would see to it that she had her pay docked.

He caught sight of his reflection in the porthole glass. His skin was flaking with eczema again and his hair was thinning in two lines at his temple, making him look vampire-ish. That was Anna's fault, too: the way he'd aged with stress and worry.

Now he heard clacking footsteps on the tiles. The door opened and Edith strode in, her slim hips sashaying in her white suit. The feather on the top of her felt hat quivered. He knew how her beauty and her immaculate fashion sense turned heads wherever she went and he'd seen how some of the workers mimicked her style. He supposed she could be considered an asset of sorts, but her shrewd features and haughty beauty set him on edge. If she'd been able to have children, she might have been out of his hair and back at Darton Hall tending to their brood, but quite apart from the annoying fact that she was barren, there was also the fact that she wasn't particularly maternal. No, as far as Clement was concerned, Edith only had one real interest: herself.

'Have you seen this?' she demanded, throwing the newspaper down on the desk. The headline spoke of trouble in America on the stock exchange. She started to pull off her leather gloves and Clement noticed her slim wrists. *How easy they'd be to bind.*

'I'm sure it's nothing,' he said.

'It will be most inconvenient if it is. That certainly wouldn't be in the plan.'

Clement shook his head, rolling his eyes to himself. 'Oh, that,' he said. 'You mean that "*Every woman in the world should have a Darton Bra*".' He quoted her, and her eyes narrowed at his mean impression.

His wife was sometimes quite impossible with her outlandish proclamations.

'You think I can't make it happen?' Her blonde eyebrow arched up in a challenge. 'You have to be fearless in business, Clement. You should know that by now.'

Clement hated himself for not standing up to Edith more, but sometimes it was impossible and he had to pick his battles. It was his own fault for letting her bamboozle her way into his business life.

'So what's all this about visitors?' Edith asked. 'Mrs Dunlop said you'd been in a meeting all morning?'

Clement took a deep breath, steeling himself and cursing the secretary for her indiscretion.

'Well?' Edith demanded.

'If you must know, they were from the Lancashire Cotton Company.'

'What did they want?'

'They have plans for Darton.'

'Plans?'

'To shut us down, or, at the very least, to consolidate us with other mills. They're talking about bigger units and central planning. They want to scrap mills like ours.'

'Scrap Darton?' He noted the horror in her voice. She stood, her hands on her slim hips. 'I hope you sent them packing?' There was a pause. 'You *did* send them packing, Clement?'

'Well, it's complex, and I've been thinking,' Clement said, walking away from her.

'Thinking what, exactly?'

He pressed his lips together. He was going to tell her. To be honest. 'Well, I say we sell our shares to the LCC and get out with some dignity while we can.'

'But Top Drawer . . . everything we've done . . . the Darton Bra is making money. We should have diversified a long time ago. I've said so all along. There's so much money to be made. Every woman in the country needs brassieres, *wants* them even, although half of them don't know it yet.

No, Clement – we haven't worked this hard to give up now, no matter what they offer.' Her voice had become shrill. 'Your father would be turning in his grave at you even *thinking* such a dreadful thing.'

'They were very persuasive.'

'No. I said no.'

'Well, it might not be that simple. What if Hillsafe sells to the LCC?' Clement said.

It was his trump card to quieten her, and he saw the colour rise in her cheeks. Edith had tried to justify her bad business blunder, but they'd paid dearly for it. When the very persuasive man from Hillsafe Investments had approached Edith with the offer of some lifeline funding, she'd thought she was being extremely clever in letting them buy shares. But then Vita's awful husband, Irving, had made Hillsafe buy shares in Darton. Shares he'd given to his wife. Shares that potentially gave her power over the mill. It was a travesty that Clement fretted over most nights.

'That won't happen.'

'But what if it does?'

'You and your mother still own fifty-one per cent.'

'But Anna owns the rest.'

How he hated her for allowing this to happen.

'Well, what are you going to do about it?' Edith said.

'I'm going to find her – Anna, Vita, whatever she calls herself – in Paris. I'm going to get the shares from her,' Clement said.

'How?' Edith sounded alarmed. Clement was aware that this was the first time they'd discussed Vita in a long while. For a moment he wanted to quip about how he'd used to drag Anna around by her hair, which had usually resulted in her bending to his will.

'I'll find a way. I have to. If the LCC gets to her first, we'll be over a barrel.'

12

Darling Cups

The dress Nancy had given Vita was cut fashionably, but was uncomfortably tight, and she wasn't in the mood for a party. By the time she had settled Bertie and arrived downstairs on Friday evening, the Delaneys' smart soirée was already in full swing.

Camilla Delaney was smiling and laughing with a group of guests in the drawing room, her chenille dress the height of elegance, a diamond choker dazzling at her throat. The double doors had been pushed back, turning the room into a reasonably-sized ballroom. At one end there was a stage where the jazz trio were playing Fats Waller, the tall guy on the bass slapping the strings, the pianist rocking his head in time to the rhythm. Waiters circulated in tails and white gloves, offering the guests canapés. *There must be at least seventy people here already*, Vita thought. The Delaneys had certainly gone to impressive lengths to put on the Nancy and Nate show.

Vita knew that if Nancy really loved Nate, she wouldn't be drinking in secret. After the tea room confession, to hear that she wasn't even particularly attracted to him made Vita even more worried. But then, plenty of marriages worked without sex, surely? Her own parents' included – they'd always slept in separate rooms.

And anyway, who was she to pass judgement, when all of her relationships had failed and she'd wound up a single mother? And not just that, but a woman who would never get a husband now. Life was much easier to navigate with a ring on your finger, but who in their right mind would take her on?

She forced a smile as Nancy waved and danced over to her. Was Nancy tipsy? Right now? She was wearing a backless pale green beaded dress that showed off her long neck and the diamond clip she wore in her hair. She and Camilla had clearly been in the safe to put the family jewels on show.

'Darling, that dress does suit you. You always looked *so* good in blue.'

Vita smiled and held out the skirt of the dress. 'It's nice to wear something new. Thank you again.'

'Won't it just be so much fun when we're out of here and living in our own apartments? We'll throw big parties, like we had in Paris in the old days. Not like this.' She leant in, putting the side of her hand up as if imparting a secret.

Nancy certainly wouldn't be holding parties anything *like* the ones they used to go to in Paris, Vita thought. She had met some of Nate's college friends – a cohort of privileged young men with secret handshakes and in-jokes, who were apt to break into barbershop harmonies. Nate thought they were marvellous, but Vita couldn't see Nancy fitting in with their wives and girlfriends, all of them good Christian women.

It alarmed her that Nancy was already glorifying 'the old

days', when Vita had assumed that they'd have so much to look forward to. But Nancy seemed to have forgotten her desire to take the world by storm, to throw 'showbiz' parties with 'famous faces' and 'outrageous fun'. Hadn't that been what she'd once said was her ambition? To really *be* someone?

Irked by Nancy's lack of self-awareness, Vita was about to make a comment to that effect, when Nancy jumped up and began waving profusely. Vita was treated to a waft of her heavy perfume, along with the tang of sweat.

'Darling, darling, over here!' It was Nate she was waving to. He put up his hand in salute and began making his way over. 'Oh, isn't he handsome,' she gushed as he approached.

Nate Materson had fleshy lips and wore his dark hair in a long fringe. He was just about handsome, Vita supposed, but he had the arrogance of someone much better looking. His eyes glittered at Vita now, as he arrived and kissed Nancy's forehead. He was wearing a scarlet-and-white-striped waistcoat which was rather brash and loud, just like Nate himself.

'Nan-Nan, isn't Vita looking swell?' he said, folding her arm under his and patting her hand. Vita's hackles rose. She hated it that Nate called Nancy 'Nan-Nan' or sometimes 'my can-can Nan-Nan' – as if making up a pet name for her made him more alluring.

'I'm just telling Vita what a wild time we'll have when we have our own apartments,' Nancy said, oblivious to Vita's feelings. 'We can pick out decorations. I saw the most darling cups and saucers at Bloomingdale's.' Vita stared at her. She knew Nancy had been on several trips with Nate's friends' wives to the fancy department store, which occupied a whole block on Lexington Avenue, to peruse gifts for her long wedding list. Even so, it was hard to believe her old friend, the daredevil dancer at the Zip and Les Folies Bergère, was now talking about 'darling cups'. *She was so much nicer when she was poor*, Vita thought.

'Well, that's if there's any money left to go shopping,' she said, wanting to bring Nancy back to reality. 'After what happened this week.'

'Now, now, don't you be a sourpuss, Vita,' Nate said, jokingly pointing a recriminating finger at her. He'd stolen another of Nancy's phrases, she noted, but she forced herself to smile.

What was wrong with her? Was she jealous of Nancy? Or was it just that she was terrified of her own future and her social debt to Renata King? Deciding that the only way to cope was to take the edge off her feelings, she grabbed a glass of champagne and downed half of it.

'Steady on, old girl,' Nate said. The way he said it made Vita want to down the rest of it.

13

Intimidating Women

Vita's attention was caught by a man who came up and tapped Nate on the shoulder.

'There you are,' he said. He was tall and slim and looked suspiciously casual for the party. He wore a gold necklace with a Star of David on it in his open-necked shirt. His sun-streaked brown hair was swept back from his forehead, which was spattered with freckles.

'Daniel, you old devil,' Nate said, and the two men shook hands firmly. 'When did you get into town?'

'It's just a flying visit. I had a stopover here. I didn't realize there'd be this much chaos.'

He was clearly referring to the markets – almost gleefully, Vita noted. 'Chaos? Gracious, no. Everything will be back to normal next week,' Nate guffawed.

'You think so?'

'Of course. It's all going to be just swell,' Nate replied, but Daniel only raised his eyebrows. 'I say, why don't you stick around and come to the wedding next Saturday?'

Nancy looked annoyed. Adding another guest was simply impossible after the seating-plan wars that had taken place.

Vita had to bite down a smile at the thought of this new arrival ruining such carefully laid plans.

'Aren't you going to introduce us?' Nancy said pointedly to Nate, adding a slightly aggressive, 'Darling?'

'Oh, of course. This is Daniel Myers,' Nate said, clumsily remembering his manners. 'I told you about him, Nan-Nan. My tennis partner back in the day – although he trounced me every time. I'm so glad you could call in. This is Nancy, my betrothed . . .'

Vita cringed at the way he said 'betrothed' in such an obsequious way.

'You're one of the college friends?' Nancy checked, shaking Daniel's hand.

'Nancy, Nate – can you come?' Mrs Delaney called, clearly wanting the couple to greet some new guests.

'Sorry,' Nancy said, waving her drink between Vita and Daniel. 'Mingle, you two,' she added, with a pointed look at Vita.

There was an awkward pause. Vita stole a look up at Daniel and he raised his eyebrows, as if meeting Nancy and Nate had been an ordeal. She blushed.

'So, how do you know the happy couple?' His accent had a trace of Eastern Europe about it. Another immigrant who'd done well for himself, she surmised.

'Nancy is my best friend,' she said, looking over to where Nancy and Nate were greeting more guests. Nancy's laughter trilled out, carrying across the room.

'Best friend,' he repeated. 'Huh. You're British?' She nodded. 'Well, if she is your *best friend*' – he mimicked her accent – 'you should warn her about that fiancé of hers.'

'Warn her?' She looked up at him. He had the most disarming hazel eyes, she noticed. What did he know about Nate? Some awful secret? Vita prepared herself to receive some scandalous news.

'His false optimism is doomed. What happened yesterday is just the start. In fact, I'd say it was the beginning of the end.'

Oh, he just means the markets, she thought, disappointed.

'The beginning of the end? Surely not? Nate says just the opposite.'

He made a kind of snort of derision. 'It's just gambling.'

'Oh, I see. And you're a puritan?' He didn't look it.

'Not a puritan. Just someone who recognizes that it's dangerous for business to go unchecked like it has been.'

'I thought the business of America *was* business,' Vita said, quoting President Calvin Coolidge who, according to Mr Delaney, correctly thought that the government shouldn't interfere with businesses – or individuals, for that matter.

'That may be so, but do you really think it's right that a handful of people, like your host here, should wield all the power? You must admit that it's dangerous for so few men to be in control. There's no government supervision or regulation of the stock market. It's gambling that's rigged by the professionals. It can't, and won't, go on.'

'Nonsense,' Vita snapped, annoyed by his sanctimonious speech. What an objectionable person he was. How dare he preach such doom and gloom while drinking the Delaneys' champagne?

Even more infuriatingly, his eyes were amused at her discomfort as he looked at her over the top of his glass. Then he said, 'Oh dear. Not you as well. Are you heavily invested?'

It annoyed her that he seemed able to read her so easily. 'So what if I am?'

'If you are, then you're surely going to lose everything,' Daniel said.

'How do you know?'

He laughed. 'Don't sound so suspicious. I have my sources.'

'Well, they're wrong,' Vita said.

'Oh. And are *you* an expert on the financial markets?' he said, in an equally combative tone.

She felt her face flushing. Did he think she wasn't an expert because she was a woman? She was tempted to argue her case, but something about the way he was looking at her made her feel flustered and cross.

'I'm going to *mingle*,' she said, making to leave, but he clutched her arm and she looked up at him, surprised.

'Don't leave,' he said. He had dimples in his cheeks when he smiled and slightly crooked teeth, but his whole face lit up. 'I'm sorry if I was too direct. Don't leave me on my own. You're easily the most interesting girl here.'

Vita wished a pithy retort would present itself. He didn't know the first thing about her.

'I'm a West Coast man. I find these New York girls far too intimidating,' he confided.

'And you don't think I'm intimidating?' Vita asked, offended.

He laughed. 'No.'

'Well, you should.'

14

The Pacifier

As she walked away, Vita was glad she'd said it, congratulating herself for putting Daniel Myers firmly in his place. But at the same time, she knew he was watching her as she went to do her duty, graciously shaking hands with the Delaneys' friends and dropping subtle hints to increase everyone's expectations about Nancy's wedding dress. But knowing that his amused eyes were on her from across the room made her feel self-conscious in a way she hadn't for years.

'I've heard it's incredible,' one of Mrs Delaney's friends said in a confidential whisper, drawing Vita aside for a quiet word. 'And, although nobody knows it yet, I'm fairly sure that my daughter's beau is going to propose any day. We're just waiting for Nancy to have her turn, you understand. But we'll be looking in earnest at dresses from the New Year. If you wouldn't mind me keeping in touch . . .'

'Not at all,' Vita smiled, feeling excited at the prospect of her first commission. But just then, the band struck up with the familiar introduction to 'Baby Face' and Nancy came to grab her, apologizing to the woman as she pulled Vita away, insisting that Vita dance to one of the old numbers from the Zip Club.

Vita, who by now had drunk several more glasses of champagne, allowed herself to be reluctantly dragged in front of the band, wracking her brains to remember the old routine and laughing as she shimmied around in unison with Nancy, wiggling her hands. When the dance ended and the crowd called for more, she followed Nancy's lead, laughing at her crazy kamikaze Charleston style. She noticed that Mr Delaney was tapping his foot, smiling at the spectacle, and Nate was looking around at the crowd to make sure everyone knew what a swell girl his wife-to-be was. Only Mrs Delaney pursed her lips in disapproval. Nancy threw Vita a look. Her mother had no idea how they *really* used to dance. What would she say if she knew that when Nancy had been a dancer at Les Folies Bergère, she hadn't worn knickers under her ruffled can-can skirt?

Afterwards, completely out of breath and hugging Nancy as they soaked up the applause, Vita was relieved when several couples resumed dancing to the band. She walked back into the hallway, passing Daniel, who hadn't moved from where he was leaning up against the doorway.

'That was a most impressive display. Where did you learn to dance so well?' he asked.

'Which one? I learnt the first one in London and the Charleston in Paris,' Vita explained, still woefully out of breath.

But now Vita was interrupted by Evelyn, who was looking for Bertie's pacifier. Knowing that Bertie was probably bawling, and it was only a matter of time before he disturbed the whole party, she hurried to find her bag in the cloakroom, tipping the contents out onto the table in the hallway. She handed Evelyn the paper bag with the new pacifiers, jumping when she realized Daniel had followed her.

'Is everything all right?' he asked.

'Perfectly,' she said, still out of breath.

He was standing next to her, and looked down at the contents of her bag as she started to reload it. It felt oddly personal that he'd caught her out – especially as he now picked up the copy of *Sylvine* which had partially fallen from its paper bag.

'Oh, no . . . no . . . I'll take that,' she said, holding out her hand for it.

'This looks interesting,' Daniel said.

'Vita – Vita, I think you should come?' Evelyn called from upstairs. Torn, Vita looked at Daniel, who seemed to be enjoying her discomfort.

'I have to go.'

'Go where?'

'I have to attend to my baby.'

'You have a baby?' If he was disappointed, he didn't show it. She watched his face for the flicker of judgement that must be coming, but instead, he smiled. 'I'm a sucker for babies. Your husband is a lucky man.'

So he'd made an assumption, Vita realized. Before she could stop herself, she opened her mouth to disabuse him of it.

'I don't have a husband,' she said.

He held eye contact for a moment, as if trying to understand what kind of misfortune had put her in such a position. She knew the drill. She knew that men like him – decent men – ran a mile at such an admission, but Daniel's eyes didn't reproach her and she felt flustered as she went upstairs.

On the top landing, she took Bertie from Evelyn's arms and soothed him.

'When they get that tired, all they want is their Mamma,' Evelyn said in a wise way. Vita thanked her, but it felt all wrong to be holding her baby while she had champagne on her breath. She shushed him and walked softly into his room to lay him down in his cot, stroking his hair and singing a soft lullaby. She stepped out of her shoes for a moment, looking at the rocking chair in the corner of the room, thinking how wonderful it would be to sit in it and close her eyes. But she couldn't. Not while the house was still full of guests and Nancy was expecting more from her.

She gently pushed the mobile she'd made around so that the shadows of boats and aeroplanes danced across the soft blue walls. Bertie sucked noisily on his pacifier, and then, quite suddenly, he fell fast asleep.

Vita crept out and shut the door softly, assuring Evelyn that she'd done the right thing in fetching her.

Back downstairs, to her horror, Daniel was still reading Archie's book, standing where she'd left him by the table in the hallway.

'Oh, please don't read that,' Vita said.

'Why? I like the writing,' he said. 'A. S. Fenwick,' he read from the front cover. Hearing him say Archie's name made Vita's heart thud and a lump come to her throat.

'No,' Vita said, harshly, before she realized she was even going to speak.

'What do you mean, *no*?' Daniel laughed. 'No, it's not good writing, or no, you don't want me to read it?'

'I'll have it back, if you don't mind.'

'Oh, I'm intrigued now,' he said. 'Do you know this guy?'

'It's really none of your business, Mr Myers.'

'It's no matter. I'll get my own copy,' he said, deliberately noting the Argosy Books paper bag on the table. Angrily, Vita shoved the book back into her bag.

'Are you coming back to the party?' she asked him. She was keen to find another drink.

'Actually, I think I'll make a move,' Daniel said. 'A few minutes is all I can ever really take of Nate's crowd.'

She laughed at his candour. 'I suppose I'll see you at the wedding?'

'Oh, no. I'm back to the West Coast where I belong. I'm getting out before next week.' Then, his face taking on an expression of concern, he stepped closer and lowered his voice. 'But be warned: I sincerely doubt there'll be a wedding at this rate.'

'What a dreadful thing to say,' Vita said, shocked, stepping back away from him. He shrugged as if it were inevitable, and his casualness made her blush.

'I hope we bump into one another again, Vita,' he said.

Despite herself, a smile started playing on Vita's lips. Daniel had been the first man to notice her for a very long time. What a shame he had such deluded opinions.

15

Free-fall

When Nancy arrived at breakfast the next morning, Vita knew she had a stinking hangover.

'Who was that man?' Vita asked. 'Daniel?'

She regretted the question immediately when she saw Nancy's stern look. 'An old college acquaintance of Nate's. I think he's a Bolshevik. And a Jew to boot. Don't tell me you like him?'

'No,' Vita said, feeling defensive. She didn't like Nancy using mean labels. What was it to her if Daniel was Jewish or not? Those were Nate's prejudices talking, not Nancy's.

'Good. I'm so relieved he had to leave town. I would have had nowhere to put him. It was so naughty of Nate to invite him to the wedding.'

With Nancy in this kind of mood, Vita didn't have the heart to tell her about her conversation with Daniel.

Mrs Delaney felt that praying collectively for their good fortune would help, so on Sunday she insisted that they all go to church together. Besides, in less than a week's time, Nancy would be getting married – they had to present a united front as a family. Nate came with them, trying to be jolly, but Vita couldn't help remembering Daniel's words and how he'd predicted that there wouldn't be a wedding. Why was she even thinking about a man who'd said such dreadful things?

By Monday, the house was a hub of activity as preparations for the wedding started in earnest. Vita had almost forgotten about the markets when they heard a newspaper boy cycling along the sidewalk, shouting, 'Extra, extra, read all about it.' Nancy rushed out with her two cents.

When she came in, she threw the bulletin directly into the bin. Vita went to fetch it. Reading about how shares across the market had fallen again, she was conscious of an uneasy feeling settling in the pit of her stomach.

On Tuesday, as trading started, Vita went to the ticker tape machine and called for Nancy to come and have a look too. The markets hadn't rallied, but had gone once again into free-fall.

'It's worse than Thursday,' Vita gasped, holding the tape between her fingers. 'Much worse.'

As the morning wore on, the codes stopped coming through altogether. When Nancy tried to telephone her father, the lines everywhere were jammed.

'I'm going down there,' Nancy said. 'There must be some mistake.'

'I'll come with you,' Vita said. 'Do you mind watching Bertie for me?' she asked Evelyn, who nodded, taking the baby with a grave look on her face.

It was easier said than done to get to Mr Delaney's office on Wall Street. The Delaneys' driver got stuck in gridlocked traffic and Nancy and Vita had no choice but to abandon the car and walk.

By the time they made it to the financial district, a huge crowd had gathered outside the New York Stock Exchange. Nancy stood on tiptoe, trying to see past the sea of brown hats.

'What's going on?' Vita asked, unsettled by the strange, restless atmosphere hanging over the scene. They were jostled from behind, the crowd crushing them together. At the end of the street there was a line of mounted police on horseback, the horses restlessly trampling the sidewalk.

'Western Union have put out a notice saying they'll sell our securities unless we can come up with more cash. But where are we supposed to get more cash from?' she heard one man say. Nancy glanced at Vita in alarm.

'Let's ask the shoeshine boys. Father says those boys always know what's what.'

But it was impossible to move to the row of raised leather seats. Instead, they listened to the rumours that flew through the crowd about how the General Motors stock was going down and down. When Vita asked if anyone knew the price, she realized it was way, way below what she'd paid for it. Had all of her investments really been wiped out? Why had she let Nate talk her into borrowing so much and taking such risks? Why had it not occurred to her sooner that she might lose everything? She felt a tight knot of panic in her stomach.

'Hey, lady, watch out,' a gruff voice said as Nancy and Vita shouldered further through the crowd towards the brokerage office. A siren wailed close by.

'Someone has jumped,' a man told them. 'A woman, from the top of one of the buildings. Forty-four floors. The shares, they're falling and falling. The ticker tape can't keep up. The whole system has crashed.'

Once again Vita pictured Daniel's face, his eyes smiling over the top of his champagne glass. He'd predicted this, but Vita hadn't wanted to believe it. He'd been right, though: Nate's optimism had been too good to be true.

'Oh, Vita, Vita – this is terrible,' Nancy said, and Vita saw that she was shaking. 'Nate said that if the markets didn't rally, then . . .'

'Then what?'

But Nancy shook her head and wouldn't say. 'Let's find Father.'

It took another half-hour and some serious sweet-talking of the doorman, the elevator boy and then the secretary to be admitted to the Delaney's Brokerage office, where all the telephones seemed to be ringing at once.

'Daddy, is it true?' Nancy asked, walking through the carved oak door straight to Mr Delaney's desk. He sat with his head in his hands, his elbows on the green leather writing surface, while strands of ticker tape curled and spilled around him like angry snakes.

Vita didn't need him to answer to see straight away that the worst had happened.

'It's a disaster,' Mr Delaney said. 'A disaster. I never thought it possible, but . . .'

'Where's Nate?' Nancy asked, her voice steely.

'He left earlier. I thought he was coming to see you.' Mr Delaney finally looked up, his eyes bloodshot. 'He was terribly, terribly upset. We're all upset. And I . . . well, goddamn it,

I allowed Nate to make a call last week when the pressure was on. I put it on him, to give him some experience, and he was sure things would swing up. So I followed his advice and doubled down. If I hadn't, well . . . I might have been able to salvage . . .' He shook his head.

Nancy used the telephone to ring home, but Vita could hear Mrs Delaney on the other end and she listened to their short conversation. 'He hasn't been here, although a telegram came.'

'What does it say?'

Nancy looked at Vita, her face serious, as she waited for her mother to fetch it and read it. Vita craned in towards the telephone to hear what Mrs Delaney was saying.

'All it says is . . . Oh, Nancy. It says, "I'm sorry. Forgive me."'

Vita saw real panic cross Nancy's face as she replaced the receiver. 'I'm going over to his place,' she said.

'Maybe I should come with you,' Mr Delaney said, standing up, but Nancy shook her head.

'I'd rather you didn't. This is personal, not business. Vita will come with me.'

Nancy reached for Vita's hand. Vita tried to smile reassuringly at her, and at Mr Delaney; but in truth, Nate did not strike her as the kind of man who could lose face and easily bounce back.

16

Nate's Apartment

The block where Nate lived was far more modest than Vita had envisaged. As they stepped out of their cab, the wind from the Hudson River was whistling through the narrow streets. Nate had done a very good job convincing the Delaneys that he was 'the right sort' and from 'good stock', but the damp stairwell in his building spoke of another kind of reality.

No wonder Nancy doesn't like coming here, Vita thought. Why, she wondered, had the Delaneys been so keen on the match to begin with, when they set such great store by their social status? Seeing Nate's living situation made her suspect that Mr and Mrs Delaney were simply intent on seeing their daughter married, no matter what. Perhaps the wedding of the year was a more desperate event than anyone around them had realized.

She and Nancy hadn't discussed the wedding on the way over here, but Vita knew her friend well enough to be sure that the implications of today's events were whirring in her mind. Last week, she hadn't wanted anyone to be in a bad mood because of the markets, but that would be impossible now. Today had been cataclysmic. A financial volcano had erupted, wrecking everything and everyone in its path.

Upstairs, Nancy led the way along a narrow corridor to Nate's apartment.

'Nate,' she called, bashing on the door with her kid-gloved hand. 'Nate, honey, it's me, Nan-Nan. Let me in.'

She looked at Vita, then banged again, this time with the flat of her hand, rattling the door handle.

A man emerged from one of the doors further down the hall. 'Have you seen Nate?' Nancy asked him. 'My fiancé, Nate Materson? He lives here.'

'I saw him earlier. He was drunk. Everyone is drunk. Everyone.' The neighbour retreated into his apartment, mumbling.

'Don't mind the old man. Nate says he's quite crazy,' Nancy said. 'I'm going to get the concierge. He'll have a key.'

She ran down the corridor. Vita stared at Nate's door and the glass spyhole in it, feeling uneasy. In a little while, Nancy was back with a bunch of keys, but Vita could see her hands shaking as she tried several in the lock. Eventually, one of them fitted. She turned the handle and pushed.

'Nate? Nate?' she called as she opened the door.

The room was comfortably furnished, with an iron bed, the brown blanket folded over the white sheet and tucked in at the corners. Striped pyjamas were neatly folded on the pillow. There was a wardrobe with a mirror on the front and a table on which a comb and an ivory clothes brush lined up. On a shelf there was a stack of newspapers and magazines and a picture of Nancy in a silver frame. It seemed too big and too grand for the room. Nancy marched to the kitchenette – perhaps, Vita thought, to check whether Nate was on the small balcony. But the apartment was eerily quiet.

There was one other door to check. Vita walked over to it and turned the handle. As she did so, a shiver up her spine told her that, without a doubt, she would find something dreadful on the other side.

The room beyond was a small bathroom. Nate was in the bathtub, his head submerged below the water, his eyes open. He was still wearing his suit, and his gold cufflinks glinted as Vita's eyes followed the line of his arm drooping over the side of the tub. A whiskey bottle had rolled away from his fingertips. There was an empty brown bottle of pills in the puddle on the floor next to it.

Nancy was coming back into the living room. 'Oh, well, I can't think where he could have gone,' she said, 'but he's not—'

She stopped, seeing Vita's face, and then in two steps she'd crossed the room and was pushing past Vita. A moment later, Vita caught her as her knees buckled in shock.

17

Competition at the Hairdresser's

At Madame Mensforth's salon, Edith admired herself in the mirror in front of her, putting a manicured nail to the white-blonde kiss curl that was sculpted to her forehead. It had taken her several hours to style her hair before coming here this morning to have it restyled.

'Really nothing more than a wash and dry,' she instructed Miss Keys, taking off her hat and handing it to her. In the mirror, she noticed the gaggle of women by the basins and the frisson of drama her appearance at the salon this morning had caused. Edith was somewhat of a celebrity here. 'I don't have time for colour.'

'Are you sure?' Miss Keys asked.

'You think I need it?'

Edith turned to Miss Keys, whose cheeks coloured. 'No. No, you're right. Today you can manage with just the set, Mrs Darton.'

Edith nodded, pleased not to have been contradicted, although to be honest, she didn't mind prolonging the trip here. It was infinitely preferable to being in Darton Hall with Clement and her mother-in-law.

She let Miss Keys lead her over to the basins, thinking

that it was hardly the Harrods Ladies' Hairdressing Courts. Back in the days before she'd come out in society, her mother had taken her there, and she vividly recalled the modern decor, the fresh flowers and the sense that within the luxuriously furnished inner sanctum, she was mixing with the cream of society. She hadn't been able to stop staring at the glamorous women who were there for massages, slimming treatments, manicures and chiropody. She remembered how she'd had her hair cut in an individual beauty nook which had an ivory telephone and a tray beside the chair that swung into place, so that one could write letters or eat a meal while being pampered.

Oh, those were the days.

How Edith longed for such refinement now. She sometimes ached for London, for society, for the kind of glamour she'd taken for granted. Her beauty was wasted here, where there was hardly anyone to notice her. Clement barely gave her a passing glance these days. What good was looking as fine as she did, when there was nobody to behold her efforts?

'That's a pretty ring you have,' Edith said, smiling in the mirror at Miss Keys.

'Oh, Mrs Darton,' the young woman gushed. 'You noticed. Yes, yes, I'm engaged,' she said, her ruddy cheeks shining as she grinned.

'Congratulations,' Edith said, fingering the opal ring she wore on her own finger. Her engagement to Clement had been a contract of sorts, but with their relationship as strained as it was these days, she wondered now, as she did quite often, whether she'd made the right decision.

It infuriated her that Clement had decided to find Vita again and it unnerved her, after what had happened to Marie, to think about what might happen during another confrontation with his sister. He'd shut down any suggestion that she approach Vita herself and remained incommunicative about his plans. If she hadn't been so shocked and angry before he'd left, she might have told him everything she'd learnt about Vita . . . about her affair with Archie Fenwick on her honeymoon, and how her husband had collapsed when he'd heard the news.

She knew it was vital information and powerful gossip that Clement might well use to his advantage, but she'd deliberately kept quiet. She would keep her powder dry and her secrets close to her chest.

Even so, the whole situation was intolerable and had to be sorted out soon. They had to get control of Darton, because the idea of the LCC getting hold of it and shutting them down was outrageous. No, they had to make a stand and forge forward with her business plans. She'd worked too hard to see everything wasted.

Because without Darton, what did she really have? Her beauty, of course, but that wasn't enough to outweigh her terrible marriage, the spite of Susan and the dreadful fact that she could never bear her own child. And now, as she so often did, she pictured Vita holding her bonny baby, which must have been born by now – and her heart hardened with bitter jealousy.

'It's like a dream,' Miss Keys continued, interrupting her thoughts. 'When Christopher asked me . . . well, I thought I was going to burst.' She touched the back of her ring with her thumb, holding it up so that the pitiful stone caught the light. 'We'll be just as happy as can be,' she said. 'I cannot wait to be married. Is it wonderful being married?'

'It has its moments,' Edith said, breaking eye contact. The girl's puppy-dog look of adoration was too much. Edith had only been in love like that once. Now she thought about Quentin and how, for those heady few months when she'd been a debutante, she had felt on top of the world. Quentin had told her over and over again how beautiful she was, until she'd felt quite radiant. At the time, she hadn't minded the scandal, the shame her parents had felt at their eligible daughter running off with a man with such a womanizing reputation. She hadn't cared about their feelings at all. She'd been so in love, she'd been prepared to walk over hot coals for her lover. That was until he'd shattered her heart, having ruined her reputation and chances for good.

Now that she was married, she wondered if she might ever get to feel like that again – that addictive, all-consuming passion. It was bad enough to be barren, but to never feel love?

She was being ridiculous, she told herself, closing down the stupid, girlish train of thought. Her position at Darton and in society in general more than made up for the shortcomings of her marriage to Clement. She had money and power. That was worth far more than the dreamy, silly look on her hairdresser's face.

'I can't believe it's nearly November already,' Miss Keys said conversationally as she led Edith over to the chairs, a towel now wrapped around her head.

'It's my least favourite month,' Edith admitted. 'I suppose

it's quiet for you at this time of the year?' she asked. She found it awkward to indulge in this kind of chit-chat, but she knew it was important not to appear snobbish. Besides, the salon was a hotbed of gossip, and Edith liked to know what was going on.

'Oh no. It's been busy,' Miss Keys said. 'We went over to the St Hilda's school yesterday to cut the girls' hair.'

Edith looked up at the name of Susan's school. She'd placed Susan in the prestigious school as a bribe to get Marianne to go to Paris. It had taken some clever subterfuge on her part. When Clement had brought the child home from Paris, Edith had kept her on at the school and, although the adoption papers weren't official, she liked to think of herself as Susan's mother.

'Oh?' Edith said, her interest sparked. 'You may have cut my daughter's hair? Susan Darton? Do you remember her?'

'Maybe,' Miss Keys said. 'I didn't catch all their names. They all have long hair and it took an age, since we had to towel their hair.'

Edith thought of Susan in boarding school and felt glad that she had this small connection, that they might have had their hair touched by the same person in the same week.

She had so hoped that Susan would soften and thaw towards her, but the girl hadn't been able to wait to get back to school. It was almost as if she couldn't bear to be under the same roof as Edith, which was so unfair, when Edith had done so much for her. She'd given Susan a start in life that she could never normally have experienced as a mill worker's daughter. She'd brought her into Darton, into their family – but Susan refused to be grateful or even to treat her as a friend, let alone as a mother. With life at Darton Hall so terribly dreary, Edith had longed for Susan to be an ally; but she'd been anything but.

'A few of the girls there want to go into the beauty business.'

Edith's eyebrows shot up. She would have hoped that after such an expensive education, girls from St Hilda's would have higher aspirations.

'Do you like being a hairdresser?' she asked.

'Oh, yes,' Miss Keys said proudly.

'And you make money?'

'I started on three shillings a week, but now I've trained for four years I'm on thirty shillings. It's much better than working over in the mills.' In the mirror, Edith saw that her cheeks had coloured. 'I'm sorry, Mrs Darton . . .'

'No, it's perfectly all right. Go on. I'm intrigued to know what the appeal is of hairdressing over mill work.' It was always good to keep an eye on the competition, after all.

'I used to be a mill girl,' Miss Keys admitted. 'Over in Bolton. I had a cousin who worked at Darton and I nearly went there, but . . . well, I got the chance to train here. There's a few of us mill girls who work here. Madame Mensforth says she likes us seeing as we're good with our hands and we're good at concentrating. It's no bother after staring at a machine all day. And it's easier to talk and get to know the clientele.' She said *clientele* proudly, her Lancashire accent slipping into faux French. A new word she'd learnt. As if that could ever make her sophisticated.

'Very interesting,' Edith said. In business, there was always a threat, but she hadn't expected hairdressing to be one.

As Miss Keys combed her hair, Edith picked up a copy of the *Daily Mirror* from the table beside her.

'Goodness,' she said aloud, reading the headline. '*Wall Street's Panic Day. The worst crash in the history of Wall Street, when thousands of people were ruined.*'

So much for Clement saying that it would blow over. This looked far more serious than he'd made out.

'I don't understand all of that,' Miss Keys said. 'Those greedy Americans. Got what they deserved.'

'Quite,' Edith said, her mind whirring. Lancashire was supposed to be the beating heart of cotton production in this country, but Edith knew that this year, for the first time, there were more spindles in the USA than in the UK. If the stock market had crashed, there was bound to be a knock-on effect for their business.

What had started as Top Drawer had expanded and evolved and now brassieres in several ranges and twelve different sizes were being shipped all over Britain, and out to Paris too. And Edith had her sights on America, and had been in correspondence with an import agent in New York.

If only she had enough control to go to New York herself, to make the connections she knew she could. After all, she'd been the one who'd saved Darton once already, when she'd raised finance from the sale of the shares. Yes, it had been unfortunate that the shares had landed up in Vita's hands, but there'd been much-needed investment nevertheless. She smarted as she thought of how Clement had frittered half of it away, making one bad decision after another.

And now, as she watched Madame Mensforth talk to some of the girls and saw them scurry away to do her bidding, she realized that she wanted to be the boss on her own terms. Quite suddenly, as she met her own hard stare in the mirror, an altogether new thought started taking shape in her mind. What if *she* were to get Vita's shares, instead of Clement? And perhaps her mother-in-law's, too? What if she, Edith, owned the lion's share of Darton? What then?

18

A Pitifully Small Service

In the aftermath of Nate's death, the days were dark, a recriminating rain lashing down. Vita could sense a terrible, tense atmosphere hanging over New York City. *The beginning of the end.* Wasn't that what Daniel had said? It certainly felt like it.

Almost overnight, businesses folded along with the banks, and the city, which had always seemed so vibrant, took on a grim atmosphere as whole families lost their livelihoods. The Salvation Army stopped talking about the dangers of alcohol and had to be more practical; soup kitchens began springing up everywhere to feed queues of hungry men. Mrs Delaney and Evelyn took blankets and clothes down to the mission, and Vita gathered up all of Bertie's old baby outfits and packed them up too. It broke her heart to think that people had babies they couldn't feed or clothe.

In the face of seeing so many others in dire need, Vita felt terribly guilty that her thoughts were often selfishly focused on money. She had nobody to commiserate with about the shock of losing all her investments, and with them her dreams. She desperately wanted someone to tell her that it was all going to get better; but that wasn't going to happen, given the state of the Delaneys.

Mr Delaney was distraught about Nate and also about what had happened on the stock market. Keeping Nate's name out of the papers had taken a lot of phone calls, some of which Vita had overheard. Nate wasn't the only young man to have taken his own life in the aftermath of the crash, but the shame of it hung heavily around the family. And a sense of guilt, too. She'd overheard Patrick Delaney weeping to Camilla, saying that it was his fault for heaping so much pressure onto Nate's shoulders.

Camilla Delaney, her eyes also red-rimmed, but from lack of sleep, had to take on the awful task of cancelling the wedding. Nancy, meanwhile, made herself absent. For a straight two weeks she stayed in her room in a fuzzy haze, thanks to the tranquillizers the doctor had prescribed – and, no doubt, the vodka under the bed.

Vita crept around the house, looking after Bertie, doing what she could to help the family, and trying to wrap her head around the calamity that had befallen the world.

Nate's funeral was held on a grim day three weeks after the crash. Only Vita, Nancy, her family and a few colleagues from the brokerage office were in attendance. Nate's mother had insisted that he be buried in New York, but she didn't travel for the small ceremony, claiming that her nerves couldn't take it. It had taken a hefty contribution from the Delaneys to allow Nate to be buried in consecrated ground; Vita wondered how Camilla had managed to square this with her staunch Catholic beliefs. Not for the first time, she recognized that there really was one set of rules for the wealthy and another for everyone else.

With some gentle coaxing, Nancy had managed to pull

herself together in the last few days and had obviously decided to make the 'grieving widow' look as fashionable as possible. She was wearing a chic black crepe suit, cinched at the waist, her make-up perfect and her lips painted a deep red. There was a spray of black feathers on her veiled hat.

They drove in the car to the funeral chapel. 'When I think of all the people who were so eager to come to the wedding – but they couldn't turn out for this,' she said with a sigh as they stepped out into the chilly air. The slate of the chapel roof glistened with the fine rain. Two undertakers stood by Nate's coffin next to the open door. Inside, the pews were almost empty. 'Poor Nate. He thought he was so popular.'

'People don't know what to say,' Vita said, trying to find a way to comfort her friend. She pulled the fur stole that Archie Fenwick had given her around her neck and looked across the graveyard.

Vita had never been a particular fan of Nate's, but there was something unspeakably sad about the pitifully short ceremony. There was no music, just a few prayers. As Nancy pressed a handkerchief to her eyes, she reached out and held Vita's hand tightly and didn't let go.

Afterwards, Mr and Mrs Delaney were silent as they walked away from the chapel, leaving the funeral directors to take the coffin to the grave. Mr Delaney put his arm around his wife's shoulder, and Vita saw she was crying. They followed, heading back to the car, but Nancy stopped.

'Vita, I need a drink,' she said.

'Oh goodness, so do I.'

'Didn't you say you knew of a speakeasy?'

'Yes. Paul's place. Let's go!'

19

Le Monsieur's in Harlem

They made their way downtown in a cab after dropping the Delaneys back at home and changing. Vita had written down the address of Paul's speakeasy, but as they arrived at a grubby milk bar next to a bakery, she began to wonder whether she really had it right.

'This is it?' Nancy asked, disappointed.

'I think so,' Vita said, recalling that Paul had told her the bar was a secret and that, as he was New York's greatest bootlegger, it was to stay that way.

The milk bar was empty except for an old woman eating a cream bun in one of the booths. She glanced up at them with dull, bloodshot eyes. An Italian-looking man with bushy eyebrows was behind the counter. He looked at them suspiciously.

'I'm a friend of Paul's,' Vita said nervously in a quiet voice, then added, 'Le Monsieur's,' remembering his nickname in Paris. The man's chin jutted out and he flicked his eyes towards a plain brown door next to the restroom. Vita took a step towards it and then looked back at the man, whose chin jutted out a second time. She guessed that meant she should keep going.

Now she noticed that there was a sliding wooden panel in the door. She and Nancy jumped when it moved an inch and a small section of a man's face appeared, his eye menacingly close.

'I'm a friend of Paul's,' Vita said again, as Nancy clutched onto her arm.

'Le Monsieur's,' Nancy added dramatically. Vita wondered whether Nancy believed her at all, but she seemed to be enjoying the adventure. Paul knew some very shady people, but now Vita felt apprehensive. Was this really a safe place for two unaccompanied young women?

The panel slid shut and there was a moment of silence. Vita looked at Nancy, about to suggest that they retrace their steps and run as fast as they could up to the street to the safety of the main road; but Nancy's eyes were glittering with excitement. And then the door opened.

An old, Spanish-looking man was on the other side, smoking a cheroot. He nodded down the grey corridor ahead to another door at the end, before sitting back on his stool and picking up a newspaper. He didn't say a word.

Vita and Nancy, clinging onto each other, made their way to the door at the end. As they approached, Vita turned and saw the man by the door pick up a telephone. He nodded to them and waved his hand for them to go forward.

The catch on the door in front of them gave, and she pushed it.

They stepped through and found themselves on a balcony that seemed to be suspended in space, as if several floors of a building had been excavated below them. And suddenly, there it was – a heady rush of jazz and smoke.

It was like being transported back in time, to Chez Joséphine in Paris.

Nancy gasped and clutched Vita's arm even more tightly as she took in the scene below. 'Jeepers creepers, Vita! You knew about this place all along, and you never told me?'

Vita smiled. It was good to get a glimpse of the old Nancy back, after the trauma of the past few weeks.

'It's not like I've had the chance, is it?' she said.

At their eye level, a glittering chandelier was suspended from the ceiling. Way down below them was a dance floor with tables; along the back of the room ran a row of booths with red leather banquettes. At one side was a bar, glass bottles lined up along the mirror.

Heads turned as Nancy and Vita made their way down the spiral cast-iron staircase, past the rough brickwork, their shoes clattering on the metal as they went down and down.

A few couples were dancing in the smoky haze, draped over each other. The guy at the piano, his hat at a rakish angle, was playing effortlessly while smoking. A trumpeter and a drummer were improvising with him.

There was one large table at the back. Vita heard the guffaws from the men who sat there, napkins tucked into the necks of their shirts, cracking lobster claws.

They approached the bar and ordered, Nancy insisting on cocktails, delighted that the barman would make her a '75. Then Vita saw a man approaching from the table of diners.

'Vita? Vita, is that really you?' he called.

'Paul!' Vita exclaimed. He was wearing a suit and he stretched his arms out wide, a look of jubilation on his face.

'My goodness. Look at you!' he said. Vita yelped as he lifted her up and swung her around. She was too heavy these days to be manhandled like this, but today was different to every other day.

'Oh, Paul, Paul. I had no idea if you'd be here.'

'How can you say that? I've been waiting all this time for you to walk into my bar. Welcome to Le Monsieur's.'

'Is that what you called it? Le Monsieur's?'

'Just as you suggested, my dear. But where have you been all this time?' he said in his Irish brogue, pretending to be put out, but his eyes were twinkling.

'With Nancy.' She pulled Nancy forward, and Paul kissed her hand.

'*This* is Nancy? Mr Wild's Nancy?'

'And you're Le Monsieur,' Nancy said excitedly. 'I never got a chance to thank you for rescuing Vita and bringing her over.'

'Anything for my Vita. Any time,' he said. 'So – what do you think of the place? It's quiet now, at this time, but by midnight this place is jumping.'

'It's wonderful,' said Vita. 'I meant to come before, but I couldn't. The baby . . .'

'Of course,' Paul said, putting his hands to his cheeks and remembering. 'A boy?' he checked, and Vita nodded, laughing at the memory of Paul and the boys making bets about her baby. Paul slapped the wooden bar with his palm. 'I knew it. Didn't I say?'

'Yes, you did.'

'He's a darling,' Nancy chipped in.

'I called him Bertie.'

'Bertie, that's a fine name.'

The cocktails arrived now, and Paul looked at the barman. 'On the house, Dino,' he said. 'For my great friend Vita here. I'm glad I've got someone to celebrate with.'

'Celebrate?'

'Best day for me yet,' Paul said. 'I'm making a fortune out of the crash.'

'Sir,' Dino said, 'there's a telephone call for you.'

'Excuse me, ladies, I've got to go. Drink up, and have more besides. Dino,' he said to the barman, 'anything they want. These ladies are my special guests.'

20

A Daring Plan

Dino led them over to a table with chairs upholstered with gold cushions.

'So that's the famous Paul,' Nancy said, once they'd clinked glasses.

Vita nodded and took a sip of her drink. 'He's a riot.'

'And likes you,' Nancy smiled. 'You didn't tell me you had a good-looking Irishman up your sleeve.'

'Oh,' Vita said, interpreting her meaning and shaking her head. 'He's not for me. Or, actually, more that I'm . . . *we're* . . . not for him.'

Nancy took a moment to get Vita's meaning. 'Oh – well that's a shame. All the good ones are the other way inclined. Cheers,' she said, holding up her cocktail, and they clinked glasses again. 'God, I've missed this,' Nancy added, taking a sip and holding it in her mouth as if savouring sweet nectar. She swallowed and sighed.

'Take it easy,' Vita said, recognizing the approaching clatter of Nancy publicly falling off the wagon. But at the same time, being here, in this place, together, was bringing them back to who they had been before Nancy's spiral into drugs in Paris – before Bertie, or Nate, or the wedding.

And as the drinks went down, Vita had to admit that it was lovely to smile and laugh, even when things were so dark outside.

'Poor Nate. I guess this is a blessing, in a way,' Nancy said.

'How can it be a blessing?'

'If all of this had happened and he *hadn't*, you know . . . done away with himself . . . then I could never have married him,' Nancy said, looking up at Vita now. Her eyes were candid. 'Not if he was' – she leant forward – '*poor*.'

She said it like it was a dirty word. There was a moment's pause as Vita let this rather unpleasant admission sink in. What was Nancy really saying? That she'd have gone through with her marriage vows – in sickness and in health, for richer or poorer – but she wouldn't have meant them?

'Does that make me terrible?' Nancy asked.

'Yes. But you shouldn't have agreed to marry him in the first place, if you felt like that.'

'I know. I know you're right. And I feel a cad about it, but I just kept thinking that it would all come good. But you know . . . I couldn't really imagine actually marrying him. Not when it came to it.'

'What do you mean? You've been talking about nothing else for months.'

'I thought . . .' Nancy sighed. 'I thought if I concentrated on the details, then the actual moment would come into view. But then – when we went to the tea room – I realized the reason I couldn't picture it was that it wasn't going to happen.'

So that was what Miss Cuba had said. *That* was why Nancy had been so strange afterwards.

'What do you mean, it wasn't going to happen?'

'It wasn't my fate. That's what Mikette said.'

'She actually said that?'

'She said that marrying was not my destiny. Those were her exact words.'

Vita took a moment to absorb this revelation. What would have happened if the stock market had stayed rising and the wedding had gone ahead? Would Nancy have jilted Nate at the altar? At the very last minute?

'And she was right,' Nancy continued. 'I *haven't* married Nate. It wasn't my destiny.'

'Then what is?'

Nancy grinned and knocked back her drink, smacking her lips. 'Well, I've been thinking . . .'

Vita's eyebrows drew together. Nancy clearly had a plan.

'What if we just . . .' She fanned her hand out in an arc. '. . . Went?' Her eyes were glittering. Vita had a sudden recollection of how her friend Percy had once described Nancy as someone who liked to detonate things and leave a mess. Was that what she was proposing to do again?

'Went? Where?' Vita asked.

'To Hollywood.'

'*Hollywood?*'

'What if it's not too late?'

'For what?'

'For us. For our dreams. Like *you* said the other day.'

'We can't just—'

'Think about it,' Nancy cut her off, gripping Vita's hands. 'We could just skip town. You, me, Bertie and Mr Wild. We could take the train. We could just . . . go.'

'But . . . your parents will be distraught.'

'They've got too much to worry about already. It'll be a relief if I'm out of the way.'

They couldn't just go, could they? Leave poor Mr and Mrs Delaney? But at the same time, the thought of being free of the impending meeting with Renata King – well, that certainly appealed. Vita was supposed to be going to her apartment to present Bertie next week. Besides, she reasoned, what was left here for her in New York, now that Nancy's wedding was off? What hope was there of any other commissions?

'But how will we survive?' she asked, remembering just what a tight financial hole they were in. She'd lost all of her money, and Nancy had too.

'I'm going to make it in the talkies,' Nancy announced, and Vita laughed.

'But you don't know the first thing about acting,' she said. She regretted it immediately, but Nancy was too thick-skinned to be offended.

'Well, how hard can it be?'

'I'm not sure, but I'd say fairly hard.'

Nancy waved her hand in dismissal. 'Rubbish. I have my contacts.'

Vita recalled the hurried phone call she'd made from Paris, when she'd told Nancy that she was coming to the States; at the time, she had really had nowhere else to turn. Nancy had been tremendously excited and had mentioned going to Hollywood to make it in the movies, explaining to Vita that she'd met a producer at the clinic. But very soon afterwards, she'd met Nate and dropped all her plans.

'Come on, Vita, drink up. Let's go and get our tickets before we change our minds.'

'Really? Now? Right now?' Vita realized her head was spinning, and not just from the alcohol.

'Where are you going?' Paul asked, coming over. 'I was just about to bring champagne.'

'Oh, Paul, we've made a big decision,' Vita said, her eyes meeting Nancy's. This illicit pact was quite thrilling. Would she regret it? Would she wake up and think she'd made a terrible mistake, once she was sober?

'Oh?'

'We're heading out west. To Los Angeles.'

'We're going to get our tickets. This very instant,' Nancy said drunkenly, although Vita doubted that either of them was sober enough for that.

Paul laughed and rubbed the side of his face.

'Sounds like you two have made up your minds. Allow my driver to take you over to Penn Station,' he said, clicking his fingers to call Dino over. 'But only after we've had a glass of champagne to celebrate. You can tell me all about it.'

21

Paris in the Lights

Clement sipped his small but surprisingly tasty coffee in the little Parisian café he'd found near his hotel. The window next to him was painted with gold and red letters and, beyond it, the fine rain was blurring the buildings to a soft haze. In the past few hours, he'd seen all manner of passers-by – chic women with little dogs on leads, men in fine suits with umbrellas, smart cars and trams taking people around the busy, bustling metropolis.

Yes, Paris had its charms, he had to admit, looking around the café with its dark wood panelling and the counter filled with delicious-smelling pastries, the radio playing some crackly jazz. If he were a different sort of man – the kind Edith wished he was – he could see, objectively, how he might consider a city like this romantic.

It was the class of the place that he'd never realized before. Naturally, as an Englishman, he'd always considered himself far superior to the continentals, but they did things with a certain style here. The Christmas displays in the shops, for example, were particularly impressive; Clement thought the shops in Manchester would do well to take note. And knowing that this was exactly the type of thing that would impress Edith, he felt even better that he was here without her.

He'd arrived two days earlier and, never having had the chance to look around before, he'd spent time exploring – although admittedly he was as jumpy as a cat at the thought of a chance meeting with his sister. He missed Rawlings, the private detective who'd tracked her down in London. He'd been such a practical and reassuring influence, and he'd have been perfect for dealing with his sister again. Clement had enjoyed their brief friendship and when he thought about Rawlings' tragic demise in front of that bus, while he'd been chasing Anna, it caused an unusually sentimental sensation of grief followed by a much harder spike of bitter fury.

But, like it or not, Clement was here in this strange city by himself. The previous night, to calm his nerves after a bellyful of steak and a bottle of particularly good French claret, he'd managed to procure himself a prostitute outside the Moulin Rouge. She'd taken him to a narrow doorway in between two shops and up the rickety wooden stairs to a tiny room, where a sleepy-looking colleague had left the bed so that the girl and Clement could have the place to themselves. There'd been a red shawl draped over the light, spotted with singe marks, and the room had smelt unpleasantly of onions and decay. The girl had demanded money first, then had dropped to her knees in a desultory fashion. Clement had enjoyed putting his hands around her throat, almost choking her as he finally felt a release he hadn't experienced in months.

Now he turned the pages of the *Continental Daily*, the only English-language newspaper he had found on the wooden rail. These days, doom and gloom seemed to pervade the pages of all the papers. There was no denying that the ripples of the Wall Street crash had already reached far beyond the United States, where the economy seemed to have completely collapsed and the government seemed powerless to stop it. The newspaper reported that car production had all but ceased, and building construction with it. Clement didn't care about other businesses; he was more concerned about Darton, and how their orders from the United States had dried up.

With all this financial misery everywhere, it was good to be away, and not just for a break from Edith, but also to get a little perspective on the situation at the mill. It seemed to Clement that for months now, he'd been firefighting on all fronts. Quite apart from the spectre of owing money, which meant he hadn't been able to return to the club or play poker, the LCC had swung their searchlight attention onto Darton. There had been a rather unpleasant investigation into working conditions, which had taken up the whole of the end of November.

Clement had been, and remained, incensed about it. It was outrageous that Darton, of all the mills, had made the front pages of the local paper, the *Daily Dispatch*.

The inspectors had turned up early one morning and when Clement and Edith had arrived at the mill, they'd found men with clipboards and shamefaced workers who'd obviously been forced into talking ungenerously about the management. After the inspectors had left, Edith had told Clement in a rather fierce voice to stay in the office – which was probably just as well, as he was so angry, he might have fired half the workforce. Edith, however, had somehow managed to settle the situation, although not without dismissing a few of the ringleaders herself.

But in one way, at least, the heat on Darton had played into his hands. Edith had been so keen to placate their customers, going on a mission to restore their reputation, that she'd been somewhat distracted. And with her out at meetings so much, Clement had been able to dabble in some light forgery in order to lighten her personal bank account by a few hundred pounds.

It was becoming an increasingly complicated business, keeping their real financial situation away from her. Not even Tantum, his right-hand man, understood the full extent of how stretched they were or the complexity of juggling their creditors. They needed more orders in, and fast. Either that, or they needed to sell Darton – but at a price that would mean Clement could pay off his debts and start a new life. Yet, after the LCC's little antics with the newspaper investigation, he doubted that they'd value Darton at even half of what it was worth.

Maybe Edith was right. Maybe they would be better keeping hold of Darton, although he'd hate to have to acquiesce to her business plan, which she kept banging on about like a monkey with a drum. One thing was certain to him: if he didn't play this very carefully, he could end up with nothing. Less than nothing. And that was a prospect that weighed very heavily on his mind.

He'd tried, of course, to go directly to Hillsafe to get his sister's shares, but that plan wasn't going to work either. From his rather terse conversation with Mr Heal, their contact at Hillsafe, Clement had got the impression that he'd only made the situation worse. The man was infuriating and had steadfastly refused to give out any information about Anna, or Vita King as she now called herself – even though Clement was family. The only way the shares could be transferred was if proper papers were drawn up and Vita were to sign them herself, in person, he'd told Clement.

He wondered if Heal would have been so unhelpful if Vita were dead. *Well, there might be one way to find out.*

He paid for his coffee now and folded up the newspaper, shrugging on his heavy woollen overcoat. Instinctively, he started to pull out his pocket watch to check the time, but then remembered where it was.

He curled his lip in displeasure. It was time.

22

The Ford Model A

Vita gripped the large steering wheel of the blue Ford Model A roadster as she and Nancy pulled away from the garage. The handsome manager, smiling and rubbing his hands on a rag, grew rapidly smaller in the rear-view mirror. Nancy had hired the car for a month, sweet-talking him with a smile and a flash of the ever-diminishing stack of notes she'd procured from Goldie before they'd left New York.

Vita had only learnt to drive in France, thanks to Irving, who had teased her about how she drove far too fast and with little regard for the road markings or traffic signs. She gave a startled laugh as they sped up, then indicated onto a main road and swerved round the corner. In the distance, the hills were brown and wild against the vivid, cloudless blue sky.

Nancy whooped, her hair flying in the breeze, the collar of her pale-yellow dress flapping. Vita grinned at her. She'd certainly dropped any sign of being a grieving widow, and it seemed to Vita that the further she got from New York, the further she got from the person she'd been in the Delaney household and the more she became the Nancy of old – from London, from those brilliant first weeks at the beginning in Paris.

It was thanks to Nancy's daring attitude that they'd managed to find accommodation at the Beverly Hills Hotel, and at a reduced rate. When she'd first announced that this was where she intended to stay, Vita had scoffed that it was impossible. Undeterred, Nancy had put on her finest suit, tucked a gardenia into her buttonhole and applied a hefty slick of red lipstick, instructing Vita to look put-upon and to stay behind her at all times. Then, bold as brass, she'd strode into the hotel lobby and informed the young man on the reception desk that she was an actress, a star on Broadway, here in Hollywood for a major role in a movie. The man, clearly not impressed, had informed her that the hotel was fully booked and that there was nothing he could do without a reservation.

Nancy had kicked up an almighty stink, insisting that her agent had booked a suite for her, her baby and her assistant. Vita had slipped easily into the role of assistant, although she'd almost burst out laughing when Nancy had shouted at her for not attending to Bertie properly. Then Bertie had started to yell and Nancy had produced some 'real' tears of her own. The young man, clearly flustered and keen to stop Bertie's racket, had quickly moved Vita and Nancy into one of the hotel's prestigious bungalows.

Nancy had kept up the act, lounging by the poolside in a very ostentatious way, until the hotel manager had cottoned on to the truth. He clearly had more contacts on Broadway than Nancy did. He'd told them that even by his standards, Nancy's had been an audacious lie, but nevertheless he seemed impressed . . . amused, even. He'd given them the number of a realtor and Nancy had fixed up a meeting to view an apartment this morning.

Vita was rather taken with her new city. She hadn't expected Los Angeles to be so well established. In the past few weeks they'd explored everywhere, by tour bus, tram and taxi. The City Hall was a buttressed skyscraper that was just as impressive as the buildings Vita had seen in New York, and the rubber baron's headquarters of Samson Tires with its crenellated tiers was like an Egyptian palace. The houses were outlandish, too – full-scale Spanish missions and Tudor mansions that looked as if they'd escaped from the movie lots. It seemed to Vita that people lived here as if they were in a permanent movie themselves. They'd ridden past John Barrymore's estate in Beverly Hills, where the tour guide told them he had an aviary stocked with three hundred rare birds and a private zoo. Greenacres, Harold Lloyd's estate, had a miniature fairy-tale house for the children and a forty-room Italian Renaissance villa. Just to be in the same city as these people, with these extraordinary visions, felt daring and exciting.

Now Vita turned to check that Bertie was still settled in his Moses basket on the back seat, but he seemed undisturbed by the hot breeze from the open window. Mr Wild sat on the seat next to the crib, his tongue lolling out. Vita laughed, thinking how much Mr Wild behaved like a patient nanny.

'Good boy,' she said, patting his head. Nancy righted the steering wheel, forcing Vita to concentrate, although the roads were so wide that there was room for several cars side by side. The cracked asphalt ahead seemed to go on for miles.

Nancy unfolded the giant map of Los Angeles on her lap, the grids of blocks so different to the layout of London and Paris and a million miles away from the streets in English villages. Vita had been studying the map since they'd bought it, trying to familiarize herself with the strange geography. Now, glancing down at it, she pointed out where they were and the cross that marked the location of the apartment.

She'd just about got to grips with Hollywood, Beverly Hills and West Hollywood and Brentwood to the north, but she was longing to see the coast, and they planned to go to Santa Monica and Venice Beach. There was so much of the city they had yet to explore – south beyond Culver City, all the way down the long boulevards to Long Beach, as well as the hills surrounding the city, although Vita knew it was wild out there once the lights faded. The starlit nights were filled with the howl of coyotes, and Nancy had told stories of cowboys and Indians to scare her.

'Oh, look, look, Vita. There it is,' Nancy gasped, pointing between the buildings. 'The Hollywoodland sign! There, look. Up on the hill.' She leant right up against the windscreen.

Vita, more used to the car now, relaxed a little bit and looked too, wishing she had time to stop and take another photograph of it, but it was time to turn into Hollywood Boulevard, which was dappled by the shade of the leafy palm trees that grew along its edges. A convoy of trucks was coming towards them from the other direction. One of them honked its horn.

'Look,' Nancy said, pointing to the van with the MGM Studios logo printed on the side. Vita looked in the wing mirror. Lolling in the back of the van were several tanned actors dressed as Roman centurions, smoking cigarettes. They waved at Nancy, who twisted out of the window to wave back.

'Oh my,' she sighed, with a happy grin on her face.

Nancy had taken to reading back issues of *Variety* wherever she could find them, asking everyone they met about the studios and how to get an 'in'. She studied 'the competition', as she called it, relentlessly, imitating the wisecracks of comedienne Carole Lombard, then declaring her feet to be 'exactly the same' as Norma Shearer's as she stood in her footprints on the sidewalk outside Grauman's Chinese Theatre.

She seemed so upbeat and positive about her future in movies, but Vita knew that willing it to happen and it actually happening were entirely different things. Nancy's attempts to track down Mark Zamburg, the producer she'd met in the clinic – so far, at least – had come to nothing. She'd called his office so many times that the secretary hung up on her now at the sound of her voice.

'Where exactly are we going?'

'It's here,' Nancy said, and Vita turned down the road. 'Pull over. This is it.'

23

Yet Another Mrs King

Clement approached his sister's house from where he'd been sitting watching it, from a bench in the formal Parisian square. As he walked up the front steps, looking at the freshly painted railings onto which Marianne had fallen to her death, he felt a shudder up his spine and his resolve to settle this matter hardened.

He pulled the brass chain by the door and heard the bell ring inside. The maid answered. Clearly intimidated by his hard stare, she said that he could wait.

He followed her into the light-filled hallway that swept up to a half-landing, where there was a marble table with a mirror and an impressive display of flowers.

On the first floor, he was shown into a drawing room with a view over the square. The walls were painted in gold at the bottom, with a scene of palm trees and exotic monkeys above. A pianola filled one side of the room, along with some velvet-covered sofas. An ornate gilt mirror above the marble fireplace reflected him as he waited, holding his hat.

'Mr Darton?'

He heard a voice with an American accent and saw a middle-aged woman entering from another door. Edith would find her appealing, Clement thought, with her trim figure, elegant burgundy dress and mane of red hair; but to his mind, she had that kind of American over-confidence that always annoyed him. It infuriated him that women, as they got older, were often under the misapprehension that they had some power, when the only currency they'd really ever had was youth and beauty. In his opinion, women had always been and would always be the weaker sex, and he resented any modern views to the contrary. This woman before him clearly had an inflated opinion of herself, and he instinctively drew himself up as she approached.

He shook her hand, feeling annoyingly self-conscious beneath her searching gaze. She looked too groomed to be a housekeeper; but why would such a well-dressed woman be living with Vita and her husband?

'I'm Alicia King,' the woman said. 'Irving's wife. Can I help? My husband is in his study on a long-distance call and doesn't wish to be disturbed.'

Clement was confused. 'But I thought . . . I thought Mr King was married to . . . someone else? My sister, in fact,' he blurted, immediately blushing for having spoken so clumsily. Did the man have two wives? What kind of terrible, immoral arrangement had Anna got herself into?

'You're Vita's brother?' This woman – Alicia King – obviously knew about him, because she folded her arms defensively across her torso. 'What is your business with Vita?'

'I would like to talk to her, that's all,' Clement said. 'I would like her to come home.'

'You're mistaken, Mr Darton. She's not here. She left a long time ago.'

'But what happened? I mean, I don't understand. She was married to Mr King and—'

'My husband gets most upset about that dreadful business with Vita. We've moved on and . . .' She looked at him now, as if a realization was dawning. 'You've been here before, haven't you? Weren't you the one who was here on that terrible day when Vita's friend fell? Yes, I remember. The police said they'd questioned you.'

Clement didn't say anything. His brain was scrambling to keep up. Why was Vita no longer married, and how did this other wife know so much about him? He didn't like the sly tone she was using, hoping to catch him out. He had no idea how much she knew, but now she stepped towards him, her eyes narrowed, and lowered her voice.

'Only, I would *so* like to know what happened. There was the most frightful stink after Marianne fell out of the window. The maid became quite hysterical and we had to dismiss her. The police still want to question Vita further.'

Clement gripped onto his hat, feeling at once cornered and relieved. She didn't know, then. She didn't know why he'd been here, or how Marie had come to fall.

'They said it was an accident, but we've found it so suspicious. If you were here, then I would like to know what went on.'

She stopped as they both heard footsteps out in the hall and a man's voice calling, 'Lys? Lys, you up here?'

A man in his late forties appeared in the doorway. He held a sheaf of papers in his hands, and was reading the top one.

Clement stared at Irving King. He was wearing a moss-green tapestry smoking jacket, a hefty gold ring on his little finger. He looked fat and unhealthy, a smouldering cigar clamped between his fingers. There was something unpleasantly fleshy about him; but then, in Clement's experience, women would forgive men anything so long as they were rich.

Irving's smile faded when he saw Clement, and he took off his reading glasses.

'Oh, Irving dear,' Alicia said, her hand fluttering to her neck, her look darting between Clement and her husband. 'This is Clement Darton. He's just called in. *To find Vita*,' she added dramatically.

Irving King's eyebrows shot up. 'You have the gall to come here? To this house?' he said in a menacing voice, stepping into the room and throwing down his cigar at a nearby ashtray. He missed, and it rolled onto the carpet.

Alicia let out a startled noise, then walked towards it and picked it up. 'Irving,' she scolded. 'That's no way to treat our guest.'

'He's no guest in this house.'

'Won't you stay for tea?' She rang the bell, but Irving turned on her furiously.

'That won't be necessary. He's not staying.'

'I don't know what my sister has told you about me—' Clement began.

'Enough,' Irving said. He raised a hand to his chest and Alicia looked at him in concern, taking the sheaf of papers from his hand before they fell.

'Come and sit down,' she coaxed. 'He has a weak heart,' she said to Clement, as if this were his fault. 'He's to avoid all stressful situations. You'd better leave, Mr Darton.'

She walked with Irving to the sofa and made him sit

down. Clement paused for a moment, then made his way out of the door and back to the stairs.

'Don't you dare come back here. She's not here and she never wants to see you again,' Irving shouted furiously after him.

Clement walked with difficulty down the stairs as the maid hurried up past him, clearly torn as to what to do. He let himself out of the front door, but as he reached the pavement, Alicia King called his name. Turning, he saw her slipping through the door and pulling it softly closed behind her. She glanced up at the windows above them, not wanting to be seen.

'She's in New York,' Alicia whispered. 'I pay my mother-in-law's maid to keep me informed.'

'Your mother-in-law?'

'Renata King. Vita went to see her. Just a few weeks ago.'

New York? His sister was in New York?

'And take it from me, Mr Darton: if your sister thinks she's getting her hands on my girls' inheritance, then she's got another think coming. She's caused this family quite enough trouble as it is.'

24

The Realtor-Stroke-Actor

Vita parked at a rakish angle by the kerb and turned off the engine, relieved that they'd made it in one piece.

'Actually, it's not too bad,' Nancy said, opening the door. She stepped out onto the running board of the car, then down onto the grass verge with a dancer's leap. She slid her sunglasses down her nose. 'Well, what do you think? Let's take a look.'

It seemed a shame to wake Bertie, but Vita couldn't leave him in this heat, so she pulled the seat forward and lifted him up. He was heavy and sweaty and his head lolled onto her shoulder. Mr Wild jumped out and sniffed around the spiky grass.

Ahead of them was an iron gateway covered in flowering purple bougainvillea. It led to a pathway, on either side of which were Spanish-style bungalows with wide porches and screen doors. Everything here was so lush, Vita thought. And so new.

'Miss Delaney?' Vita turned to see a young guy looking eagerly at them. He had very white teeth and his cotton shirt had a fashionably wide collar. He introduced himself as their agent.

'You can call me Matt. I'm your realtor – well, realtor-stroke-actor,' he said, lifting his trilby hat with its plaid band. He opened the swirly metal gate, making an elaborate bow and sweeping his hand out towards the pathway. He was so dramatic that Vita had to stifle a giggle as he did a Laurel and Hardy double step to follow them. Nancy took it all in her stride, however, keeping her head held regally high as they walked past the tall palm tree in the middle of the shared garden. Matt opened the screen door to the condo at the end, jiggling his thick black eyebrows like a vaudeville magician.

'The best part is use of the pool,' he said enthusiastically, as Nancy walked into the small apartment. 'It's shared with another complex, a block away.'

'A pool,' Vita said to Bertie, bouncing him on her hip. He sucked his thumb. 'Imagine that.'

And now an image flashed into her mind. Of Hartwell. Of Archie diving naked into the lake . . .

'There's a lifeguard there who teaches all the youngsters to swim,' Matt assured Vita. 'You'll be able to get lessons.'

'A lifeguard. There you go, Vita,' Nancy said and Vita blushed at her insinuation, forcing the memory of Archie away.

Vita followed Nancy and Matt into the sun-filled space, seeing the open kitchen with its work surfaces and sink. Two doors led off the main room, two bedrooms and a small bathroom with a basin and little cloakroom with smart lavatory. Nancy turned on the tap, which spluttered, but then clean water came out.

'We'll take it. Just for a month,' Nancy said, disdainfully looking down her nose at Matt.

'Why only a month?' Vita asked, surprised. Surely it was perfect?

'Because it won't be long before I'll be in a movie. We'll have paid work and we'll move into a proper home up in Beverly Hills with all the other stars,' Nancy said, with a confident nod of her head.

It was Matt's turn to suppress a smile now as he glanced at Vita.

'You don't believe me?' Nancy said, her nose flicking into the air.

'Forgive me for saying, Ma'am, but broads like you are a dime a dozen in this town.'

Vita doubted Nancy had ever been called a 'broad' before.

'I've been trying to make it in the movies for two years,' he continued. 'I took acting classes for two years before that, and I've only had a handful of call-ups.'

'But you've been in the movies?' Vita asked, impressed.

'Sure I have.' He grinned widely, like it was the best thing ever.

'What's it like? Behind the gates, I mean. On one of the sets?'

'Fine, if you follow the rules.'

'The rules?' Vita asked. She glanced at Nancy, who was trying hard not to appear interested.

'There are lots, but mainly, you have to be invisible.'

'I don't intend to be invisible,' Nancy snapped.

'Lady, you can have all the airs you want, but there are plenty of highly qualified actors I know—'

'I don't care what kind of two-bit actresses you consort with. My name will be on the marquee before you know it.'

She stared him down, then he hurriedly produced some paperwork from his leather document case. Nancy signed the flimsy piece of paper he gave her with a flourish.

'He'll be sorry he ever doubted me,' Nancy said, watching him go.

'Oh, Nancy, go easy on him. Everyone here has the same dream,' Vita said.

'Don't you believe me either?' Nancy snapped. 'Someone has to make it. It might as well be me.'

Vita laughed. 'Of course it will be you, darling. Let's see someone try and stop you.'

'Good. Because we're not staying in this pokey place a second longer than we have to,' Nancy said.

Mr Wild barked as if in agreement and Nancy picked him up and snuggled him, clearly mollified. Vita looked around their new home and smiled. Here on the other side of the world, hidden away behind the flower-covered gate, was a perfect place to start their new life.

25

Candles and Choir Song

The chapel at St Hilda's School for Girls was lit by candles, the warm light flickering over the walls and along the mantles of the stained-glass windows. Edith sat in the front row, happy to let people think she was a visiting dignitary. *Because, in a manner of speaking, I am.* She fingered the bound programme for the girls' Christmas concert, the date – 16 December 1929 – surrounded by childishly drawn holly, and realized that she probably should start saving these kind of mementoes for Susan for when she was older. Edith wanted the child to be in no doubt that she had done her motherly bit.

She tried not to turn too obviously to look at the other parents filling up the pews behind her. She was curious to know what kind of stock Susan's cohort came from. From what she'd seen, she was gratified to note that she was wearing the finest hat in the room . . . by far. She'd already drawn some admiring glances for her matching lilac coat with its fox-fur-trimmed collar, and it was just as well she'd had the foresight to wear it. It was freezing in here.

Clement didn't seem to realize how important it was, after the scrutiny of those dreadful men from the LCC, to show that at Darton, at least, it was business as usual. That was why it annoyed Edith so much that he had gone to Paris when he had – the timing designed to guarantee that she couldn't go with him.

Ever since he'd returned, having failed to find Vita, he'd been quite impossible. Edith brooded now, thinking of her husband and how he seemed to be permanently angry. The mill was losing money hand over fist; she had fought with him about using her part of the business to buoy it up. Used to having some of her most blasphemous thoughts in church, she wondered now whether being a widow or even a divorcée might be preferable to her current situation.

She looked up as a man and woman approached the end of the pew.

'Would you mind if we sat here?' the man asked.

Edith, unsettled at being addressed and frankly annoyed that her status in the front row was now to be shared, turned. The man took off his hat. He had a wide smile and was disarmingly handsome, with dark hair that he wore long so that it curled at his neck. His warm brown eyes, now locked with hers, caused Edith to feel an unusual sensation – one she hadn't felt since the early days of her romance with Jack Connelly, the owner of the Zip Club.

Disconcerted, she shuffled up as the man sat beside her, guiding a woman into the pew beside him. She was beautiful, Edith saw, her glossy auburn hair held in an ivory clip. Her long silk coat with kimono sleeves was a more elegant garment than Edith had seen for some time. She noticed that the man seemed to be holding her hand in a strange way.

Edith didn't want to stare, but she couldn't help it. The woman's eyes were roaming the top far corner of the chapel.

'Oh, isn't this lovely, Nicky,' the woman said. 'Are there candles?'

'Yes. Lots,' he replied.

'I knew there would be. Who is this?' she asked, leaning forward, as if sensing Edith's presence. 'Your child is performing?' The question was unsettling and far too direct. Edith recoiled at being addressed, but then, in a sudden flash of understanding, she realized that the woman was blind. She told herself to stand down from being so riled that she'd taken the most prestigious spot in the chapel.

'Yes, my daughter, Susan. Susan Darton.'

'Oh,' the woman said, with a delighted smile. 'Susan's mother. How very wonderful to meet you at long last.' She beamed as if this were the best news she'd ever received, but Edith was confused.

'How do you do. I'm Nick Bamford,' the man said, turning awkwardly now that he was shoulder to shoulder with Edith and proffering his hand.

Edith shook his hand, wondering why his name sounded familiar. Close up, he was even more handsome than she'd first realized. 'And this is my wife, Helen,' he said, leaning back so that Edith could shake the woman's hand, directing Helen's hand to Edith's.

'Susan and Lettice are great friends,' Helen said. She didn't have a trace of a northern accent like Nick had.

'Lettice?'

'We're Lettice's parents,' Nick said, as if this should mean something to Edith. He smiled brightly at her. Why was she feeling so flustered? She could smell his cologne. She stole a glance upward, taking in the collar of his shirt, visible beneath his stylish coat. It was so rare to see a man these days who dressed properly, and Nick Bamford had panache. She felt a sudden urge to run her fingers into the lustrously thick dark hair at the nape of his neck.

'You signed the form for Susan to come to us on the last exeat weekend. Oh, they had a fine time,' Helen said, her eyes twinkling as they scanned the engraved stone above Edith's head.

Edith didn't let her face so much as flicker, as she realized the extent of Susan's lie. She must have got one of the older girls to forge Edith's signature. In fact, she must have made up all manner of subterfuge to make such a plan happen. So much so that Edith didn't know whether to be furious or impressed; but she made a note to take Susan to task when she could. Maybe she was more like sneaky Marianne than Edith had given her credit for. However, she was not going to lose face in front of Nick Bamford.

'Oh yes, of course. How kind of you—'

But she was interrupted by a murmur and general shushing of the crowd as the chapel lights were dimmed. Edith watched Helen grip onto Nick's hand. His other hand rested on his leg, so close to Edith's. She studied his strong fingers and clean nails, the chunky signet ring he wore on his little finger and, surprisingly, a knotted leather bracelet just under the cuff of his white shirt, which looked rather ethnic and exotic. Compared to Clement's eczema-scarred hands, Nick's seemed alluringly touchable and for a wild moment, as the vicar started a communal prayer, Edith wondered how it would feel to have such a hand touch her . . . to cup her bare breast.

'She's a charming child,' Helen said in a whisper after the prayer had finished. 'Quite the singer. She and Lettice were singing non-stop, weren't they, Nicky?'

26

A New Year's Invitation

Edith's head was in a complete spin as they sat through the service of lessons and carols. Not just because of this new information about Susan actually having a friend, but because each time she stood up, she became more and more aware of Nick's physical presence next to her.

As the congregation bowed their heads in prayer, she pressed her thigh a fraction against his, wondering if he could sense the quivering feeling going on inside her. Had he noticed? She couldn't tell, but the moment stretched and stretched and – with it – her held breath.

Then, all too soon, the service had ended and Mrs Lanyard, the headmistress, misty-eyed with sentiment, invited the parents to the refectory for mulled wine.

'Would you mind if I came along with you?' Edith asked, as they filed out of their pew. 'I hardly know any parents here.'

'We don't either,' Nick said. 'When we came back from abroad, Lettice joined halfway through the year. Susan has been very kind.'

'Oh, where were you abroad?'

'India, mostly,' Nick said. 'But we're back now,' he said, patting Helen's hand.

'India? Oh, how wonderful. I've always wanted to go.'

'I was there running a newspaper, and Helen's parents ran a plantation.'

'You're a journalist? Publisher, I mean?' she corrected herself.

'Yes, I run the *Daily Dispatch* now.'

'It's the largest daily published outside of London,' Helen said, proudly.

Edith felt her mouth fill with saliva and her cheeks flush. The *Daily Dispatch* was responsible for the exposé on the working conditions in Darton. Did Nick know this? Did he realize what his paper had done?

She hardly knew how to broach the subject as they walked through to the refectory, where she picked up a small silver tankard of steaming wine and toasted Nick. Her eyes locked with his as she took a sip. Did he have no shame? He was clearly not going to mention it, but he must know exactly who she was.

The girls filed in now, anxious to see their parents. Edith spotted Susan's blonde head and saw that she was talking to a smaller girl with messy brown hair.

'There they are,' Nick said.

Edith saw Susan's smile fade as their eyes met and she saw who Edith was talking to. Edith held her gaze as she walked through the clusters of people towards them. As she drew nearer, Edith noted the defiant lift of her chin. *God damn it*, she thought. *That girl's quite impossible. And it's only going to get worse when she gets older.*

'You were quite magnificent,' Nick said, exuberantly hugging a small, scruffy tomboy of a girl. She was pretty, in a way, but before she developed too much further she'd have to sort out her hair, and tame her unruly eyebrows, for that matter, Edith noted – although a blind mother would hardly be up to that task. Lettice had her father's eyes, but her mother's smile. Edith wondered if Nick Bamford was studying her and Susan for genetic similarities too.

Edith, who always tried her hardest to control the flow of information, felt a new and uncomfortable sensation as she met Nick Bamford's smiling eyes. What did he know about her? She felt worried now, that her family situation – secrets that should stay in Darton – had somehow leaked out via Susan and Lettice to these people. Did they know about the circumstances of her adoption? About Marianne and Clement?

'Dad,' Lettice said, giggling at Nick's exuberance and fatherly pride. As far as Edith was aware, Susan had never once called Clement anything other than 'Sir'. Not even Father, let alone Dad. The easy, tactile way the Bamfords had made Edith's heart ache. Lettice took her mother's hand and kissed the palm of it before turning and folding herself against her mother's front. It was such an affectionate gesture that Edith couldn't help but stare. Nobody had ever kissed Edith's palm.

'This is the famous Mrs Darton,' Helen said to Lettice.

The famous Mrs Darton. So Helen knew, Edith thought, flinching at her description. It couldn't be a casual comment.

'Susan has told us so much about you,' Helen clarified.

'And I'm sure you know a fair bit about Darton from your newspaper, Mr Bamford,' she said, archly, directing her gaze at Nick.

He rubbed the side of his face and looked bashful. 'Ah,

yes. Darton. I remember now. The editor did rather go to town,' he said.

'Yes, well, his sensational claims were rather exaggerated. Unfairly so, in my opinion.'

'I just publish the damn thing,' he said, with an embarrassed smile. 'You can't hold me responsible for the copy.'

'On the contrary – I always think that the boss should be the one accountable.'

In this duel of words, Edith had hardly been paying attention to anyone else, let alone Susan, who now tugged at her sleeve.

'Please, Mother, not here,' she whispered.

Edith snapped around. 'Darling,' she said, trying to smile. 'You should have introduced me to Lettice and her family before.' Susan's gaze fluttered to the floor. She knew she'd been caught out.

'You must come to ours for New Year,' Helen said, trying to smooth over the situation. 'We're having a few friends. Lettice would be thrilled if Susan came too.'

'I'm sure someone as well connected as Mrs Darton already has plans,' Nick said with a light laugh. He was clearly embarrassed that she'd called him out on his newspaper's report. 'It's a big one . . . seeing in a whole new decade. Who can really believe it's 1930 already?'

'We don't have plans. In fact, I'm sure that Susan would be delighted to come to your house *again*,' Edith said, seeing Susan squirm. She looked directly at Nick Bamford, still rubbing the side of his face, and noticed his cheeks were slightly flushed. *Goodness, he's handsome*. And now, here was a perfect opportunity to see him again.

27

A Lead at the Laundrette

It was early, but Vita was already overwhelmed by the heat and by everything being dirty. She looked at the clock on the kitchen wall and decided to head out to find the laundrette she'd heard about, before it got too hot for Mr Wild to walk on the sidewalk. Nancy loved the heat, but it brought Vita's pale skin out in a heat rash and she hated being constantly aware of the sheen of perspiration on her skin.

She stood up and stretched, noticing her shirtdress was looser than it had been a few weeks ago. She was definitely losing weight, which was a good thing, at least. She picked up the postcard she'd written at the small kitchen table to Evelyn with news of Bertie, admitting that she hadn't appreciated just how much the housekeeper did for her. Not just all the cooking, but the laundry too. It was a full-time job looking after Bertie, not to mention Nancy and Mr Wild.

She thought of the last time she'd seen Evelyn and how she'd pressed a Bible into Vita's hand.

'You take care of yourself, and my little angel.'

That 'little angel' had kept Vita awake most of the night. Now she put her head around her door and saw that he was fast asleep in the crib. She'd wanted to buy him a proper cot, but Nancy was putting everything on hold until they found a bigger place. As much as Vita wanted to turn their little house into a home, Nancy was equally determined that it was only temporary. In fact, she talked non-stop about their future. Planning it now seemed to be her full-time occupation, leaving Vita to manage the practical details of the here and now; of shopping and cooking and washing.

Nancy didn't seem to fret that time was running out before their next month's rent was due, waving her hand dismissively every time Vita voiced her concerns. *If only there were twelve more hours in every day that I could use to work*, Vita thought with a sigh. Her sketchbook hadn't been opened for weeks, and she thought now of all the grand plans she'd had for setting up her business in New York.

It had all seemed so tantalizingly close, but it had come to nothing. Since they'd left New York, Vita had felt that she was no better off than she had been in Paris when the dancers at Les Folies Bergère had referred to her as Nancy's 'little wife'.

Now Vita opened Nancy's door. She was lying on the bed on her front like a starfish, the fan clattering around, the thin linen curtain billowing up.

'I'm going out. You're in charge of Bertie,' she said. 'Nancy?'

Nancy groaned and flapped her hand.

Vita made her way with difficulty onto the front porch with the heavy canvas laundry bag. Mr Wild scampered past her through the screen door, heading to the patch of grass.

She noticed two butterflies dancing and the air was thick

with the sound of cicadas. The vine growing up the porch was covered with pretty sprays of red flowers. It was going to be another scorching day.

Never in a million years, as a child, could Vita have imagined such a concept as sunshine at Christmas. She thought of Darton at this time of year; how Martha brought ivy and holly in from the garden and twisted it in a garland up the dark stairs, the wind whistling down the chimneys, the valley shrouded with freezing fog. And here she was, in California, in the sunshine, free to do whatever she wanted.

At the laundrette she walked into a cobbled yard, where washing lines were laden with white sheets drying in the sun. A cat was curled up on a bench next to a pot of red geraniums.

'No dogs, lady,' the woman yelled. She was Chinese, Vita saw, in blue overalls, her sleeves rolled up to her shoulders, impressive biceps on display as she operated a heavy mangle. 'Leave it in the office,' she added, nodding towards Vita's bag and waving to the next door along.

Vita wasn't the first in this morning. In the office, a woman behind the counter was helping a lady customer in linen slacks who was collecting what looked like a lot of dancers' costumes. Watching her gather up the snow-white tunics with their net skirts, it was all Vita could do not to reach out and touch them.

She looked towards the back of the office, where it opened up into a living room. A girl came forward, holding two dresses up on hangers. She had glossy brown hair, some of which was in rollers. Her cream silk robe didn't disguise her lovely figure and Vita felt a yearning for those days in the dressing room at the Zip Club; Wisey, the dresser, had been like a mother to them all. And dear Percy. She longed to tell this girl that she wasn't just another customer, but someone who knew all about the thrill of being in the wings.

'This one. I'll wear this one,' the brunette said, deciding on the pale-pink dress and handing it to the older woman, who noticed Vita standing by the door.

'Excuse us,' she called out. 'You can leave your washing there, honey. We're just getting this one ready,' she said.

'Mom,' the girl said, annoyed. 'Hurry up.'

Mom – how funny the girl sounded. Vita wondered how she'd feel when Bertie first called her that. Would he have an American accent? She hoped not, but maybe he would, now that they were living abroad. He'd grow up with hot dogs and jazz bands and baseball; he wouldn't understand about pies and gravy, hymn singing or cricket.

Vita put her bag down, her nose crinkling at the smell of Bertie's nappy squares. 'Could I come back for it all later today?' she called to the woman.

'Oh, you're English,' the girl said, 'I can do English, can't I, Mom?' She beamed at Vita. 'Roast beef and the King of England,' she said in a plummy voice, and Vita laughed.

'She fancies herself as an actress.'

The girl rolled her eyes at her mother. 'I *am* an actress. In fact, I'm going for a casting this morning.'

'She goes most mornings,' her mother said, as if her mission always failed. Vita wondered if she sounded the same herself, when it came to Nancy.

'Today will be different,' the girl said, with the same

determination that Nancy often had – undaunted by the odds that were clearly stacked against her.

'Oh? How so?' Vita asked, unable to restrain her curiosity.

The girl swept Vita with an assessing gaze. Obviously deciding that she wasn't competition, she came forward and spoke confidentially, as if revealing a secret.

'The studio call this morning is at nine, although they've advertised it for nine thirty. I happen to know that today they're looking for ten pretty girls to be factory workers in a particular scene. I think I'm in with a good chance.'

28

The Early Bird

Back at the condo, Bertie was grizzling in his crib. There was no sign of Nancy.

'Nancy, get up,' Vita shouted as she picked Bertie up. She found his pacifier, dusted it off and put it in his mouth. She kicked open the door to Nancy's room and turned off the fan, while Bertie clung to her. 'I mean it. Get up.'

'Vita . . . what the hell? What's going on?' Nancy groaned.

'A casting. In half an hour. I just heard about it. Come on – I can get you there in time.'

She hurriedly explained what she'd heard at the laundrette. For a moment, she thought Nancy was going to groan again and roll over, but after a second she jumped out of bed.

'What will I wear?' she squealed, tearing over to the mirror to check her face.

'This,' Vita said, giving Nancy Bertie for a moment and pulling garments out of the wardrobe, laying them on the bed. Nancy blew a raspberry on Bertie's neck.

'Oh, he's stinking,' she said. 'Here, take him.' She handed Bertie back and surveyed the outfit Vita had set out for her.

'All of that, plus the red shoes,' Vita said.

'Red? Are you sure?'

'Yes. Get dressed. Go go go.'

Half an hour later, as they approached the studio in the car, Vita could see a crowd of around twenty hopeful girls already pressing against the gate. Nancy, who had eaten a roll on the way at Vita's insistence, checked her lipstick in the rear-view mirror, turning it around to face her in the passenger's seat.

'Well, won't you look at that. You were totally right, Vita. There are only half the people. I guess the early bird catches the worm,' she said. 'That's what Nate would have said, God rest his soul.'

Vita glanced across at her, seeing her eyes shining. Nancy rarely mentioned Nate, and Vita was surprised that she did so now. Their life in New York already seemed so long ago.

'Is it terrible that I'm excited? That I don't miss him at all?' Nancy asked.

Vita shook her head. 'He'd have wanted you to be happy.'

Nancy nodded, satisfied, then turned and tickled Mr Wild under the chin. She pressed her red fingernail into Bertie's tummy and smiled her glossy red smile when he giggled.

'Right. Here goes . . .'

'Good luck. Remember what I said about the rules I heard from the girl at the laundrette,' Vita told her, adjusting the spray of flowers from the balcony she'd hastily attached to Nancy's hat. 'You must *never* talk to the director or look at the camera. And all the food you see on set? That isn't for you. It's either for the crew, or a prop.'

'Yeah, I got it. Thanks, kiddo,' Nancy said, air-kissing her cheek. 'I mean it. What would I do without you?' She held Vita's chin and made eye contact for a moment, and Vita felt a surge of love for her friend. It had been no mean feat getting Nancy up and out of bed in such record time. It was nice that she'd remembered to say thank you for once.

Vita put her hand on the gear stick next to the steering wheel, watching for a moment through the open passenger's window as Nancy stepped out of the car and walked forward into the crowd, her hips swinging. From the back, she looked pretty good. From the front, she was clearly sensational: Vita saw the crowd part as Nancy strode up to the gate.

'Atta girl,' she muttered. 'Let's hope today is the lucky day,' she said to Bertie, thinking suddenly of Paul and his advice about the University of Life, and how tenacity was the key. You just had to get through the door. Vita said a silent prayer that that was exactly what Nancy would do.

Because once Nancy had made it, then she could follow, right? She was convinced there must be a job for her inside the studios. She wasn't fussy about what. It was just that seeing all those costumes at the laundrette had made her hanker for the sense of a show going on, the warm camaraderie of the girls, the all-consuming thrill of being part of something amazing. And now she thought of how much fun it would be to work again doing something that she loved.

Bertie started grizzling and she sighed, turning the rear-view mirror back so that it was trained on him, remembering how complicated her life was. 'All right, darling. Where to? The pool?'

29

The Two-Piece

Matt, the realtor-stroke-actor, hadn't been wrong when he'd said that the best thing about the condo was access to the large communal swimming pool, with its diving boards and comfortable loungers. At this time of day, Vita quite often had the place to herself.

Ted, the lifeguard, had taken upon himself to teach Bertie how to swim. At first Vita had been nervous, but Ted had insisted it was easiest to teach babies when they were tiny.

Ted was fascinating to look at. He had auburn hair, a chiselled jaw, the whitest of teeth and a deep mahogany tan, the likes of which Vita had never seen before. He also had an incredible body – his arms bulged with shiny biceps. But despite this macho exterior, he had a gentle nature and Bertie adored him.

'Come with me, little guy,' he said, as Vita handed the baby over. 'Let's let your mama go and put her feet up, now.'

Vita smiled gratefully. As she headed to the end of the pool where Mr Wild had found a spot in the shade of the tree, she felt guilty at the thought of how nice it was to have a break from Bertie, even if only for half an hour.

She knew she didn't have a choice about parenting Bertie

all by herself, but now, watching Ted throw him gently up into the air, she felt a familiar stab of guilt. Would Bertie become mollycoddled, or shy? How would she stop that happening? What if she wasn't a good enough mother? What then?

Because there was absolutely no chance that she'd find anyone romantically in this town, even if she wanted to. Who would pick her, when every other girl was far, far more beautiful? Not to mention young and carefree, without a baby to look after, or a needy best friend and a naughty dog.

The cicadas trilled loudly as she settled herself, but she was already sweating. Perhaps today she'd have a swim herself, Vita thought, although she hated the swimming costume she had. It was woollen and as soon as it got wet, it clung in unflattering swathes around her curves.

She watched a parrot with its array of colourful feathers take flight from the tree above her. Mr Wild barked and she shushed him, pulling him towards her into a denser patch of shade. She suddenly thought disconcertingly of her mother, and her birds in the aviary in the conservatory at Darton Hall.

How happy her mother would be if she knew about Bertie, she thought, remembering her mother's smile. But almost as soon as the unsettling thought had come, it burned out like a snuffed candle. Vita would never be accepted by her parents, even if they knew about Bertie. She could imagine all too well how they'd shun her for being a single mother and bringing shame on the Darton family.

And now she thought of Clement and Edith and what they'd done, and with that came a fresh stab of pain. Because it wasn't just that Edith had stolen Vita's ideas for her business – she'd stolen her family too, which in many ways was a much greater crime.

To distract herself from these painful thoughts, she picked up Nancy's magazine, flicking through to the fashion pages and an article on new trends in tennis dresses. Immediately absorbed, the images made her think of a pink dress in Madame Jenny's collection in Paris that she'd admired, with its dropped waist and box-pleat skirt. Back then, she'd felt she had her finger on the pulse of the latest fashions; now she had a miserable sense of being sidelined, of time slipping by while her talent was wasted. But who would want her underwear designs here, where everything was so new and modern and fresh?

Her attention was caught now by a girl approaching the poolside. She took her robe off and flung it onto a lounger near the diving board. Vita slid her sunglasses down her nose to take a better look.

The girl was young and had a curvy figure. Her honey-tanned legs were long and shapely, and Vita watched as she climbed the steps to the diving board. She stood at the top, putting her arms up to the sky, giving Vita a proper view of the yellow two-piece swimming costume she wore. Against the blue of the sky, she looked very striking. She bent her long legs and took off, executing a perfect dive into the deep end.

The girl swam in a few languid strokes to the steps near where Vita was sitting. As she emerged from the pool, Vita saw that her costume had stayed perfectly in place. The girl stopped on the top step, undid the chin strap of her swimming hat and shook out her blonde hair.

Vita quickly grabbed her bag, got out her diary and her

pencil and made a sketch, keen to get a closer look at the fastening on the back as the girl started walking back to her lounger. Vita stared at the metal clip in the middle of the two strap pieces.

When the girl stretched out on her lounger, Vita continued sketching, her mind whirring with ideas.

'Are you drawing me?' the girl called.

'Yes, I'm sorry. Yes, I am,' Vita admitted, embarrassed, turning the diary around.

The girl swung her legs from the lounger and walked over. 'Let me see?' Vita handed over the little leather-bound book. 'Hey, that's not bad.' Her voice sounded similar to Jean Harlow's.

'I was just . . . so intrigued by your swimming costume. I'm a designer, you see.'

It was the first time Vita had defined herself that way for a long while. So long, in fact, it made her realize that who she was in her head and who she was in reality were two very different things.

Up close, the girl, who now introduced herself as June, was probably Vita's age. She had a distinctive beauty spot above one corner of her mouth.

'May I touch the fabric?' Vita asked.

'Sure. Go right ahead.'

The material was stretchy and unlike anything she'd seen before. If she could only get hold of material like that, then how wonderful would her bras be? It would open up a whole new world of possibilities. And the elastic that was attached to the underside of the material? Vita poked her finger underneath it and pulled.

'Sorry,' she said, realizing how she was mauling this poor girl. 'It's just that I've never seen it like that before.'

'It's so comfortable. I kept it from a shoot,' June confessed. 'The picture isn't out yet. But I'm in the pool scene.'

'You wore that in a movie?'

'Sure,' June said.

She sat down on the lounger next to Vita and as Vita questioned her, she heard about how June had been in ten scenes in the movies. It was a slightly better tally than Matt the realtor, but June had clearly put in an enormous amount of effort for a small return. Being an actor here obviously required hard work, patience and tenacity, and Vita hoped Nancy was up to the challenge. June described how she'd come from a farm in Wyoming and had run away to Los Angeles to make it in the movies, but that she missed her large family back home and struggled to make ends meet.

Now Ted came over, holding Bertie against his ridiculously muscled, tanned chest. She saw June angle her shoulders and her lips slightly purse. Vita knew the pose well enough to know she was breathing in.

Ted handed Bertie over and then they discussed the swimming lesson for a while before he sauntered away. Vita smiled, noticing June's gaze follow the lifeguard's tight shorts. June turned back and raised her eyebrows in acknowledgement of her crush.

'He's got quite a body,' Vita said.

'*Tsss*,' June said, miming burning her fingertip on something hot. 'I'll say.'

'But then, everyone around here is so beautiful. It makes me feel so . . . old,' Vita admitted.

'Not at all,' June said. 'And anyway, what could be better than being this little fella's mom? He's so adorable.'

Vita rubbed Bertie's back with a towel, remembering suddenly that she hadn't paid Ted. She snatched up her bag. 'Could you watch him for a second?'

'Sure.'

When she came back, June had dressed Bertie and he was sitting on her knee, giggling. He looked delighted with his new friend.

'If you ever need anyone to watch him, I'm around if I haven't had a casting,' June said. 'I miss my baby brothers back in Wyoming. Family is everything, ain't it?'

30

Stop Sign

Vita left the swimming pool and wedged Bertie's basket securely against the seat before settling him down into it, smiling as he kicked his chubby legs and grinned at her in the way that never failed to melt her heart.

'Well then, a new friend,' she said, thinking of June. But as she drove away, she thought of Marianne and how she, too, had seemed like a friend. She'd infiltrated her way so easily into Vita's life. She'd been right there when Nancy had run out in front of a car outside the club and had come to Vita's aid. Vita had trusted her so readily. Now she wondered, could she really trust this stranger with her baby?

June had given her all sorts of wonderful information about second-hand costume shops and a material emporium on a street south of Culver City, where Vita would be sure to get some elasticated material to make a two-piece for herself. Maybe she could also make something to send back to the Delaneys for Christmas, Vita thought. Things had been terrible for them in New York: Mr Delaney had had to let most of his staff go, and Mrs Delaney was run off her feet coping with the needy at the mission. But at least they still had their home, and Evelyn. So many of their friends had lost everything.

Vita looked briefly at her watch, hoping that Nancy had got through the gates and landed a part. If not, she'd be waiting on the corner by the studio in the usual place. Vita drove fast down the wide road, past the giant hoardings advertising new homes, washing powders and sodas, then past the Twentieth Century Fox studio, which looked like a temple with its large tower, followed by the RKO studio, where the street outside was lined with cars. She glimpsed the water tower on stilts beyond the lavish gateway. Then, just along the road, she saw the hopefuls still loitering by the studio and she slowed down, not recognizing Nancy in the crowd. She wasn't waiting on the corner, either.

'Yes!' she exclaimed, grinning, before indicating to get back onto the road going south. She took out a large map and spread it on the seat beside her, trying to work out the best way to the fabric shop. With one eye on the map and one eye on the road, she didn't even see the stop sign, let alone stop for it.

There was an almighty crash and Vita cried out as her head hit the steering wheel. The car span round once, then twice, lurching up onto two wheels like a scene from a car chase. Gritting her teeth, her eyes squeezed shut, she waited for it to right itself and come to a halt. She sat still, hyperventilating, then opened her eyes.

She was facing the wrong way in the middle of a junction. A car beeped loudly and swerved round her. A little way off, a brown car – a very expensive-looking, open-topped one –

had come to a halt with steam pouring out of its bonnet and an ugly dent in its side.

She turned her head, noticing her neck hurt terribly. Unbelievably, Bertie was asleep in his crib, which had only moved slightly. Thank goodness he hadn't been hurt. She couldn't breath as she put her hand out to place it on his chest just to check that he really was as peaceful as he seemed – he was.

She put a hand to her head where she'd hit it. There was blood, but she was in such shock, it didn't hurt. She looked now at the crumpled bonnet of the car Nancy had hired, and a shocked sob escaped her.

She leant down to the footwell of the passenger's seat, where Mr Wild had been flung. He whimpered, but then licked her hand. She gathered him in her arms.

'Are you all right?' She heard a man's voice and straightened to see a familiar face peering in through her window. She let out a startled yelp.

'Goodness, it's you,' he said. And then she recognized him. It was Daniel Myers, the man she'd met at Nancy's engagement party at the Delaneys'.

'Here,' he said, helping her out of the car and leading her to the pavement. It was disconcerting to be walking right across a junction, but she was glad of his assistance as her legs were shaking so badly. Other cars waited for them to cross, but one driver swerved round them and swore out of the window.

'Oh, pipe down, won't you,' Daniel called after him. 'Some people,' he muttered as he led Vita and Mr Wild to the shade of a tree on the sidewalk.

'What about Bertie?' Vita cried, pulling away to head back into the traffic, but Daniel stopped her.

'Let me get the car to safety,' he said and she nodded mutely, too shocked by the crash and the fact that it was Daniel Myers that she'd crashed into.

Tears fell as she hugged Mr Wild to her chest. 'Oh, Mr Wild.' It had all been going so well, but now this.

Daniel couldn't start the car and he opened the door, leaning inside to steer the wheel as he pushed. Soon he'd managed to navigate to the kerb beside Vita. He pulled the handbrake and wiped sweat from his brow. Bertie woke up and started crying, and Daniel moved the seat forward and gently lifted him out.

'Here you go. Here she is,' he soothed, handing him over to Vita, who let Mr Wild down on the kerb and pulled Bertie tight towards her.

'He's perfectly all right,' Daniel said. 'What a fine little fella.'

But Vita couldn't be comforted, and she rocked Bertie as tears fell. 'I'm so terribly sorry I hit you,' she managed eventually, trying to wipe her tears away with the handkerchief that Daniel offered. She put her hand on Bertie's head. *Thank God.* Thank God she hadn't hurt him.

She waited as Daniel went to get his car – the smart one with the dent in the side – and parked it behind hers. Her little Ford looked pathetic next to his brown-and-chrome beast. It was going to cost a fortune to fix, but Daniel didn't seem too concerned, assuring her that he had a man he knew from a garage with a truck who would sort out the cars.

'Didn't you see the stop sign?'

'No. I didn't.'

'Oh!' Daniel said, then smiled. 'You're shaken. Come on. Let me buy you a cup of coffee.'

31

Apple Pie

Daniel gently took her elbow and walked with her around the corner to where there was a small diner with a person-sized sculpture of a pink-and-white milkshake outside. Vita called to Mr Wild not to cock his leg on it.

'You've never been here?' Daniel asked, pushing open the glass door. 'It's kind of an institution around here.'

A bell chimed above the door as Vita and Daniel walked into the narrow diner. A man was behind the counter cooking, a hiss of burger steam coming up from the grill. He pointed to a booth with two green leather seats, a brown table in between. It reminded Vita of being on the top deck of a Lancashire bus. Mr Wild jumped onto the seat, turned around and then settled his head on his paws. He looked up with his big brown eyes through his bushy eyebrows at Vita.

'I'll get you a treat,' she told him, sliding in next to him on the banquette with Bertie.

'Back so soon?' asked a large woman behind the counter. She came over to the table, pulling a pad from the pocket of her frilly apron and reaching for the pencil stub that was tucked behind her ear. 'Oh, and a baby,' she cooed. 'Ain't he just good enough to eat?' Then she saw that Vita was holding Daniel's handkerchief to her head. 'Are you all right, honey?'

Daniel explained about the crash, and Vita realized he was on first-name terms with the waitress.

'Delores, this is Vita. The last time I saw her, I said I hoped we'd bump into each other again, but she took it a little far,' Daniel teased. Vita, still shaken, smiled despite herself. He really was being very good about the accident. Delores stepped into action, coming back to the table with cotton wool and ointment for Vita's head.

'Coffee?' she asked.

'May I have tea?'

'You English and your tea,' Delores said with a smile. 'Coming right up.'

'Tea solves everything. So they say,' Vita said shyly, as Daniel leant towards her, looking concerned.

'And some pie. My friend here needs some sugar,' he called, as Delores bustled away. 'Here, let me,' he said, taking the ointment and spreading it on the cotton wool before gently administering it to Vita's brow. His hand was warm and comforting and as her eyes met his, she saw genuine concern. 'It's not too bad. There'll be a bruise, but no scar.'

'What are you doing here?' she asked. 'I mean, here in Los Angeles?'

'I work just around the corner.'

'At the studios?' Vita asked. Because where else *was* there to work around here?

Delores brought over two cups of tea and a stainless-steel pot. Vita tipped some sugar from the glass jar with the metal spout into her cup and took a sip, but it wasn't the same as

English tea. She'd managed to get Evelyn to make her proper English tea in New York, but she hadn't had anything close in Los Angeles yet.

'Yes, at MGM,' Daniel smiled, playing with Bertie, who razzed with delight. 'I'm a producer.'

Why hadn't she or Nancy bothered to find out this fact about Daniel when they'd met him at Nancy and Nate's party?

'And what brings you out west?' he asked. 'You looked pretty comfortable in that fine house in New York.'

Was he teasing her for being the Delaneys' house guest? She couldn't help but hear the barb in his comment. 'I'm here with Nancy,' she said.

'Nancy who married Nate?' Daniel looked confused.

'Oh, dear,' Vita said. This was just getting worse and worse.

'What is it?' Daniel asked.

Gently, she told him what had happened to the Delaneys after the awful stock market crash – and finally, what had happened to Nate. What he'd done.

'I had no idea,' Daniel said. The twinkle in his eyes now was subdued. There was a beat as they stared at each other. She wondered if he was thinking what she was: that the last time they'd spoken, he'd predicted that there wouldn't be a wedding. 'Poor Nancy.'

'She's getting over it. She's trying her hand at the movie business. We've been every day to the studio gates for weeks.' Then she told him about the tip-off she'd had at the laundry, and how they'd been early this morning for the casting.

'She was a striking girl, as I recall,' Daniel said. 'And a

great dancer. Here.' He reached inside his jacket, taking out a gold card case. 'Take my card. Tell Nancy to bring it tomorrow and show it to Mrs Styles.' He wrote a message on the back of the card.

'That's very kind,' Vita said, smiling and staring at the MGM Studios logo.

'It's the least I can do.'

'No, it's more than generous, given the circumstances. There's a rather large dent in the side of your car because of me.'

'But it's worth it to have run into you,' he said. 'Or the other way around.'

She laughed.

'Oh, here's your pie,' Daniel said, seeing Delores coming over. 'The best apple pie in the whole of California.' Delores simpered at his flattery.

Daniel went off to use the telephone to call the garage, waving away her concern about the expense. He was clearly the kind of person who had other people to sort out problems like that for him. *Just how important is he at the studios?* Vita wondered.

She ate her pie, giving Bertie some of the stewed apple from inside. When he came back, Daniel took over, making 'choo-choo' noises as he wound the spoon towards Bertie's mouth. Bertie giggled with delight, then grabbed the spoon and flicked the apple in Daniel's eye.

Vita dabbed at his face with a napkin, embarrassed. 'Oh, goodness, I'm so sorry. Bertie and I are not covering ourselves in glory, are we?'

Daniel laughed, taking the napkin from her, his hand

touching hers for a long moment. 'It's my fault. I was showing off, pretending I could feed him,' he said, 'when I really don't know the first thing about babies.'

Except that he did, Vita thought. He knew how to make her son laugh.

They chatted for a while longer, and then two tow trucks turned up from the garage. Daniel called Vita a taxi to take her home. He was remarkably calm and unflustered, she thought, thinking how nice it was that someone else had sorted out her problems for once.

When they came to say goodbye, he smiled down at her. 'Next time we meet, can we make it a little less violent?' he said.

Did he want there to be a next time? Vita smiled at him, very much hoping there would be.

'I'm not here for Christmas, but I'm having a little New Year's Eve party. Why don't you and Nancy come along? That's if you can find a babysitter for this little one.'

'That would be lovely,' Vita said, immediately wondering if she'd be able to persuade June to watch Bertie, her earlier misgivings going out of the window. This was too good an offer to pass up.

He told her his address, and she thought about the other houses she'd seen up on Mulholland Drive. Did he really live in one of those fancy mansions? She couldn't wait to tell Nancy.

He ruffled Bertie's long curls.

'Well then, see you there, Vita.'

She smiled back, liking the way he said her name.

32

The Bamfords' Perfect Life

Thank goodness Clement isn't here, Edith thought, as she and Susan arrived at the Bamfords' house for their New Year's Eve party. She'd had to call ahead to tell a white lie, saying that her husband had caught a slight chill after the Boxing Day hunt. She didn't dare tell Clement about Nick Bamford and his connection to the *Daily Dispatch*. He would be furious if he knew she was consorting with the enemy.

She hadn't told him about the party until the very last minute, when she and Susan were getting ready to leave Darton earlier. He'd been drinking heavily over Christmas and, after the hunt, had gone to Manchester, although he hadn't explained why he'd gone or with whom. Frankly, she didn't care. The less he spoke to her, the better.

Now, as the Bamfords' butler took away her long cape to reveal her figure-hugging cornflower-blue beaded dress and matching long silk gloves, Edith liked to think she perceived a lull in the conversation. As Susan disappeared off to find Lettice, Nick left some of his other guests – men in tuxedos and women in shapeless dresses – and came across the hall past the lit-up Christmas tree to greet her.

'Mrs Darton,' he said, and he kissed the back of her gloved hand gallantly, his eyes staring up into hers.

'Oh, Edith, please,' she said.

He searched out her eyes from under his floppy fringe, and all of her resolve to make him grovel immediately evaporated. He was even more dashing than she remembered.

'I'm afraid you have a rather poor impression of me after the newspaper reported on Darton. I had no idea of your involvement in the mill, but I have been hearing some great things about your lingerie business. I can't wait to learn more about that.'

He'd done some homework on her, then, Edith thought, with a little shiver of satisfaction.

'And I can't wait to enlighten you,' she said. 'What a lovely home you have.'

A small dog, like a miniature fawn-coloured whippet, shot around the corner, startling Edith. She hated dogs.

'Fig, Fig, come here,' Helen Bamford said, with a laugh in her voice. The dog stopped and went obediently to her, and she stooped and picked it up. 'Oh, Mrs Darton, you're here,' she said, coming to where Edith and Nick were standing at the foot of the stairs.

She was wearing long silk trousers and an elaborate beaded kimono in a deep green pattern that made her hair look particularly bright. Her hostess had dressed far more casually than Edith had for the evening, although diamonds and emeralds sparkled at her ears and throat. But then, Edith thought, she couldn't see what she looked like, so she supposed it didn't really matter what Helen Bamford wore. Even so, she had such an air of confidence and her casual style seemed so *à la mode* that Edith suddenly felt annoyingly overdressed.

Helen waved her palm in Edith's direction, then addressed the newel post. 'What colour are you in? Don't tell me . . . green?'

'Blue,' Edith said.

Helen smiled, as if this made perfect sense. 'I bet it's lovely,' she said, taking Edith's hand and leaning forward to kiss both her cheeks.

'I'll say,' Nick said, his eyes not leaving Edith's. 'Mrs Darton . . . *Edith* . . . is simply dazzling.'

Was he flirting with her? She smiled, thrilled at his praise. She wondered for a moment whether he could sense how many times he'd entered her thoughts since they'd met at Susan's school. She hadn't been able to stop daydreaming about him in a way she hadn't since falling for Quentin all those years ago. She'd hoped that seeing Nick again would make her realize how delusional she was being; but if anything, it was having the opposite effect.

'Come in. Come in and meet everyone,' Helen said, and Edith smiled at Nick as they walked together to the crowd. Any nerves were dispelled now by the roaring fire in the hall, the pretty lights and the friendly atmosphere.

Three other couples were at the Bamfords' New Year's Eve party – an Indian man and his English wife, who Edith thought were decidedly too foreign for her taste; a boring couple from Manchester; and another couple who, like her, had lived in London and seemed to have a little spark about them. Although the wife, Jane, with her terribly overstyled hair, kept telling Edith how very wonderful their hostess was.

Edith agreed politely, as they went for cocktails in the drawing room. Like the rest of the charming house, it had been decorated with lovely print wallpaper and stylish lamps along with duck-egg velvet chairs. Nick and Helen sat together as if posing for a portrait, Fig settled comfortably onto Helen's lap. Jane sidled close to Edith, marvelling at the lovely drapes, and told her that Helen had employed a 'name' from London to restyle the house in the very latest designs.

Listening to Helen recall her life in India and their adventures visiting foreign embassies and dining with ambassadors, Edith couldn't help but notice how the men – and women – fawned over her words. She tried to counter with her own anecdotes, but she only really came to life when she was talking about the Darton Bra. It was Nick who seemed most interested, and she was delighted when she discovered that she was sitting next to him at dinner. Soon they were all invited into the dining room.

The long dining table was majestically laid up with cut-glass goblets, gleaming china and a central floral display. It was much more upmarket than anywhere Edith had dined for a very long time, and she was pleased to find herself spending New Year's Eve somewhere worthy of her stature.

The Bamfords had a French chef and, as the five courses started coming, each more delicious than the last, Edith was more and more impressed. It was a far cry from the stodgy staples Martha served at Darton. Helen joked that the chef was her great extravagance and that if she was missing one of her senses, then she'd indulge the others. As Nick smiled across the table at her, Edith could see the love in his eyes. It seemed to her that it was utterly wasted on his wife.

She set about shamelessly hogging his attention, not letting Jane, who was seated on his other side, join in the conversation. Soon they got onto business and she told him all about the first presentation she'd done of Top Drawer to Withshaw and Taylor in London, when she'd choreographed a dance routine and song with Nancy's help.

'She sounds like a character,' Nick said.

'Oh, she was. She was my best friend.'

'Was?'

Edith sighed. 'It's rather a sad story, but . . . someone else stole her away.'

'You can't steal a person, surely?' Nick laughed.

Edith smiled and took a long sip of champagne, thinking, *Of course you can steal a person. That's exactly what I'm doing right now.*

She told him about how she'd refurbished Darton and trained the machinists, not scrimping on detailing her achievements. 'Your newspaper didn't print any of that,' she said, with a tilt of her head.

'Ah. I knew you hadn't really forgiven me. You'll never let me live that investigation down, will you?'

'No, I don't intend to,' she replied. 'In fact, I'd rather like the chance to show you the good side of Darton.' She pressed her lips together, wondering if she dared ask him. 'You know, I was thinking of doing an advertising shoot for the Soirée collection,' she said, although she knew this was something Clement had expressly forbidden when she'd suggested it in the past. 'I was going to pull in some contacts in London – I have a friend at the *Daily Sketch* . . .'

'Why go all the way to London?' he said immediately,

and she was delighted he'd taken the bait. 'Why don't you advertise in the *Dispatch*?'

'Well now, I—'

'I could hire you a studio and fix some preferential rates. Perhaps that would go some way towards building bridges between us?'

'I'll give it some thought,' Edith said. Inside, she was applauding furiously.

33

The Right Party Crowd

Daniel's home was unlike anything Vita had ever seen before. Sitting in a prime position on Mulholland Drive, it was made of glass and steel and was – to Vita's mind, at least – thrillingly modern. She hoped they would fit in.

Vita looked at the figure-hugging oyster silk halter-neck dress that she'd altered for Nancy so that it fell flat over her stomach and into a fishtail just below her knees, flaring to a train at the back. She'd thought at first that it was too over the top, but Nancy had said there was no such thing. And now, as they left their coats and walked into the thick of the crowd, Vita realized Nancy had been absolutely right. Everyone at Daniel's party was dressed to impress.

Vita herself felt decidedly less dazzling in a straight midnight-blue crepe dress with a sailor neckline and flouncy white bow in the front. She'd spent all day at the hairdresser's having her hair styled properly, and now she touched her glossy curls self-consciously.

'You look swell, kiddo,' Nancy whispered.

'I'm worried about Bertie.'

'Please just relax and enjoy yourself. He'll be perfectly safe with June. Promise me you'll let your hair down tonight?'

Vita smiled and nodded as a waiter passed them. He was dressed in a lion's head, the mascot of the studios, Vita noted.

'Oh, Leo, from the bumper,' Nancy said, as he offered them drinks. 'That's clever.'

'Bumper?' Vita asked.

Nancy had taken it upon herself to learn everything there was to know about MGM Studios, and she was forever coming up with new facts.

'The bumper is the technical term for that little clip that's like a movie logo,' she said. 'So for MGM it's Leo the lion, although the first lion they tried to record wasn't called Leo at all, but Slats, and he refused to utter a peep. The current one is Jackie, and he roared properly when they recorded him. But what a terrifying job. Just imagine sticking a microphone in front of a real lion!'

They both took exotic red and orange drinks in gold-rimmed crystal glasses from the tray Leo was carrying. Nancy raised her eyebrows at Vita over the elaborate concoction, decorated with slices of pineapple and a paper umbrella, and took a sip of it through the straw. Her eyes widened as she flicked a glance over Vita's shoulder. 'Don't look now,' she said, prompting Vita to turn around.

A woman with dark hair was walking in from the gardens, surrounded by three men who were clearly hanging on her every word. 'Is that Tallulah Bankhead?' Vita asked. Nancy nodded, her eyebrows high.

Nancy had completely changed her tune about Daniel Myers. She no longer referred to him as a Bolshevik or a Jew, because his, it seemed, was a very impressive name to drop. Unlike the tiny bit part she'd landed on the day of

Vita's crash, Daniel's name had opened the gates – this time at the prestigious MGM Studios. Nancy had reported that she'd been treated completely differently once she was armed with Daniel's card. In fact, before the studios had closed for a couple of days over Christmas, Nancy had walked straight into five days' solid work on her first movie.

She'd loved every minute of it, and Vita had been a little jealous. Particularly of Nancy's pay cheque, which she'd squandered on over-the-top Christmas presents – a brand-new sewing machine for Vita and a stroller and cot for Bertie.

As grateful as she was, Vita desperately wanted to get through those gates too. But now she was one step closer, because here they were at their first proper Hollywood party. From where they stood, she could see a net across the whole hallway in which hundreds of balloons were suspended. Enormous screens with '1930' projected onto them flanked the garden, and music blared from the full orchestra. She heard the shriek of laughter and the pleasing pop of corks as they walked past a central table where a waiter on a stool was tipping champagne in a cascade down a pyramid of glasses.

'Ah, Vita, there you are,' Daniel called out, waving and then shouldering his way through the crowd to reach them. He looked very dapper in white tails and a white bow tie, his hair slicked back. He had a piece of glitter stuck to his cheek, and lipstick smudges where someone had kissed him.

Vita complimented him on his home, and Nancy offered profuse thanks for his help in getting her some work. But just as he had done with the car, he waved his hand as if it had been no problem to do her such a favour.

'You two had better be up for dancing. I've got the whole of Kid Ory's band here. You know that guy? Plays the trombone like you've never heard it. Come into the garden. There are some people I'd like you to meet. And Nancy. Well! You look divine. What a dress.'

Why had he noticed Nancy's dress and not hers? Vita thought.

'You had no trouble leaving the little guy?' he asked her, and she thought it was sweet that he was concerned, but now she second-guessed his comment. Did he just think of her as a mother?

'Our neighbour, June, is with him tonight,' she said, smiling to hide how uncomfortable she felt about leaving him.

'Then the night is ours,' Daniel said. 'Shall we?'

He offered them each an elbow and they laughed, linking arms with their host as he led the way out to a large garden dominated by a square pool, lit up from below. A fountain danced in the centre of it, the spray lit up with coloured lights as it plumed into the air.

'Walter – he's a gaffer at the studio,' Daniel explained. Then, seeing Vita didn't understand, he added: 'One of our lighting technicians. He's a genius when it comes to lights.'

Beyond the pool, the garden sloped down, and for a second Vita stopped, awed by the view. It looked over the whole of Los Angeles, the lights of the city twinkling.

'Jeepers creepers,' Nancy said.

'You like it?' Daniel asked, pleased with her reaction. Did Daniel like Nancy? He certainly seemed to be paying her lots of attention, but Vita realized that she was being ridiculous. Why wouldn't Daniel be dazzled by Nancy? Or, for that matter, any of these young beauties that seemed to be everywhere?

'All these people . . . are they all in the movies?' Vita asked.

'No. That guy over there . . .' He pointed to a man in a tuxedo who was laughing. 'That's Maddux – he's in aviation. Oh, and that's Harry Culver, the real-estate developer. Not to be confused with Harry Chandler, who built the Hollywoodland sign to advertise his real-estate development.'

Mr Culver approached and shook Daniel's hand. He looked up and down at Vita and Nancy.

'How's it going, Harry? Business good?' Daniel asked.

'I can't keep up,' Culver said with a hearty laugh. 'I got seventy ships lined up at the port to deliver me lumber.'

'Harry makes houses,' Daniel explained to Vita and Nancy.

'Not houses, *homes*, Dan. Homes. A Ford Model T in the garage, a cuckoo clock, furniture, linens and . . .' he chuckled, 'in some of them, we even provide a photo album filled with pictures of ancestors. Makes it more authentic, you know?'

Daniel was greeted now by more guests. He'd seemed out of place in New York with Nate's friends, but here people adored him. *You're the most interesting girl here*, he'd told Vita at Nancy's, but that clearly wasn't true tonight. Not when every single girl at this party was stunning.

They went past the pool to a bank of flowering bushes and through a jasmine-covered archway to where a dance floor had been set up. A full jazz orchestra was playing and a whole crowd of people were dancing on a canvas floor on the lawn. Daniel had described this as 'a little party', but there must have been several hundred people here already.

Vita saw a girl in a shimmering sequinned outfit and was reminded of their more outlandish costumes at the Zip Club. This was clearly a party at which to be seen. Beside her, Nancy stood taller, jutting out her chin.

'This is more like it,' she said.

34

Impressing Lester

On the far side, across the lawn, tables were loaded with flickering candelabras, the low banquettes around them crowded with guests.

'Ah, there's Lester,' Daniel said, waving.

'Does he mean Lester Heffman?' Nancy whispered to Vita as they crossed the grass.

'I have no idea who that is,' Vita said, her head turning at the sight of a semi-naked man riding past on a unicycle, juggling.

Daniel led them over to one of the tables where a large man was smoking a fat cigar. The crowd of men around him – five of them, Vita counted – were all laughing raucously. There was a woman, too, who wasn't smiling. She wore a figure-hugging slip of a dress, a tuxedo draped round her shoulders. She was smoking a thin, mint-green cigarette in an ebony holder and looking off into the distance as if she was utterly bored. She raised an eyebrow as Vita caught her eye.

'Ah, Daniel,' the man with the cigar said. 'Come and join us.'

'These are the girls from New York I was telling you about, Lester,' Daniel said. 'This is the one who trashed my car,' he added, flicking his head in Vita's direction, and she gasped. He leant down and whispered in her ear, 'Don't look like that. I'm teasing you.'

'Ahh,' the famous studio boss said, shifting in his seat to get a better look. 'Are you both actresses?' he asked, his beady eyes moving from Vita to Nancy and back to Vita again – specifically to her chest.

'Me? No – but Nancy is,' Vita said, suddenly put on the spot.

One of the men reached for the bottle of champagne in the ice bucket and waggled it. Daniel, noticing it was empty, called to a waiter.

'Shame you don't come as a double act.'

'We do on occasion, but you see, Vita is a fashion genius,' Nancy said. 'She invents underwear.'

'Is that so? And do you model it for her?' Lester asked with an amused grin as he sucked on his cigar, his eyes assessing Nancy. She met his enquiring gaze coolly.

'I have, Lester, in the past,' she replied, cheekily using his first name as if they were already well acquainted. Vita was amused by how risky she was being. 'We were dancers together at the Zip Club in London, then we went to Les Folies Bergère, in Paris. You've heard of it, of course?' she carried on, sliding into the seat next to him. 'And you see, I had this wonderful idea . . .'

'Let's leave those two to get acquainted,' Daniel said, in a low whisper close to Vita's ear.

They walked away. Vita heard the trill of Nancy's laughter as she was introduced to the others around the table. She was relieved not to have to sit with them and bolster up her friend's outlandish claims.

'Lester likes a new actress.'

'Oh dear,' Vita said. 'Should I warn her? She's bound to say something to get her into trouble.'

'That's fairly impossible in this town. And anyway, I think she can handle herself.'

There was a beat as he smiled at her.

'You've got lipstick . . .' she gestured, pointing bashfully at his cheek. Embarrassed, he took out his handkerchief and handed it to her. She carefully wiped the lipstick away.

'A hazard of being a host,' he laughed. And then he was greeted by a whole new crowd of people, and slowly Vita felt herself separating from him.

She had to *do* something, she thought. To make him notice her. She had to be daring. *Sixty seconds*, she told herself, willing herself to remember how brave she'd once been.

Spotting her moment as the band started a slower number, she placed her empty glass on the tray of a passing waiter and, excusing Daniel from his guests, took his hand and headed towards the dance floor. 'Let's dance,' she said.

'If you insist,' he said, smiling down at her.

He pulled her closer, his hand on the small of her back. A shimmer of desire ran through her as they started dancing, his leg between hers, leading her. He certainly knew how to move, she thought. She hadn't been with a man who could dance so well since Archie.

'Tell me more about you and your friend Nancy. It sounds like the pair of you have had a lot of fun,' Daniel said, and she wondered if he was making conversation to break the intimate atmosphere that seemed to encase them as they danced.

So, she pulled away and looked up at him as she told him about going with Nancy to the Zip Club, and how they'd gone to Paris together on the Blue Train, and boarded with Madame Vertbois, and how they'd got jobs at Les Folies Bergère. Daniel's eyes locked with hers and she was conscious of her hips pressed against his.

'It sounds like a riot.'

'It was,' Vita smiled, before telling him about working for Madame Jenny and everything she'd learnt, and how she'd come to marry Irving. It had been a long time since she'd talked to anyone about herself. Telling Daniel now made her realize what an adventure it had been, and how far she'd come.

'And you want to be a designer again?'

'Oh, yes. More than anything. June – she's the one who's babysitting Bertie tonight – well, I met her at the pool. I was staring at her because she was wearing the most fantastic two-piece costume and she caught me sketching it. She said she'd kept it from a shoot.'

'Oh, she's stolen something from the studio?'

'Oh, oh no, I didn't mean to snitch,' Vita gasped; but then she saw that Daniel was teasing her. Before she could say any more, he was interrupted by a robust-looking woman who demanded his attention and Vita was suddenly in the arms of her husband – a very sweaty man, much shorter than her. She missed Daniel's altogether more intimate embrace.

As soon as she could, she extricated herself and walked to the buffet table, where there was the most majestic spread. She took a prawn on a stick and ate it, gazing into the dancing crowd. It crossed her mind that while she'd been dancing with Daniel, she'd totally forgotten about Bertie. Would he be asleep, she thought guiltily? *What if he isn't? What kind of terrible mother am I being here, enjoying myself?*

Oh, but it felt so good to just be herself again. She saw Daniel looking for her and she waved at him, smiling as she ate, seeing what a charming host he was being. She felt a deep flush, remembering how good it felt to be noticed. Yes, Daniel Myers had turned out to be quite a surprise.

35

A Moment Alone with Nick

Nick's study was a small, cosy room, but reassuringly male. None of Helen's designer's feminine touches in here, Edith noted. There was a large desk topped in green leather and a matching chair; a brocaded chaise by the window, and floor-to-ceiling bookcases lining the walls. An elephant tusk was mounted above the door. Edith pressed the button on the green reading lamp on the desk, hoping the light was flattering. She looked down at the silver-framed pictures on the desk of Nick and Helen and him holding Lettice as a baby.

'Edith! What are you doing in here?' Nick asked, coming in. He was carrying a bottle of champagne and some glasses.

'I'm sorry; I saw the Study sign on the door and I couldn't help myself. I'm hopelessly nosey, and I was so intrigued by what you were saying about your first editions,' she said, her eyes raking his face for clues. 'I hope you don't mind?'

He walked towards her, the door shutting behind him, and her heart pounded as he put the champagne down just an inch from her hand. She could smell his delicious cologne as he went behind the desk and reached up to a high shelf. Then he took down a book, although Edith didn't give two hoots about books. In an unbidden flight of fancy, she imagined him lying on top of her on that chaise longue, her legs wrapping around him.

He smiled and turned and she blushed, wondering if he could guess what deliciously sexual thoughts she was having. 'This is my favourite. A first edition Dickens. Take a look at this beauty,' he said, handing her the brown leather volume.

Edith took it, looked at it briefly, then put it down on the desk and stepped towards him. She reached out her hand and put it on his lapel. She could feel the heat of his body beneath his clothing. She looked up at his face – his dear face – noticing a little line of freckles on his cheekbone. His eyes were soft as they looked down into hers. If she reached up on her tiptoes, she'd be able to kiss him. She looked at his full lips, already savouring their taste. Couldn't he see how much she wanted him?

'I'm so very glad you came, Edith,' he said. 'Meeting you properly has been quite . . .'

He didn't get to finish the sentence, because now the door opened. Susan was standing in the doorway, watching them.

'Susan,' Nick said charmingly, breaking away from Edith and going to the door as if nothing had happened. 'I was just getting . . .'

He held up the bottle of champagne, smiling too brightly. 'I mustn't keep the others waiting. It won't be long until midnight. I hear you and Lettice are going to join us grown-ups?'

There was a tense moment. Edith couldn't bear the feeling she had now of being caught out, especially by Susan, who continued to stand, watching and judging with her pale eyes.

Nick scooted past her and back to the drawing room. Susan was wearing the grey and blue chiffon shift dress Edith had bought her, but it was too big and it slipped down her shoulder, revealing the thin strap of her petticoat. A wisp of blonde hair fell against her pale neck, the headband Edith had insisted on wonky on her head. She looked childish and small, but her eyes blazed.

'You're making a fool of me,' she said in a scornful voice, and Edith experienced a sickening flash of recognition. She was just like Clement. Before she could help herself, she was marching furiously towards Susan.

'Don't you dare speak to me like that,' she flared, her voice lowered into a menacingly low hiss.

'You ruin everything,' Susan snapped, and Edith, unable to control the impulse, pushed her, so that Susan stumbled back into the corridor. It took every ounce of strength she had not to hit the girl for her impudence.

'Edith, dear. Is that you? Are you coming for the countdown to midnight? We're tuning in the wireless now for the chimes of Big Ben.'

Helen was coming down the corridor, her hand on the wooden panelling. There was a moment where Edith's eyes flashed a warning at Susan. Thank goodness Helen couldn't see them, their faces an inch apart.

'Is everything quite all right?' Helen asked, coming over. Her cheeks were flushed and for once her eyes met Edith's directly. It was unnerving.

'Oh, Helen,' Edith said. 'Susan and I were just . . .'

'I'm so sorry, Mrs Bamford, but we have to leave,' Susan blurted, not letting Edith finish.

'Leave? But you're staying, surely? We have rooms ready for you. Lettice is so excited—'

'I'm afraid I don't feel terribly well. I'd rather wake up tomorrow in my own bed, if you don't think that terribly rude?'

Helen laughed, placing her hand on Susan's sleeve and then patting upwards to feel her face. She cupped her chin and smiled. Vita noticed the intricate set of three diamond rings she was wearing. Had Nick knelt down and asked for her hand in marriage? Edith would bet money that he had.

'Of course I don't think you're rude. How wonderful it has been to have you celebrate the New Year with us. And you, dear Edith.' She smiled and reached out for Edith's arm, although this time she was looking over Edith's shoulder.

'I think she's coming down with a fever,' Edith said, embellishing Susan's lie. 'I'm sorry to say, but there's been a lot of illness at Darton. I really can't risk staying and having her infect you,' she said.

And that was it. The evening was ruined. Crushed. They stayed for an awkward countdown to midnight but Susan had already insisted that Hetherington, the driver, bring the car around. He was clearly disgruntled to be out in the cold, instead of drinking in the kitchen with the Bamfords' jolly housekeeper.

They said some hasty goodbyes at the door, keen not to let the chill into the warm house. It was snowing lightly, the ground dusted with an eerie white layer in the muffled moonlight. Susan put her head down and headed for the car. Nick lingered at the door, but Edith couldn't look at him when she knew Susan was watching her. The humiliation was too strong. She wanted nothing more than to reach up and kiss him, but instead she shook his hand and thanked him for a pleasant evening.

As they drove away, she rubbed her glove on the glass and cast one last lingering look at Nick, but he went back into the house. And as the door shut, sealing him with Helen into their warm house, Edith vowed that whatever happened in this new decade, she would make Nick Bamford hers.

36

After Midnight

Nancy was still holding court in Daniel's back garden and, as far as Vita could make out, didn't have any intention of moving. As she approached the tables, still out of breath from dancing, she tried to catch Nancy's eye. At this rate she'd miss the midnight countdown, but Nancy was in her element.

'And I'm telling you boys, the nineteen thirties will be the decade of women,' Nancy was saying.

The man in the white tuxedo next to Lester looked amused, but Vita could see that he was interested in the point Nancy was making, as was the woman on the other side of the table. Her heavily lidded eyes reminded Vita of Marlene Dietrich.

The man nodded at Lester, then glanced at the woman, and Vita saw her raise one thin eyebrow. There was some sort of unspoken conversation going on between all three of them. Nancy's eyes darted between them, trying to fathom it out.

'Go on,' the man said.

'It's women who are on the cover of every fan magazine in the country. Women who go to see other women at the box office. Obviously, you can put in a man with a pretty face, but it's women that have all the power.'

'Is that so?' the man said. He glanced again at the woman, and Vita saw her smile.

'Yes, it is,' Nancy said. 'Women, just the same as me, want to see women *like* me.' She put a red fingernail on his lapel. 'Fact.'

'Women like you?' He rubbed the side of his face. 'And what makes you so special?'

'I'm modern. I have sophisticated tastes, I'm single and I'm very definitely not a virgin.'

Now the woman across the table let out a snort of surprised laughter, and Vita watched the man smile too. He stabbed the end of his cigarette towards the woman. Vita looked on in fascination, wondering whether to intervene, but she had to hand it to Nancy – she'd certainly pitched herself.

'This one's for you, Ericka,' the man said, nodding towards Nancy.

Nancy glanced up and saw Vita, who now wondered whether she'd been right to interrupt.

'It's nearly midnight,' she told Nancy.

'I've got to go. Excuse me, gentlemen,' Nancy said, choosing her moment to leave while she was getting maximum attention. She shimmied out from beside Lester, not leaving him in any doubt as to the slinky curve of her derrière.

'Hey, wait!' The woman with dark hair now came after them. Vita took a sip of her drink, amused at these two assessing each other. 'I didn't ask . . . do you have an agent?'

'So what if I do?' Nancy raised one eyebrow, like Bette Davis. Vita had seen her practising this very expression in the vanity mirror at home.

'Cut the crap, honey,' the woman said. 'There'll be time enough for that.'

She shifted onto her other foot and glanced back at the table. 'I doubt you're represented, but just in case you are, a word to the wise.' She tapped the side of her nose. 'Get rid of them and come with us.'

'Us?'

'Mr Clifford would like to take you onto the books. Although I would be responsible for you, God help me,' she added. 'I'm Ericka. Ericka Brookes.'

Nancy was silent for a moment. Vita knew her well enough to be sure that she was torn between jumping up and down with excitement and keeping up her cool facade. Even Vita had heard of Clifford Associates, the famous actor's agency.

'It depends,' Nancy said.

'On what?' Ericka put out her arms and laughed. 'You've played your game well enough, Nancy. Now drop the act and let's drink champagne to celebrate and I can tell you exactly what I can do for you. Do you mind if I steal her?' she asked Vita, hooking her arm though Nancy's.

A short time later, as the band was blasting out the Charleston, there was a great noise as the percussionist clapped a pair of giant cymbals to begin the countdown. The atmosphere was electrifying as the balloons were released inside. Cascades of paper streamers went up from cannons around the edge of the jumping crowd, which seemed to Vita like a sweating, shimmering beast. She was laughing as she stumbled away from the middle of the throng to catch her breath.

'There you are,' Daniel said, pushing through to her. 'I lost you. Come with me.' He grabbed her hand.

He led her up a minimalist staircase to the balcony, holding two glasses of champagne in his other hand which splashed and spilt. They arrived at a glass-sided platform, sliding doors opening onto a softly lit room beyond. A bedroom, Vita saw, with a low bed and a cowhide on the polished floor. The door beyond it was open onto a corridor and she saw a man and woman chasing along it, the woman barefoot and giggling with excitement as she arrived in Daniel's room. Then, seeing Vita outside on the balcony, she backed out again.

Daniel laughed. 'There are quite a few people getting overexcited,' he said.

'It's the night to do it,' she agreed, following his gaze. 'It's an amazing party.'

She leant on the balcony next to Daniel as suddenly the sky lit up with fireworks. The crowd below burst into applause and gasps of awe.

'Goodness,' she smiled, putting a hand to her chest.

'I wanted you to have the best view of them.'

Vita gasped as more fireworks lit up the sky. They were so high up that they could see displays going on all across the city, a sparkling array of distant pink, gold, green and blue starbursts. She looked at Daniel's face, his skin red and orange in the light; but now she remembered the fireworks in Monte Carlo, and making love to Archie. Bertie had come into existence beneath a sky just like this. Where was Archie tonight? she wondered. Was he with Maud? Would he be thinking of her?

She forced the thought away. Archie was consigned to the last decade, she decided. She must concentrate on her new life here.

'Happy New Year, Vita,' Daniel said. 'A whole new decade. A whole load of new beginnings.'

'I'll drink to that,' she replied, smiling at him. They touched champagne glasses.

Then he reached forward and kissed her very gently on the lips. It was a tender kiss, given without expectation. When he pulled back, she saw him looking at her anxiously and she grinned back.

'Dan! Dan, come on down,' someone yelled from below.

Then they heard a big splash. Vita looked down and saw that Nancy had jumped, fully clothed, into the swimming pool.

'Oh, she's ruined that lovely dress,' Daniel said, pulling a face at Vita.

Nancy came up for air, grinning, clearly delighted at the applause, and Vita heard yells as several other people jumped into the pool too.

'Daniel,' she said. 'I want to thank you. For tonight. For being so lovely to us.'

'It's my pleasure. It made my night that you came.'

There was a moment of stillness as they smiled at one another. Vita's breath caught in her throat. Was he going to kiss her again?

'Come on – after midnight is always when the party really starts,' he said.

She sent up a silent prayer of thanks for the good fortune that had brought them to Hollywood. The year 1930 was most definitely looking good.

37

Not Again

'I thought you were staying over?' Clement asked, leaning on the banister and watching as Edith and Susan arrived at the top of the stairs to the first floor.

The cold that had seeped under Edith's cape, making her shiver all the way back from the Bamfords', now made her teeth chatter. If it hadn't been so late, she'd have asked Martha to draw her a hot bath. But all she wanted to do now was lie down and remember everything that Nick had said. She didn't want to have any form of conversation with her husband.

Besides, he'd been drinking. A bottle of port and a nearly empty glass sat on the mahogany dresser in the room behind him.

'Happy New Year, Susan,' Clement called, as Susan walked away down the corridor towards her own room at the very end. The blue and grey chiffon dress made her look like a ghost. She turned and glared back at her father, then at Edith.

'Is it?' she asked pointedly.

Clement watched her disappear through her door, then looked at Edith. 'Had another altercation?' he probed nastily.

For a second, Edith wanted to pick up the china dog from a nearby ornamental table and smash him over the head with it.

'I'm going to bed too. I have a headache,' she said.

She glanced past him. If she were to walk through his room to their shared dressing room, she'd get to her bedroom, but she knew the door was locked on her side. Now, though, she saw that there was a suitcase open on the ottoman by Clement's bed. And some of the hangers in his dressing room were empty.

'Where are you going?' she asked, suddenly alert. Why was Clement packing? Was he . . . was he *leaving* her?

'I'm going to Liverpool tomorrow.'

'Liverpool? Why?'

'I'm sailing to New York.'

'New York? *Now?*' Edith was horrified. How had he organized this behind her back? Was that what he'd been doing while he'd been away? She was sick of him being so secretive. Was this what he'd been brooding on all of Christmas? Or what he'd been laughing about with the men who'd passed through on Boxing Day? It made her furious that he'd been planning to leave while she and Susan were away at the Bamfords'. What had he been intending to do – leave a note? Or leave it to his mother to break the news for him? His appalling cowardice made her flare with anger.

The timing was particularly spiteful because he knew how badly Edith wanted to be involved in any trip to America. How she'd said, time and again, that she wanted to go and meet the agent so that they could get things moving over there for the Darton Bra. And yet he was clearly planning on going alone.

'You're going? Just like that?' she said. 'Shouldn't we discuss this?'

'I've heard that my sister is in New York.'

This was a shock to Edith. She'd thought that Vita was still in Europe with Nancy. What else did Clement know about her? Why was he taking matters into his own hands like this? Why hadn't he included Edith, if he knew Vita was in New York?

She stared at him. 'How long will you be gone?' she asked coldly, but her cheeks were burning with fury.

'It doesn't concern you. I've made arrangements at the mill. Everything will continue as normal until my return. I've put Tantum in charge.'

'Tantum? But—'

'Don't challenge me on this, Edith,' Clement said, his tone ominous. 'Tantum is experienced. He shares my view.'

'He's an idiot,' she spluttered. 'And if you think I'm going to take orders from him, then you're very much—'

He swiftly stepped towards her and smacked her hard across her face. 'I've had just about enough of your insolence,' he snapped, his spittle landing on her cheek. Close up, she saw that his face was pale and drawn, his eyes red-rimmed and blazing with pent-up anger. He looked brutal. 'It's my business. *Mine*. You will do as I say.'

He'd been rough with her before, of course. She'd always seen his temper and had been at pains to keep it at bay, but he'd never used outright violence towards her. Shock coursed through her as she ran past him and into her room, slamming her bedroom door furiously and locking it from the inside, although it was difficult to turn the key when her hands were shaking so much.

'Edith,' she heard from the other side. 'Edith, open the door.'

She backed away from the door, hating his voice. Hating everything about him.

And then another thought struck her: was this how Vita had felt, too? Was this why she'd run away? Because of Clement? Because he'd hit her too . . . or worse? Because here, in this dark room, it was as if a veil was being drawn back. Were the things he had told her about Anna all really true? Or were they a smokescreen for a more terrible truth?

She thought of Nick, of how kind he'd been to her. The contrast with her own domestic situation could not have been more profound. She heard Clement thump his fist once against her door.

'Goddamn it, Edith,' he said, in a low hiss.

She let out an anguished yelp, flung herself down on the bed and wept, pounding her palm against the needlepoint cover in sheer fury. Because she hated Clement. She did. She hated him. And the whole tangled mess she'd found herself in, when all she'd wanted to do was run a business. She hated being trapped here in this miserable house, with her uncaring, cruel husband, while women like Helen Bamford got someone like Nick. It wasn't fair. Nothing was fair.

She must have cried herself to sleep, but she woke, her teeth chattering. As she was kneeling by the hearth to light a fire, she saw a thin line of light appear beneath her door. Then she heard voices.

She unlocked her door and opened it a crack. Clement was in the corridor, his back to her. Beyond him, Edith could see Theresa Darton – her hair in rags beneath a linen cap, her long nightdress and gown making her look strangely tall. Or maybe it was just that her shadow loomed along the corridor.

'No, Clement,' her mother-in-law said, backing towards Susan's bedroom door, blocking Clement.

'Get out of my way.'

'Leave her alone,' Theresa Darton said. She'd spoken too loudly and now she lowered her voice, but in the silence of the hall, Edith heard her hiss, 'I'm warning you.'

Edith was about to intervene and open the door to find out what on earth was going on, when she saw that Theresa had one of Clement's hunting guns in the folds of her gown. She pulled it up now, with effort, hoisting it against her shoulder with a wide swing. She aimed the barrel at Clement's head.

'Mother,' Clement said, tutting. 'Put that down.'

Theresa aimed more accurately at him. 'Not again,' she said. 'Go back to bed, Clement, and stay there tonight.'

Clement put his hands up in surrender and backed away. 'The women in this house . . .' he said in a drunken slur, as if he were subjected to madness all around him.

Edith closed the door quickly before he saw her, but as she turned the key silently, Theresa's words clanged in her head . . . two of them in particular. *Not again.*

Her knees buckled and she hung onto the door handle, momentarily winded.

Was Clement interfering in some way with Susan? Was that why she was so sullen? So keen to be anywhere but Darton?

Turning towards her dressing room, she saw the blue beaded dress on the floor where she'd taken it off in a hurry. It lay on the carpet like a sad puddle and she picked it up, hugging it to her, smelling the perfume on it, picturing herself in the study with Nick, although that already felt like an age ago.

And that bold, confident woman was someone else, too. Because since then, everything had changed. Edith could no longer pretend to herself about who she was: she was a woman who was married to a monster.

38

The Crème de la Crème Service

Daniel's had easily been the best party Vita had ever been to, but now, five days later, she was still hopelessly low on sleep. She was up again early on Sunday morning, washing Bertie's bottles at the sink, looking out at the bright blue sky, her mind filled with thoughts of Daniel: the way he'd smiled at her, the way he'd sought out her company, that kiss. *Oh, that deliciously simple kiss.* Since giving birth, she hadn't even considered the thought that she might have sex again, but now she noticed the return of her libido with a vengeance.

Suddenly, the screen door banged and Ericka swept in, making Vita jump. She was wearing a tailored grey and white striped trouser suit that showed off her statuesque figure, and her short hair was oiled back from her high brow. She threw a leather briefcase down on the kitchen table, looking around the apartment disparagingly. Vita lifted Bertie out of his highchair, at once annoyed by this sudden intrusion and embarrassed by the toys on the floor.

'Is she here?' Ericka asked in her deep, husky voice.

'Ericka?' Nancy emerged from her room, pulling a robe around her. 'What's going on? It's a Sunday.'

'I haven't interrupted you going to church, have I?' Ericka

said, looking at Nancy and then laughing. 'I thought not. Sunday or no, fame doesn't work on a time schedule. We got work to do, sweet cheeks.' Opening the case, she pulled out a sheaf of papers and a gold fountain pen. 'I've got papers for you to sign.'

'Sign?'

'As I told you, Monty says you're to be my pet project. They want me to prove myself, so I shall. I shall prove to them all that I can make you a star.' She tapped the heavy gold pen against the papers with a thump, as if the proof was all there.

Nancy looked at Vita and sat down at the table next to Ericka. They'd discussed meeting Ericka, of course, and how she was clearly a Hollywood player; but even so, seeing the black and white typed contracts on the kitchen table was still a shock for them both.

'And what makes you think you could do that?' Vita asked, seeing Nancy's face and worried now that Ericka might be about to take advantage of her. She knew there were a few powerful female agents, but Ericka looked too young to be one of them.

Ericka threw back her head and laughed. 'Sweet cheeks, I know everything about this goddamned business. I've been in it since I was his age.' She pointed a long finger at Bertie. 'I've watched and I've learnt from the best, and I know what it takes. Which is lucky for you, Nancy Delaney, because you're about to get the crème de la crème service.'

'What do I have to do?' Nancy asked.

'Exactly as I say.' Ericka turned to the pile of documents. 'So, listen up.'

She pulled out a list from her sheaf of papers and went

through the items: a commitment to work with a calisthenics teacher and a tennis coach four times a week, along with a special diet that didn't involve as many cigarettes and cocktails. No more trips to the drive-in sandwich shop, she warned. There would be acting, dancing, singing and elocution lessons, with a whole variety of acting coaches to fit in too. She'd also already booked a dentist for Nancy to have her teeth whitened and a hair appointment to have her hair restyled. 'We're going to make a statement.'

'Oh,' Nancy said, clearly taken aback and touching her hair.

'You really think all this is necessary?' Vita asked.

Ericka pulled a sceptical face. 'If Nancy's not prepared to put in the work . . .'

'I am, I am,' Nancy protested.

Ericka's dark-brown eyes looked at her sternly. 'Good, because I have a screen test lined up for you.'

'A screen test?'

'It's a picture called *The Sister Returns*. I happen to know that one of the stars is about to drop out. Time is of the essence as filming has already started. So we've got to get you ready.' Ericka stood, pulling down the waistcoat of her suit. 'And what about you, kid?' she said, addressing Vita. 'Are you and Daniel Myers an item?'

'Oh, I'm not sure,' Vita replied, blushing at how direct Ericka was.

'What you waiting for? Daniel's one of the hottest catches in Hollywood and he's got eyes for you. There's no time to hang around. I heard him talking about how he'd like to make an honest widow out of you.'

'Widow?'

'Didn't your husband die? Leaving you alone with that kid? That's what I heard.'

After Ericka had left and Nancy had shown her out to her car, Vita waited for her to come back into the kitchen. Nancy, who was clearly prepared to jump up and down with excitement, saw Vita tapping her foot and her smile faded.

'What's the problem?' she asked, genuinely confused that Vita seemed upset.

'The problem? You heard what she said about Daniel. Did you tell him I was a widow?'

Nancy shrugged. 'So what if I did? What's the big fuss? That way you're still eligible. It's simpler.'

'But, but – Irving is still alive.'

'So? We're on the other side of the world.'

'But I don't want to start out with a lie.'

'Everyone lies. Everything is a lie. Hadn't you noticed? You've got to play the game. You heard Ericka. You gotta be tough to get ahead. And besides, you can't do anything at all to rock the boat with lovely Daniel. I mean it, Vita. Everything rests on this for me. You can't wreck things by shooting your mouth off about the past.'

'But—'

'I've said it before, but I'll say it again. It's just a stitch in time. A little white lie now, to gloss over the finer details. It'll save you a whole load of heartache in the future. Believe me, kiddo, OK?' She gently gripped Vita's chin. 'OK?' she checked.

Vita met her eye and nodded in acquiescence.

39

Muscle Beach

On Saturday, Vita tried to ignore her misgivings when Daniel picked her and Bertie up in his new car for a day out at the beach. As they drove south along the coast road, she was determined to find a moment to set the record straight in the most natural way possible, even though Nancy had cautioned her not to.

She smiled as he put his foot down and the open-topped car roared and sped up, the ocean sparkling as far as the eye could see, the waves so close at points that Vita could feel the spray on her face. She turned her face up to the sun, letting her hand fall out of the window, idly letting the warm breeze lift it up and down. In the back, Bertie gurgled contentedly.

When the traffic became heavier towards Santa Monica they slowed down, chatting for a while about Daniel's week at the studios.

'If you want some insider gossip, I heard that Nancy's screen test was a big success,' he said, and Vita felt a shiver of excitement. The lead-up to Thursday had been exhausting. Vita had never seen Nancy so nervous.

'You mean that part? In *The Sister Returns?*'

Daniel nodded, and Vita did a victory drum roll on her knees.

'I so hoped she would get it.'

'She'll have heard by now. We did the contracts yesterday. Believe me, she's going places, that girl,' he said. 'But don't you tell her I said so. Ericka is playing hardball with us on her fees. She seems to think Nancy is Bette Davis already.'

'Oh,' Vita said. Was this good news?

'I saw the screen test. She looks good on camera. That's the main thing. Some pretty girls can't pull it off – the camera doesn't bring out their best side, but Nancy, well . . . she's got it. Whatever "it" is. She's made for the talkies.'

'It's her dream to be in the movies.'

'You're going to have to keep her feet on the ground,' Daniel said, looking across at her. 'I mean it. I've seen heads spin in this town.'

They drove past Santa Monica beach, where Vita could see deckchairs and umbrellas lined up on the white sand, surfers with long wooden painted boards running into the white waves.

'What's that?' she shouted above the growl of the engine, and Daniel slowed down. She pointed to the pier that jutted out into the ocean.

'La Monica. The ballroom. I've only been once, but I'd like to go again. We should go dancing.'

Did he want to take her dancing? Vita smiled at this hint at a future date.

'What's that noise?' She could hear a faint mechanical rattle and distant screaming.

'That'll be the Whirlwind Dipper. It's a rollercoaster.'

'Nancy would love that,' Vita said. 'She made me go on the Big Dipper in Coney Island back in New York. I was terrified.'

'You're not into thrills like that?'

'Not anymore,' she said. 'These days I'm much less of a daredevil.' It was the first time she'd realized this was true. Being a mother had changed her in so many subtle ways, and she marvelled now at the risks she used to take. 'I used not to scare so easily. I rode horses when I was young and I used to gallop and jump fences without a care in the world.'

'Well, there's a carousel with forty painted horses. We could go on that later. Bertie could come too.'

'That would be lovely.'

Further down from Santa Monica, Daniel said he wanted to stop for a minute and show her something. They found a space to park at the end of a long row of cars that lined the cliff edge, and got out to walk down onto the boardwalk that stretched across the hot sand. Vita pulled the sunhat she'd made for Bertie down over his face and rubbed some cream into his chubby thighs, carrying him on her hip.

She was surprised to see a crowd of young people on the beach. A line of girls in swimsuits stood on the raised walkway, posing for the crowd. A man was taking photographs.

'Goodness,' Vita replied, laughing, remembering the line-up of girls at the Zip. How she'd once been the one on show. How long ago that seemed now, seeing these young hopefuls.

'You've never been to Muscle Beach?' Daniel asked, as they walked on to where there was a crowd around a platform covered in sand. At either end there were iron bars. In the space in the middle, a girl with a lithe showgirl figure lifted up a steel ball with the number 100 printed on it. Her muscles bulged. Then a man in a costume, with straps over his shoulders and knee-high lace-up boots, picked her up and held her aloft as the crowd cheered and clapped.

They watched the show for a little while longer. Vita held onto Daniel's arm in fear, her breath held along with the crowd's, as two men swung a girl by her ankles and wrists in a pendulous arc that went perilously close to the ground, then flung her up in the air. The girl did an acrobatic twist and turn, then landed in the arms of another pair of muscle-bound men, as easily as if she were a beach ball.

'Come on, it's getting hot. I know a little cove nearby. We'll swim there,' Daniel said.

40

The First Step

They drove on for ten minutes, then pulled into a sandy lay-by. Daniel took a panelled umbrella on a long pole from the back of the car and a coolbox that clinked with bottles.

After Muscle Beach, Vita was expecting to feel self-conscious about her figure, but Daniel made her feel so relaxed that, before long, she took off her sundress and lay out in the homemade costume she'd copied from June's. She was still self-conscious about her stomach, but when they took Bertie to splash about in the waves, she saw Daniel looking at her and liking what he saw. In fact, the way he was looking at her made her feel sexy for the first time in ages. She noted his tanned arms, his trim torso and the gold star necklace he wore around his neck. He had muscly legs too, and when he did a handstand in the surf she clapped. In return, she did a cartwheel and when she overbalanced, he caught her in his arms and their faces were close together and she almost kissed him.

They moved to the back of the beach near the cliff to get more shade and ate the picnic Daniel had picked up from his favourite delicatessen. Vita tucked into a delicious pastrami sandwich and let her feet sink into the warm sand, thinking how lovely this was. After lunch, they played games and took turns building sandcastles for Bertie to smash down with a spade. The beach had filled up now with families with their beach chairs and umbrellas. The air was full of the sound of children playing in the waves and Vita shaded her eyes, smiling at the sight of everyone enjoying themselves in such a beautiful setting. She saw several guys with long boards on the top of their cars drive down to the water's edge. Soon they were paddling out and catching the surf.

As they sat on the rug sipping bottles of beer, Bertie tipped forward and started crawling over to Daniel, putting his podgy hands on Daniel's knee to push himself up.

'That's it,' Daniel said, holding his fingers out so that Bertie gripped onto them. He held him upright as Bertie took two tentative steps across the tartan rug to Vita. 'There you go,' Daniel encouraged.

Vita knelt up too and they let Bertie stagger between them, their fingers touching as they transferred Bertie's grip from one to the other. Then, on one of the turns to get to Daniel, Bertie, who was concentrating very hard, let go of Vita's fingers and walked a solo step towards Daniel, a big grin on his face.

Vita gasped and clapped.

'He took his first step,' she said. 'For you.'

'Excuse me,' she heard a woman say. 'I couldn't help watching you two with him. Did you just say it was his first step?'

'Yes,' Vita said, still astonished that Bertie had walked. He sat down on the rug with a thump, exhausted by his efforts.

'Well, won't you look at that,' the woman said, her eyes

soft with delight. She saw Vita's camera lying on the rug. 'Would you like me to record the moment? Take a picture?'

'That would be lovely,' Vita said, setting up the camera and handing it over. She held Bertie up so that he was standing between her and Daniel, and they leant in close together.

'I was married like you two, with a young son, once upon a time. He's grown now and long gone, but you remind me of how we were. So in love. You're as pretty as a picture.'

The woman handed back the camera and after she'd started making her way back up the beach, Vita pulled a face at Daniel.

'That was embarrassing.'

'Was it?' he said, his eyes staying locked with hers.

Later, Bertie napped and Daniel lay beside Vita, his finger moving over her skin. They talked easily about his break into the movies and she leant her head in her hand, liking listening to him and getting to know him. He told her that he'd been engaged to his childhood sweetheart in Poland, but she'd jilted him at the altar, prompting his move to the States.

'Were you desperately in love?' Vita asked, feeling the pain of this sad story.

'I had my heart broken, but I'm not so sure that it was the same as being in love.'

'How so?'

'I was always looking for the hurt – expecting it, almost. I think that love – real love – is like the kind my parents had. Strong, you know. Unbreakable – even when tested by war, or tragedy, or illness. It's built on friendship and respect.'

'Are you close to them?'

'They're dead now,' he said.

'Oh, I'm sorry,' Vita said.

'It's better that they're together. One would have withered without the other,' he said with a shrug. 'What about yours?'

Vita sighed. Lying here, with the surf breaking way across the white sand, it seemed impossible to connect to Darton.

'They own a mill in Lancashire,' she said. 'Darton Mill. They make all sorts of fabric.'

Daniel leant up on one elbow, his necklace falling across his chest.

'You didn't tell me.'

'I ran away.'

'Why? If you like fashion. Surely you liked being around textiles?'

'Yes, I did, but I didn't like being around my father, or my brother.'

Daniel listened as she explained how stifling Darton had been, how downtrodden her mother was, how domineering her father. How she'd found out about a plan for them to marry her off to a fat, rich mill owner, like a prize calf, and she hadn't been able to bear it a moment longer. And she told him, too, about Dante and how Clement had thrashed her horse. She didn't tell him about locking Clement in a stable and how she'd left him for dead.

'Don't you want to go back?'

She shook her head. She couldn't tell him – tell anyone – about the secret fantasy she harboured of going back to

Darton and getting what was rightfully hers. How she sometimes fought with Clement and Edith in her dreams.

'Family is strong.'

'Not my family,' she said, getting up. 'No. It's just me and Bertie now.'

41

Santa Monica Pier

As the sun got lower, they packed up the remains of their picnic and drove back to Santa Monica. Daniel insisted that they head for the kiosk by the carousel so that Vita could try some clam chowder. She liked the fact that even though he clearly had money, he seemed to enjoy the simple pleasures in life. Looking down at the deep blue sea far below the boards of the pier, she felt a thrill at walking so far out over water. But then, everything about today had been new and wonderful.

As they got further along the pier, the air was filled with the smell of hot donuts and the sound of the cars rattling over the rollercoaster track. They wandered past a booth that had a crystal ball outside, and Vita laughed and told Daniel about Mystic Alice in London.

'Do you believe in all of that?' he asked.

'Not really. Nancy does, though,' Vita said, thinking how thrilled Nancy would be when she heard about the fortune teller on the pier. She'd demand to come here straight away. After all, Mikette Cuba in New York had been right about Nancy's fate.

'Come in, come in,' the woman said, emerging from the booth and seeing that Vita and Daniel had stopped.

'Oh, no, really,' Vita said, backing away.

'Why not? You go. I'll look after Bertie,' Daniel said. 'It'll be fun.'

Vita pulled a face. 'Just for a moment, then.'

Inside the kiosk, the tiny space was dense with candle smoke, the shell curtain rattling as the woman came to sit opposite her on a tiny bench.

'I really don't believe . . .' Vita began, as the woman held her palm against the velvet-covered box between them and looked at it. Vita suddenly remembered being at Mystic Alice's in London, and how she'd warned her to look out for a dark stranger.

The woman made a grunting sound and was silent for a long time.

'What can you see?' Vita asked, starting to feel unnerved.

'You are not here long.'

Vita was startled. 'You mean I'm going to . . . to die?'

The woman rubbed her palm, looking down her nose intently. Her thumb nail was grubby. 'I see air and sea. I see you travelling a long way.'

'Where?'

'To where you call home.'

Vita made her excuses and left as soon as she could.

'What did she say?' Daniel asked, when she joined him outside.

'Some nonsense,' Vita said. She busied herself with tucking Bertie in, keen to change the subject. They walked to the end of the pier, and she shielded her eyes from the low red sun.

'What are those?' she asked, seeing a group of ships on the horizon.

'They're gambling ships. They stay three miles out in the bay to avoid the law. You can get a water taxi out to one of them.'

Vita thought of Irving and how he'd spent the whole of their honeymoon itching to gamble. She should tell Daniel the truth about Irving, about what had happened – and perhaps this was her moment, but she was too upset by what the fortune-teller had said. Here, at the other end of the world, the idea of going home to Darton seemed impossible.

No, she vowed. Not ever. Her future was here.

'What are you thinking?' Daniel asked her. 'Vita, are you quite all right?'

'Never better,' she said. Then she stepped towards him and kissed him as the sun sank onto the horizon, casting a golden glow across the purple sea towards them.

42

Hooverville

It was bitterly cold in New York, and Clement's bones ached. Not for the first time, he cursed his sister for putting him through this ordeal as he saw the last cab leave from the rank in Times Square.

He had only just recovered from the journey here, which had been beset by bad weather, the ocean liner pitching so hard it made Clement feel too nauseous and weak to leave his cabin. It had been the worst five days of his life. When he'd eventually found his sea legs he'd joined the card tables in the salon, but he'd lost at every hand.

He sincerely hoped that his luck would change in New York. After all, this city was supposed to be where dreams were made. The lure of it had caused several Darton families to pack up their lives and leave on the ships from Liverpool in the hope of a better life. But Clement didn't feel so much free, as bewildered.

He put his arm up for another cab, shivering. Beside him in a doorway, a beggar approached and held up a hand for money. He looked raw with hunger and desperation, hunched over in scrappy overcoat, a flat cap and worn shoes. Clement shooed him away.

A cab stopped now, and Clement got in quickly and slammed the door. The beggar's gaze followed him as they drove away.

The driver was clearly hoping for a conversation, but Clement was too suspicious of his dark skin to respond. Instead, he looked out of the window to where the shops were boarded up. It was clear that more businesses were going bust every day, and he saw queues around the block for free soup.

As they drove past Central Park he could see that a shanty town had sprung up of homeless men. Hooverville, they were calling it, the cab driver informed Clement – after the President, whom many blamed for the financial crash.

One man in the crowd saw Clement's cab passing and walked into the road, his trousers tied up with string, cardboard on his feet, his face covered in grime. As they passed, the man spat on the cab's window, startling Clement.

He wished, for a moment, that he hadn't parted on such bad terms with Edith and that she was here with him. He could do with some moral support.

He remembered how he'd had such a fiendish hangover on New Year's Day that they'd barely spoken two words when he'd left. She'd been particularly distant and he remembered it now as odd, because he'd been expecting her to protest more about his departure. She'd barely reacted, but perhaps she was sulking about his little smack. But he was in charge, Clement consoled himself. It was only right that a man should bring his wife into line occasionally.

Deep down, though, he knew the real reason Edith was sulking was because he'd come to America alone, when he knew how much she wanted to meet their agent in New York. He'd packed samples of the Darton Bra, but now that he was here, he knew that he wouldn't present them alone. He had other, more pressing matters on his mind.

Clement paid the cab driver and stepped with difficulty down onto the pavement with his stick. The driver was clearly expecting a tip, but Clement wasn't prepared to give one to a man who had been overfamiliar. What was it with these ghastly Americans? The driver muttered a curse as he drove off, brown slush from the gutter flicking up onto Clement's tweed trousers. The damned impertinence.

He looked up at the towering building above him, snowflakes falling on his face. He'd seen Irving's smart house in Paris, but this was another level entirely. He could only hope that Renata King would prove less hostile than her son. He just wanted to get this whole awful business over with and go home to England.

43

Darton's Finest

Nick had arranged for Edith's shoot to take place at a studio across the street from the newspaper's offices in Manchester. It was a cavernous old brick warehouse and the studio was on the third floor. The vast space with its iron girders and bare brick walls now had a set at one end of it which had been made up to look like a silk-draped boudoir, although the bed was made from old crates which Edith had dressed herself with red silk and cushions. It was so creative, she thought, feeling a buzz of excitement. *This* was what she wanted. Damn Clement for never letting her do this before. *Damn Clement full stop.*

Two spotlights illuminated the girls who were positioned around the set. The eight girls she'd selected from the mill were all giddy with excitement at the prospect of a photo shoot for the full-page advertisement in the *Daily Dispatch*.

Underneath their coats and scarves the girls were all wearing different pieces from the Soirée range, although Clarry, in the front, was stealing the show. She seemed to be the girl with the least qualms about showing off her body for the cameras. Edith had given them a pep talk about how important it was that they were proud of the product they made. She had assured them, however, that the shoot would be tasteful and that they'd all get a bonus for their time and patience.

The photographer – a man who looked positively French in his beret, with buckled canvas shoes and stripy T-shirt – shouted out instructions for the girls to move into position and disrobe, while he twiddled with the dials on his enormous black camera. Edith collected the coats, murmuring words of encouragement, as the make-up artist made the final touch-ups using brushes from a leather holder fastened at her waist, a large palette of make-up in one hand. She stood back to view each girl objectively.

'Hey.' Edith heard a voice and turned to see Nick.

'You're here,' she said with a smile. He wore a blue jumper over his shirt and a natty silk scarf with his herringbone overcoat. He looked stylish and suave, and his gorgeous eyes locked with hers, making her insides flutter.

She hadn't seen him since New Year, but they'd corresponded by letter and they'd spoken once on the telephone too – although Helen had been there, making suggestions in the background and insisting that Nick honour the favour he'd offered at New Year.

He was accompanied by another man who Edith recognized as Eddy Postlethwaite, the editor. He was typical of some of the northern men she'd had to deal with, with his balding head and rotund belly.

'We came to see what all the fuss is about,' Mr Postlethwaite said, looking Edith up and down after introducing himself.

'Well?' she asked, addressing both of them and spreading her arm out to the girls. 'What do you think?'

'You've picked some fine beauties there, Mrs Darton, if I say so myself,' Mr Postlethwaite replied. His ruby red cheeks shone in the bright lights of the studio. 'Half of those girls could pass for actresses. It's true what they say . . . that there's none finer than Lancashire lasses. And they're all mill girls. Well, well,' he said, shaking his head. 'You'd never know it.'

'They're mill girls, but they're also modern young working women,' Edith said. 'They go to the hairdresser's, to the cinema and dancehalls. These are the girls who influence fashion. I'd be wary of dismissing them as just mill girls. These girls are Darton's finest.'

Eddy pulled a face at Nick as if he was amused at being chastised by Edith, but she was warming to her theme.

'In actual fact, I think these girls are the best advert we've got for Lancashire,' she said, remembering how annoyed she'd been by Miss Keys at Madame Mensforth's. It was up to Edith to make mill work more desirable than a career in hairdressing; and now an idea was taking shape.

'I dare say you're right,' Eddy conceded.

'And so, if you'll permit me, here's an idea for you, Mr Postlethwaite,' Edith said.

'An idea? Go on – I like ideas.' He nudged Nick. 'You told me this one was a live wire.'

Nick had really described her that way? She looked between the two men, wondering whether what she was about to say was a stupid idea, or inspired.

'What about having a competition between all the mills to find the best mill girl? Like a May Queen, only on a bigger scale. A Cotton Queen . . .'

She looked at Nick.

'Edith, that's a great idea,' he said. 'We could run pictures of all the pretty mill girls.'

'Now that's a licence to print money,' Eddy said, pointing a stubby finger at Nick and Edith. 'Pretty girls always sell newspapers.'

'And it could be so much more than just a competition. The winner could be an ambassador for the cotton industry. A spokeswoman, if you like. Goodness knows we need some good news stories, when so many of the mills are going bust.'

'I can see it now,' Eddy said. 'We'll call it the Cotton Queen Quest. Something like that. We'll picture all the girls and get the readers to vote on their favourites.'

'And at the end, there could be a pageant,' Edith suggested.

'Yes, you're right. In the summer,' Nick said.

'In Blackpool,' Eddy said decisively. 'We'll make a big fuss of it.'

'That sounds wonderful,' Edith said, grinning at them both.

'I don't mind saying it, but I misjudged you and Darton,' Eddy said.

Edith smiled. 'I'm glad to hear you say it.'

'I think Mrs Darton might have just come up with the best idea of the year,' Nick said, grinning.

'I want to discuss it more,' Eddy said. 'Come into the office.'

'Now? I think it's been a long day for Mrs Darton already,' Nick said.

'In the morning, then,' Eddy insisted.

'Well, I . . . I was going back to Darton with the girls later,' Edith said.

'Stay in town,' Eddy said. 'Nick will book you a room at the Midland. And you should show her the paper's appreciation, Nick, and take Mrs Darton out for dinner.'

'Oh, well, that would be wonderful,' Edith said, smiling at Eddy and then at Nick, who nodded.

'That's settled then,' he said.

44

A Business Arrangement

In Renata King's impressive penthouse apartment, Clement followed the maid to a large dining room, where he was pleased to see that breakfast had been laid out. Bagels and juice. How very exotic compared to the porridge at Darton. He had to hand it to the Americans: they knew how to do breakfast. His stomach rumbled.

At the other end of the table, a man was packing up what looked like architectural drawings. The rolls of paper were large and unwieldy.

'I'll see myself out, Mrs King,' he told the woman at the far end of the table, bowing his head.

'Do what I asked and don't come back until you have,' Renata barked in reply. Clement was intrigued to see that the man was so cowed by his hostess – especially as she was such an old woman. 'They come crying to me,' she confided, addressing Clement now. 'These silly men who can no longer finance their own projects. Caught with their trousers down by the crash. More fool them.'

He was surprised by her candour, and saw that the departing man had also heard the cruel observation. Renata King didn't care.

'So . . . Mr Darton. All the way from England,' she said, as they shook hands. Her fingers flashed with an impressive array of rings and Clement thought of his gold pocket watch – a status symbol of his own that he sorely missed.

Renata King was wearing a striped red and black dress that made her look strikingly like an insect. Clement tried to summon some of the charm that Edith told him he should muster when they went to meetings together.

'Since you've come all this way, would you care for breakfast?'

They sat at the table and the maid poured coffee silently from an engraved silver pot, her eyes scrutinizing him. Was this the one on Alicia King's payroll?

He saw Renata give the maid a scolding look as some coffee splashed into the saucer. 'Be careful, Iris,' she said. 'For goodness' sake. I expect you have staff in England, Mr Darton?' she said, the missing 'better' in the sentence clear for the maid to hear.

Clement thought of Martha. She wouldn't keep her mouth shut like this maid, or keep the house so immaculate.

'Oh yes, several staff, but I came without my butler,' he lied.

'I never travel without staff,' she said, as if this were a gross oversight on his behalf. 'Although these days I prefer to stay here and let people come to me.'

After his recent gambling losses, Clement hated nothing more than feeling poor in the company he kept. But for now, at least, Mrs King hadn't judged him as lacking.

'So, I suppose you're here to talk about your sister,' the old woman said, with a disapproving tone.

'I understand that you met her?' Clement looked up and his eyes connected with the maid's. She looked hurriedly away.

'Let me be frank, Mr Darton. That girl seems to have run rings around my son.'

'It doesn't surprise me very much. I shouldn't say this of my own kin, but she's rather a disgrace to the Darton family. She is somewhat of a slippery character.'

'How so?'

Clement decided to tell his story. About how Anna had run away to London and got herself into all sorts of trouble. He told of his dismay and upset when he'd heard she'd become a cheap dancing girl. All he'd wanted was for her to come back to Darton and stop besmirching the family name, but she'd eluded him once again and had gone to Paris, where she'd clearly used her charms to ensnare Irving.

'She *is* slippery,' Renata agreed. 'I asked her to bring the boy here, and the next thing I hear, she's skipped town.'

'The boy?'

'You didn't know?' Renata said. 'About the baby?'

Anna had a baby?

'My grandson. The boy I've always wanted. He's Irving's child.'

'I didn't know . . .' Clement said, his mind whirring.

'She made a fool of me. And I don't take kindly to that.' Renata glared at Clement, as if expecting him to apologize.

'Mrs King, you don't need to tell me how that feels,' Clement said. 'She's not only slippery, but really quite dangerous. I have to walk with a stick because of the injuries she inflicted on me.'

'Is that so?' Renata said, surprised. 'Then perhaps you and I can help each other.' She paused, looking at him with her shrewd, dark eyes. 'What is it that your sister has that you so desperately want?'

Clement wiped his mouth on his napkin, buying time to compose himself before he spoke. 'Your son, Irving, gave her shares in a company called Hillsafe – who then bought a substantial share of Darton Mill. That's my family business. I need control of the company. There are some necessary changes.'

'I see.'

'It doesn't seem right that Anna . . . Vita . . . has any say over the family business she ran away from.'

'I see. Well, perhaps we can come to an arrangement.'

'An arrangement?'

'If you help me get what I want, then I have a chequebook large enough to finance anything you desire. People often misunderstand me – my son included. Because I can be very generous when I want to be.'

They chatted some more, about Darton and about Edith's underwear plans. Renata was surprisingly receptive to becoming involved in their business. And, as he talked, Clement started to realize that she was absolutely serious. It was rather exciting to have a proper business discussion, and without Edith contradicting him he managed to paint an impressive picture of Darton as a solid investment opportunity. He'd thought that talking about brassieres with a woman – any woman, let alone one Renata King's age – would be embarrassing, but they might as well have been discussing pork bellies.

'So you see, it's important that I find Vita. Do you know where she is?'

'They're in California, so I gather. Vita and her friend, Nancy. She has a role in a movie and your sister is with her.'

'California?' Clement asked, surprised. This was a shock. He'd been expecting to find her in New York. 'Are you sure?'

'My dear Mr Darton, I know everything. My maid, Iris, sings over in some church in Harlem on a Sunday. She's friends with the Delaneys' maid, Evelyn. Your sister has quite taken advantage of that family too, so it seems.' She looked at him again, but his mind was whirring with this new information. 'Aren't you going to ask me what I wish for in return?'

'Of course. Whatever it is, I'll be happy to help,' Clement said, remembering that this was the bargain she'd struck.

'Then bring me the child,' Renata said. 'He certainly doesn't need a mother like Vita – or Anna, as you call her. I can have him brought up properly here in New York. He should be with this side of his family.'

Clement swallowed hard. This wasn't how he'd expected the conversation to go at all. 'You want me to bring you Vita's child? But . . . but how?'

'You're an inventive man, Mr Darton. I'm sure you can figure it out.'

And quite suddenly, Renata rang a little bell on the table, and Clement took his clear cue to leave.

It wasn't until he was back on the sidewalk that the shock of what Renata King had suggested really struck him. She wanted him to steal a baby. *A baby.* His own nephew.

But what better way to hurt his sister than to spirit her son away to the top of that skyscraper?

Yes, he decided, setting off. He would find a way.

45

L'Heure Bleue

Edith stopped in the foyer at the bottom of the lift in the sumptuous Midland hotel. She took the gold and crystal atomizer from her bag and sprayed another squirt of Guerlain L'Heure Bleue perfume onto her neck, then pressed the romantic scent between her wrists.

She walked towards where the hotel pianist was playing a jaunty version of 'Makin' Whoopee'. She almost wanted to break into a dance, she was so excited. She adjusted the sparkling paste necklace she was wearing for her dinner date with Nick. It would be lovely if she had real diamonds like Helen Bamford's, but it was impressive in any case. She'd had to do some very speedy shopping in a boutique just before closing time in order to prepare for tonight.

She stood for a moment, scanning the faces of the people at the bar and the waiters moving between tables, expecting to be noticed. She was gratified to see a few heads turning as she walked down the steps. Nick was waiting for her, perched on one of the high stools, and he smiled as she arrived. Like her, he'd changed for dinner, into dashing black tails, and she wondered, with a skip of delight, whether he might be staying himself at the Midland tonight.

'Do you always make such an entrance?' he asked.

'If I possibly can,' she quipped back. 'What are you drinking?' She nodded down at the small bourbon he was nursing, before insisting on ordering a bottle of champagne.

'What are we celebrating?' he asked as she sat next to him on the purple velvet stool. She noticed him looking at her legs as she crossed them, the slit of her long skirt falling open. She hoped he liked the view. She'd bathed, shaved and moisturized her skin with more care and attention than she ever had for Clement.

The start of us, she wanted to tell him, but she didn't. 'The Cotton Queen, of course.'

'That was certainly an inspired idea. I've never seen Eddy so fired up. Dancing . . . fashion . . . business. You're quite something, Edith.' She bloomed under the compliment. They chatted more about the shoot as the waiter brought over the champagne and poured it, before pressing it down into the watery ice in the silver bucket. Left alone, Edith raised her glass to Nick's and looked directly into his eyes. He didn't look away.

'I had such fun today. Thank you,' she said.

'I hope your husband will be pleased with the results.'

'I doubt it.'

He looked at her, his eyebrows raised in surprise, clearly waiting for her to say more. The comment hung between them, needing an explanation, and her brain scrambled to brush the moment away.

'You and Helen, you're so happy and . . .' She couldn't keep the bitterness out of her voice. 'Well, it's not quite the same for us.'

'I'm sorry to hear that. We haven't known each other

long, but I'd like to think we're friends,' he said. He placed a warm hand over hers. 'I know it's not my place to say anything, but Lettice mentioned that Susan . . .'

Has Susan told Lettice about Clement? Edith thought. *About what he's done to her?*

'. . . I don't mean to be indiscreet, but I get the impression that your husband is a hard man to live with.'

'What did Susan tell Lettice?' she asked, her heart pounding at the shame of it – of Nick knowing the kind of man she lived with. 'You see, she won't talk to me, but I know her relationship with Clement is . . . complicated.'

'She only said that she wasn't very happy at home. And, Edith, I can't for a second imagine that it could be your fault. You're the sweetest, kindest . . .' He trailed off, and she saw the colour in his cheeks. 'How did a woman as brilliant as you . . .' he began, before stopping again.

She knew what he wanted to ask her: why she'd married Clement. But she didn't have an answer for him. The feeling that she'd had at New Year – that she was married to a monster – was only confirmed now by Nick's suspicion of her husband, and his obvious incredulity that Edith was with him.

'Let's make a pact,' she said. 'Let's not talk about Clement. He tends to sour any occasion.'

'I'll drink to that,' Nick said, and his smile made her insides melt.

They chatted easily after that and she found his company even more fascinating than she had at New Year.

'What about you?' she asked, as they ate a steak dinner. 'Do you love what you do?'

'Mostly, but . . .' Nick hesitated, looking bashful. 'I often wish I could be in a business like yours. Running a company. Not having to make compromises.'

'Compromises?'

'Morally . . . yes, I often get compromised in my job. Being a publisher and working on a paper like the *Dispatch* – well, it can be a grubby business.'

'Grubby?'

'Just some of the people I have to deal with. Like this man I'm meeting tomorrow morning. Warren. He'll be in early, before you come in to see Eddy. He has fingers in every pie.'

'He sounds interesting.'

'No. Not interesting. He's nothing more than a low-rent mobster from Liverpool, but he has contacts in the States. He's connected to the kind of people who like to catch out stars in compromising positions. The kind of scandal that Eddy loves to print. And that I have to pay for.'

'That sounds interesting to me,' Edith said, intrigued by his fascinating world and his connections to the people who mattered.

After dinner, Edith persuaded Nick to join her for a spot of dancing. She linked arms with him as they crossed the foyer from the small bar to where a band was playing in the lounge. Nick said they should probably call it a night, but Edith insisted they stay just for one dance, and he relented.

'All right then. Since you're insisting. Shall we?' he asked, holding out his hand for her to join him. She laughed and spun into his arms. 'What would Helen say if she could see me?' he said. Then he faltered, looking embarrassed, and stepped on her toe.

It was a strange thing to say, Edith thought, when of course Helen *couldn't* see him. 'She always used to tease me about my dancing.'

They danced two dances; then Nick ordered drinks and they chatted and laughed together. Edith wanted the night to go on forever, but after a few more dances, he yawned and told her that he'd have to call it a night.

'Which floor are you?' he asked, heading towards the lifts.

'Oh, the second. But walk me up,' she said. 'I don't like those damned contraptions.'

It was a lie, but she couldn't bear to say goodbye to him.

They walked to the second floor and along the soft carpet to Edith's door. She slowed as she took the key from her bag.

'Would you like to come in for a nightcap?' she asked.

He pressed his lips together and put his hands in his pockets. She knew he was torn. That even being outside her hotel room was a step too far.

'Edith . . .' he began.

There was a moment, and she touched his lapel just as she had in his study. This time, like then, the feel of his clothing made her long for the release of her flesh against his – where it should be.

'I can't betray Helen,' he said, finally meeting her eye. And there . . . he'd said it. He'd acknowledged this thing between them.

'She wouldn't need to know,' she whispered.

'She might not be able to see, but she'd know. *I'd* know. I can't do this.'

'People have affairs all the time,' she said. 'Surely you've had one before?'

'No. I never have. And I never would. I'm sorry if I gave you the impression that I'm that kind of man. Goodnight, Edith.'

'Nick, I'm sorry, I—'

'Goodnight, Edith,' he repeated, but he wouldn't look at her as he turned away.

Every fibre of her longed to run after him, to beg him to stay. She hugged the door, knowing how her slim figure would look to him. At the top of the stairs he turned and glanced back at her, then raised his hat in a sad salute.

Damn it, she cursed herself. *You damned fool.*

46

The Magic Behind the Gates

'Hey – hey! Miss Casey!' Vita heard someone call, as she tried to make her way through the throng of hopefuls at the MGM Studios gate. She saw Matt, their realtor, waving, and remembered that he was trying to be an actor. He was wearing a brown suit and was as good-looking as ever. 'You here for the auditions?'

'No, my friend has arranged a tour,' she said, blushing slightly as she thought of Daniel. When he'd dropped her back home after their date in Santa Monica, he'd kissed her for a full five minutes, until she'd giggled, feeling self-conscious in front of Bertie. It had been lovely – not as passionate as how she'd felt when she'd kissed Archie, but that was different, and this thing she had with Daniel was different too. She was a grown-up now, a mother, and that kind of crazy romance that had made her lose her mind was not practical. And it wasn't as if Daniel wasn't romantic. Yesterday, a glorious bouquet of flowers had arrived with a note from him saying that he'd organized a studio tour for her this morning.

Matt pushed a way forward for them both, then put two fingers in his mouth and whistled. On the other side of the gate, a uniformed guard ambled over slowly and Matt nudged Vita.

'Mr Myers is expecting me. It's Miss Casey. Vita Casey?' Vita said, annoyed that she was being jostled from behind.

The guard went off to talk to another man, who came over to the side gate with a key. He was in his fifties with a very tanned face and a bushy moustache.

'Miss Casey, my apologies,' he said, introducing himself as Alec and shaking her hand. 'Mr Myers is in the sound studio. I'll take you there, but we can have a look around on the way.'

'Thank you. I'd like that very much,' Vita said, walking with him past an office, a queue of girls snaking out of the door. Alec picked up on her curious look and how she lingered, looking at the noticeboards where the films in production on the sound stage were listed, along with the directors.

'That's the casting office. Oh, and that guy over there, he's Robert McIntyre,' Alec said, pointing out a serious-looking man with his sleeves rolled up, squinting at the list on the clipboard an assistant was showing him. 'He has the final say for casting. He's pretty important around here.'

'I need another young guy,' she heard Mr McIntyre call out. 'Bring me one more from the gates.'

Vita turned to Alec. 'There's a guy out there waiting, called Matt. I know him and he'd be good for any role,' Vita said.

Alec nodded and walked over to where the casting director stood. Vita could see them talking. Then Mr McIntyre called out to the guard and, in a moment, Matt was let through. She saw him grinning and he raised his hat to Vita. She was pleased to have been able to help.

Vita smiled now at Alec as he came back.

'That's so kind of you,' she said.

'Not at all. That's this business for you. It's who you know,' he said, tapping the side of his nose. 'Always remember that. Oh, and that what goes around comes around.'

He walked her across the busy road to a small flatbed truck with open sides. Vita climbed onto the slatted bench next to him. They started zipping along the tarmac at surprising speed and she held onto her hat, her eyes drinking in the sights. Alec explained that they had forty-three acres to cover and there were forty-five buildings, including fourteen stages. Somewhere in one of those buildings, Nancy would be on set, she thought. And Daniel would be, too.

'So this is Lot One,' Alec explained. 'It's mainly offices and sound stages.'

'What's that?' Vita asked, pointing across to a two-tiered building.

'Those are the dressing rooms. All the women dress on the upper deck. There's a matron who oversees them all. She keeps everyone in order.'

They came to a stop as they turned down a narrower street, waiting for a gaggle of girls to cross.

'Oh, my goodness. Look at them. Look at their costumes,' Vita said, seeing the girls in sequinned bodices.

'They'll be off to the dancing school over there,' Alec said. Vita could hear the sound of a piano coming through the open windows, and what sounded like a room full of dancers. Someone shouted, 'Five, six, seven, eight!'

'I had no idea there'd be so many people employed here.'

'It all starts over there,' Alec explained, pointing to some low buildings. 'That's where the writers are, near the canteen. The stories that come in get read over, then the production assistants organize the scenario writers. Eventually, there's a presentation and the next films are decided.'

'It sounds like quite a conveyor belt,' Vita said.

'Sure is. It's a big operation making a motion picture,' Alec said, as they drove further on.

Then, suddenly, a whole waterfront town came into view, along with a galleon. It looked exactly as she would imagine a dock in London might have looked a few hundred years ago. Alec stopped the truck so that Vita could get out and take a photograph.

'Is that a real lake?' she asked.

'It's concrete-lined and it's not deep. They call this Waterfront Street. They adapt it and repaint the buildings for each movie.'

They drove on. She turned and could see the struts holding up the facades of the buildings. It was all just a front, but it looked so *real*.

'You'll like it down here,' Alec said, turning into another set.

This time it was a Wild West set, complete with a saloon bar and brothel, a wooden building with a sheriff's office sign and hitching posts for the horses, as well as a blacksmith's shop with an anvil. Vita asked to take a closer look and pressed the half-door of the saloon, but it didn't creak like they always did in the movies.

They walked further on, Alec telling her anecdotes about the Westerns that had been made here, until the Wild West street stopped and, ahead, Vita could hear the sound of saws and hammers. As they turned the corner, at least two dozen men in overalls were building another set.

'What's going on there?'

'They're building New York,' Alec said. Vita watched for a moment, recognizing a typical New York street scene, the cramped apartment buildings with their fold-down metal ladders. To see something that was so familiar being built right before her eyes was astonishing.

'Morning, Mr Tate,' Alec said, tipping his cap to a man. 'He's one of the guys in charge of the set design,' he told Vita. 'Those guys are something else. They can make anything from a toothpick to an ocean liner.'

By the time they'd driven around Lot Two and made it to Daniel's sound stage, Vita's head was whirring with the scale of it all. 'I always wanted to know what was behind the gates,' she told him.

'Magic,' Alec said proudly. 'That's what's here. We make people imagine they can have a better life: a better love life, a bigger home, a more exciting job, go all around the world on an adventure. Oh, I dare say the do-gooders, those God-fearers, would say it's unrealistic and childish – immoral, even. But let me tell you, while there's a need for those stories, it ain't gonna stop. Not any time soon.'

47

And If You Could Make My Dreams Come True

Vita's head was spinning with everything Alec had shown her by the time they stopped next to an enormous building with black numbers painted on one side. Alec parked the truck in the shade.

'This is where Mr Myers is today. You'll have to be very quiet,' he said, putting a finger to his lips as he reached for the handle of the small door.

Vita stepped silently into a cavernous studio, the sudden contrast from the bright outdoor sun blinding her for a moment. She took off her sunglasses and looked up at the ceiling stretching into shadows high above.

The studio was vast. Far across the concrete floor, a truck with giant tyres had a platform extended up towards the lighting grid. A camera was perched on the platform, the operator behind it with a flat cap, next to a man in dapper slacks with a cone-shaped loudhailer in his hand. They were watching the scene before them intently, the cameraman slowly turning the handle on the camera round and around.

Opposite them, one half of the building had been transformed into a nightclub, the incredible set ablaze with pillars of light and a fan of lit glass framing it above. Below the balconies at the back was a complete orchestra plus a shiny grand piano, and now it struck up, filling the studio with music. Vita watched, entranced, as tap-dancing girls in sequinned bras twirled across the polished black floor.

Other dancers came now, glamorous couples whirling and twirling through the tap dancers. The on-set 'audience' watched attentively and Vita's eyes were drawn to the elaborate dresses and the smart evening wear the men wore. She crept closer and closer, holding her breath in wonder as the musical number came to an end.

'And . . . cut. Hold for a still, people,' the man shouted through the loudhailer. Vita watched as a photographer with a flashbulb camera took photographs of the whole set frozen, then Vita heard the sound of the clapperboard again, and the people in the set collectively breathed out and relaxed. She had to resist the urge to burst into applause. She watched a couple of the dancers bend forward, out of breath.

Now that she was closer to the set, Vita couldn't help marvelling at the detail. Then she saw Daniel and he came over, grinning, and kissed her on the cheek.

'So this is what all the fuss is about,' Vita said. 'I can see why Nancy is smitten.'

'Have you enjoyed the tour so far?'

'I'll say.'

'There's lots more to come. I've asked Mrs Chafin to show you around the costume department. Then I'll take you for lunch. It'll only be the canteen, but I'll have a little break at two.'

'Sounds perfect.' She grinned at him.

At his invitation, she stayed next to him, watching as the director called for the next take. There was something about seeing Daniel at work that made him even more attractive. She remembered how Ericka had described him as a hot catch in Hollywood. And as Vita admired him in the dark, he reached out and squeezed her hand.

'Take two, scene five. If you could make my dreams come true. Into positions, please. We're taking it from the top,' a man shouted. 'Positions *please*, people.'

'It's so exciting,' she said, stepping even closer to Daniel.

She didn't just mean the movie, she realized. She meant being here with him, watching the actors, dancers and musicians find their places on the set. Might this be her one shot at happiness? What if he really was prepared to take them both on? Her *and* Bertie? She glanced up at him, seeing his face in profile, and felt her heart do an involuntary flip. Sensing her eyes on him, he turned his head and smiled at her. She smiled back.

'And *action*,' the director called.

48

The 21

At Penn Station, in a small public telephone booth, Clement held the Bakelite receiver close to his ear as the line crackled. He shifted uncomfortably, having been standing in the cramped wooden booth for far too long. His back and hip ached, and he longed to sit in a comfortable chair – preferably with a drink, although that seemed to be impossible in this city.

The switchboard operator had made him hold for the long-distance operator, who'd kept him waiting to connect him through to a different office who could dial London. He'd heard a British voice and then another connection to the exchange in Lancashire and finally, now, he could hear the telephone ringing in Darton Hall. He thought of Martha trudging along the dark corridor, and silently cursed her for taking so long.

'Where is Edith?' Clement demanded when she answered.

'She's not here, sir,' Martha said.

'And Mother?'

'Doing the church flowers. Shall I take a message? Are you coming home?'

She sounded guarded, but then, he and Martha had never

seen eye to eye. She was frightened of him, he suspected, remembering now the times over the years that he'd lost his temper or had blamed Martha for little things that had been his fault – smashing his mother's favourite vase, treading mud through the house, stealing money. Martha had watched him with her disapproving stare, and he'd despised her for not having the backbone to stand up to him.

He wanted to know where Edith was. Maybe he should have called the mill instead of the Hall. He instinctively reached for his pocket watch to check the time and calculate the time difference, but then remembered where it was. *Damn it.*

'Tell Edith that the plan has changed and I'm going to California,' Clement said. 'She'll understand.'

'California?' Martha reacted as if he'd announced that he was going to Mars.

He replaced the receiver before she had a chance to question him, tucked the train ticket into the inside pocket of his jacket and pushed open the half glass door. If Edith had been home, he would have told her about Renata King and how he might have found a way to save Darton even without Anna's shares. But now she'd forfeited her right to know the truth.

'Excuse me.' He heard a voice and turned to see a man waving. 'You left your hat.'

'Oh, thank you,' Clement said, grateful that his oversight had been noticed. He didn't trust anyone around here not to steal the coat from his back.

'It's a fine trilby,' the man continued, brushing the rim of it with his gloved hand. From the dapper way he was dressed, he was clearly a fellow who appreciated the finer things in life. He looked inside the hat and saw the silk label. 'Hawkes of London. I have several of these myself.'

He was a slim man, younger than Clement, with snake-like hips and a Clark Gable moustache, but there was something appealing about his style. The lining of his coat, which now flashed as he put his hand in the pocket of his wide pinstriped suit, was a vivid pink.

'I say. Are you in a rush?' the man asked, although it was none of his business.

'I have a train to catch, but it doesn't leave until later tonight,' Clement said weakly, taking the hat. Renata King's incentive was playing heavily on his mind. He had better get going to find Vita in California before he lost his nerve.

'Ah, you're a Brit,' the man said, smiling as he noted Clement's accent. 'I can always spot a gentleman.'

Clement nodded, raised his hat in tacit thanks and turned to leave.

'Say . . . if you don't mind me saying . . . I hope I'm not speaking out of turn, but you look like a man who could do with a drink. Am I right, or am I right?' The man had caught up, and was falling into step beside him. 'You ever been to the 21?' he asked in a whispered aside.

Clement stopped now, seeing that he wasn't going to shake off this stranger.

'What's the twenty-one?'

The fellow stood back and opened his arms out wide, as if this were an outrage.

'You can't skip town without going to the best bar there is. Say, I like you. Why don't you come with me? I was on my way there anyway. Then I'll bring you back in time for your train.'

Clement was about to refuse, when the man smiled at him and his resolve weakened. It had been a long while since he'd seen a friendly face; and he really could do with a drink. Even so, could he trust this stranger? The man, who was clean-shaven with smooth skin and white teeth, shrugged.

'Oh, shoot. Look at me, being so forward,' he said, as if embarrassed, waving his hand for Clement to forget the whole offer. 'My ma always says I'm too forward with folk. I'm sorry, sir.' He smiled again, nodded at Clement and turned to leave. 'I'll let you get on.'

'No, wait,' Clement said, surprising himself with his impulsiveness. 'You're right. I could do with a drink.'

'You sure?'

Clement nodded.

'Well, that's just swell. Let's find us a cab.'

In the back of the taxi, the man, who'd introduced himself as Tebby, sat close to Clement and regaled him about the famous speakeasy.

'Turns out, they'd just opened when the developers came in to say they were building the Rockefeller Center right on the site.'

Clement could believe it. There was development going on everywhere he'd looked in the city, and despite so many fortunes having been lost in the crash, others were clearly still being made. Some of that work was being financed by Renata King. Again he thought of the tenacious old woman and the offer she'd given him.

'So this New Year, they invited all their best customers to

arrive in ball dresses and tuxedos and when they arrived, they gave them all a pickaxe and they all got drunk and razed the place. Then they tore off the iron gate and marched it over three blocks north to 21 West 52nd Street. And the "21" was born.'

Clement was amused by how chatty Tebby was being. This was an enjoyable glimpse into a New York society he'd had no idea existed. It felt thrilling.

'Why don't they get caught by the authorities?' he asked.

'They don't keep liquor on the premises.' Tebby leant in close to stop the cabbie overhearing. He smelt of smoke and pomade. 'The word is that they put the wine in the basement next door. I heard they hold the private wine collection of the President. But those boys – they get the best wines from all over the world. Canada, South America.'

'Really? But how do they get it in?'

'Up the Hudson on boats, or in from Canada in the hoods of cars. Or they sail in boats via Long Island, bringing hooch from Bermuda and the Bahamas.'

'Surely they must get raided?' Clement asked, at once excited and nervous to be going to an actual speakeasy.

'You're either in bed with the mob or the police. The cousins have the police chief in their pockets. You'll see a fair few well-oiled officers in the bar and the restaurant. Oh . . . I didn't even tell you about the restaurant. You like oysters and martinis?'

'I've never tried—'

'What kind of backward swamp did you sail in from anyway?' Tebby teased. 'I thought you Brits were supposed to be sophisticated!'

They arrived at the club, with its famous iron gate, and

were waved through by the doorman. Tebby shook hands with him as if they were long-lost friends.

In the rather lovely, darkly panelled bar they drank bourbon and, much more at ease now with the warming flush of the alcohol inside him, Clement found that the conversation flowed easily.

If only he could talk to the chaps at the club like he could talk to Tebby, he thought. He liked the way Tebby found his Englishness funny and charming. He'd spent all of his life trying and failing to fit in, but somehow here, it was being different that seemed to be winning him points. And it was comforting that Tebby seemed respectful, too, of his superior status as a Brit. Maybe he'd been wrong to be so suspicious of New Yorkers. Because for the first time in a very, very long time, Clement was enjoying himself.

'Hey, I like you, Clem. You're a swell guy. Come on, let's grab some food.'

They got a table straight away in the crowded restaurant and Clement looked around at the sophisticated clientele. He'd been expecting speakeasies, from the way the papers talked about them, to be dens of vice and iniquity, but the crowd here seemed well heeled and well educated. It was a world away from the poverty he'd seen on the streets and Clement felt himself relaxing.

Tebby ordered more cocktails and oysters, and they chatted more about Clement's plans to go to California.

'I got connections, you know. In the movies,' Tebby said, slurping an oyster.

'Have you? Because I'm looking for my sister. She's with her friend, and . . .'

He stopped, worried that he sounded too eager. He didn't want to let his guard down. Could he really trust Tebby? Although they were getting on well and Clement was enjoying his company, he mustn't become careless.

But Tebby was clearly a well-respected figure at the club. The other diners who stopped by their table to greet him seemed to find him charming and funny. Clement liked the feeling of dining with someone influential.

'You know, I was planning on taking a trip out west sometime soon,' Tebby said, a while later. 'Say, why don't I come with you and show you around?'

Clement smiled, feeling excited and nervous at the same time at the thought of a travelling companion. But then, Tebby, in one short evening, had made him feel more welcome than he ever had at his own club. Perhaps it would be good to have someone on his side who knew the lie of the land.

'You don't need to say yes or no. It's me being impulsive again. But you never know. It might be an idea. Hey, barman. Another round,' Tebby said, gesturing to his empty platter of oysters. 'Put it on my tab.'

49

Ladies Who Lunch

Tucked away between the Royal Opera House and Covent Garden on Henrietta Street, Boulestin had been Georgie's restaurant of choice when Edith invited her for lunch. Edith baulked now at the prices of its fancy French fare but she calmly folded the leather menu and handed it to the waiter, Georgie having insisted that they order the signature *foie de veau*.

Edith hadn't seen Georgie since that last night they'd all been together at the Zip Club. There was no doubt that in the intervening years, having married dull but wealthy Douglas Trewin-Coutts, Georgie had done well for herself. She was wearing a tailored suit and a rather lovely cream hat, and her nails were perfectly manicured. It seemed that all of Edith's old contemporaries were living quite spectacular lives. Not for the first time on this trip, Edith thought that if she hadn't married Clement but had found herself someone decent in London, she too might be a lady who lunched all the time in places like this.

'You know,' Georgie said, 'my friend Cecil Beaton says that this is the prettiest restaurant in London.'

Edith had forgotten what a frightful name-dropper

Georgie was, and just how much she regarded herself. But now, as she looked around the restaurant with its circus-themed murals and sumptuous drapes, she could see that the famous photographer might have a point.

Her idea of approaching Georgie had first come about when their mutual friend Annabel Morton claimed that Georgie had 'stolen' her idea of a world tour. Annabel was most put out that Georgie had purchased a first-class passage on the ship Annabel was hoping to sail in, leaving for South America via California. Annabel had told Edith that Georgie would be spending a fortnight in Los Angeles and she'd added that – according to Mrs Clifford-Meade, the dress-maker, who kept in regular touch with Nancy's mother – Nancy and Vita were now together in California, where Nancy was trying her hand at the movie business. This vital piece of information was all Edith had needed for a cunning plan to start taking shape. She just had to make sure that she could execute it before Clement got to California and found Vita himself.

'So,' Georgie said, buttering a roll. 'Tell me everything. It's been so long since all those parties. And look at us now. Both married. You haven't got a little one on the way yet, have you?' Her loud laugh turned the heads of other diners, but Georgie was oblivious. 'Obviously not . . . I mean, look at your wonderful figure. You always were the most stylish of the bunch, Edith.'

'Thank you. That's very kind of you.'

'Whatever happened to that ghastly girl, Vita? You know – Nancy's friend?'

'Vita?' Edith pretended to be surprised that Georgie

remembered. 'Oh, well, there's a story. You see, she ran off to Paris with Nancy.'

'I thought *you* were going with Nancy.'

'Things didn't work out. But it's no bother, I've quite landed on my feet. My lingerie business is taking off,' Edith said.

'So I hear,' Georgie said, leaning forward. 'I bought two ensembles from the Soirée collection at Withshaw and Taylor. They're so terribly daring and chic.'

Gratified, Edith told her about the shoot and her idea for the Cotton Queen Quest, and about the orders in Paris. When Georgie was so much a part of the London swim, it felt good to fly the flag for her business.

'Oh, that sounds so marvellous. Edith, you are a genius. Fancy achieving all of that. You put the rest of us to shame,' she said. Edith's smile was genuine, because this was exactly the reaction she'd been hoping for. She might not have Georgie's money or her fine lifestyle, but she had something far more precious: her respect. 'But I'm confused,' Georgie continued. 'Wasn't it Vita who did something with those bras?'

'Vita? No – goodness, no. It was my idea right from the start,' Edith said, keen to set the record straight.

The corners of Georgie's mouth went down and she shrugged, accepting this as the truth.

'Anyway, I want to hear about you. Weren't you living in Nancy's flat?' Edith asked, keen to move the conversation on.

'I was for a while, but then her mother took it back and we've rather lost touch.' Edith detected a trace of the same bitterness she felt herself. Perhaps Georgie had wanted to be Nancy's friend too, and had also been dropped like a stone.

'Nancy is in California, so I hear,' Edith said.

'California? Well, I'm going there,' Georgie beamed.

'Really?' Edith asked, feigning surprise. 'Oh, I'm so envious. It seems that California really is the place to be. One day I'd like to travel there myself. You must look her up. She's with Vita.'

'What are they doing in California?' Georgie asked.

'Trying to make it in the movies. Easier for Nancy, of course, than Vita. She was always the one with more style. And I expect Vita has lost her figure after, you know . . .'

'What?' Georgie paused. Edith made a show of looking embarrassed. *She doesn't know*, she thought with satisfaction. She'd hoped that would be the case, but it had seemed just possible that Georgie too would have heard the gossip from Belinda Getty, as Edith had. Belinda Getty had been on Cassius Digby's yacht when Vita and Irving had come on board, so she'd known exactly what had happened. Belinda had reported that Archie Fenwick had secretly been on board too, and Belinda had seen him and Vita kissing on deck with her own eyes.

'Didn't you know?'

'Know what?'

'I shouldn't say,' Edith said. 'Sorry, Georgie. I really thought you'd have heard. Everyone was talking about it.'

'About what?'

Georgie's eyes were hungry for gossip. Edith glowed with pleasure at having reeled her in so thoroughly. She paused dramatically, then said, 'Vita had a baby last year.'

'A baby?' Georgie was confused. 'Then why is she with Nancy in California? Where's her husband?'

'That's the point. There *is* no husband. He . . . well, he *let her go*.'

'Let her go? That's rather a scandal.' Georgie's fork clattered to her plate.

'Well, yes, it is rather. You see, she was married briefly in Paris, but . . . then she had something of an affair on her honeymoon.'

'No!' Georgie's eyes glittered.

'That's what I heard. And everyone suspects that the husband isn't the baby's father.'

'Then who is?'

The waiter arrived to top up their wine glasses.

'Well,' Edith sighed. 'I heard it from Annabel Morton, who heard it from Belinda Getty, who'd been on Cassius Digby's yacht . . .'

'I know her . . . not well, but . . . go on . . .'

'The baby . . . the baby is . . . I can't. I shouldn't.'

'Tell me, Edith,' Georgie implored, holding Edith's arm.

Edith leant forward and said in a low, conspiratorial voice, 'The baby is Archie Fenwick's.'

Georgie's smile faded.

'Archie's?'

'You know they always had a thing for each other? They met in France. When he was there writing and Vita was on her honeymoon. They met on Digby's yacht and, well . . .'

'Archie?' Georgie gasped. 'Are you sure?'

'Quite sure,' Edith said, taking a mouthful of steak. Across from her, Georgie sat back in a stunned silence. 'Isn't he your brother-in-law?' Edith added after a moment, clamping her hand over her mouth as if she'd just realized this faux pas.

Georgie nodded, her eyebrows drawing together. 'But my sister, Maud . . . she'd be devastated. Oh, Edith, you have no idea. It would destroy her. She's been trying so hard, you see. So very hard to have a baby of their own. And, and . . . oh my goodness.'

'What?' Edith asked innocently, seeing that something else had occurred to Georgie.

'Archie is in California. He had a writing opportunity last month through his agent. And Maud is coming with us when we sail so that she can join him.'

'But . . . what are you saying? That Archie and Vita are in California *together*?'

This was news indeed – and a better twist than Edith had been expecting. 'You don't think he's been seeing Vita all this time?' Edith asked, pretending to be horrified. 'Is he carrying on the affair right under your sister's nose?'

'I have no idea – but I intend to find out. I intend to find out, and do something about it.' Georgie looked resolute.

'You absolutely must. I don't think it's very fair that Vita should get away with doing something so wicked.'

'Oh, believe me, she won't.'

They talked some more, but Georgie was fuming over the bomb that Edith had dropped. She was glad she'd saved this information and used it wisely, when it had the greatest effect. She was glad, too, that she'd kept it from Clement. He was a loose cannon when it came to such things. He had no idea how to finesse gossip like she did, to use it to her own advantage.

'I did do the right thing, didn't I?' Edith feigned concern. 'Telling you?'

'Of course. Yes, of course you did, Edith.'

They talked some more, then Edith leant forward again. 'The thing is . . . now we're being so open . . . can I tell you something else?'

Georgie nodded, keen to hear.

'You see, just between us, there's rather a sensitive issue involving Vita. One I need to resolve. It's caused quite a conflict between me and Clement.'

'What is it?'

'It's rather sensitive, but . . . Vita has something that I want. That I need very much.'

'What kind of thing?'

'She has some shares that rather interfere with what I'm doing in the business. And I need complete control.'

'Well, of course you do,' Georgie agreed.

'Oh, Georgie, it's so very good to talk to someone who understands.'

'Go on.'

Edith explained about Hillsafe and how the shares needed to be transferred, but that would only be possible if Vita signed some papers.

'And *I* can't ask her,' Edith. 'Quite apart from the fact I'm here and she's there, we don't exactly see eye to eye. I can't risk sending the papers to her by courier.'

She glanced up at Georgie, who was listening intently. 'I need someone I can really trust. Someone with tact.'

'Well, I can do that for you,' Georgie offered, her eyes glittering. Edith knew she was the least tactful person on the planet, but she gasped as if it was the best idea she'd ever had.

'You . . . well, you would be *perfect*.'

Georgie grinned.

'All I need is a squiggled signature from Vita. The less time she has to read the papers, the better. And I doubt she'll be interested, in any case.'

'Leave it to me,' Georgie said, reaching across to touch Edith's wrist. 'We're friends, and it's good to be able to help.'

'Oh, Georgie. You are a lifesaver,' Edith said. 'Let's get some champagne. My treat.'

50
Fixing the Problem

A week had passed since Vita had first set foot inside the studios. She'd come in early this morning with Nancy, who was shooting on *The Sister Returns*. Vita was a bundle of nerves, but excited about the trial day Mrs Chafin had arranged for her. She was determined to prove herself, although she knew it was going to be difficult. Mrs Chafin hadn't beaten around the bush when they'd last met.

'The girls here have worked very hard to earn their positions. Each of them is very skilled in her own way,' she'd told Vita. 'All of them have qualifications, but the only thing that counts in the studios is experience. You can start at the bottom and in three or four years you might . . . *might* . . . be in with a chance of becoming a designer. In the meantime, you'll have to earn your stripes, like everyone else.'

Now Vita walked into the quadrangle where the design studios were housed in low buildings on all sides of a central garden planted with cherry trees. Their fallen petals lined the path to the door like confetti.

'Here goes,' she said, putting her best foot forward. She was determined to make a good impression.

She pushed through the doors into the busy studios and

Mrs Chafin waved her over. She was in her late thirties, her hair in a sensible centre parting, a double string of pearls around her neck. Her shoes looked practical and comfortable, which they had to be, Vita supposed. From the sound of it, Mrs Chafin was on her feet all day.

Once again, Vita drank in the details of Mrs Chafin's studios – the tailor's dummies, machines and mirrors. She gazed at the exotic prints and textures of the bolts of fabric on the bench, remembering how much she'd loved being at Dreyfus, the fabric shop in Paris.

Mrs Chafin took her through to another room where two women were seated at a high bench, working on a lace train. Another set of women were embroidering what looked like an Elizabethan doublet.

'Look at that,' Vita said, fingering the edge of the material on the cardboard bale. She'd never seen mirrored fabric like it.

'It's a sample just in from Italy,' Mrs Chafin explained, 'although I'm not sure we'll be using it for the current slate. But we have to keep on our toes. I'm sure it'll get used in no time.'

In the next room were more women working intently at their machines; they hardly noticed Vita as she came in. Behind them, along one wall, was an open-sided wardrobe filled with padded silk hangers on which hung some beautiful silk and lace dresses. Vita walked over to a tailor's dummy clad in pristine white silk.

'That's Greta Garbo's dress form. It's been padded to her dimensions,' Mrs Chafin said.

'Could I see her dresses?' Vita asked, before explaining

that she'd previously worked at Madame Sacerdote's in Paris. Mrs Chafin looked impressed.

'I know Jenny's designs well,' she said.

'So how does it work around here?' Vita asked, as she went over to inspect the dresses. 'Who is the head designer?'

'We had Gilbert Clark,' Mrs Chafin explained, 'but between you and me, everyone said he was more impossible to work with than the divas he was trying to dress.' Vita laughed, thinking of all the larger-than-life characters she'd encountered in the fashion world in Paris. 'Adrian is Cecil's favourite now,' Mrs Chafin added. She meant Cecil B. DeMille, the hotshot director making all the movies.

'Mr Adrian designs everything for Garbo. In fact, he's probably the most influential man in fashion. Everyone looks to us for the current trends, so we have to be absolutely *à la mode*. Everything the stars wear has to be glamorous and modern. Women the whole world over will try to emulate what they see on screen. So you see, it's quite a responsibility.'

'I can imagine,' Vita said, feeling fizzy with excitement. She'd wanted to have her finger on the pulse of fashion – well, here it was.

Mrs Chafin put her to work in a section of the studio, sorting and filing fabric samples, a job Vita was more than thrilled to do. She was so absorbed she hardly noticed the time passing and she jumped when Mrs Chafin came over to assess her work. She gave an impressed nod. 'Very good, Vita. I have to go over to see Mr Adrian. Would you like to come?'

Vita followed Mrs Chafin along a carpeted corridor to some smarter offices, where she knocked on one of the doors before opening it.

Mr Adrian was a man in his fifties and he was sitting on a floral sofa, surrounded by sketches. Behind him, frilled curtains were draped over the blind. There was a modern rug on the parquet floor, full of geometric shapes, and against every surrounding surface picture boards were stacked up. He looked up, his pencil poised over the sketch-book on his lap.

'Who is this young beauty?' he said, pushing his glasses down his nose and looking at Vita.

'Mr Adrian, this is Vita Casey,' Mrs Chafin said. 'She's a friend of Mr Myers. She worked for Madame Jenny Sacerdote.' Vita was pleased that she had some credentials with which to impress the great designer.

'Is that so?'

Mr Adrian continued to sketch as he talked to Mrs Chafin for a while, and she went over to his large desk to look for the production file she'd come to fetch. Vita looked around the rooms and instinctively stepped towards the boards. They each showed a view of a woman in a dress, hand-painted in watercolours.

She picked up one of the boards, admiring the line of the dress, the short sleeves and the romantic headdress, but Mrs Chafin gave her a sharp look and Vita put it down.

'You can wait back in my office,' Mrs Chafin said to her. 'I have to take this over to the production office and check a few details, but I'll be back soon and then we can work out where we're going to start you.'

Vita nodded, conscious of having been put in her place. She was just a junior – lower than a junior, she remembered. She mustn't put Mrs Chafin's nose out of joint, but seeing

Mr Adrian and having a glimpse of his genius was so exciting. *This* was the place where she could make a difference. She knew it right in her bones.

Vita went back to Mrs Chafin's office, seeing the girls leaving to go out together – presumably for lunch. She wished they would invite her, but she had to get to know them first.

She stood in the office, admiring the photo stills from all the movies. Then she heard a commotion as a young man came in. He looked like he'd been running a long way.

'Where's Mrs Chafin?' he asked, breathless and flustered.

'She'll be back soon. Can I help?'

'I doubt it.'

'What's the problem?' Vita asked.

'The director hates these costumes. He's been screaming and shouting. He told me to bring her here.' He gestured out of the door and a girl stepped forward. She was a brunette with a slim dancer's figure, her pretty face pulled into a sad pout. The young man roughly pulled her forward.

'Hey!' she said.

'He says this all needs fixing by yesterday. Or else we're all fired.'

'Mrs Chafin is at the production office,' Vita said, looking at the girl and seeing why the brown costume with its unflattering lines hadn't met with the director's approval. It wasn't nearly dazzling enough for a showgirl. For a start, it wasn't nearly revealing enough.

'I'm going to get her,' the young man said, clearly not trusting Vita. 'Stay here. And don't move,' he told the girl. 'Oh goodness, can this day get any worse?'

Vita could see that the girl – who now introduced herself as Alma – was upset.

'The director was shouting and shouting. He said we looked nothing like showgirls.'

'Why don't I see if I can help?' Vita offered.

'How?' the girl asked.

Vita went through to the workbenches, her mind whirring. She found a tape measure and set to work, cutting out pieces from the glittering material until she'd formed a crude bra. She instructed the girl to put it on, telling her that this was no time for modesty, as she tucked her small breasts inside. She pinned it securely at the back, then set to work on the bottom of the costume, ripping away the baggy material. Alma squeaked as Vita revealed her stomach.

'Where are those pearls?' she said to herself, going over to the basket she'd seen, looping a string of pearls on each side of Alma's thigh and attaching a belt of shimmering jewels around her stomach.

She stood back, assessing the look so far, her finger on her lips. 'Feathers. You need feathers,' she said, remembering the girls at Les Folies Bergère. She went into the cupboard, selected four white ostrich feathers and wound wire around them to attach them to a hair grip, which she stuck into Alma's hair.

Vita was so absorbed that she was surprised when the young man came back with Mrs Chafin. He stopped when he saw Alma in her new costume.

'Where did you get that?' he asked Alma.

'She made it,' Alma said, pointing at Vita.

'You wanted showgirls. And when I was at Les Folies in

Paris, the girls used to wear costumes just like this,' Vita explained, blushing now as she saw Mrs Chafin assessing her efforts. A smile was playing on the woman's lips, and she nodded at Vita as if impressed.

'Why don't you see what the production designer says now?' Mrs Chafin said to the young man.

'Well, yes – yes, I will,' he said, grabbing Alma by the wrist. She mouthed a hurried *thank you* to Vita as she was rushed away.

Vita and Mrs Chafin went to the window, watching the young man pulling the showgirl across the quadrangle. Vita was just about to turn back when she saw someone stop and talk to the couple, and they pointed up to the offices.

Vita held her breath and looked closer, wiping the glass. A familiar figure was coming up the path.

It couldn't really be *him* . . . could it?

51

Seasick

A ship's horn penetrated through the fog of Clement's hangover and he put a hand to his face, feeling the pain now in a sudden wave that made him sit up and groan. His lips were sealed shut with dried blood and he tore them apart with an anguished yelp, trying – and failing – to move his jaw back and forth. He tried to open his eyes, but one eye socket was so bruised that he couldn't. He touched his beaten-up face, wincing at his sore knuckles. The bed rocked, and for a second he thought he might be sick.

He swung his legs round, noticing he was still in his clothes from last night – minus his hat and overcoat. Where the hell was he?

He staggered to the door, the floor of the room swaying disconcertingly. Was he drugged? He could hardly keep his balance.

The door opened onto a small galley, and he slid back the wooden hatchway above his head to reveal a cold grey sky accompanied by a blast of freezing wind.

Shivering, he climbed the steep steps with difficulty and found himself emerging onto the deck of a boat. He clung to the edge of the wooden hatchway to stop himself falling over as the boat dipped to one side in the roiling grey waves.

A rough-looking man in a dirty brown oilskin coat and hat came over now from the wheelhouse. Clement staggered to his feet, not quite believing the scene around him: the ugly swollen sea, the petrol smell of the engine and the craw of the seagulls as they followed in the wake of the boat. He gasped as a wave of spray hit him in the face.

He must be dreaming. He must be . . .

The man was standing now before him, water dripping from his black beard. Clement's swollen bottom lip chattered agonizingly.

'What's happening?' he asked the man.

'What's happening, sir, is what happens when chancers like you don't pay their debts.'

Clement blinked more sea spray from his eyes, panic making him even more queasy as the events of last night reared up before him. How he'd excused himself, drunk, from the table, trying to leave the speakeasy when he'd lost, but the waitress had tried to stop him and he'd . . .

He retched now, spewing up a foul load of bourbon by the man's boots. His guts still twisting, he looked up again into the impassive face of the sailor.

'You can't . . . I mean . . . I . . . this is outrageous . . .'

The man didn't move, he just laughed, then shifted his hand to his waist so that Clement could see the shaft of a knife in his belt.

'We figured a run to the Bahamas might sober you up.'

'We? Who is *we*?'

'My associates.'

'You mean Tebby?' Clement realized, remembering the man he'd met at Penn Station. The man he'd thought was his friend. The man who'd taken him to the 21, got him riotously drunk and then persuaded him to play in a high-stakes poker game at another speakeasy across town. It had a French name, he remembered.

'You go to a speakeasy with a well-known gigolo like Tebby and expect to be treated like a gentleman, when you insult the staff . . .'

Details swam towards Clement from the poker game last night. Of losing . . . of seeing red . . . of throwing over the table, because the game had been rigged. He'd known it straight away. And Tebby laughing at him.

'This can't be happening,' he mumbled, suddenly close to tears. 'I'm supposed to be going to Los Angeles.'

'To Jimmy's Backyard, no doubt?'

Clement shook his head, not understanding. 'Please . . . please just let me go. Take me back to shore. I'll pay what I owe.'

'Nope. Captain's orders. You're to stay below deck. Out of sight.'

'Don't you know who I am?'

'I don't care if you're the king of England.'

The man took Clement's arm and he winced, the vice-like grip digging into his bruises. He felt himself being pushed back down the steps into the wooden galley, then the man with the knife gestured to a black boy, who nodded. A second later, he closed the hatch.

'I shall be informing the authorities. This is outrageous—' Clement croaked.

The young boy couldn't make any sense of his mumbling fury.

'Take no notice of Rodriguez, Mr Darton,' he said. 'He's a tough guy. Works for Le Monsieur, cleaning up his business. You were just in the wrong place at the wrong time. Would you like some salve for your lip?'

Clement nodded, swallowing down tears of rage and pity for himself. The boy might be a negro, but a few kind words went a very long way. In a moment or two, the boy was back. Clement allowed him to anoint his lip, the mocking tone of Rodriguez ringing in his ears. When he'd recovered his breathing, he thanked the boy.

'What's your name, boy?'

'Drum, sir.'

'What's Jimmy's Backyard? Do you know?'

The boy's eyes were brown, and Clement noticed the smooth soft-looking line of skin by his collarbone. 'It's a club in Los Angeles where men go. Men like your friend Tebby.'

And, with blood rushing to his cheeks, Clement suddenly understood what Rodriguez thought of him. He thought he was a homosexual. He blinked up at the young man in shock, but he just smiled softly.

'You can't help what you are, sir. Same as I can't.'

52

The Brown Derby

The Brown Derby on North Vine Street was just around the corner from the studios. An attractive building with its four arched doorways, little turret, tiled roof and Juliet balconies, it was a favourite with movie actors and studio executives.

As Vita and Nancy queued at the maître'd's station Vita could see that the booths around the back of the restaurant were already full, even though it was still early for supper. There was a premier tonight at Grauman's, by the looks of things. A smart-looking foursome passed by on their way out, the men in white tails, the women in shimmering evening gowns. Waitresses and waiters – no doubt all would-be actors – were carrying trays of cocktails aloft and plates of food from the kitchen. Vita could see the busy chefs in clouds of steam behind the pass.

Since Ericka had taken her on, Nancy's physical appearance had changed dramatically. Her dark hair was now platinum blonde, which, surprisingly, suited her rather well. She'd had several long treatments in the beauty salon and her skin was gleaming.

It was Vita's turn to step up to the podium. She smiled at the short man, who looked up at her with suspicion, but

Nancy stared him down. Vita told him who they were meeting.

'He's already here. Follow, please,' the man said, clicking his fingers. A young waiter appeared and was given instructions.

Vita felt her heart pounding and a smile spreading over her face. She couldn't help it. She'd been smiling ever since she'd seen her old friend Percy Blake at the studios. Just as it had been when she'd seen him in the Riviera on her honeymoon, Vita felt as if their paths were fated to cross. And having another true friend here, as well as Nancy, had filled her with a new confidence.

'It really is him,' Nancy gasped, as if she hadn't believed Vita's story. She squealed with delight as they arrived at the booth and Percy swept her clean off her feet in a bear hug. Then he held her by the shoulders and looked her up and down.

'Well, well. Nancy Delaney! Look at you.' He smiled and Nancy did a little curtsey, pleased to see that Percy approved. 'And dear Vita.' He hugged her too and she kissed his cheek and they sat down.

Percy Blake, their friend from London, had grown into his looks. His boyish round glasses had been replaced with rather more stylish wooden-framed ones. He was wearing a fashionable cream suit with a dashing cravat and caramel shoes. These surroundings were certainly a far cry from his messy studio in Covent Garden. Vita remembered the racks of costumes and the workbenches where the girls from the Zip had come up with a dance routine to promote her first bra.

'I couldn't believe it when Vita said you were working in

the studios,' Nancy said, taking out her silver cigarette case. 'Whatever did you do when you saw each other?'

'She screamed,' Percy said.

'I didn't scream,' Vita said, laughing, as the waiter came with an ice bucket and a bottle of champagne. 'But we certainly gave Mrs Chafin a shock.'

'Look at us. All reunited from the Zip Club.' They clinked glasses.

'So. Nancy. Do tell,' Percy said. 'Vita said you've got a speaking part? That's quite a coup.'

Nancy was happy to regale them with the story of her day on set – apparently the lead actor was unspeakably vain and had kicked up a big fuss about the lighting, but despite the waiting around, Nancy was loving the whole thing. She was still talking, hardly pausing for breath, as the waitress came to take their order. When Percy said that it was on his expenses and they were to order anything they wanted, Vita plumped for the lobster roll.

Then, finally, Vita spotted an opportunity to ask Percy about how he'd wound up in Los Angeles. He explained that he'd fallen in with a musical director in the South of France, and had come out to California at his invitation. It didn't surprise Vita to hear that his talent for costumes had been recognized straight away at RKO, and then Mr Adrian had poached him.

'Oh, goodness,' Nancy said suddenly. She'd been only half listening, distracted by the glamour of their surroundings. 'There's Mark. I simply must go and say hello.'

'She knows Mark Zamburg?' Percy asked, impressed, as Nancy slipped out of the booth.

'Apparently so. She met him in the clinic where Irving sent her to dry out. When we first arrived, he refused to take her call – but now she's got a part . . .'

They watched as Nancy patted her hair and then confidently approached a table a few booths away. They could see a man, presumably Mark, standing up and introducing her to his companions. The sound of Nancy's laughter reached them as she put one hand on her chest and accepted a seat. Vita could see the woman next to Mark bristling like a riled cat.

'Nancy was made for Tinseltown,' Percy observed, and Vita laughed. 'But I want to know about *you*,' he continued. 'The last time I saw you, you were on your honeymoon.'

'Oh, yes . . . Irving.' Vita pulled a face.

Percy listened, his brow creasing into a frown as she told him about Irving and their disastrous marriage. How he'd swept her off her feet in Paris, taking her out for dinners and buying her lavish gifts and begging her to marry him; and how she'd quickly realized that Irving, although kind and thoughtful, had serious health issues.

'Did you ever bump into Archie Fenwick?'

Vita put her hands over her face, then looked through her fingers at Percy.

'You saw him?'

Vita nodded.

'Oh, goodness, Vita, you're a dark horse,' he said.

Their food arrived. They decided not to wait for Nancy, who was still over at Mark's table. To avoid telling Percy all about Archie and what had happened in Monte Carlo, Vita filled him in on how they'd come to be in Los Angeles.

'So you're running around after Nancy, as usual?' Percy said, with a sad shake of his head. Then, picking up Vita's look, he added, 'All I'm saying is that Nancy is the kind of person who looks out for number one. That's all. She can be tremendous fun, but . . . I've seen that look she has before.' He nodded towards the table where Nancy was holding court.

'What look?'

'The look people have when they are resolutely clambering over others to get to the top.'

'I want her to get to the top.'

'Yes, but what about you?' Percy put his hand over Vita's. 'What about Top Drawer? You are so talented – you should be designing. What about *your* ambition?'

'Oh, Percy, you know how much I want that. But what can I do here? I have no money, no contacts—'

'Well, then, you need to be working in the studio.'

She sat back with a sigh. 'Oh, if only. Being in the department – oh, it was just glorious, but Mrs Chafin has made it very clear that it'll be years and years before I'm designing. I don't want to tread on the toes of the other girls.'

'Yes, but what you did today with that showgirl . . . well, I heard all about that. It was certainly the kind of quick-thinking flair we need around the place. And I said as much when I talked it through with the production team.'

'Talked what through?'

'You. Coming to work with me. Full-time. Come on, Vita. What do you say?'

'But what about working my way up?'

'You've just bypassed all that. I need you designing by my side.'

'Really? Really, Percy?'

'What are friends for?' he said, winking at her and filling her glass. 'We're going to make the best team, Vita. I just know it.'

53

Tea for Two

As Edith waited in Manchester's Piccadilly Station, scanning the faces of everyone who passed through the barriers, she could barely contain her delight. These past few weeks had been so exciting – and now she was about to see Nick again.

Nick – oh, Nick.

Her heart lurched now as she saw him and she ducked behind a pillar, then peeked again, watching him sauntering up the train platform as if he had all the time in the world. He was approaching the ticket collector now and she skirted around to the other side of the pillar, careful not to let him see her, pretending to check something in her bag so that she wouldn't look suspicious to passers-by. She waited and waited – and then, as he walked past her to the exit, she ran a few steps and bumped into him.

'Goodness – Edith,' he said.

'Nick!' she exclaimed. 'What a surprise.'

'What are you doing in town?' he asked.

'I was meeting a friend here before my train back, but I've just found out that she can't make it.'

'I'm sorry,' he said, although he looked confused that she was sharing these details with him. She'd rehearsed her story over and over in her head, but now there was an awkward pause.

'Nick . . .' she said, putting her hand on his sleeve, 'I'm glad to have run into you.' She made a show of looking bashful. 'About the other night . . . I think I might have embarrassed myself. You see, I drank far too much. I'm so terribly sorry.'

'It's me that should be apologizing to you,' Nick said, but he sounded relieved.

'Not at all. I've been feeling so wretched,' she lied. 'It's been so long, you see, since I've been out to dinner, or gone dancing with anyone – and I had such a wonderful time. But what I said was most inappropriate, and I'm utterly ashamed. I mean, what must you think of me?'

He nodded and smiled at her properly for the first time. He put his hand out and squeezed her arm.

'Please, don't mention it again. If anything, I was flattered.'

'But . . . but what must Helen think? She must have been horrified.' Edith attempted a shocked laugh.

'I didn't tell her,' he admitted.

'You didn't?' Edith felt a burst of victory as she glanced up at him coyly.

He shook his head. 'Your secret is safe with me.'

'Only, I had hoped to see you when I went in to see Eddy the following morning, but he said you hadn't come in. I hope that wasn't because of me.'

'No,' he said, but she didn't believe him. 'I hear he's very keen on the Cotton Queen idea. You've certainly impressed him.'

She nodded, glad that in that respect, at least, she'd gone up in Nick's estimation.

'I met your associate,' she said. 'Warren.'

'You did?' He didn't sound very pleased about it.

She nodded, losing her nerve. 'He really wasn't as dreadful as you made out.'

Nick frowned. 'Don't judge a book by its cover,' he said, with a look at his watch. 'He's as shady as can be.'

Edith smiled bashfully and there was another awkward beat as she looked at her feet. This wasn't how she'd expected their conversation to go. In her fantasies about this meeting, she'd thought she might share the burden of the secret that burned within her. She'd hoped she might tell Nick what she'd done. How she'd employed Warren herself for a very special task . . . but now that fantasy popped. She couldn't tell Nick. He would never condone what she'd done.

'So . . . I guess I must . . .' he said, nodding towards the crowds heading for the exit.

'What are you doing now? Would you like a coffee at Meng and Ecker's?' she asked innocently. 'I have time to kill before my train.'

Nick relented and in the coffee house they were shown to a table laid with a white cloth. They sat down, and Edith smiled across at him.

'Isn't this lovely?'

'Yes. It's nice to encounter someone in a cheerful mood.'

'Well, it's been an interesting few weeks.'

'Oh? How are things at work?'

'Apart from interference from Clement's dreadful lackey, Tantum, everything is great,' she said, confidentially. 'I've had a wonderful response from the advert in the *Dispatch*. The Darton Bra is going from strength to strength. Withshaw and Taylor have tripled their order, and there are customers lining up.'

'Oh, Edith,' he said. 'That's great news. And is your husband back from America?'

She looked at him, weighing up the thing she most wanted to tell him, but he didn't need to know. Not yet.

'No, he's not. And I don't expect him back for some time. Between you and me, it's so much better not having him around.'

'Well, you look good on it,' Nick said, and he smiled at her.

'Don't give me compliments, Nick. I'll get quite giddy,' she said. 'And we don't want that happening again.'

54

Nancy's New Place

In her dogged determination to move into a dream home, Nancy had signed the lease on a house up in Beverly Hills. It was almost as smart as Daniel's, although not as large. But, according to Ericka, it was definitely in the right location.

'I'm going to throw a huge party,' Nancy announced as she flounced through the empty rooms, arms outstretched. Vita followed with Bertie on her hip. 'Ericka has already started on the guest list. It'll be for the cast and crew of *The Sister Returns*, and everyone else who is anyone.'

Vita could easily imagine this spectacular modern villa filled with Hollywood types; but as a home? She couldn't help noticing hazards everywhere. The French windows opened directly onto the pool outside, and it was all too easy to see Bertie falling right through the gaps in those lethal-looking glass stairs.

Nancy had insisted they come up here early, before her tennis lesson, and now she tripped over to the glazed doors with her white tennis skirt flapping against her toned thighs. She was even more giddy than usual and Vita suspected that there was something she wasn't telling her. She knew what Nancy looked like when she was harbouring a secret.

Turning the key, Nancy did a little pirouette onto the terrace in her white plimsolls. Vita followed, smiling at her friend's exuberance as they looked out at the view. Nancy grinned, her newly whitened teeth flashing in the morning sunshine.

'Isn't it wonderful!' she said, holding out her arms again as if she could embrace the city below. 'Don't you just feel on top of the world?'

'It's quite something,' Vita agreed. But Bertie was tired, and suddenly he threw the teddy bear he was holding onto the slate tiles at Nancy's feet and began to cry noisily. Nancy winced. She could never bear it when Bertie was anything other than well behaved. His cries reverberated around the empty space.

'Sorry,' Vita apologized. 'Shhh,' she said, bumping Bertie up and down.

Nancy picked up the teddy and waggled it in front of Bertie, then pretended to hide behind it and leapt out, like a character in a Charlie Chaplin sketch. This clown act was also something new – no doubt an exercise from the acting classes she'd been taking – but it worked. Bertie stopped grizzling and Nancy blew a raspberry on his chubby hand. Vita gave her a grateful look.

'So I guess I'll start packing up the condo while you're at the studio today,' Vita said. She tried to keep the jealousy out of her voice. She'd thought very seriously about Percy's offer and she'd talked it through with Nancy too, but there was no way she could work full-time when she had nobody to look after Bertie. June had landed a few weeks on a film, and Vita had drawn a blank trying to find anyone else.

'Well, here's the thing,' Nancy said, and Vita recognized a sheepish tone to her voice that meant she was about to confess whatever it was that was bothering her. 'Ericka says I have to think about my image.'

Vita nodded. Most of Nancy's sentences these days started with 'Ericka says'.

'That makes sense.'

'Oh, Vita, I knew you'd be reasonable about it,' Nancy cried. 'And I've been so worried.' She put both hands to her chest and groaned as if with relief.

'You mean . . . you mean, you want me to stay at the condo?' Vita said, suddenly picking up on what Nancy was really saying. Her mind started whirring. How would she ever afford to pay the rent by herself?

Nancy looked startled, and then laughed as if Vita was being absurd. 'No, not at all. I chose this place because it's got a little gatehouse that you and Bertie can have. Just along the drive. Isn't that just the perfect solution? Clever Ericka.'

She was scanning Vita's face for a reaction. Vita found that unexpected tears were forming and she swallowed them hard, nodding. She couldn't help feeling that Ericka thought of her as a useless hanger-on. And now that Nancy clearly had her sights set on a real shot at fame, maybe she was right.

She thought about what Percy had said too – about how Vita was running around after Nancy. She'd been quick to dismiss the accusation, but if they moved here, Vita really would be a full-time servant, but with none of the benefits of living in the big house. Because how else was Nancy going to fend for herself? She had no idea how much Vita did for her.

As Nancy showed her around the rest of the house, Vita

tried to find the positives. For a start, it would be good to have her own space with Bertie, a place to which she could escape – certainly from Ericka. A place where she could start designing and planning in earnest.

She was so busy trying to imagine how it would be, she hardly registered the chime of the doorbell downstairs. Nancy tutted as Mr Wild started barking.

'Honey, can you get that?' Nancy said, flapping her hand at Vita, who bristled as Nancy took Bertie out of her arms. It was just as she'd thought: Nancy was already treating her like a servant. She jogged down the stairs and shushed Mr Wild, picking him up and opening the wood and glass door with its frosted panels. The shape of someone wearing a hat was visible on the other side. It must be Ericka.

But it wasn't Ericka. A black taxicab with a chequered trim was pulling away. The person it had dropped off turned, picking up a heavy carpet bag.

'Evelyn!' Vita cried, astonished to see the Delaneys' housekeeper on Nancy's doorstep. 'What on earth are you doing here?'

'Oh – I didn't know if I'd got the right house,' Evelyn said. 'And then I heard Mr Wild. Didn't Miss Nancy tell you I was coming?' She looked genuinely surprised, as Vita rushed over to kiss her cheek. How had Nancy kept this quiet? Vita ushered Evelyn inside the house, taking her bag and putting it down.

'Well, rest my soul,' Evelyn said. 'Won't you look at this place?'

'Oh, you're here,' Nancy said, beaming as she carried Bertie down the stairs. 'What do you think?'

Evelyn didn't answer. She only had eyes for Bertie. 'Where is my angel?' she cooed, scooping him up from Nancy's arms. She cuddled him, pressing her round cheek against his and breathing him in. 'And look at you!' she exclaimed, taking in Nancy for the first time. 'Lord have mercy, what have you done to your hair?'

'You like it?'

Evelyn pulled one of her sceptical faces. 'Your mother thinks you've gone off the rails again.'

'Then you'll have to set her straight. I'm honestly better than ever, aren't I, Vita? She'll tell you,' Nancy said, looping her arm around Vita's shoulder. The two of them smiled as Evelyn buried her face in Bertie's neck. He giggled with delight.

'He's still good enough to eat.'

'But I don't understand. You didn't tell me Evelyn was visiting,' Vita said.

'Visiting? No, she's coming to live with us,' Nancy said, grinning like a cat and clearly enjoying how dumbfounded Vita was. 'If you're going to work – and, by the way, I've told Percy that you are absolutely starting at nine sharp on Monday – then we need someone we can really trust to look after Bertie,' she explained.

Vita stared at her, realizing just how much Nancy had done to make her dream happen.

'Oh! Oh, goodness,' she said, grinning. 'Nancy – you didn't have to . . .'

'Of course I did. And besides, it's good to be the one giving you a break for a change,' Nancy said. 'Isn't that what friends are for?'

55

It Still Works

Vita and Nancy wasted no time in leaving the condo for Beverly Hills. As they settled in, it very quickly became apparent that neither of them could have coped without Evelyn there to help out.

On Monday morning, Vita took Bertie up to Evelyn at the big house before driving to the studio with Nancy, who, thanks to Ericka, now had her own parking space on the lot. They both enjoyed the feeling of driving straight through the gates to the sound stage, seeing the longing faces of the hopefuls waiting there patiently – although Nancy was dismissive of them as if she'd never been in that position herself.

Percy was thrilled to welcome Vita and threw her straight in at the deep end, insisting that she get to know everyone in the department. She felt guilty about leaving Bertie, especially as she didn't even have a second to call Evelyn on her first day. She'd thought she would be nervous around the seamstresses and designers, worried that they'd think she'd used her friendship with Percy to get a leg up, but as soon as she started making suggestions, everyone listened. Within the first week, she'd designed period costumes for a king and queen as well as dancers' costumes for a musical. She'd also helped Mr Adrian with his schedule and had not only found some valuable lost costumes in the vast store but repurposed them for Mr Adrian too.

Now, on Saturday, it was a relief to have some time off in order to sort out the gatehouse. It was a cheerful little cottage with a whole wall covered in pink roses – exactly the same shade as the roses that had grown round the doorway of Madame Jenny's in Paris.

There was a large bedroom with a stylish iron and wooden bed and French windows that opened onto a private patio and lawn, which Mr Wild adored. Vita had covered the bed in a counterpane made from intricate squares of patchwork, which one of the talented seamstresses at the studio had sold to her. It gave the room an immediate homely feel.

There was a separate nursery for Bertie, and an open-plan kitchen leading to a lounge area where Nancy had insisted Vita install the gramophone for company. It was the first place that Vita had ever had to herself, and she whistled along to the crackly records as she unpacked the box in her bedroom. Once she'd hung up all her clothes in the closet and smoothed her lingerie into the chest of drawers, she turned to her shoebox. She'd left Paris in such a hurry, she hardly had any possessions to her name; but the few she had meant a lot.

There was a framed silver photograph of the showgirls at the Zip – one that her old roommate, Betsy, had found and sent to Nancy in America. A poker chip that she'd kept from Paul's boat on her journey over to America. A Metro ticket from Paris. Bertie's first rattle, and the first shawl she'd wrapped him in. And finally, her papers – her passport and some paperwork, including old share certificates and the copy of *Sylvine* she'd bought in New York, still in its paper bag. She opened the top drawer and shoved it beneath the folded-up slips and bras.

'Hello? Vita, are you here?'

The voice came from her front door – it was Daniel. She hadn't been sure what time he'd get away to come and see her today, but now she called out, 'I'm in here,' and hastily piled her things back into the box, putting it on a chair.

'Hey,' he said, coming into her room. He was carrying a large bunch of flowers in one hand, and a gorgeous green and pink china vase in the other. 'Moving-in present,' he explained. 'Oh, and a congratulations-on-your-new-job present.'

Vita laughed and thanked him, taking hold of the vase and placing it on the drawers, then putting the flowers in it. The whole ensemble went beautifully with the new counterpane.

'They're lovely,' she said, suddenly flustered that he was standing so near and that they were on their own. She put her hands in the back pockets of her dungarees, wondering if she should have dressed a little more smartly, although she had a pretty headscarf in her hair and she knew that the figure-hugging blouse she wore beneath the dungarees was flattering to her arms and neckline.

'What do you think of the place? You like it?'

'It's great. But where's Bertie?'

'Evelyn has taken him, so I can have some space to fix things up.'

'Do you want a hand?' he asked.

'I'm more or less done,' she said with a shrug, her eyes not leaving his. 'I don't have many things.'

'And we're all alone?'

'We're all alone,' she confirmed. And in a moment, he was kissing her.

Still kissing him, she yelped and laughed a little as he tipped her over onto the bed and they landed together on the soft mattress.

'Hello, you,' he said, smiling at her and stroking her hair away from her face. Vita kissed him deeply and fully now, and soon she was lifting up his shirt. Then Daniel was on top of her, her dungarees flapping down and his hand reaching inside her knickers . . . and then she froze.

'What is it?' he whispered, as she pulled away from his touch.

'I'm nervous,' she said. 'I haven't . . . I mean, since Bertie.'

'You had a baby, Vita,' Daniel said tenderly. 'I've heard women's bodies have a tendency to forget and spring back to normal. Trust me.'

He kissed her again, and she tried to relax. 'We don't have to do anything you don't want to do,' he whispered, but his hardness was pressing against her. 'You mustn't be self-conscious. You're beautiful, Vita.' He traced a finger over the mole on her shoulder. 'All of you.'

Afterwards, they lay spent and sweating on the counterpane.

'I knew you'd be knockout in the sack. I knew it the first time I saw you.'

She laughed, punching him playfully on the arm.

'So it still works?' Daniel teased.

'It still works,' she agreed, turning to face him and grinning. She was embarrassed now, realizing that she must have made some noise – but oh, it had been so good to feel the sexual release she'd missed so much.

'This . . . this makes me happy,' she said, addressing the ceiling, and he laughed.

'Are you sure? You sound like you're still making up your mind about me.' He leant close and looked searchingly into her face. 'Are you?'

She laughed and placed her hand on his cheek. 'I have made my mind up,' she said. 'And I'm sure. I like you, Daniel,' she said, kissing him. 'I like you a lot.'

He rolled over on top of her. 'How much?' he teased, and she giggled as they started to make love again. After a moment, though, they heard a noise coming from the kitchen and suddenly froze.

'Oh no, it's Evelyn. Quick,' Vita whispered urgently, bundling Daniel off the bed along with the quilt. He laughed as he raced to put on his clothes.

Vita dashed across the bedroom and pulled on her kimono, tying the belt up before opening the door.

She went into the kitchen, where Evelyn was taking Bertie out of his stroller. He had chocolate around his mouth; she suspected that Evelyn had spoilt him up at the big house.

'Thank you, Evelyn,' she said.

'He was no bother. We made some cakes.'

Vita smiled at her, but Evelyn's face said it all when she saw Daniel come into the kitchen a moment later. He hadn't done up his shirt properly, and he looked as relaxed as if strolling out of Vita's bedroom half-dressed was the most normal thing in the world. Vita felt her cheeks growing hot.

'Evelyn, isn't it?' Daniel said, putting out his hand. He smiled his disarming smile. Evelyn shook his hand loosely, looking uncertainly at Vita. 'Would you be able to look after Bertie again tonight?' Daniel continued politely. 'I'm taking Vita out.'

'You are?' Vita was shocked by his presumptuousness.

'Yes. I'm picking you up at seven.'

He smiled at them all, then said his goodbyes and left.

Evelyn turned back to face Vita, her eyebrow arched in surprise. 'I don't know if I approve,' she said, 'but I like him.'

'You do?'

'Anyone who puts a smile on your face and some colour in your cheeks is fine by me,' Evelyn told her. 'I'll say no more. This place . . . well, it ain't like anywhere I've ever been. It seems that anything goes, so who am I to judge?'

56

Sundowners

The following few weeks were a whirlwind of work at the studios with Percy and then parties and dinners with Daniel.

Now, on Saturday afternoon, having left Bertie napping and Evelyn making soda bread, Vita walked around the back of the big house to the terrace to join Nancy. She'd hardly seen her – not just because her own days were filled up at the studio with Percy, but because Nancy's schedule for *The Sister Returns* was much more demanding than either of them had expected. The days on set were excessively long; quite often a chauffeur brought her back at gone midnight and collected her early in the morning.

As Vita arrived, she saw two lighting men packing up their equipment and she remembered that Ericka had organized a photo shoot at the pool. Nancy, in full make-up, was still wearing the glittering two-piece Vita had procured for her underneath a vivid green silk robe. She looked every inch a starlet as she waved over to Vita and proclaimed that she'd arrived just in time for cocktail hour.

Ericka was sitting at the low terrace table, dressed in her usual monochrome – this time, white palazzo pants and a black sleeveless silk top. Since coming into their lives she'd been a permanent fixture by Nancy's side and she seemed, if not exactly to distrust Vita, certainly to be suspicious of her. She jutted out her chin as Vita called out to say hello.

Picking up Mr Wild – who greeted her effusively, undoing the ridiculous bunches that had been tied above his eyebrows – she walked over to where Nancy stood behind the bar, squeezing oranges for a cocktail and sloshing around the remains of a bottle of vodka. She sniffed at the bottle. 'I think it's vodka,' she said to Vita. 'Although I hardly know these days. Do you know, it's two months since I've had a drink.'

'And you look fabulous on it,' Vita said, meaning it. Nancy looked utterly radiant. 'How was the shoot?'

'Same old,' she said, and Vita smiled that all this attention was already second nature. 'That's Max, the photographer, and his assistant, Luke. Oh, and that guy talking to Ericka is from *Variety*. He's been here all day, doing a profile piece. Ericka says that I have to get into all the papers,' Nancy said conspiratorially. 'Turns out she's not just an agent, but a pretty fine publicist too.'

'You're making a hash of that, Nancy,' the young guy, Luke, said, joining her behind the bar. 'Let me.'

'You're a darling,' Nancy said, blowing him an air kiss before linking arms with Vita and tottering on her high heels over to Ericka.

Ericka, ever focused on business, was mid-conversation about the press and the importance of profile with Max the photographer and the *Variety* journalist. Nancy sidled onto the sofa next to her. If Ericka minded that their hips were touching, she didn't show it, or move.

'So, what's the trick?' Nancy asked, cheekily. 'I mean, if one wanted to be famous? Properly, properly famous.'

'I'd say you need to be newsworthy. I mean, your life needs to be newsworthy,' the *Variety* man told her. He had red cheeks and looked too hot in his grey suit.

'Newsworthy?' Vita asked. 'How do you mean, newsworthy?'

'It helps if you're involved in a scandal,' Ericka said.

'Only a minor one. Either that, or a revelation. A star these days needs a back story,' Max chipped in, as he lit a cigarette and handed it to Ericka.

'I've got plenty of back story,' Nancy said, intercepting the cigarette and taking a drag. Ericka frowned and Nancy handed it to her.

'You mean Nate?' Ericka said. 'Sorry, but nobody has sympathy for rich bankers.' Vita looked at her in surprise, amazed that she would say something so callous. 'It's simply not sexy enough,' Ericka explained. 'But without a new story attached to a star, it's impossible to differentiate anyone these days.'

'That's why the party is important,' Nancy jumped in. 'You'll come, won't you, Max?' she said, putting one of her hands on his thigh. 'Take all the right pictures. I was thinking we could set up a red carpet and some lights when people arrive, and you could do a snap of them that I could send out afterwards.'

'If you want me to.'

'And bring your journalist friends.'

'How many are on the guest list now?' Vita asked, fighting down her distaste at this little gathering and how calculated Nancy was being.

'Everyone who is anyone is coming,' Ericka said, with a flick of her wrist, as if it was no matter. Vita wondered how Nancy was going to pay for it all.

It wasn't long before Daniel arrived, but he refused a drink, telling Vita that it was time they got going to the movie theatre.

'Oh, what a shame you're leaving. But have fun, you two,' Nancy called.

'I think it's going to be a long night,' Vita told Daniel as they got into his car. 'They're talking non-stop about this party. I'm rather dreading it, if I'm honest.'

'Was that Toogood from *Variety* I spied? He's a dreadful little toady,' Daniel said as they drove away.

'Well, there's only a certain amount of column inches. The trick is to fill them as often as possible,' Vita said, doing an impression of Ericka.

Daniel laughed, but then made a face. 'Yes . . . Ericka.'

'What about her?' Vita asked.

'There's talk. Talk about . . . you know? About what's going on between her and Nancy.'

'What does that mean?'

'What do you think it might mean?' Daniel said.

Vita sat back in her seat as they drove down the hill. The sky was a wash of indigo, mauve and pink.

'Do people really think . . . ?'

'Don't sound so surprised, Vita,' Daniel laughed. 'Ericka's preference for the fairer sex is well noted. And you're telling me that Nancy isn't a lesbian too?'

Vita thought now about how Nancy always seemed to

be draped over Ericka's shoulder. And now other things started to slot into place – about how she'd often seen Ericka's car in the drive very early in the morning.

Vita knew she ought to be happy for Nancy, but now her relegation to the gatehouse appeared in a different light. Did Nancy not really want her here at all? Did she want Ericka now instead? On a more permanent basis?

Vita was still mulling it over as they got to the Fox Beverly. Daniel bought a bucket of popcorn and some sodas and they settled down together in the deep red velvet seats. She looked up at the almost circular proscenium arch and the lavish red and gold decor, reminiscent of a Chinese temple.

'Don't worry about Nancy. I know she's your friend.'

'I'm not worried,' Vita lied.

'You know, this might sound crazy, but to be honest, I had my suspicions about you and her – you know, when you first arrived here,' Daniel said, leaning over and whispering in her ear. 'You seemed like a perfect little family unit.'

'Oh,' Vita said, taken aback and blushing. 'No, no. We're just friends.'

'I know that now, of course. It's just, she seemed to want to be a father figure for Bertie. And call me old-fashioned, but Bertie needs a real father.'

Was he offering himself for the role? Vita didn't know whether to be more shocked about this revelation or about his comment that she and Nancy had seemed like a family, with everything that implied.

As the newsreel came on, Daniel slid his arm around her. She liked the way she fitted against his tall frame. She liked the way he made her feel petite and dainty.

'You're the only one I want to see movies with,' he whispered.

Vita laughed. 'That sounds serious.'

'I am serious. You must know that, right?' He lifted her chin and gazed into her eyes. 'I'm crazy about you, Vita.'

Vita smiled, looking up at the screen, feeling something that she hadn't felt for a very long time. She felt completely safe.

57

The Silk Cotton Tree

In the bowels of the boat, Clement crouched, listening to the rhythmic slap of the waves across the wooden boards. It reminded him of the sound of the giant water wheel at the mill, the engine like the thrum of the spinning jenny. He closed his eyes for a moment, transporting himself in his mind to Darton.

He pictured himself standing at the giant wooden back doors of the mill and greeting the truck drivers who brought in the raw cotton bales from the docks with a smile, for once.

And – not for the first time in recent weeks – he made a pact with whatever God might save him that if he could only get home, then he'd be different. He'd give a raise to Jed, the most senior of the overlookers, who kept the machines working and mended the broken threads. He hadn't wanted to admit it before, but with some perspective, he could see that the *Daily Dispatch* might have had a point in its critique of the practices at Darton. He vowed now that he'd pay to get the ventilation fixed in the blowing room, where the cotton was cleaned and the workers had complained about recurrent lung infections and coughs.

How far away the green hills of Lancashire seemed now,

though. Rays of sunshine beat down through the wooden grille above him and he felt his shirt sticking to his back. He couldn't wait to make his move. He only wished he could see Rodriguez's face when he realized that Clement had gone.

That bastard, Clement thought, trying to stop his mind plotting the revenge that had come to obsess him. As soon as Clement had stopped throwing up, Rodriguez had ordered him to work on deck, scrubbing the boards like a common navvy. Clement hadn't experienced anything like it – the relentless hours and the loss of freedom. It had been such an assault to his ego, he'd been close to tears many times.

It was only the open sea that had provided any distraction, especially as they'd got further south and the sun had come out. And then it had been like a scene from the illustrated copy of *Treasure Island* he'd had as a child. All he'd seen were palm-fringed cays with turquoise water, Rodriguez navigating the small boat between sandbars where emerald waves broke. At times, the water was so clear it was like looking through glass to the bottom of the ocean, where patches of coral were picked at by a dazzling array of fish. Conch shells rocked on the bottom of the white sand, and Drum, the cabin boy, nudged him occasionally when stingrays four feet wide crossed underneath the hull.

Rodriguez had line-caught fish the likes of which Clement had never seen before: silver fish with bright yellow fins, fish with spears for noses. Drum, who'd been tasked with keeping an eye on Clement, had deftly cut them up, frying the delicious steaks under the stars for the crew.

Clement kept his own counsel, not listening to their jibes or how they teased him for being an English gentleman. They clearly enjoyed the sport of kicking a dog when it was down. But he waited, and he listened, and as he did he put the background of the crew together, realizing that they all worked for Le Monsieur. The name rattled round and round in his head, and Clement plotted his revenge. Oh, yes: Le Monsieur would rue the day he ever crossed Clement Darton.

He was only saved from going out of his mind by Drum, the only person who treated him with any respect. Clement didn't dare admit the real feelings he had for the boy, who shared his small cabin – and, since one very stormy night, his bunk too. He'd woken to find the boy's thin frame wrapped around his; he'd been quaking with fear. Clement had let him stay, and he'd crept into Clement's bed most nights since. The physical contact was the only thing that calmed Clement's mind.

Then, last night, Drum had whispered that the exchange was taking place. Confused as to what he might mean, Clement had followed Drum's lead and crept on deck with him, belly to the boards. By the bright light of the full moon and a million stars, he'd seen that they were anchored next to a larger vessel, and Clement's heart had leapt when he'd seen the ship was flying a British flag.

There'd been two smaller boats rowing back and forth between the ships and he'd seen Rodriguez hauling over large barrels, which Drum had told him were full of contraband whiskey. Rodriguez's men had rolled them down a gangplank to the bottom of the ship, stowing them away beneath the iced fish boxes.

The small boats had gone back and forth for what seemed like hours, until Rodriguez had signalled that the ship was full. He'd thrown a canvas bag, which Drum said contained bundles of banknotes, over the side to the men in the small boat.

Clement had watched this shocking exchange and been tempted to jump ship himself, imagining swimming to the British ship and begging for a safe passage home; but the water was too terrifying in the dark. And besides, when they'd crept back to their cabin, Drum had told him that Rodriguez was planning on making a short stop at Nassau to take on supplies. There, if Clement waited for his signal, he'd be able to make an escape.

Now, as Drum appeared above him and lifted up the wooden grille, Clement knew that this was his moment. With Drum's help, he climbed out onto the deck and bent down, hiding in the shadow of the wheelhouse.

They were moored in a busy harbour, on the far end of a wooden dock which ran down to the quay where there was a white building and a flag fluttering from the white pole.

Civilization. At last.

Drum tapped him on the shoulder, and Clement took the bag that he handed him with his few possessions. Then he jumped down onto the dock, the hot planks already scorching beneath his feet.

He hurried as fast as he could to the shade of the low white building, looking around the corner as he put on his shoes. It felt weird to be on dry land, his legs jelly-like, his stomach rocking. He walked between two trucks, heading along the sandy road towards the town. It wouldn't be long before Rodriguez saw that he was missing. How long could

Drum mask his absence from the boat? Long enough for him to find a policeman, or a British consulate? Long enough to give him time to raise the alarm?

Ahead, he could see the land, where low white buildings stretched down to the water's edge in between the palms. Still masked by the trucks, he walked from the dock over a gangway, seeing that shells littered the white sand below where a noisy surf broke. He heard singing and followed the direction of the traffic, noticing a group of women in thin cotton dresses stopping to stare at him, bundles and baskets on their heads. Street hawkers approached him now, offering him small bunches of bananas.

It was only a short walk to the centre of town, but it was hard without his stick. As he hobbled, Clement practised what he was going to say when he arrived at the police station and told them that he'd arrived in a boat that was now filled with illegal whiskey. At the very least, he hoped Rodriguez would be arrested. Clement might even be rewarded for this valuable information.

He crossed the square, his attention caught by what he thought was confetti in the air. But when he looked up, he saw that he was standing in the shade of a vast tree. He stared at its immense brown trunk, which emerged from the ground in giant folds. The canopy had to be at least a hundred yards across.

'Isn't it magnificent?' a woman said conversationally. She had a lilting American accent and was walking underneath a white parasol. Clement drank her in – her pretty, clean clothes – and wanted to cry, because for a second he'd thought she was Marie. She had blonde hair tied up at the nape of her neck and Clement rubbed his eyes, thinking that he must be seeing a vision. He hadn't shaved, and he was all too aware of his patchy beard and crazed appearance.

'It's a ceiba – a silk cotton tree,' she said. 'The finest in all Nassau. It's been here for years. It's the best cotton in all the world,' she added. 'Here.'

She stooped down and picked up a fluffy ball of cotton from the ground, handing it to him. Clement took it, hardly able to feel the light substance between his cracked fingertips. For all the years he'd spent working in a cotton mill, he'd never stopped to consider where the cotton actually came from.

'You're new in Nassau? Just off a boat?' she guessed.

Clement nodded. 'Do you know where the police station is, ma'am?' he asked, coughing slightly in order to find his voice.

'It's right over there,' she said, pointing to a building on the other side of the square.

Clement thanked her and started walking towards the building, but then he heard the whine of a truck. It halted, blocking his path. He tried to move around it but was stopped by the sound of a familiar voice – and the unmistakeable pressure of a gun barrel against his back.

'I don't know what you have planned, Darton, but believe me: you don't want to be shooting your mouth off anywhere near here.' It was Rodriguez.

'Let me go,' Clement hissed, desperately turning to see if he could appeal to the young woman for help.

'Easy now,' Rodriguez said, pushing the gun further into his back, forcing him around towards the back of the truck. 'You know, your fag gave you up with very little persuasion.'

Clement tensed at the sneering accusation in his voice. He wasn't going to acknowledge his remark about Drum, but his stomach lurched at the thought of the boy being hurt on his account. 'Please, let me go. I won't say anything. I just wanted to find the British consulate—'

'You're damn right you won't be saying anything. Because you won't be staying here,' Rodriguez said. 'And I don't want your lily-livered face on my boat. Luckily, my friend Bill here happens to be going to New Orleans. And he can take a guest.'

Clement was pushed into the truck. He fell against some hard boards, and below him the engine started. He heard Rodriguez slap the back of the vehicle, and it lurched away.

He fell forward, crushed by boxes as he scrambled to look out at the disappearing view of the cotton tree; but it was blurred by a thick cloud of black smoke from the truck's exhaust. Then another lurch sent him tumbling backwards. He struck his head on one of the boxes, crying out in anguish and fury. When would this hellish nightmare ever end? What if it didn't? What was going to happen to him now?

58

A Certain Glow

At Darton Hall, Edith stood before the tallboy with its oval mirror to remove her gloves and her new hat, thinking that she really had given the parishioners at St Hugh's a treat this morning. She touched up her lipstick, letting her thoughts turn to Nick. What would he be doing now? Did he and Helen go to church and then have Sunday lunch together alone? Would he be thinking about Edith the way that she was thinking about him?

As she walked through to the sitting room, she looked out towards the double doors to the conservatory. They were closed against the chill, but the green hills beyond were dazzling against the pale-blue sky. A flock of sheep was moving over the crest, heading for the patchwork of hedgerows that ran down to the river. In the distance, snow-capped hills glistened in the sunlight.

Her mother-in-law, Theresa, stood by the fire warming her hands. She was a small, slight woman with brown hair streaked with grey. Her customary black dress was buttoned up to the neck and she wore no make-up. She had a stooped, timid demeanour, as if she expected someone to hit her at any second. She jumped slightly and turned when Edith came in, and Edith was shocked by the intensity of her blue eyes, the one good feature she'd passed on to Vita.

'Let's stoke that up, shall we?' Edith said, taking a log from the stack in the pile and throwing it onto the fire. She took one of the heavy brass fire irons and shoved it into the grate, sending a shimmer of sparks up the chimney, and the fire caught. 'That's better,' she said. 'Shall I pour some coffee?'

She sat down opposite Theresa on a chair in front of the fire, noting the look of suspicion on her mother-in-law's face. Edith smiled, trying to be as friendly as she could; but the truth was that although they lived in the same house, whenever Susan was away at school Edith deliberately kept different hours in order to avoid them being alone together.

Since the dreadful business when Theresa had found out about Paris and the row that had followed, there'd been a gradual thawing of relations, but she was still frosty even though Edith had given the lonely old woman a grandchild. Susan adored her and, if she was honest, Edith was a little jealous of their closeness and the way they seemed to share secrets.

But now, with a secret life of her own, everything was different. Edith could finally see a clear path to happiness.

'Father McDougal was asking after Clement again at church,' Theresa said.

'What did you tell him?'

'The truth. That I haven't heard from him. And you haven't either?'

'No. Of course I haven't. Not since he called Martha. He'll be away for at least a month, I should imagine.'

Theresa was eyeing Edith suspiciously. 'Have you done something to your hair? You seem . . . different.'

'How?'

'You just have a little glow about you.'

'It's living without Clement,' Edith said, candidly. She saw that this had surprised her mother-in-law, and there was a pause while Theresa sipped her coffee. Edith bravely went on, 'Theresa, can I be honest with you?'

'What is it you want to say, Edith?'

'The fact of the matter is that Clement has gone to California because Anna is there. And he's going to get her shares. The Hillsafe ones. In her name.'

Theresa blinked once, then twice, like one of the birds in her aviary, as this news sank in.

'He's gone to find Anna? He knows where she is?'

Edith sighed. There was so much her mother-in-law didn't know. So much she'd kept from her.

'But I thought she was in Paris?'

'Not anymore. She's with her friend Nancy. As far as I know, they're working in the movies.'

Theresa had a faraway look in her eyes and the hint of a smile played on her lips. 'The movies.'

'Exactly,' Edith said, trying to keep her focused. 'So she has no interest in Darton,' she went on, bluntly. 'In coming home. In being part of this family. We're nothing to her.'

She'd hit home, she saw, because now Theresa's eyes blurred with tears.

'We have to stop him this time. Because his plan – once he has those shares and has control, at least – is to sell Darton out to the LCC.'

There was a small moment of silence. Then Theresa's eyes widened. 'No, no – he couldn't. Edith, tell me it isn't true?'

'I'm afraid it is.'

'Well, we have to stop him.'

Edith smiled. 'Exactly my feeling. So . . .' She smiled softly at Theresa. 'I've put some things in motion.'

'Things?'

'Vita – Anna, I mean – is going to agree to sell *me* her shares in Hillsafe.'

It wouldn't be long before this was the truth. Georgie would be in California any day now.

'You've been in contact with her? With Anna?'

'Not directly. Through a third party. But when I have Anna's shares – and, say, if you were to sign yours over to me – then, you see, I would have control of Darton. I can stop Clement selling the mill to the LCC. I can save Darton. You said yourself how much you approved of the lingerie business, and—'

'You would take over from Clement? You'd stop him selling out?'

'With your help, I would. Yes.'

Theresa Darton nodded, then stood up and opened the door to the conservatory. Edith watched her walk through the double doors as she went to her aviary, taking some grains from her pocket and feeding them to the canaries. Edith rolled her eyes. She put her coffee cup down and rose, following Theresa.

'You really don't think Anna will ever return?' Theresa said, after a moment.

'Frankly, no. I don't expect she will.'

'I always thought . . .' The old woman's voice trailed off.

Edith softened her tone. 'I know I'm no substitute for your real daughter, but I'm here. And don't you think that, together, we could be a force for good? We could certainly protect Susan better.' She turned back and shut the door, so that she could be sure they weren't overheard by Martha. 'I heard what happened at New Year. The way you threatened him.'

'I . . .' Theresa's chin trembled.

Edith held her mother-in-law's gaze now and saw the truth dawning there – that Edith knew.

'I know you protect him, Theresa. I know you protect him because you're his mother, but this can't go on. I won't let it.'

Theresa squeezed her eyes shut. A lone tear fell down her wrinkled, tired cheek.

'And how do you propose to stop him?' she said. 'He's a man. You think that's easy?' Her voice was a choked whisper. Edith felt a flash of sympathy with this woman who'd buried her secrets so deeply, bearing her shame like a martyr's cilice.

'If Clement continues to interfere with her, then I will have no choice but to call the authorities.'

'The authorities?' Theresa looked startled.

'Although heaven knows, it's a scandal that the business really doesn't need. Our names would be dragged through the mud, our reputation tattered. Well, yours probably more than mine, as I'd naturally have to distance myself. We could lose everything. We might have to leave Darton.'

'We mustn't let that happen. We can't . . . I can't leave.'

'Exactly. So I was thinking that before Clement returns

– *if* he returns – then you and I should pay a visit to the lawyers. I've fixed an appointment in Manchester. We can make our arrangement legal. And then we can begin a whole new era.'

'And what about Clement? What will he say?'

'He'll hardly have a choice, will he?'

Theresa nodded as if her mind were made up. Edith took her arm and led her back through to the warm room. 'So it's settled, then? You'll come to Manchester with me?'

'Yes,' Theresa said quietly.

'Good – because there's a show on at the theatre. I've booked tickets for you and Martha.'

59

Daniel's Lunch

Vita felt bad about leaving Bertie at home on a weekend. She knew Daniel wouldn't have minded if she'd brought Bertie to his lunch party; but as Evelyn so rightly put it, Bertie was a handful now that he was on the move, needing to be constantly watched and stopped from crashing into furniture and pulling things to the floor. And besides, Vita ought to concentrate on being Daniel's girlfriend. Evelyn seemed to have become Daniel's biggest fan, positively simpering whenever he came to the gatehouse to pick Vita up.

Despite how his house had seemed to Vita at New Year, Daniel's stylish home was actually more modest when it wasn't filled with merrymakers. That said, it still astounded Vita with how modern it was. She loved the feeling of being someone who mattered in this gorgeous city that buzzed with youth and vitality. She'd felt that way in Paris once, but she felt it even more here: that this was where the pulse of everything that mattered started.

Daniel was outside in the garden, playing the last of a round of croquet on the lawn with some of the lunch guests – two charming couples whom Vita had met several times.

Vita stood watching as he swung the wooden mallet

between his cream and brown shoes and hit the ball with a satisfying *tock*. He crossed his legs, swinging the mallet over his shoulder, as everyone watched the ball shoot across the lawn. He punched the air and one of the guests, Jill, laughed and clapped her hand against his in the air.

Vita remembered when she'd first met him at the Delaneys' and how she'd found him too forthright, but she'd come to love his upfront honesty and the way he called things as he saw them. In fact, now, as he turned and waved to her, she smiled and waved back, thinking how happy he made her.

Thomas, one of Daniel's staff, came over.

'Do you think Mr Myers would like me to begin serving the starters?' he asked Vita, as if she was already his mistress.

'I don't know, Tom. Let me find out.'

She walked across the springy lawn to talk to Daniel, who looked at his watch.

'We're just waiting for one other guest. I'll gather everyone in any case. Come on, you hooligans. Lunch!' He waved them over to where Thomas had laid a table beneath the pergola, and hung back so that he could wait for Vita.

'Did I tell you how divine you look in that dress?' he whispered to her, putting his arm around her waist. 'It's good enough to take off.'

She smiled at his insinuation, pleased that the sky-blue shirtdress met with his approval. She'd bought it with Nancy last week when they'd been shopping – the first purchase she'd made with her own pay cheque.

As his hand snaked around to her bottom, he gave it a squeeze and she laughed, conscious that they might have been observed. Even so, she snuck up to give him a quick kiss on the lips.

'I'll get rid of them as soon as I can,' he said, nodding towards the guests. 'There are things I'd like to do with you this afternoon.'

'Who are we waiting for, anyway?' Vita asked, as they set off across the lawn to where the marble table and iron-work chairs with pretty yellow cushions had been set up beneath the rattan pergola.

'That's the best bit. I've got a new writer I want you to meet. He's working on the rewrites of *The Sister Returns*. I poached him from another studio. Ah, here he is. Just in time.'

Vita stopped as Daniel waved to the guest, a man in a light-blue shirt coming through the garden door.

'Vita, come over and say hello,' Daniel called, but suddenly she couldn't move. As she shaded her eyes against the sun and looked at the new arrival, the world stopped turning momentarily.

'Darling, meet Archie Fenwick,' Daniel said. He looked excited. 'You know, A. S. Fenwick, the author?'

Archie.

Her Archie . . . was here?

Vita's first and foremost emotion was terror. Terror that Archie would reveal that they knew one another. She locked eyes with her former lover, feeling as if her legs might give way. She shook her head just a tiny bit and she saw him understanding.

'How do you do?' she said, holding out her hand, and Archie shook it formally. She snatched it away as soon as she could, her body electrified by his touch.

'This is Vita, who has recently become my altogether better half,' Daniel said.

Archie nodded and gave Vita a tight smile. 'Vita,' he said, drinking her in, just as she was him.

Here in California, surrounded by Americans, it was easy to forget England and her roots, but Archie's British accent brought everything she missed about home flooding back. Everything she missed about home . . . and about him.

He's here. Really here. My Archie. In touching distance.

Daniel took his place at the head of the table, with Archie on his left and Vita on his right. He showed no sign of noticing the tension between them.

Vita concentrated on spreading out her napkin on her lap, as Thomas brought out platters of food. Her mind was racing with questions as she fought not to catch Archie's eye, but she felt him staring at her.

'Everyone help themselves,' Daniel called down the table to his guests. 'Do dig in. Oh, oh, and you've got to try this wine,' he said, pouring some white wine into Archie's glass and then into Vita's. 'Thomas's nephew makes it in a local vineyard. I wouldn't mind betting that Californian wine becomes very fashionable before too long. It's just as good as the French stuff. Cheers.'

Vita took a long slug of her wine, putting the glass down quickly, not trusting herself not to reveal that her hands were trembling.

'Good, right?' Daniel said, wanting approval.

'Delicious,' Archie said. Vita looked at his fingers on the stem of his glass, trying to stop them sparking a dozen memories. 'It's a great place you have here. I saw you have tennis courts. Do you play?'

'Not as often as I'd like. What about you?'

'I used to play at Hartwell,' Archie said. 'With my brother, long ago.'

At the mention of Hartwell, Vita thought of roller-skating down the halls of the beautiful house with him and falling into his arms in the drawing room, among the dust sheets. Hartwell, the place where she'd lost her heart.

'Then you must come for a game,' Daniel said, jovially.

The starters – cold meats and devilled prawns – were on pretty platters along the table for everyone to share. Archie picked up the one nearest him and offered it to Vita first. She had no choice but to look at him as she thanked him and picked up the silver serving forks.

'You know, it's down to Vita that you're here,' Daniel told Archie.

'Is it?' Vita asked in horror, at exactly the same time as Archie said the same words. She blushed, but Daniel laughed at the coincidence.

'When I first met Vita in New York, she'd just bought your book.'

'Is that so?' Archie said.

'You remember, Vita? At Nancy's party? You were trying to find the pacifier and you tipped out your bag on the table and the book was there. I started reading it and liked the writing. When I heard that there was an Archie Fenwick in the writing team over at RKO, I knew it must be the same guy.' Daniel looked delighted with himself, as if he'd done her an enormous favour.

'You were looking for a . . .' Archie said. 'Sorry, did I hear you correctly? A pacifier?' He frowned at Vita. 'You mean for a . . .'

'A baby, yes. Vita has a son,' Daniel said. 'From her first marriage.'

'Oh?' Archie said. 'Is that so. How old is he?'

Vita didn't say anything. She couldn't find her voice.

'He was born in May,' Daniel said cheerfully. 'It was May, right, Vita? He's a fine little fella. And strong too.'

Vita looked up now and, as Archie's eyes met hers, she saw him doing the maths and she tried to ignore the question in his eyes.

60

Mary Pickford

As Vita parked the car and walked towards the design studios on Monday morning, the knowledge that Archie was here in the same studio was almost too much to bear. Her mind was filled with him. With the questions that she burned to ask him. She went over and over how she'd behaved at the lunch on Saturday, wondering if she should have reacted differently, but seeing Archie had sent her into a complete spin. One she was still reeling from.

At the first opportunity, Vita had made an excuse to talk to the other guests, but Archie had followed her and found a way to talk to her alone.

'I can't believe you arranged it,' he'd said in low whisper, careful to look as if he wasn't talking at all.

'Arranged what?'

'For me to be hired as a writer on *The Sister Returns*.' He looked up at her, grinning. 'Oh, Vita, I knew you still cared.'

'I didn't. I didn't have anything to do with it. This is the last place . . .'

'Oh,' he said, clearly hurt. 'Is it really so terrible to see me, Vita? Well, is it?'

'Daniel doesn't know anything about us. I want it to stay that way. For once in my life, I've found someone who is loyal and means what he says—'

'Oh, but if only you knew. If only you knew how tortured I was after France. I did everything I could to get away . . . to get here to Los Angeles, hoping I'd be far enough away, but look. You're here. It's fate,' he said, sighing.

'Don't, Archie. Not here. Please.'

'Then where? When?'

'I can't.' She glanced up and saw Daniel waving to them, grinning. 'I don't want to see you, or talk to you. Is that quite clear? Pretend we don't know each other. That's the only way this will work. Now excuse me.'

But he grabbed her wrist. 'But that's the thing, Vita,' he said, quietly. 'I *do* know you.'

When the guests had left, she made a spurious telephone call to check on Bertie and told Daniel that he was poorly, as an excuse not to stay the night at his house.

On Sunday, when he telephoned in the morning, she told him that Bertie really was unwell and that she'd been up all night – which was true, but not because of Bertie. She told Daniel to go and play golf alone. He was disappointed, but she insisted.

Lying to Daniel made her feel wretched, though. Having pretended that she and Archie were strangers, right in front of him, how could she even start to unpick all the lies and set things straight? She thought about Irving, and about the 'stitch in time' that Nancy had said would save nine. That had been bad enough, but this . . . this was so much worse.

Unable to stay at home with her thoughts or to face Nancy and Ericka, she drove out to the canyon, but it was too hot to walk and she found the scenery – the dark-brown sand ravines – only increased her sense of panic, reminding her how far away she was from everything she knew and understood.

And so now, after another sleepless night, she was grateful for the distraction of work. As she greeted Percy's assistant, Alison, who waved her through to the studio, she thanked her lucky stars that her dear friend was here.

'Ahh, just who I need,' Percy said with difficulty, before taking out the large pin he held in his mouth and jabbing it into his lapel. 'Too lampshade?' he asked, holding up some gold fabric and some gold brocade.

'Too lampshade,' Vita said decisively, walking in and putting down her bag.

'This, then?' he said, selecting some more fringing from the samples laid out on the workbench.

'What's it for?'

'The musical number set in Cuba.'

They'd been working on the drawing boards all through the previous week, and Vita was immediately absorbed. Gladly so. Anything to stop her obsessing about Archie Fenwick and what the hell she was going to do.

'This one,' she said.

'Decision made,' Percy said, teaming the fabric and the sequinned fringing Vita had chosen. 'Now then, tell me about your weekend? How's the great romance going?'

He smiled expectantly, but Vita covered her face in her hands. She told Percy about the lunch and, seeing she was upset, he drew her away to the small kitchenette. In hushed whispers, she explained that Archie was the new writer on the movie.

'What am I going to do? Percy, what on earth am I going to do?' she said, tears choking her.

'Oh, goodness, Vita. That is a shock. Daniel doesn't know? About you and Archie and your history?'

'No. Of course not. And I could have told him, but now it's too late.'

There was a knock at the door and Percy's secretary put her head in, smiling. 'She's here. Shall I send her in?'

'Sure,' Percy said, waving his hand. 'Send her to my office.' He turned to Vita and put a hand on her arm. 'Come and help me now, and then we'll discuss it.'

Percy's office had two art deco sofas and a clothes rail in it. Vita went to the window, slanting the blinds so that it wasn't so light. There was a knock. Alison opened the door and Mary Pickford stood framed in the doorway.

Vita caught her breath at the sight of the beautiful actress. She was wearing a gorgeous emerald-green silk dress and she smelt wonderful, Vita noticed, as she walked in and kissed Percy on both cheeks.

'Percy, dearest,' she said, before peeling off her gloves. She sat on the sofa with a satisfied smile. 'It really is miles away over here, isn't it?' she went on. 'It took me ages from the lot. It's nice to have a break. I always so look forward to coming to the costume department.'

'I gather Carl wants a new look for your costume, is that right?' Percy said.

'Yes, apparently so,' Miss Pickford said. She turned in

her seat to look at Vita. 'Don't I know you? You seem familiar.'

'Actually, we have met before,' Vita said, glancing up at Percy, who was surprised by this revelation. 'In Paris. I worked for Madame Sacerdote.'

Miss Pickford clasped her hands together. 'I simply love Jenny's clothes.'

They talked for a while about Maison Jenny and about Laure, then moved on to discussing the new movie and the dresses Miss Pickford would have to wear. Vita realized how seriously the stars and designers took their fashion responsibility.

'Vita, perhaps you'd like to do some preliminary sketches,' Percy said.

'Are you sure?'

'Yes, yes, Vita, you must,' Mary Pickford insisted. 'It would be good to work together. Anyone trained by the great Madame Jenny is perfect for me.'

61

Just Two Normal People

Vita was buzzing with ideas as she waited for Percy in the canteen at lunchtime. She sat on the far side by the window, a sketchbook on the table in front of her. She added some lines to the sketch she'd started for Miss Pickford, remembering the boards in Mr Adrian's office and Mrs Chafin's comment about how they were creating worldwide fashion trends. She had to do something daring. Something different. She turned over the page, telling herself to be more adventurous and imagining the line, imagining what the dress might look like on screen.

She was so absorbed, she only noticed that someone had approached her table when a shadow fell across the page. Archie was standing there, a brown wooden tray in his hands.

'Mrs Chafin said you came here for lunch,' he said, by way of explanation. She noticed the surface of the coffee in his cup was trembling slightly. 'Can I join you, Vita?'

Vita. The way he said her name. The way he looked, in his soft woollen tank top, made all her resolutions dissolve.

'I'm meeting someone,' she said, but she didn't sound convincing. She almost told him she was waiting for Percy;

but explaining that it was the same Percy from London would only bring more of their shared history flooding back.

'I won't stay long . . . if you don't want me to,' he said, and he pulled out a chair and sat down.

Vita picked up her sketchbook to make room for his tray, hugging it against her chest. She blushed, thinking about the terrible, hurried conversation they'd had at Daniel's house. How awful she'd been to him.

'We've met officially, haven't we? So, it wouldn't be wrong for us to have bumped into each other here? We're just two normal people . . .' He made it sound so logical, so plausible, when there was nothing normal about this at all.

He was wearing a short-sleeved shirt under his jumper. She looked at the blond hairs on his sunkissed arms, remembering how those arms had once held her close. Remembering how she'd lain against him on a moonlit night at Hartwell, stroking her fingers along them.

'Vita. Please don't ignore me again. Can't we talk?' he asked, searching out her eyes.

She'd been dreading this conversation for so long, but now it was here, she had no idea how to start it.

'What do you want to talk about?' she said, looking out of the window.

'Vita, look at me,' he said, and when she glanced his way she saw his eyes were beseeching her. She swallowed, her throat suddenly dry.

'That night in France,' Archie said, 'on Digby's yacht.'

He wasn't here to make small talk, then. She could feel herself shaking, her emotions tumbling around inside her. She glanced once more at the door. Percy would be here any second.

'Vita, please. I need to talk to you about that night.'

'It was a mistake,' she said.

He sat back in his seat. 'A mistake? Is that really what you think?'

He stared up at the ceiling. She saw that she'd really hurt him, and for a second she wished that she could take the words back. She wished she had the courage to tell him that for so long, *that* night had been all she was able to think about.

But too much time had passed. She'd spent too long on her own. Too long trying to heal and move on. And finally, she had, hadn't she? She had Daniel. She had a new life here, a million miles away from Archie Fenwick and all the ways he could hurt her.

Except that now he was right here. In touching distance.

'And the baby?' he went on.

In her wild flights of fancy, when she'd thought about seeing him again . . . about having this conversation . . . she'd never imagined it to be like this. So hurried and whispered and illicit.

'Is he mine? Ours, I mean?' he pressed.

'Bertie. He's mine,' Vita said, but her voice was a hoarse whisper. 'That's all there is to it.'

Archie looked at her, aghast, then leant forward, his face close to hers. He held her chin and the rest of the canteen, the studios, the whole of the world melted away.

'Look me in the eye, Vita, and tell me the truth,' he said. 'Tell me it's not true. Tell me he's not mine. Put me out of this torment. I'm begging you.'

She knew exactly what she should say. The denial that would save her, that would make him go away once and for all . . . but she couldn't say the words. She watched his eyebrows crumple together, tears forming in his eyes as, in the suspended moment of silence, he understood the truth.

Her heart was weightless with the relief of it, the heaviness of the secret lifted momentarily from her shoulders.

'You had our baby?' he said in a whisper. 'Why didn't you tell me, Vita? Why?'

'What good would it have done? You're married, if you hadn't noticed. And so was I.'

'Is that why you split with that man? With Irving? Because he found out the truth about Bertie? About us?'

She didn't have to answer.

Archie put his hand to his hair and pushed it back. He let out a desperate sigh.

'If I'd known . . .'

'If you'd known, you'd have . . . ?' Vita said, suddenly feeling cross. 'Would you have left her? Maud?'

She thought of Maud, and her vile sister Georgie, and all the reasons that she and Archie had been kept apart. Because he'd married for money. Maud's money, which had ensured he could keep his precious Hartwell.

He sighed. 'Oh, Vita – I never loved her. Not like I loved you. Like I love you. Because . . . my God, when I saw you at Daniel's, I realized, I realized just how much I've missed you.'

'Don't say that. Please.'

'Because of Daniel? Because you love him? Has he asked you to marry him?' he demanded, his voice loaded with jealousy.

'No, but so what if he does? It's none of your business, Archie.'

'You expect me to stand by and let another man bring up my son?'

'He's not yours. He's mine.'

'But everything is different now.'

'Is it? How, exactly? You have your wife, your mother, Hartwell. You chose them over me long ago.'

'It wasn't like that.'

'Wasn't it? You always made me feel that I wasn't good enough for you.'

He laughed, but it was edged with a much rawer emotion. 'It's funny, that. I always felt the same. That I'd never be good enough for you.'

Vita gripped her sketchbook even more tightly.

'I have to go,' she said, pushing back in her chair. He stretched across the table, grabbing her forearm.

'I want to meet him. Bertie. At least let me see him. Just once.'

'No. I don't think that's a good idea,' she said, staggering to her feet. She couldn't bear to be here a moment longer.

She hurried away from him and he stood and called after her, but she bolted for the door – where she bumped straight into Percy.

'What's the matter? I'm not late, am I? Goodness, Vita, you look dreadful.'

'He's here. I can't stay here.'

'Oh, dear,' Percy said, looking past her into the canteen. 'Let's go back to my office. I've got some whiskey in the bureau.'

But as he put his arm around her and led her away, Vita knew Archie was standing, bereft, at the table where she'd left him.

It had been hard enough to face her feelings about Archie Fenwick when they'd had an ocean between them. But now? Now she felt as if she'd capsized.

62

One Precious Life

In the office at Darton, Edith handed Nick a glass of brandy and he thanked her as they clinked glasses. His green eyes locked with hers and she noticed the wrinkles at the corners of them, which only made him more handsome.

Nick had told her that it had been Helen's idea to follow up the Soirée collection splash with a piece about Edith, to coincide with the paper launching the Quest for the Cotton Queen. Edith regarded it as a very positive sign that Nick had come along with the reporter and photographer to make sure that everything they were going to print was to her liking. She'd spent the whole afternoon with him, showing him around the mill and introducing him to the staff.

'You know, you were very impressive today, Edith. I think you're a fine ambassador for Darton,' Nick said, before draining his brandy in one mouthful. 'But now, after a very pleasant afternoon, I'm afraid I must be going.'

Edith looked at the floor and rubbed a patch on the tile with the white leather tip of her shoe. She couldn't bear for him to go – not when just being near him made her feel as if she was being a better version of herself. Surely he could feel it, too? This chemistry? The way they finished each other's sentences and laughed at the same things? He *must* do. And she knew he found her desirable. She'd caught him looking at her and quickly looking away several times.

'I'm sure Helen can do without you for a little while longer? It's been a long day. Why don't you come back with me and have some supper at the Hall? Don't you want to see where I live?'

'But Helen will be worried.'

'Then telephone her. Tell her I insist.'

Nick placed the call to their housekeeper, making an excuse and telling her that he'd be back late. Watching him, Edith was mesmerized by his strong hands. The desire that had been building inside her all day made her knees weak with longing.

They drove back to the Hall in Nick's blue sports car, but as they approached, she couldn't help seeing the austere building from his point of view.

'It's a fine place,' he said, looking up at the facade through the windscreen.

'It could be. There's so much I'd like to do with it. That said, I don't have Helen's flair for decorating.'

'Yes, well, Helen paid someone else for *their* flair.' Edith noted that this was said with just a hint of exhaustion, and she liked the fact that Nick was opening up to her. It was a good sign, wasn't it? For him to be so candid about Helen? This little chink of dissatisfaction gave her just the boost of courage she needed.

They parked, and she opened the front door with her key and threw it onto the console table. Nick looked along the flagstone corridor and up the dark oak staircase to the gloomy floors above.

'Where is everyone?' he asked as he followed her inside.

'Oh, goodness,' she said, turning to face him with a light laugh. 'I've just remembered. Theresa has gone out this evening with Martha. It looks like we're all alone.'

She made a silly face, as if she'd been foolish, trying to dismiss the fact that she'd deliberately engineered for them to be alone and this was going exactly as she'd planned. She took him along the corridor to the kitchen. Victor, her cat, stretched as he got up from his basket by the range.

'There you are. This is my baby,' she said, picking up Victor and holding him against her face. 'Do you like cats?'

'We have Fig, as you know, but I grew up with cats,' Nick said, reaching out to pet Victor's face.

'He likes you,' Edith said, hearing the cat purr.

She put Victor down and walked over to the larder. 'Are you hungry?' she asked, opening it and then looking in the side door of the range. 'Martha's bound to have left something. Oh yes, look, she's left a pie. We can have that later.' She realized she was talking too much. 'Why don't I take you on a tour?' she offered.

She had to be calm, she told herself, but having him all alone in the house suddenly made her feel jittery and nervous. He followed her from the kitchen and she opened the door to the drawing room.

'As I said, this house is so dreadfully dark, but I don't mind it in here.' She opened the doors and walked through to the conservatory.

'Look at those birds,' Nick said, touching Theresa's aviary.

'I've always found something so tragic about birds in captivity,' he said. 'The gardener used to keep doves in our house in India. I was sad that they were never free.'

'Oh, believe me, the amount of times I've wanted to just open the cage. They're my mother-in-law's pride and joy. She talks to them, you know.'

It was so illicit and exciting having him here, but there was something too stifling about being in the room where her mother-in-law spent so much time. 'Let's go to my study,' she said.

Since Clement had been in America, Edith had persuaded Theresa to let her take over Darius's study, and she'd recently had it painted. It felt like a little oasis of colour in the otherwise drab house.

In the study, she felt more relaxed now that she was in her own space. She went over to the drinks trolley and mixed two strong martinis while Nick admired her framed prints. Once she'd given him his drink, she kicked off her shoes and drew her feet up underneath her on the velvet-covered Chesterfield. After a few moments, he seemed to relax, and when she patted the sofa he came to sit at the other end. The late afternoon sunlight from the French windows soaked the room in a golden glow.

She asked him about India and then, as she knew he would, he turned the conversation onto Helen. It was then that he seemed to remember where he was and put his glass down.

'I shouldn't . . . I can't drink that. It's strong and . . .' He looked at his watch. 'I really should get back to Helen.'

'I think it's admirable . . . your dedication to her . . .' She trailed off, realizing that she was about to overstep the mark. 'But does she really need you that badly? So badly that you can't just relax a little and enjoy yourself?'

Nick sighed. 'You don't understand, Edith. It's complicated. The thing is . . .' He sighed again and shook his head. 'It's my fault that Helen lost her sight.'

Edith was shocked. 'How could it possibly be your fault?'

'I was working on a story. I got close to uncovering something that people didn't want uncovered – and, well, they came to the house and hurt Helen.'

She reached out and touched his face. 'Oh, Nick. I'm so sorry. That must have been dreadful.'

'The worst of it is that Helen has never been angry about it. If she had been, I could handle the guilt I feel. But it gnaws at me, you know?'

He wanted her to understand, but all she could think about was that his confession was affording her the opportunity to stroke his hair. She fingered the fine brown curl that fell behind his ear as she stared into his face.

'I know. You poor darling.'

'I even feel guilty for telling you,' he said.

Edith laughed gently, moving closer still. 'You don't have to feel guilty about that. This is me. We're friends, remember?'

But when he looked at her, she saw the look she'd been longing for. That he wanted them to be so much more than friends. A flush was rising in his cheeks.

'Edith, I have to go,' he said.

She nodded, and he stood. There was a tense silence as he picked up his coat and hat.

'Perhaps we shouldn't see each other for a while,' he said, addressing the wood of the door.

'Nick.'

She knew her voice would stop him. She stood and undid the zip on her day dress, letting it slide over her shoulders. Underneath, she was wearing her finest sheer petticoat and as she walked towards him, she stepped effortlessly out of the dress. Now, as he turned, she saw him staring at her, his eyes running over her body. She put her hand on her hip, her legs apart as she stood before him.

'Edith – I . . .'

She reached out and put a finger on his lips. 'Don't say anything.'

'I can't do this. It'll destroy Helen,' he said, shifting away from her, but she stepped once again towards him so that he was flattened against the door. There was a satisfyingly hard bulge in his trousers that she'd been fantasizing about.

'She'll never know. This is just about you and me.' She snaked her arms behind his neck. 'We only get one life, Nick,' she said. 'Just one, precious life. Is it worth wasting any of it not being happy?'

She had him, she could tell. He was rooted to the spot. He didn't move as she pressed her body against his and then he let out a long, sensual sigh that ignited her loins. She felt his hands grab her buttocks and squeeze her so hard against him that he lifted her off her feet, and her heart soared. She'd won at last.

63
Marrying Hollywood

To Vita's surprise, when she asked Nancy what she was going to wear to her party, she'd announced that she wanted to wear her wedding dress. She might as well, she'd said, since her mother had sent it out in the trunk that had arrived from New York.

So, with Percy's help, Vita had altered the silk dress into a more revealing garment than had ever been intended for the wedding. She'd had it pressed at the studio and had driven home early.

Now she set off to deliver it to Nancy, scooting around the catering vans that came one after the other up the gravel drive along with the man from the flower stall, who was carrying a vast arrangement of white roses. Walt, the gaffer from the studios, was perched high on a ladder against the front of Nancy's house, a string of lights falling down as he wired them up.

The front door was wide open and inside there was a fierce-looking woman with a clipboard supervising the moving of furniture. Vita could see bunting being erected over the pool, and she heard the chink of bottles and glasses being set out on trestle tables. Keen to remove herself from the chaos, she climbed the stairs to Nancy's room, where Mr Wild greeted her ecstatically.

Nancy was in a towelling robe, her face covered by a gloopy green face mask. She announced that she was making herself beautiful before the hairdresser arrived.

'Have you seen Hugo Manners?' she asked, picking up a newspaper from the bed and thrusting it at Vita.

Vita took it and read aloud from the diary column.

'New girl in town Nancy Delaney, star of the new MGM picture *The Sister Returns*, is putting herself well and truly on the map.' She pulled an impressed face at Nancy. 'A little bird told me that party plans are afoot. Be there, or be square, is what this intrepid reporter heard.' Vita looked up at Nancy in alarm. She remembered that awful man Marcus Fox in London, with his salacious diary, and how much trouble his mention had got her into. She didn't trust journalists. 'Oh my goodness, Nancy. He's broadcast it to the whole world. Everyone will turn up now.'

'There's security, don't worry,' Nancy said, flipping her wrist. 'It's a good thing. Don't you see?' She pointed a manicured nail at the copy. 'Star of *The Sister Returns*. That's quotable. Ericka is delighted.'

Vita wasn't so sure. She put the paper down and handed the dress over to Nancy, who took it out of the canvas cover and held it against herself.

'Oh, kiddo, this is wonderful. I'm going to look like the hostess with the mostest tonight!'

'You certainly will,' Vita said, laughing at how giddy she was being. 'But give it back before you cover it in that green mess.' She took the dress from Nancy and put it carefully back in its wrapper.

'Isn't this fun?' Nancy said. 'Us getting ready . . . like it's my wedding. Only this time it's for real.'

Vita was confused. 'Who are you marrying?'

'Hollywood, silly. After tonight, *everyone* will know my name.'

Vita hung the dress up in Nancy's closet while she listed off the celebrities who were coming to the party.

'So, I have news,' Nancy said, grabbing Vita's wrist. Her eyes looked especially wide in the face mask and Vita knew her well enough to understand that she had a piece of tittle-tattle.

'What?'

'There's a new writer on *The Sister Returns*.'

'Oh. I suppose you mean Archie.'

'You *know*?' Nancy was disappointed that this piece of gossip had fallen flat.

Vita nodded. 'I've hardly had a chance to see you. To tell you what's been going on.'

'And what *has* been going on?' Nancy demanded. 'Because don't you dare tell me you're going to jeopardize everything over that' – she waved her hand – '*man*.'

Any hope that Vita would be able to tell her how she'd been feeling was now crushed. Nancy had never approved of Archie – which was why Vita had never told her the truth about Bertie.

'But don't you think I ought to tell Daniel? About Archie? That we have history?'

'What on earth for? No, Vita, don't be foolish. You can't

upset Daniel. It might ruin my chances in this film – not to mention yours and Archie's, come to think of it.'

'But I feel wretched.'

'Archie is your past,' Nancy said, pressing the end of Vita's nose. 'Distant past. And Daniel is your future.'

'Nancy?'

They both looked up to see Ericka in the doorway. She was wearing a robe that matched Nancy's. She tied it tighter when she saw Vita.

'The hairdresser is here.'

'I'm coming,' Nancy said.

'Don't say anything to Ericka,' Vita whispered as Ericka moved off along the corridor. 'Please, Nancy.'

'Don't worry. Your little secret is safe with me,' Nancy said; but Vita, remembering the look on Ericka's face, wasn't so sure. Could she really trust Nancy? Or Ericka? Or anyone in this place? Nancy might want her to forget about Archie and to think about her future, but that was proving to be very much easier said than done when Vita's whole life suddenly felt like a house of cards.

64

Never Off Duty

With so many people coming and going up to Nancy's house and Evelyn needing to be on hand to help out, Vita had arranged for Bertie to stay at Daniel's house. Thomas and his wife, Mary-Anne, were delighted to be in charge of him for the night.

'I know you like Evelyn to look after him,' Daniel said, as they got ready in his bedroom, 'but Mary-Anne will be just as good. Better, even. She's certainly younger.'

'What are you suggesting? That I leave Bertie here all the time?' Vita sat on the end of his low bed, pulling on her shoes. It had been a long day and she wished that she didn't have to go to Nancy's party, but could just lie down on Daniel's bed and read a book. She dreaded the thought that Archie might turn up tonight. What if he wanted to talk to her again?

Daniel stood in front of his silver dressing mirror, tying his bow tie, and she went over to him and put her arms around him from behind. She didn't want to think about Archie. Not when she had Daniel.

'Or you could move in,' he said.

Vita felt her breath quicken. What was he suggesting? His

eyes were soft as he met hers in the mirror. 'I can't just move in here,' she said.

'You could if we were . . .'

'Were?'

'If we . . . when we . . .' She saw that he was blushing. He broke eye contact, turning and kissing her ear. Was this a proposal? 'It's just something to think about. That's all,' he said, lightening the moment. 'Come on, we shouldn't be late.'

Nancy's house was lit up like a beacon when Vita and Daniel arrived. They had to queue at the door, Nancy insisting that the guests pose on the red carpet while the photographer flashed the camera in their faces.

'What a wonderful couple,' the photographer's assistant said as Vita and Daniel smiled for the camera. She felt him put his hand over hers.

They walked into the party. 'It's a good turnout,' Daniel said, impressed.

'I had no idea she knew this many people,' Vita murmured, dismayed by the crowd already spilling out onto the terrace.

'She doesn't. But they all want to know her. That's the difference,' he said, taking a couple of glasses of champagne from a nearby waitress with a tray. 'And it's only going to get worse. The moment *The Sister Returns* hits the screens, we shan't see Nancy for dust.'

'You really think so?'

'I've seen it happen. And I've seen enough pictures to know that she's going to be a star. But don't you dare tell her I said that.'

Vita heard music now: a man sitting and singing at the grand piano, another guy on drums. There was a double bass player, too. Outside, she spotted Nancy being greeted by excited well-wishers at the bar, like moths around a flame. Vita watched her smiling, shaking hands, kissing cheeks – it was clear that she was loving the attention.

Then there was a lull, and Vita saw Nancy puff a breath up over her face. She remembered Daniel telling her that Nancy was going to need someone to keep her feet on the ground – but the way he'd been talking just now made her feel as if, even if she tried, she wouldn't be able to hold onto her.

Vita went over and hugged her, admiring her dress.

'Everyone loves it,' Nancy told her. 'I've had so many compliments. Didn't I tell you, Vita, that we'd come out here and throw wild parties? Only this is so much better than Paris.'

'Here's the party queen,' Daniel said, approaching and offering Nancy a glass of champagne. She put out her hand.

'I'm pacing myself,' she said. 'For once, I'm sober-ish,' she added, taking a little slug out of the glass and handing it back. 'Vita, do go and get the dancing started,' she urged, gesturing at both of them. 'You too, Daniel.'

'As you wish, your ladyship,' he laughed, amused that Nancy was calling the shots. He took Vita's hand as they moved away. 'She's a better hostess than I thought. And I know you were nervous about the dress, but it's gorgeous. I can't imagine her getting married in that, though. It's rather revealing.' Vita laughed, realizing that his was the only praise she really wanted. 'Percy is lucky to have you,' he went on. '*We're* lucky to have you at the studios, Vita.'

Matt the realtor-stroke-actor was at the party, along with

June from the pool, who was now dating Ted, the lifeguard. They made a fine couple dressed up in black tie, and Vita introduced them to Daniel. June simpered, amazed to meet a famous producer, and her eyes widened at Vita.

'You're really dating Daniel Myers?' she asked in an awed tone. 'You couldn't put in a word for me, could you?'

'I can try,' Vita laughed, 'but he's off duty.'

'Is anyone really ever off duty at a party like this?' June asked, innocently. Vita had to admit she had a point.

She caught up with Daniel, explaining how she knew June. 'You said you hardly knew anyone here in LA?' he asked.

'I suppose I do know a few people,' she said with a smile, waving to Ericka and Max, realizing that he was right. This was beginning to feel like home.

After a few more glasses of champagne Vita started to relax and have fun. Daniel was so charming to people, and she liked hearing stories from the set of *The Sister Returns*.

'I meant what I said earlier,' he said, when they finally got onto the dance floor. 'About you moving in with me. Tell me you'll think about it?'

He turned her around and she was about to reply when she glanced into the house and saw Nancy throwing her arms around a tall woman, and suddenly the warm, fuzzy feeling disappeared.

65

The Powder Room

Vita carried on dancing, but as soon as she got the chance, she excused herself from Daniel and slipped through the crowd to talk to Nancy.

'That wasn't – it wasn't Georgie I saw you with, was it?' she asked.

'Yes. She was in town and telephoned,' Nancy said, with a careless shrug, as if Georgie had just happened by. She was supposed to be in England. Miles away. What was she doing here?

How could Nancy have forgotten? Didn't she remember how much Georgie had interfered in Vita's life? How she'd split her and Archie up?

'Her husband is wildly successful,' Nancy continued. 'She's rich as rich can be. They're just off on a world cruise.'

Vita remembered the first time she'd seen Georgie – at Kettner's, when she'd been dining with Archie – and how she'd been so intimidated. She hated that Georgie had inveigled her way back into Nancy's life, but she hated most of all that she was here. It was only a matter of time before they collided at the party.

She went back outside to find Daniel, but just as she

stepped onto the terrace and joined the group he was talking to, she felt a tap on her shoulder.

'Oh, Vita,' Georgie said, with a grin. 'There you are.' She was wearing a beaded dress and a headband, her tanned skin gleaming, her glossy pink lips wrapped around an ebony cigarette holder.

'Oh. Hello, Georgie,' Vita said, trying to keep her voice level.

'Darling, we must catch up. I insist. Excuse us,' she said to the others, linking her arm through Vita's and steering her back inside. 'Let's go somewhere quiet.'

She marched Vita inside and along the downstairs corridor, babbling about how fabulous it was to be in Hollywood. Vita longed to escape, but suddenly Georgie turned the handle and opened the downstairs cloakroom.

'This will do,' she announced, looking around the freshly decorated room with its deep-green walls and glass vase of lilies. She locked the door, smiling coldly at Vita as she did so. 'I always love a chat in the powder room at a party, don't you?'

She put her bag down on the side of the marble sink unit and preened her appearance in the mirror.

'I was listening to Nancy earlier. My goodness, she seems so hungry for the press. She introduced me to that man, Hugo Manners. He was quite taken with my recollection of Nancy's days in London. I was happy to oblige when he asked for details. Of course, there's so much more that I could say, should I be so inclined,' she said, with a venomous little laugh.

Vita took a deep breath, trying to stop the room from spinning.

'I think Nancy is perfectly capable of handling her own press. Without your help, Georgie.'

'Oh, Vita,' Georgie said with a sly smile, turning around. 'Still so defensive.'

Vita looked at the door, wishing she had the nerve to walk back to it, open it and run far away from Georgie's cloying perfume and calculating eyes.

She remembered now how Georgie had threatened her, and how Archie had described his sister-in-law as a terrible meddler. He'd told her in France that he'd cut off contact with her, but here she was, in Vita's life again. Meddling.

'So – Daniel Myers . . . ?'

'What about him?'

'You've snared yourself someone quite important, so I see. Interesting, though, that he thinks you're a widow.'

So she knows, Vita thought, fully sober now, her palms sweating. The feeling that she was caught in a trap only intensified as Georgie took a step closer.

'You always were such a little bundle of lies, weren't you, Anna Darton?' Georgie said, flicking her under the chin condescendingly. Vita bristled at the use of her real name. Georgie stood with her back against the door. 'Oh, yes, I know all about you. I've made it my business.'

'Leave me alone, Georgie.' She stepped towards the door but Georgie remained in place, barring her way. 'Please . . . we have nothing to talk about.'

'Oh, but we do. Because we're practically related,' Georgie said.

'What?' Vita said, confused now.

'Oh don't play the innocent, *Vita*. I know all about what

happened on Digby's yacht – and how you had Archie's baby,' Georgie said, her face close to Vita's. She raised her eyebrows in a challenge.

Vita swallowed hard. How did she know? Who had told her? *Archie?*

'And how you've been here in California with Archie all along.'

'I haven't,' she said. 'I had no idea he was here.'

'I don't believe you,' Georgie said. 'Do you know how upset my sister would be if she knew? About you two? And the baby? She'd be beside herself. You know that she and Archie have been trying and failing to get an heir. Maud is quite distraught. It's only our father's money that is keeping everything afloat at Hartwell. And it could be turned off just like that.' She clicked her fingers. 'Yes, poor Maud. I can only imagine the extent of her wrath should she ever find out the truth.'

Vita closed her eyes and then, clenching her fists, she turned to face Georgie.

'Hartwell . . . your family . . . it has nothing to do with me.'

'Oh, but it has everything to do with you,' Georgie said, with a sly smile. 'And the thing is, Vita, these sordid little scrapes you get yourself into . . . well, I'm prepared to keep them on the hush-hush and not expose you to your new boyfriend. In public, that is. That Hugo Manners strikes me as the kind of man who could make *quite* a story. "The new writer of *The Sister Returns* fathering the love-child of the producer's girlfriend."' She popped out her fingers, like fireworks going off. '*Pow*. Just the kind of salacious gossip everyone loves.' Her eyes glittered at Vita and then she put a finger to her bottom lip, as if pretending to be pensive. 'Although, I can't imagine what Nancy would say if *you* got all the press for her picture, instead of her.'

'Leave Nancy out of this.'

'Oh yes, well, that's what you've been doing, isn't it, Vita? She told me she scooped you up in New York and has paid for you all this time – brought you and Bertie to California and even provided a nanny – and yet, she doesn't seem to know your little secret? Not really how I'd want to be treated, if I was someone's *best* friend.'

'Does Archie know you're here?' Vita asked, thinking about the scene in the canteen and how he'd begged to see Bertie. Was this the way he was intending to make it happen? By sending Georgie? 'Has he sent you?'

'Archie? Oh, Lord, no,' Georgie laughed. 'Archie and I don't really speak. No, he knows nothing about this.' She flapped her hand between them.

'Then what is it you want, Georgie? Why are you here?'

Georgie smiled a sly smile, clearly sensing some kind of victory.

'Well, the thing is, I believe that your husband – your *very much alive* husband – gave you some shares, when you married.'

Vita was confused. What was she talking about? How did she know about Irving? But now Vita remembered the envelope Irving had given her. 'What of it?'

'I happen to want them. Those shares.'

'Hillsafe,' Vita said, remembering now.

This was the last thing in the world she'd been expecting.

This was to do with *money*? This wasn't to do with Bertie after all? Or Archie? She felt relief flooding through her. It was just rich people after money? She should have known. That's all they ever pursued.

'You want the Hillsafe shares?' she checked.

'Yes. That's all. You have no use for them, and I do. That's my bargain. Sign a few papers, and I'll flit away with my mouth closed.'

Vita could hear people outside in the corridor. There was a knock at the door.

'Hurry up in there,' someone called.

'Or, I could . . . well, start scattering a few home truths around the place.'

To Vita's horror, Georgie took out an envelope from her purse. She unfolded the thick papers within.

'All you have to do is sign here,' she said, taking a pen from her purse and holding it out. 'And that will be it. You'll never have to see or hear from me again.'

'You want me to sign these papers? Now?'

Georgie nodded.

'But I need time to read all of this,' Vita said, looking at the densely typed document.

Someone banged more urgently on the door. 'There's a queue,' she heard someone shout. 'Whatever you're doing in there, hurry it up.'

Vita growled with frustration and grabbed the pen from Georgie, who held it out to her. She looked at the share transferral details, her stomach turning over as she signed her name. Irving had told her they were an insurance policy, whatever that meant – but after losing all her money in the stock exchange crash, she doubted the shares were worth very much anyway. What mattered now was that she was finally financially independent, and besides, she had Daniel. Daniel, who'd offered her and Bertie security and a home. And surely those Hillsafe shares were just a link to Irving and to the past? Her life was here now. If signing this paperwork meant getting Georgie out of her life, with her threats, then surely it was a small price to pay?

'Thank you, Vita,' Georgie said, taking the pen and putting the papers back in her bag. 'That wasn't so difficult, was it?'

66

Thirty Love

By the following Sunday after Nancy's party, Vita had just about put the encounter with Georgie to the back of her mind. Daniel had quizzed her about it afterwards and she'd brushed it off, saying that Georgie was a terrible gossip and she'd wanted to talk about people from the past . . . from London. But the feeling that she'd done some kind of deal with the devil had persisted all week, along with her hangover.

A busy week at work had helped, though, and Daniel had insisted on getting her a new car, after the contract on the Ford had expired. The Buick Series 60 Coupe was a dazzling shade of blue with a black retractable roof and white-trimmed wheels, plus a spare on the side. Compared to the Model A, it was enormous, with enough room for five passengers. Vita felt like a queen driving it.

Now she turned into Daniel's driveway, parked the car and lifted Bertie from the back seat, worrying that she was a little early for their lunch date. She walked around the side of the house to where his tennis court was shaded by a line of trees. Four men were playing, two with their backs to her. Daniel waved between shots.

'Thirty love,' she heard him call. She heard the thwack

of a winning serve and saw him slapping his partner on the back, who Vita saw was one of the directors of photography she'd met at the studio. Then there was another serve and a rally, and then Daniel and his partner had won the game. As she walked towards the court the other men were jogging to the net, laughing and slapping each other on the shoulders.

As Vita arrived at the court gate, her step faltered. One of the players on the other team was Archie. He did a double take when he saw her, his smile fading.

Daniel jogged over, opening the gate and kissing Vita, and then kissed Bertie on the head. 'Hey, champ,' he said, but Vita could hardly respond, because behind Daniel, Archie was coming nearer and nearer. His eyes were fixed on Bertie.

'Let's go and get some more drinks,' Daniel said, skipping past Vita towards the side door of the house. The other two players followed, wrapping white towels around their necks, and Vita was left standing with Archie.

'Hello,' Archie said, reaching out to touch Bertie's hair. Vita noticed his eyes were filling with tears. She'd never realized that seeing Bertie and Archie next to each other would be such a monumental shock. Because they were so very alike.

Bertie blew out a raspberry and Archie laughed. 'He's gorgeous,' he said, but there was a catch in his voice. 'He's just like you.'

She looked behind her to make sure Daniel and the others had gone.

'What are you doing here?' she demanded, but her voice sounded strange.

'Daniel's the producer,' Archie said. 'I couldn't exactly refuse his invitation to play, could I?' He stepped closer. 'I promise you, Vita, I'm trying very hard to stay out of your way. I didn't come to Nancy's party, even though Maud wanted to go.'

Vita bristled at the sound of her name. Georgie had talked about Maud at Nancy's party, but Vita hadn't realized she was actually here in Los Angeles. 'I didn't know you'd been invited?'

'Everyone on *The Sister Returns* was. I was the only person who didn't show up, and I've had it shoved down my throat all week, that I missed *the* party.'

Vita shook her head. She didn't care about him missing out. She was glad he'd stayed away. Bertie giggled and reached out and grabbed Archie's fingers. She saw the longing in Archie's eyes, the joy as he drank in Bertie's face, and she moved, breaking their contact.

'Georgie came. She locked me in a cloakroom with her.'

'Did she? What did she want?'

Vita looked behind her, again to check that they couldn't be overheard.

'To blackmail me.'

'Blackmail you?'

'Yes, about you. She knows. She knows about Bertie. And you and me and France. She knows it all. She threatened to expose it all.'

Archie looked ashen. 'How?'

'I don't know. I haven't told a soul.'

'What did you do?'

'Gave her what she wanted.'

'Which was what?'

'She wanted some shares,' Vita said, relieved to be telling

him about the dreadful encounter. 'Some shares of mine that Irving gave me when we got married. In a company called Hillsafe Investments.'

'Why did she want your shares?' Archie asked, confused.

'I don't know,' she said. 'That's what's puzzling me. She made me sign some papers, but something is off. I mean, why would Georgie want shares? Isn't Douglas wealthy?'

'Very,' Archie said. 'Why don't I call Bobby Chartwell in London? He'll do some digging.'

Vita pressed her lips together, remembering the dreadful drive back from Hartwell in the rain, when Archie's friend Bobby had insisted they go back to town. Little had she known that they were driving to Archie's stag night.

'Please don't raise any suspicions, Archie. She said that she's not going to say anything. About us.'

'Vita, please . . .' Archie said, still looking at Bertie. 'I have to see you.'

'No, that's not a good idea.'

'But—'

'Hey, guys, come on,' Daniel called, and Vita broke eye contact and went over to where Daniel was pouring a pitcher of fresh lemonade into some glasses.

Archie arrived a moment later and Daniel handed him a glass. 'I'm afraid I have to go,' Archie said.

'Are you sure? We're going to have lunch after a dip. You should see Bertie swimming. He's hilarious. I never knew a baby so talented. Come here, you,' Daniel said, lifting Bertie out of Vita's arms.

Vita saw Archie watching Daniel, and her heart ached as his eyes followed Bertie.

'Big week this week,' Daniel said. 'We're filming Archie's scenes. You should come and watch, Vita.'

'Oh, I'll be—'

'I'd like that,' Archie said, seizing the moment, and she cast her eyes down, not daring to look at him.

'Thanks for the match, Daniel,' Archie said, putting his glass down. 'So long, Vita.'

Vita nodded, but her heart hurt as he hurried away and she glimpsed his eyes fill with tears.

67
A Close Shave

It was all Clement could do not to sigh out loud as he reclined in the chair, the hot towels caressing his face. He'd been to the barber's regularly, of course, but he'd never encountered this kind of personal care in England. But then, never had he been in so much need of some pampering.

The journey to Los Angeles had been an extraordinary adventure and now, as Clement closed his eyes and allowed himself a rare moment to relax, he found it almost incomprehensible that he'd made it this far. He'd thought he was in serious trouble when he'd been abducted into the truck in Nassau.

It could have been worse, he supposed. The truck could have been going all the way to New Orleans – but instead, it had driven onto a ship at the port. Bill, the driver, had strong-armed him to meet the captain, who had put him to work to earn his crossing with Jacques, the French chef.

Clement had never once prepared a meal for himself in his life, and it had come as a shock to find himself peeling potatoes and washing pots as Jacques regaled him with tales of his misadventures around the world. Clement had been appalled at first, but then quite intrigued. Soon, he had found himself laughing at the boisterous Frenchman's anecdotes.

Clement had planned to jump ship when they'd docked briefly at Fort Lauderdale, thinking that he might find an easier route to Los Angeles, but Jacques had stopped him, telling him that he'd be safer staying on the ship as it chugged around the coastline. He was glad he'd stayed on board, because by the time they'd reached Tampa and Tallahassee, Jacques had got Clement a place at the crew's poker table – where, to everyone's surprise, including his own, he'd won five straight nights in a row. He'd known then that his luck had changed.

His pockets full of grubby dollar bills, when they'd docked at New Orleans he'd slipped off the boat, with Jacques covering for him in return for a very healthy bribe. It had been dark and the docks had been full of hoodlums. It had taken all Clement's wits to make it to the bright lights of Storyville, the neighbourhood he'd heard the crew talking about, where prostitution was rife and anyone could find solace – rich, poor, black or white. He hadn't been expecting such a colourful scene, with restaurants on every corner, the smell of fried chicken making his mouth water. He'd eaten hungrily outside a bar, watching a brass band marching down the street and the people dancing on the sidewalks, rejoicing in his freedom. It was almost impossible to believe he'd escaped the boat. Jacques really must have covered well for him, but he knew that he'd better not stay in plain sight for long.

On a tip-off from a barman, he'd talked himself into an upscale brothel with a piano player in the salon. The old-fashioned room had ruched curtains at the windows and lots of exotic-looking houseplants in large pots amongst the overstuffed sofas. Girls lurked on the stairways in low-cut corsets, the madam keeping a watchful eye on them as she served Clement a julep in a dainty glass, simpering at the presence of a true English gentleman in the house. It had been the first time he'd been treated with any kind of respect since leaving New York, and Clement had lapped up the attention gratefully. When the madam had asked for his preferred choice of girl, he'd told her he was looking for a blonde, but instead he'd chosen Hissy, as he heard her speaking French.

Hissy was a creole of colour, the madam had explained, and one of her best girls. She had the smoothest skin Clement had ever touched, and her lustrous dark hair smelt of coconuts. She'd given him a bath and a shave and had massaged his aching body in a way he'd never been touched before, explaining that her mother had been black and she didn't know who her father was, but she'd heard he, too, was an English gentleman.

Afterwards she'd pleasured him with her mouth in the most remarkable way before opening the French windows onto the cast-iron balcony. They'd sat and watched the world go by below and for the first time in weeks, Clement had let himself relax a little. Dixieland jazz had filtered up as they'd smoked her special tobacco, which made him feel fuzzy and light-headed. Lulled by the warm breeze and so thankful to be on dry land, Clement had found himself confessing his woes and how he needed to get to Los Angeles. Hissy had pointed to the tracks leading to the Canal Street terminal and given him the name of a man he could find there, who could sort out false papers for him.

Clement applauded himself for flying by the seat of his pants and becoming a man of the world. Yes, he rather liked being 'Gerard Collier', the name on his new identity papers. In LA, he'd checked into a half-decent hotel and had been shopping in the store next door. He'd purchased a hat and a fine linen suit, which the concierge had assured him were extremely dapper. And he did feel dapper, although he didn't trust these Americans and the way they wished him a pleasant day everywhere he went. He couldn't tell if anyone was being truthful.

'You should watch your back in this city,' the barber told him now, scraping the long blade against his chin, then wiping the foam on his towel. 'There's the rich folk up in their mansions, but there's a dark side to this place too.'

'Oh?'

'There's plenty of sick folk who come here to die, there's crazy religious folk who will spirit you away to a cult if you're not careful. There's people who refuse to believe in science, and' – he leant forward and added in a confidential tone – 'a whole pansy scene.'

'Well, you might be able to help me out. I'm looking for someone from that . . . persuasion. Have you heard of a place called Jimmy's Backyard?'

The barber looked at Clement with alarm in the mirror. 'Sure. It's over on Cosmo Street. But you be careful in that neighbourhood, sir. And that bar in particular.'

'Oh, I will,' Clement said, but his resolve to get his revenge on Tebby had only hardened. If he was here in Los Angeles, as he'd said he might be, then Clement was determined to find him and make him pay.

But first he had a job to do, although it was turning out to be more difficult than he'd anticipated. Los Angeles was far bigger than he'd been expecting. He only knew that Vita and Nancy were working in motion pictures. How would he ever find out where they were actually located?

He thought of Renata King and her beady-eyed stare. *You're an intelligent man. I'm sure you'll find a way*. The words echoed in his head.

The barber wiped his chin and Clement stood up, feeling human for the first time in ages. He thanked the barber and tipped him.

'Thank you, sir. Is there anything else I can help you with?'

'Only if you could help me find my secret crush,' Clement said with a light laugh. 'It is my greatest desire to meet a certain actress. She's called Nancy Delaney.'

'Oh, celebrities aren't hard to track down,' the barber said. 'You just need to read the papers.'

'Which publication should I get?'

'Any number of them. Try Hugo Manners' gossip column,' the man said helpfully, handing over a newspaper. 'He usually charts all the goings-on.'

68

Triumph

Edith could hardly contain a smile as she sat in her chair at Madame Mensforth's salon. In fact, she was so pleased that she wanted to pinch herself. She'd never known it was possible to feel this happy.

The only thing nagging at her was that she still hadn't heard anything from Mr Warren – or from Clement, for that matter. But the longer he stayed away, the better.

Mercifully, however, after an agonizing wait, she'd heard from Georgie, who sent the paperwork that Vita had signed. It was due to arrive at Hillsafe any day now. And then . . . *then* Edith's plan would be complete. Theresa had swung completely around to Edith's way of thinking, and things at Darton Hall were better than they'd ever been.

Of course, it wasn't just because Clement was currently out of their lives. It was because of the delicious secret that seemed to fill her with light and joy.

Nick, oh, Nick.

She couldn't stop thinking about him, her mind pawing over every detail of their exquisite evening in her study. And then there had been the encounter yesterday morning. He'd called her at the office and without preamble had said, 'Let's go for a drive. I'll pick you up at lunchtime.'

She'd cancelled her meetings, then shut the office doors, redoing her make-up and changing in the small bathroom into her best suit. At noon, she'd looked out of the office window and seen the roof of his pale-blue sports car. She'd checked her make-up once more and, telling Mrs Dunlop that she was going out, tripped down the back stairs and straight into the car.

Nick had smiled tightly at her as she settled into the seat and she'd braced herself, knowing that he wanted to talk to her about Helen and how guilty he felt. But actions and words were very different, Edith thought.

'Isn't it a glorious day? Where are we going?' she asked.

'Somewhere where we can talk alone,' he said. 'Not here.'

He glanced up at the mill and she followed his gaze, feeling its eyes on her. 'I know just the place.'

They drove out to the countryside, crossing the river at the old stone bridge. Below it, the crystal-clear water bubbled over the stones and they followed the road along the river, stopping to wait for a herd of sheep to cross. The hedgerows were alive with nesting birds, the banks either side of the road filled with daffodils.

'Here,' Edith pointed, and they turned up a shaded lane into the forest. Ahead of them the trees were dense, the forest floor covered in a haze of bluebells. When Nick turned the engine off, the air was filled with the chirrup of birds.

'Oh, Nick. Look. Isn't it gorgeous?'

He didn't say anything, but he hung his head. 'Edith . . . about the other day . . . We have to talk.'

'Please, Nick, don't regret it. I don't.'

She reached out and touched his face, looking into his eyes, seeing that he was torn with guilt and self-loathing. But she saw too that he was powerless to resist her. In a moment, she crossed the divide between their seats, and they were kissing.

Her body strained towards him as his hand searched for her, moving up her skirt, and she gasped as he touched her. She pulled away briefly and flung off her hat, pulled off her jacket and began undoing her skirt, but he couldn't wait. They tumbled into the back seat and then he was on top of her, kissing her neck, her ear, her lips, pulling aside her bra to find her nipples. Daringly, deliciously, she released him from his trousers and opened her legs, easing him inside her as she moved beneath him, the heat building and building within her.

'Wait,' he said, pulling away. Moving down, he wrapped his hands around her thighs and pressed his mouth into her, and she cried out as a great crescendo of pleasure overtook her. Then, while she was still lost, he was back inside her and the sensation suddenly burst into a whole new dimension. She heard him gasp as his own release came.

Exhausted, he held her, and she looked up at the roof of the car as they both tried to catch their breath, hearts pounding.

'Oh, Edith. Oh God. What are you doing to me?'

She smiled and stroked his hair, pulling his face away so that she could kiss him. The shame and guilt that had been written all over his features before was now replaced by something else.

'Don't be sorry,' she whispered. 'I'm not. I haven't been able to stop thinking about you. About us. About this . . .'

He kissed her then – deeply, fully – and she knew that he was hers.

'You look very well, Mrs Darton,' Miss Keys said, breaking her delicious reverie.

'I am well,' she said. 'Thank you.'

'I heard about the Cotton Queen Quest,' the hairdresser went on. 'Everyone has been talking about it. We've had so many girls wanting beauty treatments and their hair styled for their photographs.'

Edith glowed with satisfaction. It was on the tip of her tongue to tell Miss Keys that it had all been her own idea, but she could afford to be modest. Instead, she raised one eyebrow archly in the mirror. 'Not so bad to be a mill girl after all, is it?'

69

Undone

At the studio, Vita knew that they were filming Archie's scenes for *The Sister Returns* today and that she'd agreed to go; but as the day wore on, she made excuse after excuse not to leave Percy's office. She couldn't bear the thought of seeing Archie and Daniel again in the same place. Then, at six o'clock, Daniel called Mrs Chafin to ask Percy to release Vita from her duties and send her over to the sound stage. She couldn't put it off any longer.

Before she left, Vita called Evelyn.

'Bertie is fine. I'm taking him back to the gatehouse now,' Evelyn said. 'Don't you fret.'

'I'll be back as soon as I can,' Vita said, realizing that yet again she'd be missing bath and bedtime. She knew Bertie was in the safest hands with Evelyn, but still she wished she could work somewhere closer – somewhere where she could just pop back during the day for a little cuddle with him. Once she'd got through the gates of the studio, the days seemed to rush past with hardly a moment to think about her life outside.

'Oh, no, please don't rush back,' Evelyn said. 'I have knitting, and besides, Mr Myers telephoned earlier on.'

'Did he?' Vita asked.

'He said he's taking you and Nancy out after the shoot.'

'Oh,' Vita said, surprised that Daniel was comfortable enough to make domestic arrangements with Evelyn. Her conscience pricked with guilt. Daniel was continuing their relationship as if they were heading towards the future they'd talked about together, but somehow, Vita had secretly put the brakes on her own feelings. She knew she owed it to him to come clean – but what would she say? It was just too complex and confusing.

'He sent a fine present for Bertie,' Evelyn went on. 'It arrived today. A big stroller.'

'That was very thoughtful of him. I'll be sure to thank him.'

'You do that. And say hello from me.'

Vita checked her make-up and, nerves jangling, walked through the small door to the sound stage.

The giant set for *The Sister Returns* had been built in sections but everyone was focused on the far side, where a bedroom scene was lit up. Daniel was sitting in a canvas-backed chair and she smiled at him, waving and walking over, deliberately not looking around for Archie.

'You're finally here,' Daniel said, standing and kissing her cheek.

'It's been a long day,' she told him. 'How's it going here?' She was distracted by the sight of Nancy reclining on a four-poster bed, the camera at one end of it.

'Vita,' Nancy called, seeing her and waving her over. 'Hey, kiddo!'

'Can I?' Vita asked Daniel.

'Sure,' he said.

Vita walked onto the set. 'Nice work to be paid for being in bed all day,' she teased. Nancy winced, holding up her forearm as a gaffer on a tall ladder readjusted the light, which was on a metal grid above the set and shining directly into her eyes.

'It may look easy, but working with Harold is somewhat trying,' she said in a low whisper, flicking her eyes towards the back of the set.

'That's him?' Vita asked, looking over to where the famous actor stood smoking a cigarette. He had greased-back hair, and his long plaid dressing gown made him look more like an old man than a Hollywood sex symbol.

'What's he like?'

'His moustache is tickly,' Nancy whispered. 'It's very strange kissing him. We've done four takes so far.'

Vita laughed. 'I wish I had my camera,' she said. 'What would Evelyn say if she could see you in that negligée?'

'Oh, this old thing,' Nancy smiled, looking down at what she was wearing. 'Actually, can you pin it?' she asked. 'It doesn't fit on this shoulder.'

She sat forward and Vita bunched in the fabric at the back, reaching into her pocket for the safety pins she always carried.

'We're almost ready to go. Places, please,' someone called. Vita smiled at Nancy and retreated from the set. 'Good luck.'

'I hope this is the last take. Daniel says we're going for dinner,' Nancy said. 'And I'm famished.'

Vita stood back, watching from the shadows as Nancy

shuffled up in the bed so that Harold could get in next to her. He took off his plaid robe and Vita saw that he was fully dressed on his bottom half, including shoes. Vita was so amused by the look on Nancy's face that she didn't notice Archie sneaking up next to her.

'Vita!'

Startled, she turned to face him.

'I was hoping you'd come,' he said quietly into her ear. 'Did you get the present I sent for Bertie?'

'What present?'

'The stroller?'

'That was from you?'

'It's the least I could do. I want to contribute.'

Vita looked over at Daniel, who was talking to the director. She'd so nearly thanked him for the gift. And how on earth was she going to explain it to Evelyn, who was bound to say something?

'I wish you hadn't. It makes things . . . complicated.'

He looked embarrassed. 'I'm sorry, Vita. It's just that ever since I saw Bertie—'

'Please don't,' she said, cutting him off. 'I don't want Daniel to see us together like this.'

She moved away, towards Daniel, wanting to be in his orbit and safely away from Archie.

'Wait,' he said, holding onto her arm. 'I called Bobby. Bobby Chartwell.' Vita turned back. 'About the Hillsafe shares,' he added.

'What did he say?'

'Well – Hillsafe, they're just an investment broker – but, Vita . . .'

'What?'

'Quiet, everyone,' Vita heard the director shout, and the lights changed.

'Bobby said he'd pulled in a favour from a secretary there, who told him that Hillsafe bought shares in Darton Mill in your name. Isn't Darton . . . isn't that where your family are from?' Archie whispered.

The room tilted.

It's all thanks to Marianne. She suggested you might want financial independence . . . Irving's words rang clearly in Vita's memory now.

She'd had shares in Darton all along? And now she'd signed them over to Georgie . . .

Vita could hardly breathe. There was total silence on the set; everyone around them was watching Nancy and Harold kissing on the bed. Then Nancy turned away and stretched, smiling luxuriously.

'That's a big smile,' Harold said. 'You look like the cat that got the cream.'

'I feel like the cat that got the cream. I feel . . . undone.'

Vita turned to look over to where Archie stood in the darkness, finding his eyes, and her insides were weightless for a second. Because those were the very words that they'd spoken to one another after they'd first made love. And as the words echoed down the years, she felt undone herself – all over again.

She turned to walk away from the set, desperate for some air and some space, and to try and stop this feeling that she was unravelling. This impossible situation with Archie was snowballing, and she had no power to stop it. As she walked towards the door, she had the urge to keep on walking. Walking and walking away. But where to?

And then it hit her. She wanted to go home. To her mother. She wanted England. She wanted Darton. And she could have had that all along.

Only now, it was too late.

70

Into the Night

It had taken forever for the sun to set, but finally it was almost dark, the sky spreading out over the city an array of deep purples and mauves. Clement looked out at the view from the back of his cab as it snaked around the hairpin bends on the way up to Beverly Hills. He was thinking that this place was far too foreign: the daylight too bright, the nights too strange, the sky altogether too wide. He longed for the drizzle and the green valleys of home.

It was the people, too, that had set him on edge. He was still reeling from his visit to Jimmy's Backyard, a terrifying club where he'd seen things he'd never thought possible: men dressed as women, women dressed as men, singing bawdy songs and making filthy innuendoes as everyone posed and preened – and not a policeman in sight! Several men had approached him and one of them had . . . Clement closed his eyes, pinching the memory away, hardly able to admit to himself what had happened. The room at the back, the naked men, the scene of debauchery that he'd never get over. The music and smoke . . . all of it seemed like a dream, but it hadn't been a dream. It made him feel breathless and shocked to even think about it. It had felt afterwards as if he'd dabbled in the very depths of sin – but that was as far as he would ever go, he assured himself. He was done with Los Angeles. Done. Very soon he'd be on his way out of here, and then back to sanity.

He clutched the piece of paper, warm in his fingers, as he craned his neck out of the window to make sure he was on the right street.

'Here, here,' he said, leaning forward to tap the back of the driver's seat. He'd been up here yesterday and the guide, with some prompting from Clement, had shown off his local knowledge by revealing that this was the very house where there'd been a big party hosted by the new star, Miss Nancy Delaney.

Clement couldn't get his head around the adulation that people in this town bestowed upon actors. They were just puppets. It was hardly a respectable way for a grown-up person to make a living.

'You'll wait. Wait here,' he said, not sure if the Indian-looking man spoke good enough English to understand.

The cab driver, who had stopped on the kerb, nodded.

'I have to pick up my kid, you see. My child,' Clement clarified.

'Child,' the driver nodded.

'Yes, and we're going to the station. You will drive us there. To the train station?'

He turned his wrist, hoping to see the time on his new watch. He'd be cutting it fine to make the overnight train, and he tapped the ticket he'd bought in his pocket. The relief that he was leaving Los Angeles felt more solid than anything had since his arrival.

Clement peeled off some dollar bills from the stack in his pocket and passed them to the driver. In this town, bribery was everything, it seemed – especially with the filthy immigrants. The man's demeanour changed.

'I wait. I understand,' he said, nodding.

Clement closed the cab door quietly and walked up to the drive of the dark mansion, limping without his stick. In the light of the street lamp, he looked down the deserted road, listening to the trill of cicadas. He wiped the sweat from his brow. A fox stopped some distance away, staring at him. The night seemed to pulse with heat and danger.

He moved across the front of the driveway, standing still by the shadow of the trees that lined its curve. Through them, he could see that the main house had fewer lights on than he'd expected. He started up the drive, but just as he came to the first corner he saw a small cottage, the windows lit up. He'd go there first, he decided, creeping up to the path that led to the front door, which he saw now was open, a screen across it. He crept closer. Inside, he could hear a radio playing. He swatted an insect that buzzed against his temple. This was most probably where Nancy's security guy lived, Clement thought, wishing he'd had the nerve to buy a gun. Instead, he reached into his jacket for the hammer he'd taken from the handyman's toolbox at the hotel, gripping and re-gripping it in his palm.

He crept up the two steps to the door and the screen squeaked as he pushed it open. A small white dog started barking furiously, trying to jump up. Clement took a well-aimed hit with the hammer and the dog skidded across the kitchen floor, where it hit a table leg and lay still. Clement wiped the sweat from his brow, looking desperately around him, the soppy voices of a radio soap opera crackling.

'What you doing, Mr Wild?'

It was a woman's voice and, for a moment, Clement thought she might be addressing him. 'Hush your mouth. You'll wake my baby—'

Now a portly black woman in her fifties, wearing a navy dress, came in from the corridor to the kitchen. She stopped when she saw Mr Wild on the floor and then, after a split-second pause, she inhaled, about to let rip a scream. Clement limped across to her in two bounds and put his hand over her mouth.

'You'll be quiet,' he said, leading her to a kitchen chair and forcing her to sit down. He took a cloth that was hanging over the rail of the cooker and stuffed it into her mouth, although the woman was surprisingly strong. She thrashed around, and he picked up the hammer that had fallen from his grip. Her eyes widened as she saw it and, with all her might, she reared up at him, but he hit her hard in the face. He heard some bones crunch, and she slumped back onto the chair. Blood gushed down her dress.

He grabbed a ball of wool that was lying in the basket next to some knitting needles on the table, then wound it around the woman as tightly as he could, the yellow wool digging into the brown flesh of her arm. Confident that her torso was pinned to the back of the chair, he tied off the wool. Then he went to the kitchen blind and, taking scissors from a drawer, cut the string and tied her ankles to the legs of the chair.

Satisfied that she was as inactive as the dog, he picked

up the hammer again and crept to the corridor she'd come through. He pushed open one of the doors and saw a neatly made bed and a row of windows overlooking a small garden. Then he pushed open the other door and saw a cot.

There was a very low light on and, as Clement crept across the rug, he saw a blonde baby lying in the cot, playing with its toes, looking at a mobile that cast shadows on the wall. Clement looked at the baby, then at the framed photograph of his sister holding the same baby.

'Well,' he said aloud, shocked that he'd found Anna's baby so easily and there was no sign of his sister.

This, then, is surely meant to be.

The baby giggled and smiled at Clement, who stared down at his nephew, shocked by the enormity of what he was doing. For a second, he felt scared of lifting up the child. Could he really take this baby out of this cot, out of this room, out of this house and into the night?

Then he thought of Renata King and what she'd offered him. In reality, he was just performing a service: delivering the baby to another relative. He stared into the baby's big blue eyes, recognizing so much of his sister in them. And for the first time in a very long while, he smiled. Because finally, *finally*, he'd found a way to hurt her.

His mind whirred into action. He knew he'd need supplies for the journey back to New York, but, never having had a baby of his own, he hadn't the first clue as to what to pack.

He found a suitcase under the bed in the other bedroom and filled it with cotton diapers and some spare clothes. Then he shut it and, carrying the suitcase in one hand, picked up the baby. He was surprisingly heavy, and Clement carried him awkwardly under his arm.

The black maid was coming round, reaching out for the child and making a terrible sound of distress, her face already swelling up in an ugly purple welt. He cursed himself for not doing a better job. The child started to cry. Clement tried to rearrange him in his arms and roughly jogged him.

'Don't cry,' he told the child, but his cry turned into a wail.

The maid made a strangled, terrified sound as Clement passed her and went to open the door. She started shuffling on the chair, trying to move it, her one good eye wide with terror.

Clement shook his head and put the suitcase down for a moment, then walked over to her and pushed the chair over. And the old woman was still.

71

Unwelcome News

In all the time that Edith had known her, Theresa Darton had never come to the mill, but ever since Edith had taken her to London to see Mr Heal, she'd taken much more of an interest in the business. Edith was surprised at her extensive knowledge of the mills, the workers and everything that went on. She was much more business-minded than Edith had ever realized. She looked more the part, too, after their lunch and shopping trip to Withshaw and Taylor, where Edith had commanded a first-class service and a hefty discount on the six outfits she had insisted Theresa purchase. Theresa had been reluctant to abandon her black garb, but Edith had been adamant, and although it had been like cajoling a child, after a while, with the fawning attention of the assistants, she could tell that Theresa had started enjoying herself. They'd been to the Harrods salon, too, where Theresa had had her hair subtly dyed and restyled and had even been persuaded into some new make-up.

Edith looked up from her desk now and waved a friendly greeting over to where Theresa was talking to Mrs Dunlop outside her office.

Today, Theresa was in the lovely green tweed suit, with

a matching green hat. With her dark hair curled beneath it, she looked ten years younger. Edith had noticed with some surprise that Theresa had a shapely figure and fine legs. *That's where Vita must have got them from*, she thought, her mind casting back to the long-ago day when she'd challenged Vita to high kicks on the roof of the Zip Club.

She smiled to herself at the memory. Vita clearly hadn't had the first clue how to dance, but she'd been so defiant. In some ways, she'd been a very worthy adversary. It was only now that time had passed, and Edith had found out the truth about Vita and realized why she'd run away from Darton, that she understood how brave she'd been.

And now Vita was in Los Angeles, Edith mused, thinking about her signing over her shares in Darton. Georgie had told Edith on the phone that it had been a very easy transaction. Vita clearly had a life there – a producer boyfriend, Edith had heard, and a job designing at the MGM Studios. She obviously no longer felt any emotional attachment to Darton and knowing this made Edith feel vindicated in everything she'd done.

Theresa walked into the office as Edith finished signing the invoices.

'Oh, Theresa. How lovely that you're in again. I've just had these samples in—'

But she stopped as she saw the expression on her mother-in-law's face.

'What is it?'

'I came straight away because I received a telegram this morning,' Theresa said, shutting the door and approaching Edith's desk. 'From Clement.'

'Clement? What did he say? Where is he?'

'He's in New York. He says he's secured investment in Darton in the States.'

'*Investment?*'

Theresa took a telegram from the snakeskin handbag on her arm. Her expression was grave as she passed it to Edith, who stood up and unfolded the flimsy paper.

'He says that we're going into partnership with King Enterprises. And look, he says that he's travelling home on the Cunard, and we're to have Hetherington pick him up on Saturday.'

Edith swallowed a rising tide of panic, reading the last sentence saying exactly that. 'Saturday?'

'What will he say when he finds out what you've done?' Theresa asked. She looked worried.

Edith scanned over the abrupt words, bristling at Clement's triumphant tone and the fact that he'd written to his mother and not to her.

This couldn't be happening. Edith had paid Warren to detain Clement in the States. That had been their agreement. She'd told Mr Warren all about Clement's weakness for gambling and whores, and he had said that he'd have no problem whatsoever helping Edith out. He had an associate, Tebby, he'd told her, who would be up to the job.

And, as the silence from the States had gone on longer and longer and Edith had succeeded in reaching Vita before Clement, she'd started to hope that Clement really had disappeared for good.

But clearly not.

Instead, he'd done some sort of deal. How could he have

secured finance in their business with King Enterprises? Because surely it couldn't be the same King as Vita's husband? What did this mean?

'Well?' Theresa demanded.

Edith had to keep her nerve. She couldn't let Theresa see how derailed she felt by this news.

'This doesn't change anything. Whatever he thinks he's done, it's too late. We can tell him about Hillsafe and our meeting with the lawyer. I'm in charge now, Theresa. That's what we agreed. He can't do anything without my say-so.'

'But—'

'Theresa, trust me. Clement's reign of terror is over,' Edith said. 'He's not going to push us around any longer. The steps we've taken mean that Darton is safe. And Susan is safe.'

Theresa nodded, acknowledging this fact, but Edith's smile felt tight on her face. She thought back to her meeting with Mr Warren again. If only she'd had the guts to ask him to do worse. He'd offered to detain Clement 'permanently', but she'd said that wouldn't be necessary. *Oh, but if only he had.*

Because what about her and Nick? How would Edith see him when Clement was breathing down her neck? She had to move things forward. She had to get Nick to commit to leaving Helen, now. Then, when he got home, she could demand a divorce from Clement, and the whole new chapter she'd been dreaming about could begin.

72

By Plane and Train

The shrill whistle woke Vita, although she could only have been dozing for the last few minutes. For one split second she thought it all must have been a terrible nightmare, but then, like a bucket of cold water being tipped over her, she remembered.

She pulled the blind a little way up next to the bed in the train carriage where she'd spent the last tormented hours, and was relieved to see the dawn light breaking across the vast American plains. She sat up and hugged her knees, the familiar tears that had overwhelmed her constantly coming again, as snatches of scenes from the past forty-eight hours flashed across her mind.

She pictured herself at the dinner with Nancy, Harold, the director, Daniel and some of the crew after they'd wrapped the scene from *The Sister Returns*, finding it unbelievable now that she'd sat in a restaurant while her baby was being snatched. She remembered how her mind had been whirring, hardly able to look at Daniel, as she went over the lines that Archie had written and the message they contained. Because it had meant he wanted her to remember the promise he'd made to love her forever. It had felt so important, so confusing, but how self-indulgent and unimportant that seemed now.

It shocked her that even as she'd driven Nancy home, she hadn't had any sense of what was about to happen. Nancy had been tired and sozzled from too much wine and Vita had driven past the gatehouse so that she could drop her right outside her door, promising that she'd send Evelyn up right away.

She remembered now how she'd reversed back down to the gatehouse, parking the car in the darkness, and then rested her forehead on the steering wheel, taking her time, wanting a few moments alone to gather herself.

It was only when she'd seen the screen door of the gatehouse was open that she'd thought something was strange. When she'd approached and Mr Wild hadn't barked, she'd called out for Evelyn. Then she'd pushed open the screen door and had cried out when she'd seen the devastating scene: Evelyn tied to a kitchen chair on the floor, her face and hair covered in blood, Mr Wild whimpering with pain. And worst, worst of all, had been the shocking sight of Bertie's empty cot – his favourite toy rabbit abandoned on the floor.

Hours had crawled past after that, each minute a torture, as the police arrived and Vita gave a description of Bertie. Ericka had turned up, armed with two journalists and a photographer, keen to snap the devastated starlet and hear about the baby that had been abducted from her home. Vita had remembered Ericka telling Nancy that she needed to be newsworthy to be famous, but she'd never thought that Bertie being abducted was the news that would do it. The press had latched on to the story, not least because Nancy had played the shocked starlet perfectly.

'He's like a son to me,' Nancy had sobbed out on the driveway, illuminated by the photographer's lights. They'd taken pictures of Bertie's empty cot, and of poor Mr Wild before the vet had come to take him.

Evelyn had been taken to hospital in an ambulance and Nancy had gone with her, the press trailing behind. Daniel had come straight over and, as the hours had dragged on waiting for news, Vita had contemplated the worst scenarios possible while he'd tried to reassure her that the police were doing everything they could. But Vita couldn't be comforted.

Then, as light had seeped into Nancy's house – the beautiful day like a cruel insult – a cab driver had heard the story on the news and come forward. He'd confirmed that he'd picked up a man and a baby at Nancy's address and dropped them near the train station. When the man, contrite and sorry, had described Bertie screaming all the way, it had almost torn Vita in two.

And then, worst of all, was Percy's visit. He'd heard the news and arrived full of concern for Bertie, taking Vita into Nancy's bedroom for some privacy.

'Who would do something like this?' she'd cried as Percy held her in his arms. 'Percy, I've got to get my baby back. They're checking the trains, but someone has already taken him God knows where . . .'

'Vita,' he'd said, mopping her tears, 'I don't want to have to tell you this, but I came over as soon as I heard.'

'Tell me what?'

And then he'd told her about how Doug, his partner, had insisted on meeting some friends and how they'd wanted to see a drag act. They'd ended up in Jimmy's Backyard, the infamous bar, the night before last, and Percy had seen a blond man with a limp. A man who had seemed so familiar that Percy had left straight away.

'I told myself I was just seeing things,' he told her. 'I thought at the time that I must be going mad . . . hallucinating . . . conjuring a painful past. But it can't be a coincidence, can it? That Clement could be here in town, and now Bertie has gone?'

'Clement?' Vita pulled at her hair in anguish. 'You saw Clement? Oh, Percy, no. No, no, no . . .'

Then Nancy had come back from the hospital, wrung out and worried about Evelyn, who'd been given a sedative. The vet had called saying that Mr Wild was in a critical condition and they'd have to operate on his head.

Vita and Nancy had sat on the sofa by the pool under some blankets while Daniel went to make coffee. Numb with horror, they'd stared silently at the telephone on the table in front of them. When it rang, they'd both yelped. Vita had leant forward to grab it.

'Is that Miss Casey?'

The woman on the end of the phone had explained in a hushed tone that she was a friend of Evelyn's, calling from New York. Vita was about to start explaining that Evelyn was being treated in hospital and still had a broken jawbone and concussion, when the woman told her that her name was Iris and she was calling from Renata King's residence. And that's when Vita had remembered the silent maid she'd met, the day she'd been summoned for an audience with Irving's mother.

'The thing is, Miss Casey, your brother has just arrived at the apartment in New York.'

Vita had been silent, thinking that she must have misheard.

'And the darndest thing. He came with a child.'

'Bertie?'

Nancy had leapt up to put her head next to Vita's by the phone. She gripped onto her wrist.

'Yes. That's the thing. Evelyn showed me a picture of that little boy. She loves him, you see, and she was so excited about going to California to look after him.'

'Is he safe?'

'Yes, he's safe. He's with me.'

'Oh, Iris,' Vita had said, with a sob. 'I'm on my way. Don't let him out of your sight.'

Daniel had pulled out all the stops, just as Vita knew he would. He'd wanted to tell the cops, but Vita had been too scared. She'd persuaded him that it was better to call them once they'd got Bertie back. Because what if Clement eluded them once again, and they lost their chance of rescuing Bertie?

She'd had to leave the house with a blanket over her head, avoiding the press who'd been camping out on the drive, while Nancy had prepared to give them an interview.

Daniel had driven Vita to an airfield where his friend Harry had booked them on one of his flights to Chicago. Vita had never flown before, but she was in no state to appreciate the experience and spent the whole time with her eyes closed, the turbulence making her panic.

In Chicago, they'd boarded an express train late last night and now, this morning, Vita would finally get Bertie back.

The door of the train compartment slid back and Daniel looked in, smiling gently when she turned towards him.

'You're awake,' he said. 'We'll be in Penn Station in an hour. I've ordered tea.'

She nodded. 'Thank you.'

'Did you sleep?'

'Not much. You?'

He shrugged lightly, not answering, and came to sit beside her, taking her hand and stroking it as if she were the most precious thing in the world. 'We'll get him back, Vita. Very soon. Then it will all be over, and we can go home. There's a return train we can catch at six tonight.'

She nodded, grateful that he'd come with her. Grateful that he was looking after her. She held his hand on her lap.

'And then – well, I've been thinking. I want you to feel safe, and I think you and Bertie should come and live at my place. I want us to be together, Vita. I want to take care of you.'

She nodded, but more tears were coming, not least of all because she knew somewhere deep down inside that she wouldn't be returning to California. Not until she'd untangled her past. Not until she'd set the record straight, or worked out the connection between Clement and that vile old woman.

She had been thinking all night about Renata King: how fixated the old woman had seemed on the idea of having an heir, and how Vita had snubbed her by coming to Los Angeles instead of bending to her wishes. She'd threatened her with rumours and Vita had been worried at the time, but she'd never imagined that Renata would stoop as low as this.

'Daniel, we have to talk,' she said. 'There's so much—'

There was a knock on the door. 'Ah, the tea,' Daniel said.

He gave her a small smile. 'Just for you, Vita. Haven't you always said that tea makes everything better?'

She nodded, feeling bereft, knowing that tea was not going to work this time.

'I'm serious, Daniel. We need to talk.' She had to tell him. She had to confess everything – about Irving and Archie and Bertie.

'Let's get Bertie back, and then there'll be all the time in the world for talking.'

He leant forward and kissed her forehead, and Vita, feeling wretched, tried to muster a weak smile.

73

Irving Makes a Stand

Vita was buzzing with lack of sleep and adrenaline as they got out of the cab outside Renata King's apartment. She stepped onto the sidewalk and looked up at the vast building, the rain stinging her eyes.

After the interminable journey, they were finally here. She hoped Iris had been as good as her word, and that Bertie was in there.

Her baby. She ached to hold him so much, she thought she might break. She just had to get past Renata first.

'Please stop worrying,' Daniel said as they went inside, but the elevator man barred their way.

'No visitors to the penthouse today. I'm sorry,' he said sternly.

'But I'm visiting Iris,' Vita insisted.

'I've got my instructions, miss. If you want Iris, try the service elevator.'

He nodded towards a door and Vita and Daniel rushed through a maze of corridors until they found themselves in a loading bay. It took a hefty bribe to get one of the porters to let them use the service elevator.

Vita couldn't stop shaking as the cage lift arrived and

they stepped out into a corridor leading to a kitchen, with two enormous cookers and a refrigerator. There was no sign of Iris. Vita and Daniel made their way through the kitchen and emerged into the marble hallway.

'Wow,' Daniel murmured as they walked through to the main room, awed by the view. Vita's eyes were already scanning the space. Remembering her previous visit, she rushed over to the far door, desperate to find Bertie. She flung it open and then stopped, her breath catching as she saw a familiar figure standing by the window. He was wearing a coat, as if he too had only just arrived.

'Irving,' Vita said, her eyes locking with her ex-husband's.

'Ah,' he said, turning to her. 'Well, well . . . Vita.' He shook his head, and she saw that he was just as surprised to see her as she was him. 'I happened to be in town and read about it in the papers,' he said, holding up a newspaper and throwing it onto the sofa, dispensing with any greeting. 'How a baby had been abducted. And then I saw a picture of Nancy, and put two and two together.'

Vita stared at him, her stomach churning. 'Your mother . . . she stole my baby,' she said. Irving shook his head and held up a hand. He clearly hadn't finished.

'In fact, I was so worried, I called on the Delaneys. I've invested with Patrick Delaney's brokerage in the past, but do you know what he told me?' he said.

Vita pressed her lips together. All the times she'd ever said a bad word about Irving rushed through her mind.

'Well? Do you, Vita?'

Vita shook her head, although she knew full well. She felt her face flushing.

'He called me something unspeakable. He called me a *wife-beater*. I'm many things, Vita, but was I ever cruel to you?'

'No, of course not . . .'

'Then what in the Sam Hill have you said to make him think that? Well?' His voice was raised.

'Irving, I . . .'

Now she felt Daniel beside her, taking her hand. 'Vita, who is this guy?' he asked.

'I could ask the same of you, sir,' Irving said.

'I'm Vita's . . . Vita's boyfriend,' Daniel said confidently. Vita noticed him puffing out his chest. 'Well, more than that. We're engaged,' he added, and she turned to him, shocked that he thought she'd agreed to marry him.

She'd never seen Daniel be anything but in control and relaxed, but he wasn't now. He squeezed her hand and smiled at her, but nervously. His eyes searched hers, waiting for her to confirm his words.

Irving gave a short, derisive laugh and tucked his hands into the pockets of his jacket. 'Oh, are you indeed?'

'And you are?' Daniel probed, riled.

'Her husband.'

Daniel stared at Irving for a long moment, then turned to Vita. She saw his mouth fall open with shock at this bombshell, but before either of them could say anything, the far door swung open and Renata King shuffled in on her frame. She was wearing a black dress with pearls around her neck and an elaborate fascinator in her thin hair.

'Oh,' she said, stopping and looking at Irving, Vita and Daniel. 'You're all here.'

'Vita?' Daniel asked desperately. 'Vita? What's going on?'

Vita shook her head. She couldn't answer Daniel. Not now.

'Mother,' Irving said in a low voice, 'you've really excelled yourself this time. Is it true that you've abducted a child?'

'Don't be ridiculous,' Renata snorted. 'I arranged to have your son brought home. He's my grandson, and, from everything I've heard about her' – she pointed a crooked, ring-laden finger at Vita – 'he's better off here. With us.'

'So it *was* you. You stole Bertie,' Vita said in a hushed whisper, her eyes blazing with hatred.

'Look at her, Irving,' Renata said dismissively. 'She's utterly incompetent and her reputation is in tatters. We need to protect our name.'

Vita couldn't bear the look on her face – the way she was so clearly delighted at having manipulated them all into this situation. And she was serious. She really *had* used Clement to steal Bertie. What was he getting in return? Vita didn't dare to think. But this had to end right now.

'Stop it,' she shouted, surprising herself with the ferocity of her voice. 'Stop. Just stop.'

'Vita?' Daniel said in a warning tone, taking her arm. She shook him off.

'Bertie has nothing to do with you,' Vita jabbed a finger back at Renata. 'Or him.' She pointed at Irving.

Now there was a tense moment as Daniel, Renata and Irving all stood staring intently at her. She felt as if they were spinning around her, and she put a hand up to her head to steady herself.

'I'm so sorry,' Vita whispered. 'Irving. Truly, I am, but this has to stop.'

'Tell me what's going on,' Renata demanded. 'What's this about Bertie?'

'He's my son. That's all that matters,' Vita said.

Irving turned away from her and back, shaking his head. 'He's *his*, isn't he? They said you were with him on Cassius's yacht. Right under my nose. On our honeymoon. I didn't want to believe them.'

She shook her head. 'I'm so sorry. I didn't mean for it to happen.'

'So he took advantage of you? He raped you? Is that what you're saying?'

'No.'

'Do you love him?'

'I did once.'

'Who?' Daniel shouted now. 'Who are you talking about? Who is Bertie's father?'

'It's Archie Fenwick,' Irving snapped, as if Daniel was too slow to keep up.

'Archie . . .' Daniel blinked very hard. 'Archie – the writer?' He stared at Vita, as if struggling to comprehend what he was hearing.

'What silly fools you men make of yourselves over a pretty girl,' Renata said as Daniel stepped away from Vita, his eyes wide.

'Daniel – Daniel, wait. Let me explain.'

'All along . . . he was in my house . . . playing tennis . . . and you and him . . .'

'He didn't know. I swear it. I only saw him for the first time at your house that day.'

He shook his head, and Vita saw that his eyes were damp. 'You made a fool of me, Vita.'

'She's made fools of you all,' Renata interjected.

'Please, please – I just want my baby,' Vita said, her voice breaking.

Then they heard a familiar cry and turned to see Iris coming from another room, holding Bertie in her arms. Vita's knees almost gave out with relief.

'Iris, I told you to stay out of sight,' Renata fumed, but Iris marched across the room to Vita and Bertie held out his pudgy arms, starting to cry. Vita took him from Iris, cradling him to her as she sobbed into his neck. She felt faint with relief.

Her baby . . . her darling boy. He was hers again. She looked up. 'Thank you, Iris,' she said. 'Thank you.'

Iris nodded, and then raised her chin defiantly as she looked at her mistress. 'I'm doing the right thing, Mrs King,' she said. 'I got my conscience to think about.'

'Oh, Mother, you fool. Vita is right. That baby has nothing to do with us,' Irving said.

Vita saw a cloud of confusion cross the old woman's face. Then she frowned heavily. She looked like a little child who wanted to stamp her foot.

'Then you should tell your brother I want nothing more to do with your dreadful family,' Renata said to Vita. 'This is a terrible business. Terrible.' She put her hand to her head and collapsed backwards into the chair.

'Oh, Mother,' Irving said, going to her.

'I only wanted Bertie because you've left me,' Renata cried.

'I'm here now,' Irving said soothingly. 'I'm here now.'

Vita turned to follow Iris, desperate to get away. It was only then that she realized Daniel had gone. She let out a sob, feeling dreadful for having lied to him and for having inflicted so much pain. But she couldn't worry about Daniel. Not right at this moment.

'Get out,' Renata shouted after her. 'Get out, you hear me?'

'Come this way,' Iris said, beckoning Vita. 'That old viper,' she added as they hurried down the corridor to the kitchen and the service elevator. 'She's the devil.'

74

Le Monsieur's Game

He liked the feeling of knowing the secrets of a city, Clement thought, as the small peephole in the door slid back and he was admitted to the hidden speakeasy behind the bakery in Harlem. This was the setting for the big game. Last time he'd been here, with Tebby, he'd been half cut, and his memory was hazy; but tonight he was razor sharp and sober.

He had a satisfyingly thick stack of cash in his pocket. The banker's draft signed by Renata King had prompted the teller in the bank earlier to become quite obsequious. It had been for two thousand dollars, which she'd described as a reimbursement of his expenses for 'procuring' the child. He wondered now whether he should have asked for more.

Clement had enjoyed his exchange with Renata, who seemed to have done quite a bit of homework on Darton since their previous meeting. She'd given him her lawyer's details and had written a letter of intent to buy Darton Mill once her lawyer had drawn up the paperwork.

Oh, he couldn't wait, he thought. He couldn't wait to show Edith his spoils and tell her how he'd saved them from the LCC. With his debts paid off, Clement could begin again.

He'd be able to return to the club triumphantly. He'd even get his pocket watch back.

Even better, Renata had been kind enough to telephone her travel agent, who had sent over a first-class ticket for his passage back on a Cunard liner. Unlike his recent terrible experience going to the Caribbean, this was going to be a fine way to travel. He would return to Darton in style. In *triumph*.

Yes, things were looking up. And now this: the chance to play in a game at Le Monsieur's. Clement wasn't going to leave New York without reclaiming some dignity and showing those hoodlums who they were dealing with – and this time, if there was any trouble, he was prepared. The gun had been his first purchase with the money Renata had given him. The shopkeeper at John Jovino's, behind the police headquarters, had shown him exactly how to use the Colt M1911 pistol, reassuring him that it was the best weapon a man could have. Clement didn't want to have to use it, but he felt better having it tucked into his trousers, and now he patted the steel reassuringly. Yes, Clement Darton was a changed man, he told himself. Nobody was going to take advantage of him ever again.

The club was already full of people, dancing and laughing as he limped down the long spiral staircase. The bartender came over to him, and he announced that he was here for the game. A moment later, a voluptuous young woman dressed in leotard and fishnet tights asked him to follow her through the club to where a thick red curtain hung in one corner. Beyond it was a door, on the other side of which was a plushly decorated room. A low lamp with long gold fringing hung over a large table, making the green baize shine while the far end of the room remained in shadow.

Clement could hear voices and saw a huddle of a dozen men, but his attention was drawn by a waitress, who asked him what he'd like to drink. He ordered a bourbon. Her bosoms were barely held in place by the outfit she was wearing, and she had a choker around her neck. She noticed him looking at her cleavage and when she turned away, he placed a hand on her backside. She flinched and moved out of the way with her tray.

Now he watched a short man with curly brown hair enter the room, clapping his hands and calling out a greeting in an Irish accent, beckoning to the men in the shadows. They all sat down at the table, chairs scraping against the brick floor, as the newcomer greeted them all and checked that they had enough to drink.

The dealer – a young man with a bushy moustache – at the Irishman's cue, took a deck of cards from the packet in his pocket and fanned them out on the baize for inspection.

Clement approached and sat at the chair nearest to him. As he settled himself, another man took the empty seat beside his, and Clement saw that he held an unlit cigar between his fingers. It triggered a flash of memory – of exactly the same brand of cigar being thrown to the floor in a grand salon in Paris.

Irving King recognized Clement at the same time that Clement recognized him.

'Well, well. Mr Darton,' he said.

The Irishman, who had been shaking hands with two of the other players, paused now and turned his gaze on them with eyebrows raised, no doubt at King's sneering tone.

'I thought you were leaving New York?' Irving King said. 'I heard it from my mother's maid.'

Irving King had been to see his mother? In that case, he must know about Bertie. Did he know about Clement's arrangement with Renata? Clement realized now that he should probably try to mend bridges with Vita's ex-husband. Irving was, after all, the baby's father.

'I wonder, Mr Darton,' Irving continued. 'Will you ever stop torturing your family? After everything you've done to Vita, you now steal her child?'

The Irishman leant in towards the dealer, and Clement heard him say, 'Wait for me. I'll be back.'

He disappeared back into the club, a brief blast of music entering the card room as he opened and closed the door.

'But the baby . . . I . . . your mother,' Clement began, unsettled by Irving King's thunderous look. 'The baby is yours, sir. I thought you'd be pleased that he was back in New York, where he belongs.'

Irving King shook his head. 'You and your sister. You are just the same with your lies.'

Clement had never been compared to his sister in such a way, and he baulked at the accusation. 'I don't understand.'

'Understand this, Mr Darton. I will see you ruined, if it's the last thing I do.'

'Now, Irving, keep it civil,' one of the other players said, glancing up at the Irishman, who was now coming back towards the table and shrugging on a smart jacket. 'You're lucky Le Monsieur didn't hear you speaking like that. He'd have us all thrown out. Yes, let's remind ourselves that this is a gentleman's game.'

The Irishman pulled a chair up to the table. His earlier good humour seemed to have vanished.

One of the other men at the table addressed him. 'You're playing, Paul?'

'Tonight, to be sure, I will,' he said. He didn't look at Irving or at Clement, but nodded to the dealer. 'Let's begin, shall we?'

75

A Refuge at the Delaneys'

Vita paced as Patrick Delaney spoke into the telephone on the side table in his lounge.

'That's right. Hold the sale of the shares. If at all possible,' he said, looking at Vita.

He signed off the call and heaved a sigh.

'Well?'

'You'll have to go and see Mr Heal in person to sort out this mess, I'm afraid. The paperwork you signed is binding.'

Her fate was sealed, then. She'd have to go back to England. There was no doubt in her mind that Georgie must have been working for Clement. Or Edith, for that matter. Why else would Georgie have insisted on her signing that paperwork? Vita let out a strangled groan. She'd been such a fool. *Such a damned fool.*

'Now then, Vita. You'd better tell me what all of this is about,' Mr Delaney said. 'Would you like a drink?'

She nodded and he handed her a brandy, which she drank gratefully. She slumped onto the green leather chair and rubbed her eyes. She couldn't remember the last time she'd slept properly.

'Once I've told you everything, if you want me to leave, I will completely understand,' she said.

Patrick Delaney chuckled. 'Nothing that you could tell me is so bad that I would throw you out onto the street, my dear. And Camilla is not going to let Bertie out of her sight after what you told us earlier, so I think you're safe to say whatever you have to say.'

Vita took another sip of brandy.

'I don't even know where to begin,' she said, but Patrick patted her knee and sat opposite her. His eyes, which reminded her so much of Nancy's, were soft. It really had been so comforting to take him up on his offer of being a safe haven if she were ever in trouble. This had been the only place she could think of to come after leaving Renata King's building with Iris and Bertie. Iris had been adamant that she was walking out on 'the old witch', and when Vita had arrived at the Delaneys' and explained how Iris had saved the day, Mrs Delaney had insisted she stay with them.

'Start at the beginning, my dear.'

So, she told him about Darton and her family, and about leaving Clement for dead in the stable and running away to London. She told him about meeting Nancy and Edith, and how she'd helped Percy and then started designing underwear. She told him about Marianne and how she'd died – but not before stealing all of Vita's designs for Edith. She told him about coming to New York, and how Nancy had lied for her about Irving so that the Delaneys would give her a home.

'I see,' Patrick Delaney said, standing up and pacing in front of the fireplace, his hands behind his back. Vita was wrung out. 'I owe Mr King an apology,' he said after a few moments.

'Irving only wanted to protect me. He's a good man. And I betrayed him. I've betrayed everyone.'

Vita burst into fresh tears, thinking of Daniel. What she'd done to him felt like the worst aspect of all this. She could only assume that he'd taken the train they'd planned to take together. No doubt he would go back to Hollywood and all of his friends would rally round, wouldn't they? She hoped he wouldn't be sad for long, but she doubted he'd ever forgive her. And why should he? She was a dreadful, dreadful person.

Mr Delaney came and laid a hand on her shoulder. 'Come along, Vita. You need to pull yourself together. What's done is done. It's what you do now that counts. Have you heard of Mary Pickford?'

Vita nodded and managed a weak smile through her tears. 'Yes. Of course. I've actually met her. In fact, I'm supposed to be making her a dress for her next movie.'

'Are you indeed?' Patrick Delaney said, impressed. 'Well, I read an article in which she was quoted as saying . . . now let me get this right. Oh, yes.' He put his finger up, as if remembering something solemn. '*If you have made mistakes, even serious mistakes, you may have a fresh start any moment you choose, for this thing we call "failure" is not the falling down, but the staying down. The past cannot be changed. The future is yet in your power.*'

'You really think so?'

'I know so. It's time for you to stop running, my dear, and take a stand.'

Mrs Delaney came into the room now, holding Bertie, his head lolling on her shoulder. Seeing that he was fast asleep, Vita got up to help her lie him down on the silk chaise. She placed a shawl over him and gently stroked his hair away from his face.

'There's a call for you, Vita,' Mrs Delaney said. 'It's Nancy.'

She nodded to her husband, and they left Vita alone in the study. She sat on the chaise next to Bertie and picked up the telephone receiver.

'It's true? He's really safe?' Nancy said. 'Thank goodness.'

'Oh, Nancy, Nancy,' Vita said, so relieved to hear her friend's voice.

She told her hurriedly what had happened in New York, and how Daniel had left. 'It didn't turn out to be a stitch in time. My lie about Irving. Oh, Nancy, it was so awful.'

'Oh, kiddo.'

'He was so upset. I know he hates me. How could he not?'

'Calm down, Vita,' Nancy said. 'What's done is done. That man adores you – and Bertie. Believe me, Daniel is bound to forgive you. Just give it a little time to blow over.'

'And what am I going to do in the meantime?' Vita asked.

Was that even what she wanted? For things to blow over, and for Daniel to forgive her? Nancy was clearly assuming that Vita would be coming back to Los Angeles; but she wasn't sure about that, either. Not now that she had a chance to get her Darton shares back.

'Well, that's why I'm calling,' Nancy said. 'Because I had a call from Paul – your Paul.'

'Paul? Paul Kilkenny?'

'He called all the way from New York. He didn't know

where you were. I thought you would have gone to my parents', and I'm so glad I was right. I'm so glad you're still there.'

'What did he say?'

'Something about having your brother Clement at his club. At a game. And he's losing. He's just lost his ticket for his crossing back to England tomorrow. Paul says to meet him at the docks in the morning and he'll give the ticket to you instead. I told him everything, and Paul is making sure Clement doesn't leave the club.'

Vita shook her head, amazed that her friends on opposite sides of the country were working together to save her. 'You did all that for me?'

'Of course.'

Nancy talked some more about the press, and how Evelyn had arrived home from the hospital. Her cheekbone would take some time to heal and her face was swollen, but she would be fine now that she knew Bertie was safe.

'Even Archie Fenwick turned up here,' Nancy added, clearly pleased that the house had been a hive of activity.

Vita felt her heart lurch. 'What did he say?'

'I sent him packing, of course,' Nancy said. 'You never told me in so many words, Vita, but I knew all along that he must be Bertie's father.'

'You did?'

'It's pretty damned obvious. I figured you'd tell me in your own good time, but I don't trust that man. He's caused you enough trouble, and I told him as much. He ruined you in London, then on your honeymoon, and I shan't let him complicate your life any further. Not now that you've got Daniel.'

'But – oh, Nancy, Daniel has gone, and I—'

'Oh, Vita darling, I've got to go. Ericka is here and I'm doing an interview. Poor Mr Wild is still at the vet's, but he's alive, and that's the main thing. They all want an update. This has been *such* good publicity for the film.'

Vita replaced the receiver slowly, equally stunned by her friend's generosity and her remarkably thick skin. She'd known all along about Archie and Bertie? Vita could hardly fathom it. But then, Nancy had always had her back.

Poor Archie. She knew that he must have been so worried about Bertie when he'd heard about the abduction. And then he'd caught the wrath of Nancy. Vita knew Nancy was only protecting her, but she didn't understand how complicated Vita's feelings were.

But what did she really want from Archie? He could hardly come after her now. Not when she was leaving tomorrow. Not when he had his career to think of, and Maud. And anyway, she told herself, resting her hand on Bertie's chest and listening to his soft breathing, she didn't need Archie Fenwick to rescue her. She had to rescue herself.

76

Confessing to Nick

In her office, Edith stared intently at the newspapers Nick had just handed her and the pictures on each page. Not least of all the startling image of Nancy, her blonde hair and stylish suit so lovely against the backdrop of a stunning mansion.

'Nancy Delaney, star of the new movie *The Sister Returns*, describes her anguish over a shocking incident during which her godson was abducted from her Hollywood home,' she read. '"Quite apart from the brutal attack on my housekeeper, who was babysitting, the intruder took a hammer to Mr Wild, my dog," Nancy told reporters. This reporter hopes that the pampered pooch will survive, but it's really touch and go.'

There was even a picture of Mr Wild: Nancy posing by the pool with the little dog in a diamond collar, its eyebrows tied up in bunches.

Edith was too stunned to read any more out loud. Her eyes were wide as she continued reading: *This paper is pleased to report that the baby has been found safely in New York at the residence of renowned property tycoon Renata King, snatched, it seems, by the child's uncle.*

'Clement,' she gasped.

All eyes now are on poor Mr Wild. Let's hope Nancy, who has nearly finished filming her new picture, is reunited with him soon.

Edith shook her head, stunned, not only at the revelation that a baby – and it must surely be Vita's baby – had been stolen by Clement, but that the reporter only seemed to care about the dog.

She knew Clement wanted to hurt Vita, but – stealing her *baby*? Why on earth would he do that?

Edith stood up and paced.

Renata King . . . Clement . . . the baby . . . they must all be connected. She thought back to Clement's message. How he'd 'secured investment' from King Enterprises. Had he done a deal with Renata King? It couldn't be a coincidence.

'Did you know anything about this?' Nick asked, interrupting her efforts to put all the pieces together.

'No, of course not,' she said, but his knowing look made her blush.

'Because that's only half the story,' he said. 'The other half is this.'

Now he produced another piece of paper and handed it to her. It was a telegram from Mr Warren, addressed to Nick. Edith scanned down it, her pulse racing as she realized that Mr Warren had explained his connection to her.

'Well?' Nick demanded. 'You know Warren? You . . . you . . . *employed* Warren?' His voice was low and menacing. 'Because that's what this is implying.'

'Well, yes – it's sort of true. That morning, when I went

to see Eddy and you weren't there, I met Mr Warren – I told you I'd met him,' she stalled, seeing how angry Nick was. 'I said I had a problem and, well . . . he said he had associates who could detain Clement in America. He made it sound easy. Like it was something he could just . . . do.'

'Just do? Can you hear yourself? People like Warren don't *just do* anything.'

'I told him that Clement wouldn't be hard to find. And then I didn't hear anything else at all, until Clement telephoned to say he was going to California. And then . . . nothing. Until now.'

Nick shook his head. 'Edith, what were you thinking? Why didn't you tell me?'

'I wanted to, but I thought you'd be angry with me.'

'I *am* angry with you. It turns out that your friend Mr Warren has had a field day following Clement. He led him straight to New York's biggest illegal gambling syndicate, which leaves Warren with his direct link to this newspaper being hunted down by some very unsavoury people. And now there's evidence of the link between you and me, and your involvement in all of this . . . You have no idea how bad that looks.'

Edith moved towards him, imploring him. 'I'm sorry, I didn't think . . .'

'No, you didn't.'

'But I had to make him stay away, to give me time to think,' she said, begging him to understand. 'Just to give me time to make Darton mine. And you see, Nick, now that I have, I can veto Clement's plans. We can oust him from Darton for good.'

'But this thing with Warren. Your connection to him . . .' Nick held up the papers. 'This whole story is going to backfire on me. I know how these things work. When you take matters into your own hands like this, you get your fingers burnt.'

'What if we just tell the truth? About it all. About Clement? About us?' She tried to smile up at him. 'Don't you understand that, together, we can get through anything?'

'Together?'

'Yes, together. Us. We make such a good team. Don't you feel it, Nick?'

He shook his head, backing away. 'Edith . . . just stop.'

'No, Nick, no,' she cried. 'You have to be patient. Just until all of this dies down.'

She launched herself towards him and tried to place her head on his chest, but he pushed her away and she started to shake, understanding what he was saying.

'Oh, Nick, Nick – don't leave me. Don't. I can't bear it if you leave me.'

He held her at arm's length, looking at her sternly.

'It was just an affair,' he said, his expression closed off. 'As you said, everyone has them. I assume you've had them before, so you know the score. They end.'

The door burst open then, and Tantum stood looking at Nick and Edith, taking in the way they were standing together. His eyebrows shot up in understanding.

'I've heard Mr Darton is coming back,' he said. He didn't try to mask the triumph in his tone.

Nick stepped away from her, picking up his hat from the desk. 'Goodbye, Edith.'

'Wait,' she said, but it was too late.

She put a hand to her forehead, fighting down tears. 'Get out,' she told Tantum, who was lingering in the doorway, sneering. 'Get out!' she shouted, more forcefully.

77

Martha

As the Liverpool docks came into view in the morning light, Vita stood on the deck holding Bertie close to her. This hiatus on a luxury liner had been a godsend, but she knew that there were difficult days ahead.

'Look,' she said, pointing out the cliffs. Ahead of them, the ship sliced through the grey water, seagulls riding the currents. Across the deck, she heard the brass band start up with some jaunty music.

'Half an hour until we dock,' she heard someone call, and she breathed in the chilly spring air.

The crossing had restored her spirits, not least because she'd finally been able to sleep with Bertie beside her. She would never lose him again, she vowed. No matter what.

The closer the ship got to Europe, the more convinced she'd become that it was time to face the past and stop running. She had to stand up to Clement before he hurt anyone else she loved. When she thought of poor Evelyn and Mr Wild, it made her stomach turn with fury.

If only she'd been honest with everyone she cared about from the start – Archie, Irving, Daniel . . . Nancy, even. She'd made a hash of all her relationships because she'd wanted to change everything about herself. She'd wanted to sever her connection to her past. But no matter how far she'd travelled or how hard she'd tried to be someone else, she hadn't been able to outrun the Darton family. She hadn't been able to outrun Clement.

Until now, she thought. Because, for once, she was one step ahead of him.

She thought of Paul at the docks when he'd given her the ticket, and how she'd given him the book she'd forgotten to give to Percy before she left. It was the sketchbook of her drawings for Mary Pickford, which she'd asked him to deliver personally to Percy when he next went to California. She had a feeling that Paul and Percy might just get along.

'Don't be a stranger now,' Paul had said as they'd parted, but she had no idea when she would see him again. She only hoped that one day she could repay the great favour he'd done her in detaining Clement.

The dock at Liverpool was crowded with well-wishers as the huge ship approached. Vita watched people throwing streamers and cheering to their family and friends as the ship pulled in, the band launching into a rousing version of the national anthem.

Hetherington, her father's driver, was waiting in the arrivals hall and Vita saw him scanning the crowd, no doubt looking for Clement. He didn't recognize her until she was standing right in front of him.

'Miss Anna?' he said, his eyes wide. Then his face lit up in a smile. He hadn't changed one bit, she thought, surprising him by embracing him.

'You were expecting Clement?' she said.

'Yes.'

'Well, you've got us instead,' she smiled, before introducing him to Bertie.

She'd never seen Hetherington in such a flap as he helped her to the car.

'They'll be very surprised,' he said. 'Should we stop so that I can telephone ahead?'

'No. Let's just go.'

'I can't wait to see the look on Martha's face when she sees you,' Hetherington said.

Whenever Vita had thought of Martha, she'd remembered her roughly brushing her hair, shooing her out of the way or telling her off for her manners. But since she'd become a mother herself, she'd come to realize that Martha had only been doing her best to bring up Anna in the austere Darton household. Hearing Hetherington talking about her made her remember the flagstoned kitchen, and how Martha and the other staff used to let her join them sometimes as they played cards in front of the range when the chores were finished. Darton had been a whole world overshadowed by Clement, but now that Vita remembered all the people who'd been part of her extended family, the prospect of seeing them all again made her shaky with excitement.

'I'll get you home as quickly as I can, Miss Darton,' Hetherington said. 'Or should I say Mrs? Are you married?'

'No. Not anymore. And that's just the problem. I don't know what Mother and Father will say about Bertie.'

'Your father?' Something in his tone alerted her.

'What about him?'

'Oh, Miss Anna.' Hetherington stopped the car and turned to face her.

'What?'

'He passed. Didn't you know?'

'No,' she said. 'No, I didn't.'

She listened as Hetherington told her about the funeral, and how Clement and Edith had been running Darton ever since Darius Darton's death. Vita fought hard to keep her tears at bay, thinking of her father and the last time they'd seen each other. They'd fought over him taking Clement's side. She'd been so furious when she'd discovered Clement's plan to marry her off to Malcolm Arkwright, the fat old mill owner from the other side of the valley – she'd had no choice but to run away. She'd wanted her father to see her as a person, not as a commodity. But now it was too late.

As they drove away from the docks Vita stared out of the car window, a lone tear falling as she thought about how much she'd missed and how long she'd been away. She remembered being in Paris in the Sacré-Coeur, and how she'd seen a clergyman who'd reminded her of her father. Perhaps on some level she must have known that something had happened. And she hadn't been there. She hadn't had the chance to say goodbye or to comfort her mother.

Perhaps Hetherington sensed that she needed time, because he didn't talk as Vita settled back in her seat, holding the sleeping Bertie in her arms. Soon they were driving through countryside and she looked out, drinking it all in. After the dry earth of California, the green, rolling hills were a balm to her tired eyes.

It was a Saturday, and Hetherington beeped the horn as

they passed a flock of sheep going off to market. The closer they got to Darton and the more familiar the hills and valleys became, the more Vita's experiences in America, Paris and London seemed to recede, as if they'd been nothing but a dream.

They approached Darton and Vita sat forward as they drove up the gravel drive, the Hall's windows and roof like a well-loved face she hadn't seen for a long time. Hetherington pulled to a stop and Vita opened the door, breathing in the cold English air. The smell of home.

The front door opened just as she was getting out of the car with Bertie. Martha stood on the threshold.

She looked the same as Vita remembered her, although her hair was grey in the bun she wore beneath her cap. Her eyes widened with surprise.

'Oh, Anna, you're back,' she said, rushing forward and pulling Vita into a hug. Vita breathed in her familiar vinegary scent. 'Oh, my . . .'

Vita looked over Martha's shoulder into the hallway of Darton Hall, a cascade of memories assaulting her.

'And who is this?' Martha asked, her eyes shining as she looked at Bertie in Vita's arms. He giggled. 'Oh, isn't he bonny?'

'This is Bertie,' Vita said. 'Would you mind taking him for a moment?'

She handed him over and walked inside.

'Mother?' she called.

She flung open the door to the study, but the scene that greeted her made her gasp. There was no trace of her father. Not anymore. The study had been painted in duck-egg blue and hung with tastefully framed prints. The huge desk had been replaced with a velvet sofa.

'Mother?' She opened the door to the drawing room next, and saw that her mother was in the conservatory beside her aviary.

'Mother,' she said, walking towards her.

'Oh!' her mother exclaimed as Vita flung herself into her embrace. 'Oh, Anna. I knew you'd come home.'

78

Playing with Fire

At St Hilda's, Edith stepped gingerly over the muddy puddles on the edge of the gravel car park and onto the field where the girls were playing a lacrosse match, even though the new hunting shoes she was wearing with her fetching woollen slacks were designed for the job. She hated this Saturday ritual of sports matches and usually sent Hetherington to pick Susan up after them, but today he'd gone to Liverpool to pick up Clement, and Edith wanted to be anywhere but Darton when he arrived. Besides, she couldn't miss the chance of seeing Nick. He'd be coming to pick up Lettice, she was sure of it.

She hadn't been able to think of anything else but that dreadful scene in her office a couple of days ago. But surely by now Nick must have had the chance to calm down and realize that he'd spoken too hastily? What they had was too important. She refused to believe it was over.

She headed towards the small crowd of spectators at the bottom of the rickety open-air stands. The girls were running around the muddy pitch, their wooden lacrosse sticks held aloft. Edith searched for Susan, listening to the calls of the girls, the grunts and screams as the ball was passed back and forth. Susan was in goal at the far end, swamped by the pads over her legs and a square-necked sports tunic that was far too big.

She was gratified to see the sports teacher – a man with a whistle in his mouth – turn his attention from the game to Edith as she approached. She slipped behind him to the other parents, recognizing Helen Bamford just along from her.

'Helen,' Edith said. 'What a surprise.'

'Oh, goodness – Edith,' Helen said, looking rather dismayed as she turned to Edith and grasped her hand.

'I wasn't expecting to see you here,' Edith said, her mind whirring. Where was Nick?

'I usually come to support the team,' Helen said. 'Lettice says that even though I can't see who's winning, it helps having me here.'

'I'm always too busy to come,' Edith said, pointedly. Wasn't it rather sad that Helen had nothing better to do than stand on the sidelines of a field in the cold? 'The mill is so busy – even on a Saturday.'

'I'm sure it is,' Helen said.

'So . . . how are things with you?' Edith asked tactfully, her tone deliberately cheery.

'Oh, fine.'

'And Nick?' she asked, thinking of how her lover's hands had gripped her buttocks as she'd wrapped her legs around his waist.

'Nick has been working hard,' Helen said. 'Rather too hard.'

She doesn't suspect, does she? Edith thought. 'Clement has been away too. Husbands can be tricky,' she said with a light laugh. She turned her attention to the game. 'Go on, reds,' she shouted.

'The blue team is Wendell,' Edith corrected her. 'They're playing in house teams.'

Edith watched as the ball bounced off the post and the red team took over, firing a shot straight past Susan. She saw Susan being commiserated by a teammate.

Edith looked at Helen now as she stamped her feet in the cold. Mud spattered up her oilskin coat and a little dot had made it onto her face. In the grey drizzle of the sports field, her hair tucked under a woollen hat, Helen Bamford no longer looked beautiful and bewitching but old and haggard, the lines on her face clearly visible. No wonder Nick found Edith so alluring. In her mind, she'd seen Helen – even given her disability – as something of a threat, but now she assured herself that there simply was no competition. In fact, if anything, Helen deserved her pity.

'Is everything quite all right, Helen?' she asked. 'You seem a little down, if you don't mind me saying.'

'I suppose . . .' Helen sighed.

'What is it?'

'Edith, can I trust you?'

'Of course,' Edith said.

'Do you ever . . . I mean, with Clement . . . Do you ever suspect that there are things going on that you don't know about?'

The irony of it, Edith thought.

'You see, with Nick, I always know what he's thinking – even when he's not with me. But lately . . .' Helen continued, then waved her hand and fizzled out. 'Ignore me.'

'You don't mean you suspect that there might be . . . someone else?' Edith couldn't help herself. It was like running her finger through a flame.

Helen shook her head and buried her face in her hands. 'I'm so ashamed,' she said, taking a breath. 'For even saying it aloud. No, no, of course not. I trust Nick completely.'

Edith nodded, not able to help how exhilarating she found this conversation, how seeing a flash of Helen's torment made her feel quite victorious.

'I suppose it must be hard for him, though. Having to look after you, as well as being a career man. It takes a certain kind of person – a selfless person, I should imagine.'

Helen's cheeks coloured now. 'Nick is selfless.'

'I'm sure he is. From what I've seen of him, he absolutely is,' Edith said, remembering him looking up at her from between her legs. His generosity in helping her achieve the kind of pleasure she'd never experienced before certainly *was* selfless. 'I just don't believe that any man – certainly ambitious men – can ever truly resist temptation, that's all.'

Nick had once remarked that Helen had a sixth sense, and now Edith was sure that something was happening as Helen's expression changed.

She knows, Edith thought, her whole body tingling at the thrill of sowing such a seed of doubt. Helen turned back towards the field, but her shoulders were stiff. The air between them felt as if it was crackling.

The final whistle sounded and Helen took a sudden step away from Edith towards the pitch. She tripped over the edge of the stand gate, falling over and kneeling in the mud.

'Oh, Helen, look at you,' Edith said, picking her up.

Helen shook her off. 'I'm fine,' she said. 'Really.'

'Are you all right, Mummy?' Lettice asked, suddenly running over from the pitch.

'She tripped,' Edith said. 'It was unavoidable. Your mother really shouldn't be out here unaccompanied.'

'But she's not. She has you,' Lettice said with an innocent, enquiring look.

'Of course, she does,' Edith replied with her friendliest smile.

She was going to have to get Lettice on side. When Lettice had weekends with her father and Edith and they were a little family unit, then they'd need to get on. But the weekends and holidays when she wasn't there, when she and Nick could be alone – oh, how wonderful they would be . . .

Edith made an excuse to wait for Susan to join her in the car. Soon afterwards she saw the small, defiant figure trudging towards her, and wished she'd found a way to love the child more.

'Aren't you happy I came to the game?' Edith asked, when Susan was settled into the passenger seat beside her.

Susan looked sullen, her cheeks still pink, as Edith started the car.

'I wish you hadn't.'

'That's a little mean, darling,' Edith said, stung by the force of her words.

'You're the mean one. You were mean to Mrs Bamford.'

'I wasn't, I—'

'I know you've been in Manchester at the same time as Mr Bamford,' Susan said. 'No wonder she's cross.'

Edith wondered how Susan could possibly know such

information, and was about to deny it, when a new thought suddenly occurred to her. Might not this be the perfect moment to be transparent?

She indicated onto the road. 'It's true. But then, Nick and I . . . we have so much more in common than I do with your father. And we've become friends.' She pressed her fingertips into her hand around the thin steering wheel. 'A little more than friends, if I'm honest.'

She felt Susan's cool blue eyes on her now.

Edith smiled across at her, then tried to concentrate on the road. 'I was thinking . . . perhaps we could start over.' She reached out a hand towards Susan, but the child flinched away. 'I certainly have felt that things are much better at home since your father has been away. He's a cruel, cruel man, Susan. And I think it's better for us if we get him out of our lives.'

'You mean, leave Darton? What about Grandmother?'

'No, no . . . It's more about us staying and your father . . . well, I think he should go. More permanently.'

There was a moment of silence and Edith smiled again at Susan, seeing her absorb this new information. Was she relieved? Was she going to confess what Clement had been doing?

'What do you mean, *a little more than friends*?' she asked.

She'd picked up on that point about Nick then, Edith realized. Susan's voice was laden with suspicion.

'We're . . . confidantes,' Edith said brightly. 'Maybe Nick then, like me, wants the chance to start again.'

She glanced at Susan, but her eyebrows were drawn together in an angry frown.

'What I'm saying is that potentially – and I think this is a long way down the line – but you and Lettice could be sisters. Proper sisters. Haven't you always wanted a sister? And you get on so well. We could be a family.'

'They already *are* a family.'

'But—'

'If you take Nick Bamford away from them, I will never forgive you,' Susan said with such force that Edith took her foot off the pedal in shock and stalled the car.

'Do not use that tone with me, young lady,' she snapped, but her cheeks pulsed as they drove back to Darton in silence.

Damn Susan, Edith thought. She was just like her father. Well, she wouldn't let her win. She wouldn't let Susan ruin her chance of happiness.

79

A Darton Welcome

Vita's mother wouldn't stop reaching out to hold her hand as they sat in the warm kitchen at Darton. It had been quite a conversation – Vita telling her all about running away to London, and how Clement had hunted her down.

Her mother listened closely, absorbing every word.

'Those designs – they were yours? Top Drawer was yours all along?'

She shook her head, trying to take it all in. Martha was listening too, her face grave.

'Your father and Clement . . . they looked for you everywhere when you ran away. Clement hired a private detective, but I wanted you to stay away. I wanted you to be away from here,' her mother said. 'Everyone missed you so terribly, though. Harrison at the mill put a collection together to help with Clement's search.'

'They did?' Vita hadn't considered how her absence would have been felt at Darton. Bless Harrison for caring.

'I'm sorry that it took me such a long time to write,' she said. 'But I did think of you often.'

'You wrote eventually. It was the happiest day of my life.

Just to know you were alive. Just to know you were safe. And now you're home.'

And in the way she said that word, and the way she took hold of Vita's hand, Vita knew that she couldn't leave again any time soon.

Vita told her all about what had happened in Paris – about working for Jenny Sacerdote, and how she'd designed with Marianne. She described her horror at the missing bras, and how she'd seen them at the Galeries Lafayette and then discovered Susan and Mr Wild in her old apartment. She told them, too, about Clement coming, and about Marie falling to her death.

'I had no idea what was happening,' Theresa said, horrified. 'I had no idea about Marianne or Susan, or I would have stopped Edith. I knew she was wicked, but when I think of that poor child's mother . . .' She put her hand over her mouth and shook her head.

'Where is she? Edith?'

'She's collecting Susan from school. It was their house lacrosse match.'

'Marianne's Susan lives here?'

Her mother nodded. 'When Marianne went to Paris, Edith put Susan into St Hilda's in Manchester. When Clement brought Susan back from Paris, Edith adopted her, although they aren't very close.'

Vita heard the front door opening now and, a moment later, a blonde girl came racing into the kitchen in sports kit.

'Martha? Martha, is there any—'

She stopped as she saw Vita and Theresa at the table. Both of them stood.

'Susan, this is your aunt,' Theresa said.

'Do you remember me? I am – was – a friend of your mother's,' Vita said, as she stared at the little girl. Susan looked so much like Marianne.

But before Susan had a chance to answer, Vita saw Edith behind her. She was standing in the doorway, wearing a tweed suit and a hat.

There was a long beat as Vita stared at her old adversary, seeing the stylish woman she'd become, remembering that arrogant tilt of her head and how furious she'd been on the first day they'd met at the Zip Club.

Edith didn't smile. Her face was hard as she started to pull off her gloves, as if preparing for a fight. 'So you're back,' she said.

80

A Formidable Woman

Edith rested her elbows on the marble mantelpiece in her bedroom and put her head in her hands. Vita was back. Back with that brat of hers, and Edith couldn't bear it. She couldn't bear the way Theresa and Martha were fawning over her every word and cooing over that wretched baby.

On Sunday, Edith got up early, deciding to make herself scarce. She drove around the countryside, stopping at a village pub and using the phone box to call Nick at home. When Helen answered she slammed down the receiver, losing her nerve about calling back again.

In the afternoon, she was relieved to find that Vita was out at the stables, which gave her the opportunity to take Susan back to St Hilda's. Susan remained silent the whole way. She clearly wasn't talking to Edith after their conversation about Nick.

'Your aunt – Anna? Vita, I mean? Has she spoken to you at all?'

Susan shook her head and Edith glanced at her, wondering what was going through her mind. She didn't look back as she walked into the school building, and Edith worried now that she was going to say something to Lettice. She should have listened to Nick about getting her fingers burnt when she took matters into her own hands.

She parked out of sight in the school lane, waiting and waiting for Nick to come to drop off Lettice. When he didn't turn up, she had no choice but to go back to Darton Hall.

Maybe he's telling Helen, she thought. Maybe that was why Lettice hadn't returned to school. Because he was telling them both the truth. About how he and Edith were going to be together. But by Sunday night, there was still no word.

With Clement still gone and Vita back, everything she'd so carefully planned was evaporating like a mirage.

On Monday she was up early again and went straight to her office without breakfast. And then at ten, as she had suspected she might, Vita arrived at Darton Mill.

If the reception at home had been nauseating, this was even worse, Edith thought. The workers fawned over Vita as if the prodigal daughter had returned. She looked down now from the porthole in the office to where the machinists had stopped working to crowd around Vita, clearly entranced by her glossy curls and tanned skin.

'Can you believe it,' Mrs Dunlop said, as she came to Edith's office a few moments later with Vita. She was beaming with joy.

'You can get back to work,' Edith said, rudely.

'Of course, there must be so much for you to talk about.' Mrs Dunlop left, but not without another effusive smile. 'Miss Darton, all grown up. It's so good to have you back.'

Vita stood in the doorway, her curvy figure accentuated perfectly by the shirtdress she was wearing, along with a fur-trimmed jacket that was so stylish it could only have come from abroad. The scrappy impostor who'd stolen Edith's best friend had grown up into a formidable woman.

'I like what you've done with the offices,' she said, walking in and closing the door.

Edith stared at Vita, noticing the way her eyes roamed around the office, as if reclaiming the space.

'What are you doing here?' Edith asked.

'You're avoiding me at home, so I had no choice but to come here.'

Edith paced in front of her desk. Vita was very still, watching her.

'Can you just stop and talk to me?' she asked, calmly. 'Woman to woman?'

'I'm not sure what we have to say to each other,' Edith shot back. She didn't want Vita here. She just needed to be alone. To call Nick, to know that everything between them was going to be all right.

'It was you, wasn't it? Who sent Georgie to blackmail me? To give up my Hillsafe shares?'

'So what if it was? What good were they to you anyway? You gave up all your rights to Darton when you ran away with Nancy. And now you think you can just walk in here as if you own the place. Well, you don't. I have control of this company now. It's up to me.'

'But only because you cheated your way to acquiring *my* shares. *My* ideas. It was *my* husband's money that paid for all of this.'

'He wasn't really your husband – and anyway, you hardly obeyed your marriage vows. I know what you did with Archie.'

'And you told Georgie,' Vita said, nodding. 'It all makes sense now.'

'What do you want, Vita? Why are you here? I'm very busy, and—'

'I want what's mine. I want my business back.'

'But it's mine. The Darton Bra . . .'

'Based on Top Drawer—'

'Might I remind you that you *gave* me the designs, in London? You swapped them for my passport and ticket. Everything I've achieved with them has been of my own making.'

Vita let out an outraged laugh. 'But that's where you're wrong. You stole everything from me in Paris. What you made Marianne do . . . that was wicked. *So* wicked. I was there when she died . . . when she fell. You have no idea how much that haunts me.'

'It's not my fault Marie fell. I was the one who saved that child,' Edith said, her voice suddenly passionate. 'You've seen how happy she is at Darton.'

Edith watched as Vita sat down heavily at the desk that had once been her father's.

'That's Clement's chair.'

Vita laughed scornfully and shook her head. 'Nancy always said you had dreadful taste in men – but I never thought you'd be so stupid as to marry my brother.'

Edith wished she'd prepared better for this confrontation with Vita. She wished that Vita didn't look so at home here. Her future – her plan to run Darton with Nick – suddenly seemed impossible now that Vita was back, her elbows on Darius's old desk.

'All right then. You want the truth? The truth is that you think I'm as bad as Clement, but I hate him just as much as you.'

Vita's eyebrows shot up as Edith made this daring statement. 'And, furthermore, I kept Paris – everything – a secret from him. I kept Clement away from *you*,' Edith said. 'If it hadn't been for me, he'd have hunted you down in Paris long ago.'

'You hardly stopped him. He came to America. He *stole my child*.'

'I didn't know he was going to do that.'

'He thinks he's done a deal with Renata King, but she wants nothing to do with him, so whatever little plan you two had . . . it's over.'

'I had nothing to do with Renata King. And I can assure you, he won't be in charge when he gets back.'

Vita nodded. 'Oh, he'll be back. You know Clement. He won't relinquish Darton.'

'That's where you're wrong.'

Edith stood now, her hands on her hips, as she explained the situation with the LCC to Vita and how much financial trouble Darton was in. And, as she told her about his treachery, she started talking about the fights she'd had with Clement about taking the business forward, how he wouldn't see how her business plan worked. Warming to her theme, she started telling Vita about her meetings in London with Withshaw and Taylor, how the Soirée range was selling well in Paris and new customers were coming on board all the time, and how she'd even put feelers out in the States and had an agent lined up.

'So you see,' she finished, 'you can't just come in here and—'

'You did all of that? With just those designs?' Vita said. She seemed dumbstruck. 'Goodness, Edith.'

'Yes. I did,' she said haughtily, glad that she'd justified herself. Vita stared at her for a long moment and her shoulders dropped.

'Then, despite everything you've done, I should congratulate you.'

Edith scanned Vita's face and saw, to her surprise, that she meant it.

Nobody had praised her before. Nobody had seen her vision. Nobody except Vita. Edith felt flustered now.

'I'm not asking you for any sympathy,' Edith said. 'I'm telling you this so that you understand how hard I've worked.'

'I can see that with my own eyes.'

She sounded like she meant it.

'And – well, the thing is, I have plans, as I said,' Edith continued. 'A vision. A way to be rich and successful, and to make women happy.'

Vita smiled. 'You're beginning to sound like me.'

'I'm not like you. I'm nothing like you,' Edith snapped back.

Vita sighed. 'Maybe not . . . but, Edith, listen to me. Why don't we work out a way we can move forward together?'

'Together?'

'Yes. You and me. Without Clement. Couldn't we build something wonderful here at Darton?' Vita asked. 'Because there's so much more we can do. There's so much more I want to design. There are fabrics that I saw in America that we could make ourselves. But I'm getting ahead of myself. Listen, I know there's a lot of water that needs to flow under the bridge, but it seems to me that we both want the same thing. I'd like it if we could give each other another chance. What do you say?'

Edith wanted to cry with sheer frustration. To stamp and rail. Because Vita couldn't just come in here offering an olive branch. She couldn't trick her into being friends. She meant it, though. Edith could see it in her kind blue eyes. But this *wasn't* the plan. Not the plan at all.

81

Clement is Back

Clement stood outside the railway station in the taxi queue, shivering. His stomach hadn't recovered from the wretched crossing, but at least he was home. On British soil. He had no intention of travelling abroad ever again.

Another wave of self-loathing mixed with indignation swept over him. It wasn't fair. None of this was fair. Quite apart from losing all his money to Irving King at the game, he'd also lost the ticket that Renata had given him and had ended up travelling back with his false papers, bunking down alongside twenty others in a filthy cabin.

He'd spent five gruelling nights fuming over the disaster at Le Monsieur's. Because far from getting his revenge, it had gone horribly, terribly wrong. It had been bad enough that Irving had told him in no uncertain terms to get out of town before he was arrested for kidnap and assault. But worse, as he'd left the club, one of the other players had pulled him aside.

'You gave me the last piece I needed,' he'd said.

'The last piece?'

'For a big exposé on this whole operation. You see, I work for Mr Warren.'

'Who the hell is Warren?' Clement had asked.

'The guy hired to detain you.'

'*Detain* me?' Clement hadn't been sure if he'd heard right. 'Someone was paid to detain me?'

'You know, to rough you up a little,' the man had said, with a laugh. 'I think Tebby saw to that.'

'You know Tebby?'

'Of course. He works for Warren.'

'And this Warren?' Clement had asked, desperate now to know what this all meant. 'He was hired . . . so, so someone paid him? Do you know who?'

'I heard it was your wife.'

Edith. Edith and Tebby were linked? Through this Warren chap? And people knew? People had followed him and set him up?

Clement had never known such an intense feeling of impotent rage in all his life.

As he brooded during the crossing home, he thought about everything that he'd gone through – from Paris to New York, and then via his incarceration on Rodriguez's ship to New Orleans and on to Los Angeles. He'd been so close to securing a future with Renata King by himself – but all the time, his wife had been intent on scuppering him. She'd reduced him, shamed him, when he'd thought she was on his side.

Well, she wasn't going to get away with it. Not if it was the last thing he ever did.

'Clement?'

The voice interrupted his vitriolic thoughts and he looked up to see Decker, the secretary of the club. He hadn't seen him for months – not since Decker had sent those thugs to demand Clement's debts be paid. And he could have paid them. He could have paid everything off and restored his reputation, if only he hadn't been swindled in Le Monsieur's game. *If only, if only . . .*

He swallowed hard, remembering his vow to repay the debt in a couple of months. Another ultimatum was the last thing he needed when he was so wrung out.

'How have you been? We haven't seen you at the club lately,' Mr Decker said jovially.

The gall of the man, to approach him like this after threatening him – and with such an innocent smile on his face – made Clement flash with anger. He had to clench his fists to stop himself punching Decker as he remembered the public house, that Irishman snatching away his father's watch and putting it in his pocket.

'I have been away,' he said, feebly. 'In America.'

'Oh, well, that explains it. I hope we'll see you before too long.' He smiled. 'There's some new Beaujolais from France in, which many of the gents are enjoying. I'd get in before it's all gone.' With a chuckle, he raised his hat to Clement before walking on.

Clement shook his head, baffled. But at that moment, a taxi pulled up next to him and he bundled inside, giving directions for Darton Mill.

He'd nodded off by the time the taxi pulled up in front of the large black gates, and he blinked in the weak sunshine, staring up at the white sky and the high windows of the austere building. He felt an emotion so strong, it brought a lump to his throat. He was back. Back home. Finally. Where he belonged.

As he paid the cab driver, he looked up at the windows again and remembered that Edith was up there. Right now. He couldn't wait to throw her out and send her packing. If she thought she was getting any part of Darton Mill, she was seriously mistaken. He'd already written to the lawyers and had sent the letter he'd had witnessed by the ship's purser.

She would get nothing from him. *Nothing*. Ever.

As God was his witness, he hated women. Hated them *all*.

As he limped through the mill, he heard the workers whispering. As he walked through the area where Edith's machinists worked, they all stopped and stared at him, but he ignored them, clambering up the metal staircase to the office. Mrs Dunlop stood when she saw him, but he scowled at her too, ignoring her greeting. He flung open the office door to confront his wife.

She was sitting on the edge of his desk in a white suit, her cheeks flushed. A man he didn't recognize was standing over her, their heads close together. They sprang apart when Edith saw Clement. Edith stood and faced him, smoothing down her white skirt over her hips.

'Talk of the devil,' she said.

If she was alarmed by his appearance, she didn't show it. Instead, she glanced at the man next to her – and in that instant, Clement knew. He knew from the look on her face that there was something between them.

He'd been all the way to the other side of the world, and

not only had Edith set him up, but she'd betrayed him while his back was turned.

'I'll leave you to this,' the man said, squeezing Edith's arm. 'Will you be all right?'

He walked out and closed the door. Clement watched Edith's face – her eyes shining as she stared after the man.

Then her eyes met Clement's and she looked him up and down, her lip curling. He followed her gaze down to his tattered suit, his ripped shirt, his dirty hands.

'Who was that?' he asked. 'Edith?'

'If you must know – his name is Nick Bamford. He's the publisher of the *Daily Dispatch*. He came to show me this. Out of courtesy.'

She thrust some sheets of paper at Clement and he limped towards her, his back in agony from the terrible crossing. 'It's the front page of the *Dispatch* they're printing tomorrow.'

Clement scanned the pages, shocked to see his own face staring back at him. A scurrilous headline that made his eyes widen. 'This all came from Mr Warren? This is your doing. You harlot, you—'

He was very tempted to hit her, but to his surprise, Edith faced up to him.

'You know, all I asked was for Mr Warren to detain you. I wanted time. But you managed to create a scandal all by yourself. Kidnapping a child, speakeasies, gambling . . . all of it *your* own doing.'

Clement took a step back, completely thrown by her tone.

'I gave them the go-ahead to print the truth about you, Clement. About the kind of monster you are.' She pointed a finger at him, her face pinched with venom.

'Monster?' he spat back. 'How dare you.'

'Don't you say another word. A monster hardly covers it. You've been interfering with Susan. All this time. I know what you've done, you brute.'

'Interfering?' Clement was shocked. He'd been into Susan's room before, but only to watch her sleep. He'd never done anything *terrible* to her.

'It's over, Clement. Don't you dare touch me.'

When he'd imagined this confrontation, he hadn't expected Edith to look so triumphant.

'But this is all lies. They can't print this.'

'They're going to. And we'll have no choice but to stand tall and get through it.'

'We?'

'Your mother, Vita and I.'

'Vita? She's here?' Clement felt as if she'd hit him.

'Oh yes, Clement. Your sister has returned.'

Edith walked around her desk and plucked the white jacket from the back of her chair, shrugging it onto her slim shoulders. Then she adjusted her hat in the mirror before picking up her white leather bag.

'Where are you going?'

'To the Hall. Vita has called.'

'She's there? At home?'

'*Our* home, yes. Hers and mine. You see, we've come to an arrangement,' Edith said. 'I have her shares. She signed them over to *me*. And with your mother's controlling interest, which she has also signed over to *me* . . .' She paused now, her eyes blazing into Clement's. 'I am in charge of Darton.'

'You can't do this,' he shouted as she walked past him to the door. 'I won't have it. You can't do it . . .'

'Save your breath, Clement. I already have.'

And with that, she stalked past him in a cloud of expensive perfume.

82

Mrs Bamford's Plea

'Is Bertie still out with Mother?' Vita asked Martha, coming out from the drawing room for a moment and seeing her just outside the door.

'Yes, she's taken him for a tour around the stables. Those new horses arrived today. She couldn't wait to show Bertie.'

'Could you bring tea into the drawing room, please?'

'Right away. And I telephoned Mrs Darton at the mill, as you asked. She's on her way,' Martha said.

Vita returned to the drawing room and smiled at the woman waiting there, who had introduced herself earlier as Helen Bamford. She sat in the chair by the empty fireplace, wringing her hands as if she were cold. She had long red hair and wore no make-up, but she was still very beautiful. Vita had realized straight away that she was blind and wondered how this elegant woman went about her daily life. How did Edith know her? Surely they couldn't be friends?

As Vita sat down, she explained that Edith was on her way and wouldn't be long. Helen nodded, but she seemed agitated.

'I didn't know that Edith had other family living here,' she said. So Vita had to explain that she was in fact Anna

Darton, and that she'd just returned from the States. But if the woman was impressed, she didn't show it.

'Maybe I should go,' she said suddenly, as if losing her nerve. But at that moment Martha came in with the tea, and Helen retreated into the chair.

Martha served tea, throwing a concerned look at Vita.

'How exactly do you know Edith?' Vita asked, keen to keep the conversation going. With some more prompting, Helen began talking about Susan and Lettice. Vita was relieved to hear that Susan had friends at school.

'I was friends with Susan's mother,' Vita said.

'Her mother?'

'Yes. Marianne. Susan's mother.'

This obviously came as news to Helen Bamford. 'But . . . I thought Edith was her mother?'

Vita was glad that Helen couldn't see her blushing at the faux pas she'd just made. 'She is now, but . . . Susan's mother was a mill worker at Darton,' she explained. 'And unfortunately, she – she died.'

'I had no idea,' Helen Bamford said slowly, as if things were slotting into place. Vita felt a spike of worry now for Susan – she hadn't meant to let slip all that information about the girl's heritage. And it affected Edith, too. How would Vita explain to them that she'd already caused a stir, when she was meant to be trying to maintain their truce and keep Edith on her side?

Now they heard the crunch of tyres on the drive. As Vita stood up to go to the door, Edith marched in, taking off her hat. She clearly wasn't expecting a visitor, because she started speaking as soon as she got through the door.

'Vita, he's back,' she said. Then she saw Helen Bamford, and stopped short. 'Helen,' she said, her eyes darting to Vita's in alarm. 'Are the girls all right?'

'The girls are fine, as far as I know,' Helen said. 'They're at school.'

Helen Bamford stood awkwardly. She'd gone pale.

'Edith, I came to talk to you about Nick. To ask you . . . beg you . . .'

Nick? Who was Nick? Vita wondered. She sensed a terribly charged atmosphere now.

'He told you?' Edith said, in a whisper.

'He didn't have to,' Helen said. 'I knew it was you. At the game. You practically told me yourself. And I never thought . . .' She started to cry now. Vita glanced through the open door to where Martha stood.

'Go away, Martha,' Edith barked.

'But there's a gentleman here, too,' Martha said. She'd only just got the words out when a man in a fine grey suit with curly hair rushed in.

'Oh, Helen, you're here,' he said.

'Nick,' Edith exclaimed.

'I was so surprised to see Arnold outside in the car.' He embraced Helen, who let out a sob. 'Why are you here?' he asked. 'Is everything all right?'

Helen Bamford shook her head and then pushed him away. 'I didn't think . . . I didn't expect to find you together, but now I know.'

Vita saw the man looking desperately at Edith.

'This can't be happening. Tell me it isn't true, Nicky? Tell me it isn't true?' Helen pleaded.

'Darling – Helen . . . I don't know what you think—'

Now Edith interrupted, her tone urgent. 'No, Nick, no. Don't lie. Tell her the truth. Tell her what's been happening. Tell her how we're going to be together.'

Helen let out an anguished moan, and Vita instinctively stepped forward.

'Leave us,' Edith snarled, clearly furious that Vita was witnessing all of this. Vita jumped at the vitriol in her voice. 'Get out. This is nothing to do with you.'

Vita retreated, but in the hallway she lingered, her hand on the door, wondering whether she should have intervened. Helen Bamford looked desperate. What on earth had Edith done? Had she stolen this woman's husband? Because that's what it sounded like.

She stood there, frozen, listening to Edith and Nick fighting and Helen sobbing. She should go back in. She should help Helen, who let out an unseemly wail now – but then she decided against it. She couldn't risk Edith's fury. Turning away, she began heading for the stairs, when suddenly the sound of a gunshot made her jump.

She leapt back to the drawing-room door and flung it open. The scene before her made her blood run cold.

Clement had arrived at the conservatory doors from the garden, looking utterly deranged. He was holding a pistol.

The man – Nick – was on the floor, and now Edith started screaming as she put her hands over his chest. Helen, shaking all over, was on her knees, crawling towards where her husband lay bleeding on the hearthrug.

Clement hardly seemed to notice the mayhem as he walked

slowly forward through the conservatory, his eyes locked on Vita's.

'You,' he snarled. '*You . . .*'

'Clement, put down the gun. Clement, please. Put down the gun.' Vita stepped past Nick on the floor, moving towards Clement.

'Anna?' It was Martha at the door. 'Oh—'

'Call the police, Martha. Call them right now,' Vita said, keeping her gaze steady on Clement. Martha scurried into the corridor.

'It's all your fault,' he said. 'All of this. Everything.'

'Please – just put down the gun, and let's talk,' she said, coming into the conservatory and taking a step closer to him. He flinched. He primed the gun again, and Vita put her hand out. 'Please, no, Clement – no.'

'Get out,' he shouted, training the gun on her. Driven by the direction of his aim, she turned and started backing towards the garden doors he'd just come through. Her eyes didn't leave his, everything in her imploring him to be reasonable, but he was deranged with fury. She'd seen that pinched look on his face before, his pale cheeks and blazing eyes; but this time, she had to stand her ground.

'Put the gun down. Let's talk, Clement,' she repeated. 'It's me. Your sister. You don't want to do this.'

He shook his head and Vita froze, knowing that he was beyond reason and that he was going to shoot.

There was a blur now and, out of the corner of her eye, Vita saw that Edith was no longer crouched over Nick's body on the floor but was running towards Clement, like a wild animal. She was holding something in her hand.

There was an awful noise as she thrust it into Clement's back.

After a moment of frozen silence, Vita watched Clement's knees buckle, and a bubble of blood appeared on his lips. As he fell to the floor, the gun went off, the shot shattering the roof of the conservatory. Glass rained down on Vita.

Vita found herself face to face with Edith, who was staring down at where she'd stabbed Clement in the back with the fire iron. She still held the weapon, looking between her husband's body and her hand as if it didn't belong to her.

'Edith,' Vita whispered, seeing a pool of blood starting to seep out around Clement. 'Edith, what have you done?'

Edith didn't answer. Like someone sleepwalking, she calmly stepped over Clement and came towards Vita, then carried on past her and out of the doors into the garden. Vita turned and watched as Edith stumbled into the grass, still carrying the bloody poker in her hand, her legs slowly giving way. Then she fell to her knees, emitting a heart-wrenching wail that made the crows launch from the trees.

83

Theresa's Confession

Theresa Darton was still fragile, but with every passing day, thanks to the distraction of Bertie and Susan, she was gradually coming to terms with what had happened at Darton. The inquest into Clement's death had hit her hard and Edith was still in a jail cell in Manchester, waiting for her trial and sentence. Helen Bamford's lawyers and the newspaper had insisted that she couldn't be released on bail, and Vita worried constantly about how Edith was coping. Her mind kept replaying the terrible scene when Edith had been taken away from Darton in the police van, her white suit covered in mud and blood. Vita had been twice into Manchester to the jail to see her, but Edith had refused any visitors.

Vita hadn't heard from Helen Bamford since that awful day, although after some deliberation, she'd sent flowers to Nick's funeral. She'd heard that Helen and her daughter were planning on going back to India. The police had said that since Helen was blind, she wouldn't be required to give evidence at the trial.

The exposé about Clement never went to press – the newspapers reported instead on how Clement, deranged in his jealous fury, had killed his wife's lover. It made for much more sordid copy.

Vita and her mother buried Clement near Darius Darton in a small ceremony at St Hugh's, the mill workers staying away. Only Tantum and a few others attended, along with Hetherington and Martha. As Father McDougal said a final prayer for Clement, Vita tried very hard to forgive him; but his face, and the way he'd primed the gun, still haunted her at night. If it hadn't been for Edith, Vita was certain that she would be in that grave instead of him.

After the ceremony, her mother surprised Vita by asking if they could go riding. Vita hadn't been on a horse for years, but the new ones at the stable were lovely beasts and soon they were both in the saddle, riding up to the top of the hill.

It was a glorious day. After a gallop up a steep escarpment they stopped, out of breath, by the ancient coppice of oak trees. Below them, patchwork fields stretched as far as the eye could see, the river catching the sun like a jewel.

'There is something I've got to tell you,' Theresa said, looking over at Vita. 'It's time.'

They dismounted and let the horses rest, Vita joining her mother on a patch of grass overlooking the view. Daisies grew all around them. Vita felt the sun on her face and leant back, but her mother sat very still with her hands in her lap.

'You look very serious, Mother. Whatever is it?'

Theresa stared out towards the horizon for a long time.

'There's something you should know . . . about Clement,' she said, her voice just a whisper. She shook her head.

'Go on.'

She turned and reached for Vita's hand, her eyes filling with tears.

'He wasn't . . . he wasn't . . .'

'He wasn't . . . ?' Vita could see that Theresa was trying hard to tell her something, but her voice cracked.

'He wasn't your father's son.'

'What do you mean?'

'There was a mill worker, you see,' Theresa said. 'He and your father . . . they didn't see eye to eye, and then one day . . .' She shook her head and took a breath, trying to compose herself. 'I was only just married. It happened so fast. I was returning from the mill. I used to help out Ruth and Meg, you see, and it was late and somehow, I was alone in the cobbled street and he was there, this man, and I couldn't escape him. He . . . he . . .' She shook her head, unable to say the words, but Vita could see the truth in her face. 'Well, he took advantage of me.'

In the moments that followed, Vita felt a long, slow breath leave her body as she took in this enormous revelation. So much of her childhood suddenly started to make sense.

'Your father . . . he . . . he was so furious.'

'What happened to the man?'

Theresa shrugged. 'He wasn't seen again.'

'Father *killed* him?'

'I'm not sure. He never said he had. We didn't talk about it. After that day, it was as if a shutter came down and the secret was trapped – locked away in here,' she said, thumping her chest. 'We never spoke of it. I've never spoken of it. Not until now.'

'Oh, Mother,' Vita said, realizing the enormity of this confession.

'We were so happy, your father and I. Until that happened – and nine months later, Clement came along.'

Vita leant forward and hugged her mother now as her tears turned into sobs.

'I always thought that your father thought it was my fault.'

'How could it have been your fault? Oh, Mother, I'm so sorry,' she said, as she finally comprehended the magnitude of the misery her mother had lived with for so many years.

This truth shone a new light on everything: how Vita had never looked similar to Clement, how her father had been so hard on him, how her mother had always been distant and prone to bouts of illness. How she'd always been aware of the terrible tension in the Hall, as if happiness couldn't be allowed.

'When you came along and were such a ray of light in all of our lives, Clement was consumed by jealousy. And, as he got older, a kind of righteousness. He had more than you in every way, and I had to actively stop paying you any attention when he was around for fear of his temper.'

'Why didn't you tell him?'

'How could I?' Theresa said. 'That would only have made things worse. But maybe I should have. Maybe we'd all have been happier. It's the biggest regret of my life that I didn't give you more,' she said. 'I should have. I should have been truthful. You deserved that.'

'You've told me now,' Vita said gently.

'And you're not angry?'

'No, of course not. I'm so very sorry you've suffered.'

She let her mother rest the side of her head as they looked out at the view. She felt Theresa relaxing, and then she took Vita's hand in her own.

'My runaway daughter,' she said, bringing Vita's hand up to her lips. She kissed her fingers. 'I'm so glad you came home.'

84

The Rightful Owner

A week after Clement's funeral, their family solicitor asked Vita and her mother to attend his office for a reading of the will. It was more convenient to go to him than to have him come to Darton. After the terrible events in the drawing room, they'd moved with Susan, Bertie and Martha to a cottage on the estate, which was far more cheerful and wasn't haunted by memories; but it was still a little chaotic, and no place to receive a solicitor.

To Vita and her mother's surprise, it transpired that Clement had written a letter while he'd been on his way home from the States, changing his will. The letter had been witnessed by the ship's purser, and the solicitor had verified it.

'The gist of it is that Mr Darton changed his will so that all of his shares would go to his mother in the case of his death. And, failing that, to Susan Darton.'

'He cut out Edith?' Vita asked.

'Expressly,' the solicitor said. 'There's a letter attached with some rather shocking allegations – I'm not sure how many of them are true.'

Theresa tutted as she read the letter, but she didn't let Vita read it. 'I've had enough of Clement's nasty words to last me a lifetime,' she said, ripping up the letter and leaving the pieces in a pile on the solicitor's desk. 'Let's not have them in our heads, my dear.'

It seemed to Vita that her mother, since her confession, was more assertive than she'd ever been before.

On Sunday morning, Vita came down the narrow staircase in the cottage carrying Bertie and saw her mother talking to two men at the back door. It seemed odd to Vita that her mother hadn't asked them into the kitchen.

'Is everything quite all right, Mother?' she asked as her mother closed the door, but not before Vita had seen the two men doffing their caps and Theresa thanking them. 'Who on earth were those men? They looked rather unsavoury.'

Theresa sighed. 'I knew Clement was gambling. I knew it from the club – I saw the letters that he tried to hide from Edith. And I knew that he wouldn't stop until he'd gambled everything away, so I took steps to stop him losing the thing that was most precious.'

'What do you mean?'

'I had to stop him losing this,' she said, opening her hand. In it, Vita could see her father's pocket watch. 'I employed those two at Mr Decker's suggestion to frighten Clement and to relieve him of the watch. Of course, Clement didn't pay off his debts to the club, so I had to, but I'm very grateful that the watch is back where it belongs. Because your father wanted *you* to have this.'

'Me?'

'Yes, very specifically, when he died. One of the last things he said was that he wanted it to go to you. You are its rightful owner.'

Vita watched her mother's hands close around hers, the gold watch warm in her palms.

'Time is precious, my love,' her mother said, her eyes softly shining. 'Which is why I want you to have all the shares,' she added. 'Mine, Clement's – all of them. Darton is yours now. Just as it should be.'

85

The Photographs

And so it was that, a week later, Vita stood on the top of the iron steps outside the offices, addressing the Darton workers.

'Since I went away, and after these terrible few weeks, I've learnt the value of honesty. And I owe it to you to be honest,' she began.

She glanced to her side, where her mother stood. Theresa gave her a nod of encouragement.

'It pains me to tell you that after seventy glorious years, Darton Mill can no longer continue how it has been.' She heard a collective groan. 'The fact is that we can't compete with the Far East, and the markets have changed. The old ways of doing things are no longer profitable.'

She put her hand around her father's watch, hoping it would give her courage.

'Will we lose our jobs, Miss Darton?' one of the workers called out.

'Not if I can help it.' Vita smiled briefly. 'What Edith – Mrs Darton – and my brother began here, with my designs . . .' She let the comment hang for a moment. She knew the workers were all aware of what Clement and

Edith had stolen from her. '. . . Has given us a head start. And I intend to keep building on that vision. We're going to make new types of fabric at Darton. Fabrics I discovered in America. Fabrics that we'll be able to use to make fine garments. And in doing so, we will diversify and grow. I know you are clever, skilled workers and I know how loyal you are to Darton. And Darton is loyal to you. Which is why we're going expand the mill to produce a Darton Bra for every woman in the country. And then every woman in America.'

A cheer went up, and Vita turned and smiled at her mother.

'What about the Cotton Queen?' Clarry called up. 'And all the girls from Darton who have entered?'

'Well, one of you is going to win it, of course.'

Despite being on a whirlwind publicity tour for *The Sister Returns*, Nancy hadn't forgotten Bertie's birthday and had sent a package containing a miniature cowboy fancy-dress outfit, which Vita thought was both hilarious and ridiculous. She'd also sent Vita an envelope of photographs, developed from the camera she'd left in California.

As they ate the birthday cake that Martha had made in the kitchen, Vita showed Susan the pictures.

'Is that really the Hollywoodland sign?' Susan asked, studying the black and white image.

'Yes, and look – this one is at the studios. That's a whole street that looks like the Wild West, but it's all just the facades of buildings. Oh, Susan, you wouldn't believe how marvellous the studios are.'

'I'd love to go there.'

'Well, you will, one day. Nancy is determined that we'll go there for a holiday.'

Susan smiled, realizing that Vita meant she'd be taking her with her.

'Who's that?' She turned around the picture of Vita and Daniel on a beach near Santa Monica, with Bertie in between them.

'That's Daniel,' Vita said, with a sad smile. *Poor Daniel.* Nancy had seen him and had reported that he was working terribly hard and hadn't wanted to talk about Vita. She hoped he'd found someone who could share his wonderful home. She wanted his story to have a happy ending. It was only now that she was far away that she realized this could never have been with her. She'd been seduced by Hollywood, but ultimately, it wasn't where she belonged.

'You look quite similar. Like brother and sister,' Susan said.

'You think so?'

'You certainly look more like Daniel's sister than . . . *his.*' She gasped, as if realizing she'd said something unspeakable, and Vita braced herself. This conversation about Clement had been a long time coming.

Vita set the photographs down and turned to face Susan. She had so much of Marianne's character in her face. The curve of her chin; the way she struggled to hide things.

'Shall we talk about him?' Vita asked, gently. 'I think it would be good if we talked.'

Susan looked down at the table, fiddling with the china bowl of eggs on it.

'Is it bad that I'm glad he's gone? That I'm glad he's dead?' she asked.

'No,' Vita said. 'If I'm honest, I'm glad too. I've been running away from him for a long time.'

'I wish I'd been able to run away,' Susan said. 'When I came to Paris with Mamma, I was so happy. And so was she. She said you'd look after us.'

'Oh, Susan. I didn't understand what she'd done, or why,' Vita said, 'not then. But I do now.'

She reached out and stroked Susan's blonde hair. 'I wish I'd known about you. I wish I'd understood. That she'd done what she'd done because of you.'

'I hated having to call Edith Mother,' Susan admitted. 'Afterwards, you know. When I knew Mamma was dead.'

Vita pulled Susan towards her. 'Oh, darling. I'm so, so sorry,' she said. 'For everything you've been through.'

They sat for a long while and Vita cradled Susan as she cried, in a way that Vita suspected she never had before.

'It won't always feel like this,' she promised her. 'Your mother was right about one thing.'

'What was that?'

'That I would look after you. Because I will.'

86

The Sister Returns

Vita threw herself wholeheartedly into learning the business, spending every day at the mill while her mother and Martha doted on Bertie. Each new day was challenging in a way she'd never imagined – particularly when she had to present her plans to the LCC, who had threatened to amalgamate Darton with some other mills. But finally she'd got them to see sense and agree to let her carry on with Darton her way. Mr Delaney in the States had helped Vita secure some much-needed investment, and it was exciting knowing that production was scaling up and orders were coming in thick and fast.

Vita had also embarked on a new training programme at Darton, sending Harrison, the foreman, and Meg out to Percy's contact in Italy to learn about the elasticated fabric. Meanwhile, Ruth and her team were booked to go to Paris to learn pattern-cutting with Laure at Madame Jenny's when they closed in August.

To her delight, Percy had sent over some yellow nylon fabric for Vita to make a two-piece swimming suit just like June's, which Clarry was going to wear in the final of the Cotton Queen pageant in Blackpool. With the fabric, Percy had written to update her on his relationship with Paul. Even though they were living on opposite sides of the country, he said that they'd been keeping in touch. It seemed the two of them had really hit it off and, from the way Percy wrote, she sensed that it wouldn't be too long before they were more than friends. She hoped so, in any case. Percy deserved to be happy and Paul did too.

As busy as work was, Vita made sure that she spent every Saturday afternoon with Susan, picking her up from her new school and taking her into town for some quality time together.

Today, they were going to buy new summer clothes for Susan now she'd grown so much. As they walked through the centre of Manchester in the sunshine, Susan pointed to the cinema on the corner.

'Look, Vita. It's playing: *The Sister Returns*.'

Vita stopped, staring up at the marquee. 'Nancy Delaney in *The Sister Returns*,' she read. 'Won't you look at that.' She smiled. 'Nancy always said she'd have her name on the marquee before we knew it.'

'Can we go and see it? Please, Vita. I'd love to.'

Vita shook her head, remembering how she'd been in the studio that day they'd been filming the bedroom scene. Quite apart from the fact that Susan was far too young for the film, she was saving it for when she could go by herself and be swept away by the emotional rollercoaster that it would inevitably be. She wasn't strong enough at the moment, after everything that had happened, to be reminded of Archie. To hear those words again that he'd written for her.

She tried so hard not to think about him, or picture him

with Maud in California. She wondered what had happened between Daniel and Archie when Daniel had returned from New York. Maybe he'd fired Archie; or maybe, in Vita's absence, they hadn't spoken about it and the matter had simply been dropped. She knew what it was like at the studios and how all-consuming the work was. They'd probably both moved on without her.

But even seeing the words *The Sister Returns* made those sun-filled days come flooding back.

'Is she really your friend?' Susan asked, awestruck, as they walked closer to the theatre now and up to the poster of Nancy. Vita smiled, seeing Nancy pouting in all her sultry glory. She could see why the press loved her.

'She's my best friend,' Vita said sadly, reaching out and touching Nancy's image, thinking of the last conversation they'd had just before she'd left for New York. She'd been so stressed and anxious at the time, so desperate to get Bertie back, that she hadn't dwelt on what Nancy had said; but now it came back to her.

'You know, that very first time I saw you standing on the Charing Cross Road, I thought "She looks like someone I could be great pals with,"' Nancy had confided.

'What do you mean?' Vita had asked.

'Well, you know about people, don't you? You know straight away if they're going to be your type. With partners, but even more so with friends. I knew with you straight away.'

'You knew I wasn't Edith's friend?' Vita had been shocked.

'Of course you weren't. I knew Edith's type, and you definitely weren't it.'

'So, when you took me to the Zip Club . . . ?'

'. . . And named you Vita?'

'You knew I was lying all along?'

'I knew, and I was impressed with your gumption,' Nancy laughed. 'Because you did turn out to be exactly the person I wanted. Mystic Alice said I was going to meet a great friend. A friend for life. And as soon as I saw you, I knew you were her.'

Vita smiled now at the memory. 'We're friends for life,' she said, looking down at Susan.

'Even though you don't see her?'

Vita nodded. 'We will. One day.'

Susan nodded. 'I miss Lettice. She was my best friend.'

'What happened with the grown-ups shouldn't stop you two being friends, if you want to be.'

'Maybe I'll write.'

'Maybe you should,' Vita nodded, taking Susan's hand.

87

A Mysterious Present

The days grew longer and balmier as midsummer came and Bertie learnt to talk and sing. Vita came home one Friday evening from the mill, looking forward to playing in the garden with him. Hetherington had put up a new wooden swing and a small climbing frame.

'Something got delivered for you,' Martha said, as she came from the front door into the kitchen.

She handed over a large packet wrapped in brown paper. There was a rose tied in the string.

'What's this?' Vita asked, putting down her bag and carefully undoing the package. It felt heavy.

'It's just a piece of plank?' Martha said, giving Vita a quizzical look as she unwrapped it. But suddenly Vita's breath caught.

'Where's Mother?'

'In the garden with Bertie. And there's a visitor with her.' Martha's eyes were twinkling.

Vita rushed out through the kitchen door to the garden, where her mother sat on a picnic blanket near the swing.

'Go on,' Martha said, a soft smile on her face.

Vita walked into the garden, hardly daring to believe what

she was seeing. Archie was crouching down, holding Bertie's hand. He was laughing as Bertie stood and walked towards his grandmother.

Theresa, who was wearing the pretty blue and white dress that Vita had made her, bundled Bertie into her arms, laughing too.

'Archie,' Vita whispered, and he slowly stood. They stared at one another. He was wearing cream trousers and a short-sleeved shirt. His hair was longer, falling across his tanned forehead; but his eyes, his gorgeous green eyes, made her insides dance.

Theresa got up from the rug and carried Bertie towards Vita, squeezing her arm. 'I'll leave you to it.'

There was a beat, and then they were alone.

'What are you doing here?' she asked, hardly able to find her voice. In all the ways she'd ever imagined him, she'd never imagined him in Darton.

'I brought you a present. I'd hoped to bring it when I could put a daffodil with it, but a rose will have to do,' Archie said, nodding to the wooden board she held in her hand. She looked down at it again, seeing the faded love heart scratched onto it, hers and Archie's initials inside it. She remembered how, when they'd first made love, he'd taken his penknife to the board below them. 'When we lost Hartwell, I had to save the most precious part of it. For you.'

She couldn't quite believe what he was telling her.

'Hartwell's gone? What about Maud?'

He shrugged, as if it was no big deal. 'I told her. About you. And about Bertie and how I felt about you both. That nothing else was important. She was upset, but too busy comforting Georgie. Her husband has left her, and now I've left Maud. I'm quite the pariah.'

He smiled, as if this was, in fact, a relief.

Vita could hardly concentrate on what he was saying, because he was walking over to her. His eyes were like two ropes that were pulling her towards him.

'I've spent too long hiding the truth,' he continued. 'From her, from you, but most of all from myself.'

She didn't move as he arrived, reached out his hand and touched her cheek.

'And Hollywood?' she asked. What about his dream? Of being a writer?

'It's not for me. All the hype. All those people. And it's far too hot.'

Vita smiled. 'So, what are you doing now?' she asked. 'After *The Sister Returns*?'

'You should know. I wrote the end of the movie explaining. I thought you'd be expecting me?'

'I haven't seen it,' she said. 'Not yet.'

He laughed, looking at the sky. 'Oh . . . all my well-laid plans.'

'What plans?'

He shrugged. 'Well, if I'm honest, there's only ever been one.'

'And what's that?'

'For you to forgive me, and let me have a chance at being the man I always should have been.'

And she knew then that he was finally hers.

'That's two plans,' she pointed out as he pulled her into

an embrace, but she didn't resist. She smiled, feeling her heart singing as she drank him in. Her Archie. The love of her life. Here at last.

'We all make mistakes,' he murmured, as his lips met hers.

Author's Note

As with the *The Runaway Daughter* and *The Hidden Wife*, I have tried to evoke an era and give a flavour of this fascinating period of history. In fact, it's a miracle the book actually got written as I became addicted to watching old movies and some amazing early footage of the studios. If it hadn't been lockdown, I would have loved to have gone to New York and LA on a research trip, so my apologies to any US readers for any inaccuracies. Thank you very much to Rory Kotin, New York resident and renowned calligrapher, for her help on Manhattan geography. I found Mick LaSalle's brilliant book, *Complicated Women: Sex And Power in Pre-Code Hollywood*, particularly helpful, and I'd like to thank Joe The Curl – my wonderful hairdresser – for lending me two very helpful books: *Designing Dreams* by Donald Albrecht and *Los Angeles: Portrait of a City* by Jim Heimann and Kevin Starr. For the English research, I found *Me and My Hair: A Social History* by Patricia Malcolmson most helpful. I have taken artistic liberties to include the Cotton Queen Quest, which was a real contest to find the 'most beautiful girl in the cotton industry' run by the *Daily Dispatch* in April 1930. I like to imagine that Clarry from Darton Mills won it in Vita's yellow bikini.

Joanna Rees
2022

Acknowledgements

This A *Stitch in Time* trilogy has been an utter joy to write and I'd like to thank Wayne Brookes and the team at Pan Macmillan for giving me the chance to bring Vita and Nancy's escapades to life. Being able to transport myself to the glamour of 1930s Hollywood during the Covid pandemic was a complete blessing. Thanks, too, to the foreign sales team for bringing my books to an international audience. I'd like to thank Susan Opie for her insightful editorial notes and the eagle-eyed Samantha Fletcher, as well as Karen Whitlock, my patient proofreader. Thanks to Felicity Blunt, my fabulous agent, and Rosie Pierce, too, and everyone at Curtis Brown.

I'd like to thank my neighbourhood buddies and early readers Bronwin Wheatley and Eve Tomlinson, along with Shân Lancaster and Louise Dumas. I'd also really like to thank all my girlfriends, many of whom have put up with me for decades and whose support means the world to me, especially Dawn Howarth, who was the very first person to take my ambition to be a writer seriously and who has held my hand through every book. I'd like to thank my family, especially Aunty Merryl for sending me a vintage 1930s dress, and my lovely sister, Catherine.

A special thanks to the Splashers and Bobbers swimming gang who accompanied my flings in the cold sea, along with

Jenni Dunn for her brilliant online yoga and Peter Deadman, who inspired my daily qi gong practice.

As a writer, you find routines and practices that see you through and I'd like to thank all the other writers out there who share their wisdom on the subject and lend their support. I'd also really like to thank all the bookshops, libraries, bloggers and reviewers who keep on finding readers, even during these challenging times.

Emlyn and I have been used to writing at home together for over twenty years, so when I was writing this book and the lockdown happened, I was convinced that we'd got it covered and it wouldn't ruffle our feathers in any way. I hadn't factored our three girls being home and the general stress of living through Covid times. So, along with Ziggy the dog, I'd especially like to thank my beautiful daughters, Tallulah, Roxie and Minty, for filling our home with laughter and joy. (I'd also like to thank the person who invented Beats headphones and the people who put together brilliant 1920s and 30s playlists on Spotify.)

Lastly, and most importantly, thank you to Emlyn for always making me believe I can write, when I sometimes find it impossible. But mostly for making me wholeheartedly believe that love will always save the day.

The Runaway Daughter

by Joanna Rees

The first book in the A Stitch in Time series.

It's 1926 and Anna Darton is on the run from a terrible crime she was forced into committing. Alone and scared in London, salvation comes in the form of Nancy, a sassy American dancer at the notorious night-club, the Zip Club. Re-inventing herself as Vita Casey, Anna becomes part of the line-up and is thrown into a hedonistic world of dancing, parties, flapper girls and fashion.

When she meets the dashing Archie Fenwick, Vita buries her guilty conscience and she believes him when he says he will love her no matter what. But unbeknown to Vita, her secret past is fast catching up with her, and when the people closest to her start getting hurt, she is forced to confront it or risk losing everything she holds dear.

The Hidden Wife

by Joanna Rees

The second book in the A Stitch in Time series.

Paris, 1928. Having fled London and been on the run around Europe, Vita Casey has established a new life for herself, keeping a low profile as a dresser at a cabaret hall where Nancy is part of the risqué dance troupe. It's a vibrant world of wild parties, drugs and jazz music.

But despite the fun, hedonistic lifestyle they lead, Vita longs for a proper career and to re-kindle her dream of designing lingerie. When an opportunity to work for famous couturier Jenny Sacerdote presents itself, Vita grabs it with both hands and is soon exposed to an altogether different side of Paris society. Before long, romance blossoms in the unlikeliest of places.

However, left to her own devices, Nancy spirals into danger and drug abuse and Vita has to save her friend. But can Vita really trust the people who want to help her? Especially when there are those back in England who wish to see her ruined and forced to pay for the past she ran away from . . .